STITCH UP

SOPHIE HAMILTON

templar

A TEMPLAR BOOK

First published in the UK in 2014 by Templar Publishing,

an imprint of The Templar Company Limited,

Deepdene Lodge, Deepdene Avenue, Dorking, Surrey,

RH5 4AT, UK

www.templarco.co.uk

Text copyright © 2014 by Sophie Hamilton

Cover design www.the-parish.com

Images © shutterstock/the-parish.com

Typesetting by Aztec Design

ISBN 978-1-84877-423-0

Printed and bound in Great Britain

For Christopher

The Skin I Live In

THE railway tracks flashed like surgical knives in the sunlight. I drummed my fingernails against the train's tinted, bulletproof window. I was getting that locked-in feeling again. The Easter holidays stretched before me. I pinched the skin on the back of my hand, counting the seconds it took to sink down. Since the revelation, I had become obsessed with skin – not any old skin.

I was obsessed with saving *my skin*.

My skin covers about two square metres, weighs around three kilograms and contains seventeen kilometres of blood vessels. I shed 30,000 dead cells a minute, 600,000 an hour, and grow a brand-new skin every twenty-eight days – that's about 1,000 new skins in a lifetime, which, in case you were wondering, doesn't make me a freak. It's completely normal. The freakish part, or the bit that was freaking *me* out big time, was my parents' plan for it. I puffed out my cheeks – exhaled slowly. It was just plain wrong. I mean, *it's my skin and I live in it.*

BANG!

A rush of air slammed against the Star Academy's chartered train. I jumped. A civilian train raced alongside, its windows blanked out by speed. Watching the grey squares spool past, like empty frames from a film, I found myself slotting images and headlines into the blank spaces, cutting together a trailer for the next tragic episode of my life. COMING SOON: TEENAGE GIRL METAMORPHOSES INTO BEAUTIFUL ZOMBIE DOLL! The images showed surgeons working on a girl in a high-tech operating theatre, followed by post-op shots of my bruised and battered face, eyes weeping blood. In the final shot I smiled to camera, my face smooth as a mask. STAY TUNED! Moments later, the civilian train was gone.

The carriage was a muss of chatter. Coco and her sparkly crew, the List – so-called because your parents had to be on the Rich List before Coco would consider you worthy of membership – were huddled over tablets, buying clothes for their holidays and acing each other's plans. Samantha, daughter of a retail magnate (Rich List number eighteen), said she would be chilling at the family villa in the Caribbean. Coco, heir to a candy empire (Rich List number fourteen) trumped her with holidaying on the family super-yacht. Anushka, daughter of an oligarch (Rich List number twenty-one) had a royal flush as she was doing both. I zoned out when they started arguing about the size of their parents' Learjets. I could outdo them all, if I cared. My dad was a media mogul and the king of the cosmetic surgery industry (Rich List number eight). But I wasn't into lists, especially Coco's. Her List ruled our class at the Star Academy, and their starry rules sucked. They were all sparkle and no heart.

WHOOSH! The train sped into a tunnel, sealing us into

a darkly mirrored bubble. In unison, the girls swivelled to check their reflections in the blacked-out windows, pouting, primping and spiffing their hair. I scowled. The List were such fakes; all they cared about was how they looked.

The plasma screen in the corner of the carriage was showing footage of burned-out police cars, a double-decker bus in flames, and hoodies looting a high street somewhere in the Edgelands way over east. The news was rolling soundlessly. The ticker tape on the bottom of the screen read: **Broken Britain. Hood-Rats Run Riot.** The girls' eyes flicked up to the screen and then back to their reflections. The Edgelands were a world away. Nobody gave a damn. Next up, my mother's perfectly-sculpted face filled the screen. Blab, blab, blab went her trout pout as she introduced the lead item on her prime-time show. My brow knitted into a frown. No escape! With my mother presenting daily shows on GoldRush TV, I often had the eerie feeling that her eyes were on me, spying on me from plasma screens, controlling me by remote. Despite the sound being turned down, I could guess Mum's angle. She'd be banging on about outcasts, hood-rats and bad civilian parenting, as if she were auditioning for the Mother of the Year award. *As if...*

I caught Big Stevie's eye in the window. My frown deepened. He was standing with the other minders, monitoring my every move. Most girls had their personal bodyguards on board, even though the Bullet Train Company employed security guards as part of the company's bespoke service. This was because our security guards doubled as spies for our parents. Every weekend our parents chartered a Bullet Train to ferry us from the Star Academy to London and back again. At fifty grand a pop, the Bullet offered a secure solution for super-rich parents as a precaution against the kidnap crews. My dad described it as the Hogwarts Express with guns.

Big Stevie was telling the other minders a joke; obviously I'd heard it a million times before. I rolled my eyes. It was weird to think that he'd been guarding me for more than ten years – over half my life. He'd outlasted every boyfriend and most friends, too. Even weirder, he knew more about my habits than anyone else in the world, including my parents. He shadowed me twenty-four/seven, and I hated him.

Suddenly laughter filled the carriage. Coco and the List turned towards me in a confection of she-wolf smiles, shimmery lipgloss and capped white teeth. Coco – the Fake in Chief – jumped up. Her blonde hair was immaculately styled and her bright pink nails clacked like lobster claws against her tablet as she walked over, shadowed by her tittering crew.

I mentally manned up.

"Oh my God, you've been *papped*," Coco smirked, as she held up a photo of yours truly attending a premiere with my parents. I was getting out of a silver Mercedes in a lacy black dress. "Totes inappropes. Totes tragic. The corpse bride look is so over, Dasha. So *last century*."

"It's called unique style," I replied, without missing a beat. "Not that you'd know anything about that." I let my eyes travel slowly across their uniformity.

The List crowded round her tablet.

"Nope. I still don't get it." Coco's eyes lasered the photo. "You have shed-loads of stylists and you still look like trash. Now that's what I call an *achievement*."

Her glittery crew burst out laughing.

"Go fake yourself!" I kept my eyes glued to the plasma, wishing for an ejector seat – preferably one that would shoot me into a parallel universe.

But Coco shoved her face up close and hissed, "If your dad's so famous for fixing everyone's image, how come he sooo forgot about yours? I'd call that child neglect!" The List tittered. Her eyes flicked up to my mother's image on screen. "And your mum's cougar-chic is tragic, too."

"You're just jealous," I snapped.

"Like how?" But she was backing off.

I fixed her with a chilly stare as she retreated.

Anushka and Samantha hovered. Anushka nudged Sam. Sam giggled and nudged her back. Immediately I knew they must have heard the rumours. Sam drew closer. "Where are you going for Easter, Dasha?" she asked.

"One of the islands," I said coolly.

I saw Coco's face cloud over. She tried to catch Sam's eye.

But Sam's desire for gossip made her break rank, and she continued in a hushed voice. "Is your dad giving you a makeover for your seventeenth birthday, Dasha?"

I shrugged. I couldn't have told them even if **I'd wanted** to – which I didn't – because my parents had made me sign a confidentiality agreement. That's the kind of brand, I mean family we were – *close*. . . But there was no harm in playing them.

"Dad's got plans." A smile twitched the corner of my mouth. Although Coco tried to play it cool, envy glinted in her eyes. And in that moment I knew that she would do anything to swap places with me.

"Chilling in the Caribbean mainly," I blagged some more. "So be afraid, be very afraid. I'll be coming back tanned and gorgeous." I waited a beat. "A new person." I flashed a dazzling smile, although on the inside I wanted to scream. But I couldn't give Coco the pleasure of seeing how terrified I really was.

Her face shifted with fury as they walked away.

Coco hated the fact that my parents owned one of the most powerful media corporations in the world, as well as a multi-million-pound cosmetic surgery business. Last year they had merged the two companies to form GoldRush Image Inc, which was the most influential image-making machine in the world. Coco was jealous as hell, but she didn't know the half of it. In two weeks' time, on my seventeenth birthday, I was going to become the brand-new face of GoldRush Image Inc. That was the reason Dad was whisking me off to one of his islands. Once there, GoldRush Image surgeons were going to give me a radical makeover. As I pinched the skin on the back of my hand again, I found myself once more dreaming of being propelled into a parallel universe.

The situation was freaking me out. It was totally intense, and there was no escape. I was twenty-four hours away from having my identity stolen, but this was identity theft with a twist, of course, because my parents were involved.

This wasn't about cracking a password, stealing bank details or personal data. My parents were physically changing my appearance for ever for their own crazy purposes.

My phone rang. I sucked in a breath. It was Dad.

"Precious?"

"Hi, Dad," I said without enthusiasm.

"How are you feeling? Excited?"

"Like a freak show," I said, chewing at my thumbnail.

"Excellent." He carried on, pretending he hadn't heard. "Everything is in place for your launch, Dash. We've had teams on it night and day. The good news is I'm now turning my focus on the star attraction. Which means you have my undivided attention, precious."

"Lucky me!" I snapped. "And I wish you'd stop talking about my launch, Dad. I'm not a perfume."

He laughed. "Okay. Okay. Your *rebirth* begins tomorrow. So how does it feel to be weeks away from perfection?"

I rolled my eyes. Rebirth was just the creepy kind of word my father loved to use.

"I'm not going to be born again, Dad. I hate your cult talk."

"The cult of Dasha Gold. We can channel that. The brand's new goddess."

"Yeah. Whatever. Get to the point, Dad." I was totally sick of his sticky sales pitch.

"A limo is waiting to take you to City Airport. Big Stevie knows the drill. Our jet is scheduled to leave at nine-thirty sharp."

"Great," I said, giving my bodyguard the evils. When he smirked back I got up and left the carriage, only half-listening to Dad as he talked me through 'the procedures' — another of his smarmy words — for about the millionth time. Then, realising this really was the last-chance saloon, I quickly gathered my thoughts and gave it one final shot: "Dad, I don't know about this. It's just not me…"

"Fine. See you at nine." He hung up.

Typical, I thought angrily, staring down at the smartphone's blank screen.

Big Stevie entered the empty carriage, as if an invisible cord attached us. I pretended not to notice him. Moments later, a cheesy ringtone jived from his Puffa jacket. He answered with a grin. "Mr Gold. Yeah. I've got my eye on her." He gave me a sly wink. "We'll be there. City Airport for nine." When he spoke, he rubbed his huge hand back and forth across his shiny head, like he was trying to warm up his brain. A barbed-wire tattoo, which circled his thick wrist, flashed from beneath his sleeve. This marked him out as one of Dad's elite security detail — the Golden Knights.

"Yeah. I heard her. The same old baloney. No worries. I'll see to it." His mafia routine was seriously toe-curling.

"Fraud," I said when he hung up. Anger was bubbling up again, pushing against my skin. I had been guarded all my life.

"Boss wants me to keep you on side, Dasha. And at the end of the day, you've gotta do what the boss says, innit?" He couldn't resist the football clichés.

"Whatever!" I zoned out.

Suburbia. London sprawl. Grim-faced houses, abandoned trampolines and cheap-looking conservatories slid past. I imagined living in one of the nondescript little homes backing onto the railway tracks, leading a civilian life, going to the local academy, hanging out with the cool kids. Doing normal things – trips to supermarkets, shopping malls and cinemas, eating burgers. Not living in billion-pound penthouses in the sky. Not attending an elite finishing school. Not going to premieres, parties and VIP everything…

The train passed an advertisement featuring my dad's goddaughter. Someone had scrawled **pretty vacant** across her forehead. Although I'd seen the poster a million times before, a shiver ran down my spine when I read the graffiti. That would be me soon, I thought. Operated on. Stitched up into Dad's ideal of beauty. Face zeroed. I screwed up my face, enjoying the sensation of my skin crinkling up around my eyes. Soon I wouldn't even be able to do that. My parents were seriously messing with me. No, they were trying to control me in every way.

I checked my watch. The charms on my bracelet clattered – one for each of my sixteen birthdays. In a matter of hours, I would be on my parents' jet heading for our private Caribbean island with its state-of-the-art operating theatre and recuperating suites. Once there, GoldRush Image Inc's most qualified cosmetic surgeons were going to use groundbreaking technology to transform me beyond recognition – or, to use another of Dad's dodgy phrases, 'turn me into a living logo'.

I pressed my fingers to my temples. My head was throbbing. All 'the procedures' sounded so sci-fi, so unreal. In six months' time I would be… *what?* I pushed my temples more forcefully. *A complete fake? A freak? A prototype?* Dad's ideal version of me!

I pictured my therapist talking me through the surgical procedures. He had spent hours trying to bring me round to Dad's way of thinking. But when he started regurgitating all Dad's slimy expressions – 'picture perfect', 'aesthetic archetype' and 'living logo' – I'd switch off and begin cloudspotting, shaping animals, fish and butterflies from the cotton-wool air. His therapy kingdom was situated on the fiftieth floor so there were always plenty of clouds. I imagined these cloud creatures had fluid, ever-changing identities, and in the stories I dreamed up, they always escaped.

A scream was building up deep inside my stomach. I closed my eyes and gripped the armrests of my seat, as if this might stop me hurtling towards my future.

Suddenly a terrible cacophony engulfed the train. Brakes shrieked. Metal screeched. Then my world was spinning and, as I hit the floor in a tangle of limbs, I saw Big Stevie was airborne, too, and rocketing straight towards me like a heat-seeking missile. I scrambled out of range moments before he crashed down, his arms splayed out like a fighter-bomber plane.

The train shuddered to a halt. An eerie silence followed. A heartbeat later, the screams started. Terrifying questions crammed my head. Was it a bomb? A kidnap crew?

A collision? I shook Big Stevie by the shoulders; he was out cold. Placing two fingers on his wrist directly below the longest spike of his barbed-wire tattoo, I checked his pulse and counted the beats out loud, because that action stopped the dark thoughts crowding back in.

Then a voice was booming over the intercom, instructing us to disembark for our own safety. The doors zizzed open. The television crackled static. The announcer's voice was rough around the edges – unofficial somehow. Grabbing my Dior bag, I crept towards the door and peered out.

All along the Bullet Train, shell-shocked girls from the Star Academy were spilling out and regrouping in hysterical huddles. Some were hugging each other and crying while the more media-savvy were filming the scene on their smartphones – their eyes, as ever, on the main chance. A minder, who was carrying a girl with a gash on her head, was shouting for help to get the injured to safety.

I jumped down. There was no sign of a bomb, no toppled carriages, no mangled metal. The train, although tilting, was still on the track. The Bullet Company's cheesy advertising jingle popped into my head – 'Bullet Trains save lives'.

The rat-a-tat-tat of gunfire sounded from the front of the train.

Then I saw them, working in pairs. Men in masks were running down the tracks, checking carriages. The girls started screaming and scrambling up the sidings while the armed security guards rushed towards the advancing snatch squads.

Oh, no, a kidnap crew, I thought in a panic, chasing after the girls from my class, my bag banging against my hip. These guys were hardcore. They were desperate enough to risk everything to kidnap the super-rich for massive ransom payouts. They didn't mess around.

The girls from my class stumbled and tottered in their high-heeled shoes as their minders shepherded them up the sidings. I was still running after them when an idea took hold. I slowed to a walk. Stevie was still out cold in the carriage. This was my chance!

I had exactly sixty seconds to change my life.

Peeling away from the rest of the group, I headed off in the opposite direction. About fifty metres down the track, I started climbing up the sidings, breaking a fingernail as I grabbed hold of clumps of weeds and grass to help me up, heels sinking deep into the claggy mix of mud and gravel. Reaching the top, I crouched down behind a bush and surveyed the scene. A freshly felled tree lay across the tracks. The front two carriages of the train were slanting precariously to the right. The girls from my class had vanished. Their minders stood guard.

Gunfire rang out again.

My heart was in my mouth.

Girls were screaming again.

More gunshots, closer this time.

I stood up slowly, edged along the fence until I found a gap and climbed through, skidding down an embankment into a grubby suburban street.

Reality Bites

AN hour later, the Thames snaked before me, glittering in the last rays of the sun as it swept London's secrets out to sea. Splashes of gold spangled the murky water, then for a moment the wind dropped, plating the surface, as if all the gold bars stashed away in the Bank of England's vaults had melted into the river. The breeze got up again, rippling the water, sending jagged gold lines shooting back and forth, like the hands of traders on the stockmarket floor. Ragged pink clouds stretched across the darkening sky. The city's skyscrapers flashed like gangsters' jewellery.

I glanced over my shoulder. No sign of Big Stevie. That was a first. He was probably still out cold on the train. It felt strange but good. Freedom buzzed and shimmered all around me. Everything was louder, brighter, more intense, as if I were experiencing life in high definition for the very first time. I walked over to the river, and standing there, soaking up the scene, all I could think was, *This is the real world, the freaking real world.*

London.

As I'd never seen it before.

Alone.

Without Big Stevie shadowing me.

"Free," I whispered, trying the word out for size. "Free,"

I said the word a little louder. I liked the way it pushed my lips into a broad, beaming smile.

I took a deep breath. The river smelled salty. It made me think of Elizabethan adventurers gliding down the Thames in ships with big, billowing sails, off to discover the New World.

London pulsed beneath my feet. *My New World.* Pressing the tips of my middle and index fingers to my lips, I kissed them and crossed myself before touching them to the pavement, like a superstitious footballer heading onto the pitch.

Straightening up again, my excitement ebbed away. GoldRush Image Inc – my parents' headquarters – loomed on the other side of the river. The network's news helicopters were zipping off helipads, hunting down breaking news, their blades glinting in the day's last light.

Before long my parents would know that I was missing, if they didn't already.

I sat down on a bench to catch my breath. An inscription on the back read: *Everyone needs time to think.*

Understatement of the year, I thought, trying to gather myself. I tilted my head back and looked up at the sky; the last rays of the sun warmed my face. The gulls swooped and wheeled over the Thames, riding the breeze, bellies stained pink in the evening sunlight. I was running. *But from what?* I took a deep breath. In. Out. Slowly my thoughts settled. The kidnappers had saved my skin for the time being. But I needed to crack on.

I stood up, hoping to walk myself into some kind of plan.

An arrow of light shot across the Thames straight towards me, as if singling me out. I smiled. I still couldn't quite believe that I had dodged the knife.

As I set off in the direction of the Houses of Parliament, the civilian world rushed towards me in a riot of sound and vision: chattering families strolled past, giggling girls sashayed by in high-street fashions, a crew of skateboarders slalomed between squawking hen parties, while beered-up boys in whack shirts whistled at girls with spray-on tans. Asian women out with their families caught my eye as their saris sparkled in the sunshine. Weaving through the crowds, I felt as if I'd wandered onto the set of a West End musical. Every millimetre of the seventy-two kilometres of nerves in my skin was supercharged. Electric pulses were racing round my body, as if it were a Formula One track. I was hyped to the max.

Down by the London Eye, a carousel whirled. Out of nowhere, a clown started shadowing me – invading my space, mirroring my every gesture and playing it for the crowds. I walked faster, but my fancy-dress stalker kept on mimicking me. His cheap joke spooked me. Even eerier, Mickey Mouse, Darth Vader and Michael Jackson laughed as I scooted past. I did a double take. They were shabby human statues. Totally freaked out now, I sprinted up the steps to Westminster Bridge, taking them two at a time. From below, laughter reached me, followed by the tinkle of change dropping into the clown's hat.

I stopped on the bridge, heart rocketing. It was as if the

creepy clown had tripped a switch in my head and, boom, the rush of excitement had changed into something dark. I leaned against the bridge as I caught my breath.

In the gathering darkness GoldRush Image Inc dazzled. It dominated the skyline, hogging the limelight, making the House of Commons, Whitehall and all the other government buildings look gloomy and irrelevant, like fusty old fossils. Dad's headquarters were a DNA-inspired design, two towers that twisted a full ninety degrees as they rose up into the clouds, resembling a double helix. One tower housed his media empire; the other his cosmetic kingdom. Dad used to be a cosmetic surgeon – one of the best. He was the go-to guy for the rich and famous. That was how he made his money. With this wealth he had built up his media empire. Dad was ahead of the game; he'd sussed out the power of the image decades ago.

Clips from my parents' TV shows flickered and flashed on the massive LED screens that encased GoldRush Image HQ in a glittering force field. An A to Z of celebrity guests winked and smiled. World leaders gave the thumbs up. Royalty waved. Superstars blew kisses. On the largest screen, footage of Dad interviewing the prime minister was playing on a loop – a twenty-metre-high love-in, a bromance special. This supersized image gave the impression that the two of them governed the country from right there on the sofa. A chill crept up my spine.

Across London, lights were flicking on. People were hunkering down for the night, cooking supper, putting the kids to bed and switching on the TV. Soon they would be turning on the news and watching the train crash story.

I steadied myself against the side of Westminster Bridge. London stretched for miles in every direction. Its lights marked out a strange, parallel world to the one I knew.

The civilian world.

Although technically I lived in London, I didn't really. I didn't walk around the streets, take the bus or hang out in its parks. I never shopped on the high streets or in department stores. I couldn't grab a coffee, chill out in civilian bars or walk the dog. I was a global, or, in other words, stinking rich – because my parents were part of the global financial elite, the one-percenters. So it was simply too dangerous. Globals inhabited secure corporate spaces – VIP retail theatres, bars and clubs. We lived in the Gates, secure gated apartment blocks, the Billionaires' quarter and the Fortress district, as well as swanky penthouses. Bubbled by security twenty-four/seven, we were chauffeured around in bulletproof limos or helicopters from one safe corporate space to the next. We were protected from the world. In fact, my feet rarely touched the pavement unless it was covered by red carpet.

I never walked around by myself. *Not like this.*

Pointing my finger at London's skyline, I joined the dots of my life: Mum and Dad's HQ, our billion-pound apartment as well as my favourite clubs, restaurants and bars – constructing a twinkling spider's web of my regular haunts.

Coco and the List would probably be out tonight, despite the crash. They were going to The Glitz to celebrate the beginning of the Easter break. Nothing – not even a train crash – would stop those girls from partying. Think of the gossip! The press would be scrumming the place, desperate to hear their stories. They would be media stars. What better way to start the holidays? I usually met my London friends at SkyLab on a Friday. Its neon sign pulsed seductively. And for a moment I thought about giving up and walking over to GoldRush HQ, going straight back into the lion's den, but I pushed the idea from my head. I could be on a jet, heading off for the mother of all makeovers. But that wasn't okay for me right now. My anger bubbled up again, hot and furious. My parents didn't own my body, not yet.

A siren wailed in the distance. Instantly memories of the night my whole life was turned upside down flooded back.

All it took was a screech of a siren, a full moon or a blast of my favourite getting-ready-to-go-out tune, which at that time was a vintage hit from a few years back, and in a flash I was back there, reliving that night, still half-believing it was a dream. Not that I needed triggers because the events of that night were with me twenty-four/seven, like a screensaver of snapshots continuously looping round, ambushing me whenever my mind wasn't occupied. Even though it had been almost a month, the memory remained raw, bright and dramatic, like blood gushing from a fresh wound. Sometimes I felt as if the memory had seeped into my bloodstream and, like grit in a shoe, it worried me constantly.

* * *

On the night in question, it had been business as usual – more or less. I'd been warring with my stylists about which outfit I was going to wear for a film premiere. I'd picked out an Alexander McQueen black mini dress with a death's-head hawkmoth design across the front, and had teamed it with silver trainers, while my stylists had been proposing something more appropriate for the GoldRush brand. When, suddenly, a bone-chilling screech rang out. The security alarm's wail invaded every corner of the house. It vibrated my stomach, turned my organs to jelly, taking over my body like some kind of sound-shifter. Then a robotic voice was ordering us to make our way to the panic room.

I rushed out into the corridor. Stevie was belting towards me. He was shouting something, but his words were lost in the siren's wail. His arms folded around me, and then he was charging up to the next floor where the panic room was situated.

When we reached the safe room, Stevie punched in the code, threw open the door and dumped me inside. It was state of the art. Space age.

"What's up?" My voice boomed in the silence of the soundproofed room.

"Intruders. A Crunch Town gang. We're dealing with it," he said, before speaking into his walkie-talkie. "Yes, sir. Dasha's secure." Then, as he turned to leave, he said, "You know the drill. Stay here until the all-clear sounds."

"Where are Mum and Dad?" I asked nervously, never in

a million years imagining that I would be shut up in the safe room all alone. In previous drills, Mum and Dad had always been there to reassure me.

"They're okay," he said. "They'll be up soon." Next minute he had lurched from the safe room and was rocketing back down the corridor.

As I went to shut the door, I hesitated. The panic room with its white padded walls, its graveyard silence and its minimalist furniture gave me the creeps; it was like an antechamber to death. I half-expected someone to arrive with my last supper, a little something to cheer me up before my lethal injection. On impulse, I crept into the corridor.

Nobody. The staff had vanished into the vibrating air. Realising the siren would drown out my footsteps, I sprinted down the corridors until I reached the stretch of landing overlooking the hallway. Then, crouching behind the banisters, I peered down into the grand entrance to my parents' mansion. It was empty.

As suddenly as it had started, the siren stopped, plunging the house into an eerie silence – not a sound, not even the soft-shoe shuffle of the maids as they went about their business. Through the vast stained-glass window above the front door, I saw the security lights snap on, revealing two of Dad's security guards approaching the house. I ducked down behind a Henry Moore sculpture, moulding my shape to its curves. The guards took up position on either side of the front door. I'd left it too late to head downstairs.

The silence deepened.

The full moon looked like a blood orange through the stained-glass window.

Noticing my crouching figure reflected in the supersized red heart hanging from the ceiling, I inched back behind the sculpture. My father had given Mum the heart for their last wedding anniversary. It was a Jeff Koons. Dad had paid over thirty million pounds for it. The truck-sized chandelier stippled the shiny, metallic heart with a million pinpricks of light. Banks of gilt mirrors were reflecting the light back, too.

My heartbeat was booming so loudly, it would have easily filled the massive heart.

Footsteps. They were coming from the corridor leading to Dad's study. From the sound of it, seven, maybe eight people were approaching. It was hard to tell because they were marching in time like troops on parade. I edged forwards again.

A phalanx of security strode into the entrance hall. At its centre, a pale-faced woman was struggling to free herself from the guards' grip. She was wearing a classic Burberry trench and a salmon-pink scarf at her throat, a shining pearl in the ugly shell of security.

The woman turned around to speak to someone out of sight.

She had dark hair. A flash of green eyes. Porcelain skin.

Heartstop. Even in the blur of movement, there was no mistaking our likeness. A jolt of electricity zapped through me. I edged out some more.

As she tussled with the guards, she shouted: "I want to see my daughter."

Her words rang out, clear and sweet as birdsong, swooping up and round the domed ceiling.

They were like an adrenalin shot to my heart.

Security clamped her shoulders more firmly, closing in around her as they propelled her towards the door. Now the woman's shouts were muffled – absorbed by the guards' expensive cashmere suits. Still I caught every word.

"You'd have to be blind not to see the likeness. You know it's the truth. I'm no blackmailer, no imposter. Mr Gold, she's my child, admit it. She's baby 9614. I can feel it with every cell of my body."

My mouth gaped open.

Next minute the goons had hustled the woman out into the night. Two police cars were waiting outside the security gates, their flashing lights bathed the neighbouring white mansions in a shimmer of blue strobe.

The door slammed shut. A gust of wind stirred the air.

My parents were standing directly below me, out of sight. I heard the click of a cigarette lighter, a sucking sound as they lit up, and then they stepped into the hallway, throwing Halloween-scary shadows up onto the hanging heart.

My father spoke first. "That's her dealt with for now. But we need to make sure it remains dealt with." He cracked his knuckles one by one, a sure sign he was feeling stressed out. "Damn it! Dasha is my life's work. The lynchpin. She's the brand's future. I won't let that woman come swanning in here and foul up our plans. Dasha is ours. We chose her. Bought her, for Chrissakes. Things must be managed carefully. I'll speak to the police chief tomorrow. We need to make sure *that woman* remains silenced."

"How the hell did it happen?" My mother dragged nervously on her cigarette. "Do you think she got our names from FuturePerfect?"

"Not a chance. We signed up with them precisely so this wouldn't happen." He stabbed his cigarette into the air to emphasise his point. "Their confidentiality clause was watertight."

"Must be female intuition. Motherly love." My own mother laughed nastily. "I can't believe how similar they look. It's uncanny. No wonder she made the connection."

"Financial necessity, more like," my father snapped.

His knuckle-crunching echoed off the walls like rifle shots.

"What if she goes to a rival organisation?" My mother took another long drag on her cigarette. "Stirs it up."

"Like she's going to do that. We *are* the media, for Chrissakes. It's our word against hers. It's easy to paint her as a blackmailer, an imposter and a money-grubbing piece of trash. It happens all the time – people turning up, posing as missing children, relatives or long-lost ancestors, and demanding money. She wouldn't come out of it well."

As they spoke, I watched the blue lights of the police cars disappear into the distance. Dad must have been watching too because he added, "The police will take care of it. They are going to caution her for blackmail, leaving her in no doubt about how serious an offence it is. The threat of jail should stop her blabbing. We need this to remain sorted."

"Dasha must never know." My mother's voice sounded strained.

Every millimetre of my skin prickled with anger.

Dad snapped his fingers. "Stevie, check on Dasha. Tell her it was a false alarm if she asks."

I retraced my footsteps at speed. On reaching the panic room, I zapped in the code. The door shut with a snap behind me, the sound of a prison door closing. Totally wired, I paced back and forth, the deep-space silence buzzing in my ears as I ran through the sequence of events.

What the hell was going on?

Was that woman *really* my mother? *For real?*

She certainly looked like me. No, she looked *just* like me.

Barely breathing, I pressed my palms against the white padded walls to steady myself while my brain slowly assimilated the information.

So, the happy family schtick had been a pretence – another lie to add to all the others which had been stacking up recently. But this was deception on a grand scale. I slowly slid down the wall, crouching on my haunches, hands clasped around my head like a crash helmet, as if this gesture might protect me from the lies. Snakes alive! One minute I was Dasha Gold, daughter of the Golds. The next minute I was… what exactly? *Adopted?* Nothing made sense any more. All I had were negatives.

I was NOT a Gold.

The Golds were NOT my parents.

I was NOT their daughter.

Each revelation detonated a massive scream inside my head.

I felt as if I had stepped on a landmine. Boom! All my knowns had become unknowns. Stunned, I sat there staring into space, waiting for the fragments of my life to fall back down to earth again, only to find when they did, and I tried to piece them back together, essential parts of the jigsaw were missing.

What really hurt was the way Dad had spoken about me, like some kind of product. It chimed with the recent bad stuff, reinforcing my fears. As I rocked back and forwards, head cradled in my hands, his words, dark as a witch's curse, filled my head – trolling me, making me feel small, insecure and unloved.

"I bought her."

"Chose her."

"She's my life's work."

"The brand's future."

His words were so cold and businesslike – so unemotional. They weren't going to win him a top-dad tribute anytime soon. I couldn't kid myself, the crazed control-freak was speaking more like a CEO of a global corporation than a doting father. What the hell was a *lynchpin*, anyway?

But my parents' conversation explained a lot, my 'makeover' for a start, and confirmed my worst suspicions. My parents didn't love me, not like parents should –

not unconditionally. First and foremost they saw me as a franchise girl. They wanted to transform me into someone else — make my face fit the brand — and that sucked. I was a brand slave! Fabulous!

Anger started fizzing up from the pit of my stomach, spreading through my body like a brushfire, finally exploding into my brain in a geyser-rush of rage. For months we'd been having massive fights about my surgery, especially after they'd told me how extreme it was going to be. I hated the fact that my parents were trying to control me in every way, right down to how I looked. The next thing I knew I was punching my fists against the padded walls, screaming into the soundproofed silence until I thought my lungs were going to pop. Slumping back against the wall, I wiped away a tear with the back of my hand. I took deep breaths. In. Out. Slowly my fury subsided.

I stared at my feet, confused by how sad I was feeling. In many ways, I should have been glad that I wasn't made up of their demented DNA. What kind of psychos would force their daughter to have cosmetic surgery, anyway? But I wasn't glad. I wasn't happy, not really.

I closed my eyes, clasping my hands tighter around my head, and, like a thwacked piñata, the happy memories came tumbling out — glittery, flashy and fun: days hanging out with Mum and Dad at GoldRush Towers, sitting with them in the edit or mucking around on set; evenings spent watching films in our private cinema; nights at VIP parties and premieres, meeting stars. I indulged in the good memories for a few more moments. There I was riding my pony, Miami; hanging out with my favourite band backstage and chilling out on our island. Dad was a laugh, Mum too, when they weren't 'outsourcing' – another of Dad's slimy words – my care to nannies, minders, stylists and gurus. They weren't around much, but that was the global way. But the glitz and the glamour had filled the space, until the dark stuff kicked off, poisoning everything.

The whiteness and underwater stillness of the panic room pressed in, squeezing the breath from me, as if I were swimming in arctic waters; my heart was slowing and I was drifting into a trance-like state. I punched the wall again, firing up my fury once more. I'd had it with their lies and schemes. I stood up, went into the bathroom and splashed cold water onto my face. *Why would I want to be a Gold, anyway?*

As I became less shell-shocked, I focused on the positives. Okay, I wasn't the Golds' daughter. But was that really so bad? I had another mother. Unbelievable! And if I wasn't their daughter, they had absolutely no right to mess with my face – turn me into some kind of brand-bot. I pictured the woman in the hallway again, her beautiful face framed by Dad's heavies. And in the silence of the panic room, I realised that this woman – if she were my mother, as she claimed – could offer a solution to my problems, if, and it was a very big if, I could track her down.

Squinting at my reflection in the mirror, I wondered why she'd described me as baby 9614. That struck me as weird.

At last I heard the bleep, bleep of the code being tapped in.

The buzz of the door opening. Big Stevie entered.

"False alarm, Dasha."

"What, like everything else in my life?" I spat the words out.

He shrugged, puzzled by my tone. "Your dad has given me your schedule for tonight. We've got to leave in thirty."

I ignored him and started walking back to my bedroom. I could hear his footsteps padding along, ten metres behind me, as per usual.

I gripped the side of the bridge, anger flashing up again at the memory.

Big Ben struck eight. A reality check – like the bongs at the beginning of the news. Two hours had passed since the train crash. I pictured Mum pacing her penthouse office mad with worry while Dad was on his mobile calling in favours. I focused on the London Eye, wanting to sync my racing thoughts with its slow spin. I could live a different life if I held my nerve. The measured turn of the wheel steadied my thoughts. The pavement felt firm beneath my feet. I was grounded now and, despite everything, I felt strangely anchored. The crash had given me the chance to realise a dream. Could I do it? Doubt zapped me. Although I had been thinking about finding my real mother more or less constantly since that night, it took the form of daydreaming rather than concrete, practical plans, because, I guess, I had never imagined even in my wildest dreams that I would ever escape the Golds. But against the odds I had given Big Stevie the slip. Like the spin of a bottle or a roulette table, my number had miraculously come up, and I couldn't blow my good luck. I had to give it my best shot.

Keep calm, deep breaths, this is your one chance, Dash. Okay? Okay? I had to get to the adoption agency. *But how?* I clutched at the silver locket, which I always wore round my neck, and considered the options. Hidden inside the locket was the address of FuturePerfect. That was a step in the right direction, at least. I had something, somewhere to aim for. I glanced up at Big Ben. But it was too late to do anything tonight.

So what now? Think straight, Dash. Calm thoughts. THINK! THINK!

I looked helplessly at the massiveness of London stretched out before me, overwhelmed by my cluelessness. How the hell was I going to get round the city when the only Tube map I'd ever studied in detail was the lithograph, 'The Great Bear', which was hanging in Dad's bathroom. The artist had replaced the tube stations with the names of famous people, so I could get to Albert Einstein, Michael Caine or Charles Darwin, but what the dib-dab-scritch use was that?

Think! I could head over to Scarlet's apartment, tell her about my situation and swear her to secrecy. That was a plan of sorts, although she was about as useless as me when it came to the civilian world. Scarlet was my oldest friend. We'd known each other for twelve years, and we were close, although not as close as we used to be since I'd been attending the Academy. But we hung out together most weekends.

We were partners-in-crime on the party circuit. We'd had zillions of sleepovers, shared buckets full of ice cream and watched a million movies together. She knew all my secrets – well, almost. Luckily she lived alone in a secure Gate on Royal Hospital Road because her parents were out of the country most of the time, which meant I could hide out there without raising parental suspicion. Her Gate was about fifteen minutes upriver by limo, so I guessed it couldn't be more than an hour by foot – not that I fancied walking, but as I'd never taken the bus or the Tube in my life, and I reckoned taking a cab was too risky, I didn't have much choice.

A siren burst into life on the other side of the river – another reminder.

I took a deep breath. My skin prickled with excitement. London twinkled and pulsed around me. I drew myself up to my full height, blew a kiss to GoldRush Image HQ and murmured, "Who's in control now?"

Figuring it would be a smart move to avoid the roads and CCTV cameras where possible, I scooted back down to the river walkway, taking the last few steps at a gallop. The section across the river from the Houses of Commons was deserted and dark – no clowns, no Disney characters, no tourists; nobody, apart from a couple kissing on a bench.

At intervals the walkway was lit by old-fashioned lamps, which cast a murky glow. The gloom gave me goosebumps. Glancing over at the Houses of Parliament, I imagined MPs, or 'my people', as Dad liked to call them, watching me from the Houses of Commons. I shivered and walked on purposefully. Up ahead, a gang of skaters were mucking about. Their boards whizzed and zipped as they did stunts. A police boat sped downriver, its hull crashing against the water like a warning drum. For a second, the darkness pressed in on me. I hesitated, but telling myself not to be so jumpy, I shoved my hands into my pockets, quickened my pace, slotting in behind the zigzagging skaters. A guy with a blond mop of hair turned around, clocked me and grinned. I smiled back, but kept my distance. I followed them over Lambeth Bridge, past Millbank Tower on the north side of the river and up to Tate Britain, where they picked up their boards and mingled with groups of arty-looking kids drinking beer and smoking outside on the steps.

Above the entrance a white neon artwork stated: EVERYTHING IS GOING TO BE ALRIGHT. I knew it was stupid, but I crossed my fingers and repeated the phrase under my breath. I couldn't help myself: it was just something I did. I was always looking for signs to reassure myself: magpies, shooting stars, lucky numbers, pennies to pick up or a vapour-trail kiss up in the sky. It was the way I was — superstitious.

The partygoers looked as if they were having such a good time that, for an instant, I was tempted to stay, but I rejected the idea at once, realising it wasn't exactly the cleverest move when you're about to trend worldwide on social media. Anyway, I'd had enough of parties for a lifetime, so I carried on walking, adrenalin spinning through me like a supernova sugar rush.

The stretch of river beyond the Tate was deserted. A great hulk of a restaurant stood empty, its roof stripped of slate. Next door, there was a boarded-up petrol station covered with graffiti. Red neon spelled out Dolphin Square across a block of art deco flats. A car swished past in a rush of steel and blank eyes. On the other side of the river, Battersea Power Station loomed like a ghostly ocean liner.

It was a beautiful night. The full moon shone on the water, shaping a silvery superhighway. I sucked a deep breath of night air down into my lungs. My blood felt charged up, as if I'd bungee-jumped right down from the stars.

A driver honked his horn and I swore under my breath as I watched the car's red tail lights glide off into the night. A taxi cruised by with its **FOR HIRE** sign lit up. My hands twitched in my pockets. I balled them and carried on walking.

I'd just passed a single red phone box when I heard footsteps approaching at speed. I glanced back, half expecting, half hoping to see Big Stevie. Instead I saw a scruffy man in a T-shirt and trackie bottoms. His face split into a leer, and then he broke into a run.

Heart rocketing, I was running, too, but my heels were slowing me down. Without looking round, I could tell he was gaining on me, because I could hear his trainers pounding the pavement in long strides while, in contrast, the tickity-tack of my stiletto steps were small and uncertain. And all I could think was, *Oh my God! What the hell am I going to do now?*

Although I knew I'd lose valuable seconds, I pulled off

my heels, fumbling and fluffing, and nearly falling over in my haste. Then, clasping a shoe in each hand, I surged forwards, like an Olympic runner sprinting from the blocks. The cool pavement felt good beneath my feet. My Dior bag bumped against my hip, unbalancing me. I used my shoes like paddles, pushing them through the air, ramping up my speed. I concentrated on planting my feet in the centre of each paving stone, forcing myself to take them two at a time, stretching myself to the limit and building up a rhythm which would propel me forwards. In my head, I was certain he would catch me if I accidentally trod on a crack.

Seeing a sprawling estate – a junk space – to my right, I thought about heading in, but picturing dead ends, poor lighting, hood-rats, I kept on running. About five hundred metres up the road, Chelsea Bridge's lights were twinkling, which meant Scarlet's Gate couldn't be more than ten minutes away. But before that I had to negotiate an underpass beneath a railway bridge, its lights smashed out by vandals. I estimated twenty metres of dimly lit terrain. I dug deep for a final spurt of energy and raced in.

The creep's stride lengthened, too. Seconds later, his footsteps were reverberating around the railway bridge. The sound of his piggy breath swallowed me up. In the distance, I saw a set of traffic lights change to green.

Go! Go! Go! A voice screeched in my head.

He was on me in three steps.

"Got you!" A wet slap of a whisper.

His breath smelled like road kill.

His hands gripped my shoulders, and then he was pushing me down towards the pavement. His lips were right next to my ear, and he was calling me baby.

No way, I thought. This wasn't meant to be happening. *Everything is going to be all right.* I repeated the phrase in my head, picturing the phrase lit up on Tate Britain in neon lights. The rhythm of the words calmed my mind. Suddenly a part of me was floating a few feet above the scene, directing my earthbound self to relax. Obeying orders, I went limp, which threw the creep off balance, and then I rammed my stiletto heel up into his armpit with all my strength. Cussing loudly, he grabbed hold of my face with a sweaty hand and turned my nose like a key in a lock. Spluttering for breath, I pushed the shoe in harder. He loosened his grip. Squirming free, I spun round to face him. Then, pointing the heels of my stilettos at him as if they were blades, I started edging away, never once taking my eyes off him, so that when he lunged towards me, I danced out of reach with ease. Then I rushed at him, stabbing the heel into his face. When he staggered backwards clutching his eyes, I started sprinting for the traffic lights.

From behind, I heard running footsteps, a thud of fist on flesh, a groan, followed by the crump of a body hitting the pavement. I glanced over my shoulder, stopped in my tracks. A tall, slim kid in a cowboy hat had knocked the creep to the ground. The boy turned. His smile was wide and crooked. He was dressed in street cleaners' overalls and was wearing a black and white chequered keffiyeh around his neck.

"You okay?" He nodded up the brim of his hat with the tip of his middle finger, and smiled reassuringly. "Looked like you were in a bit deep."

I didn't reply, just stood there goggle-eyed and gasping.

"Are you okay?" he repeated, walking over.

My eyes flicked from the boy to the heap of human on the pavement.

"*Vamos, chica.*" He grabbed my arm so I had no option but to follow him back down the road that I'd run up moments earlier.

Brainsnap! I was heading into the night with a boy — a stranger, a civilian, most probably an outcast. He could be dangerous. But at that moment, it just felt good to be whisked away from there, and to be escaping the vile creep without having to think...

As I ran after the boy, I realised that the world is a scary place when you know dib-dab-scritch about it.

The Nighter

"ARE you lost?" he shouted as we headed into the estate that I had avoided before. "It's not safe to jam round here. Get me?"

"Yes," I shouted, but my reply came out like a big, blustery gasp.

"Keep tight," he yelled, sprinting ahead.

A stitch was burning in my side and, as the distance between us lengthened, I concentrated on keeping up, eyes fixed on the bobbing, luminous Westminster logo on the back of his overalls.

The estate was a maze of dark streets and unlit walkways. Squares of light framed domestic scenes: a screaming fight, a house party and a muscle-man pumping iron. From open windows, a mash-up of music escaped into the night, pop ballads slugging it out with rap.

Terrified we might get jumped by gangs lurking in the shadows, I kept my eyes lowered, focusing on the pavement. *Don't tread on the cracks or the monsters will get you. Don't tread on the cracks...* I found myself clinging to this crackpot superstition, wanting to blank out the dangers that I imagined all around me.

After about five minutes, we headed out of the estate, past a parade of shops, a library and a school until we finally stopped by a slab-grey church, squeezed between two rows of gleaming white Georgian town houses, like a rotten tooth in a bright cosmetic smile. The church towered above me, making me feel small and wrong. I don't know why, but churches always made me feel that way.

Bending over to catch my breath, the blood rushed to my head in a twist of dizziness. A pain stabbed deep into my guts. I gripped my sides and inhaled deeply.

I straightened up slowly.

The boy in the cowboy hat was standing on the church steps. His shadow loomed up behind him, like his deputy. Although the boy's eyes were shaded beneath the rim of his hat, I could feel his gaze lasering me. I found his stillness, his watchfulness unnerving. There was definitely an edge to him. I walked over uncertainly, eyes lowered, focusing on my glittery socks, which spangled in the lamplight.

As I approached, he knocked up the brim of his cowboy hat with spindly fingers and gave me his wide, crooked smile. "Latif, all-round good guy, night-haunt drifter and sometime saviour of dames in distress. *Salaam, chica.*"

"Dasha," I whispered, shaking his outstretched hand, even though it seemed stupidly formal. "Thanks," I added, wondering when my brain was going to stop rationing the words to my mouth. ONE. AT. A. TIME. I was rarely stuck for something to say so I wasn't enjoying feeling like a prize idiot one little bit.

I studied him in the lamplight, trying to work him out. I'd never met a civilian before. Of course, my parents' army of staff – the maids, minders, stylists, TV people, chauffeurs, gurus and the rest – was always around, but they didn't count. I'd never been alone with a civilian socially before. I'd never hung out with a civilian. *Not like this.* Therefore, I had no idea how to behave. Lowering my eyes, I traced the letters on the lid of a manhole with a glittery toe: SELF-LOCKING.

Like my mouth, I thought hopelessly.

"So, you okay?" That crooked smile again. Then, nodding at my shoes, he added, "Cute weapons of mass destruction. You shanked him good."

I turned them over in my hands. One of the heels was speckled with blood. "Hopeless getaway shoes, though." Then, shuddering at the memory of the creep, I placed my stilettos on the church wall, positioning them carefully side by side, like a bloody offering to the gods. It felt good, as if I'd just stepped out of chains.

"You said it. Crazy shoes for a night walk."

"I guess," I said, eyeing him with suspicion.

An awkward silence wrapped around us. A shiver of unease chilled me momentarily. Wanting a distraction, I took a pair of trainers from my croc bag and slipped them on. But when I went to do them up, my shaky fingers tied themselves in knots.

I sat down on the wall and, resting my elbows on my knees, cupped my face in my hands. From above, the shrill squawk of neon-crazed birds punctured the silence. Thinking they sounded about as strung-out as I felt, I stared up into the darkness, hoping to glimpse them in the branches. For a moment the urge to scream into the night like one of those confused birds overpowered me. I closed my eyes, clenched my fists and pressed them to my temples.

"Don't fret, *chica*." Latif squeezed my knee gently.

My eyes snapped open.

He was crouching down at my feet with his face raised towards mine. It was the first time I'd seen him properly. His skin was a deep olive colour and his cheekbones were razor-sharp. He had long, curly eyelashes, which framed huge aquamarine eyes. And he had one of those smiles that blew you away. I guessed he was from the Middle East or perhaps North Africa.

"Thought you needed some assistance."

"I guess," I whispered, staring down at my trembling hands incredulously. "I'm not usually this much of a loser. I can dress myself and everything, honest." I tried a joke, but a sob clogged my throat so the words came out strange.

Fixing me with his aquamarines, he smiled reassuringly. "Don't let negative stuff eat you up. Move on.'"

"I guess," I repeated, even though I was thinking, *Easier said than done.*

When he started tying my laces he let out a low whistle. "Your creps are live." He flicked his fingers as if they were too hot to handle. "You must've queued all night to get your hands on these."

"What?" I blinked. "Queued?" I had never queued for anything in my life, and was about to tell him so, as well as explaining that Nike had biked them round for free and were paying me a cool ten thousand pounds to wear them when he said, "All I'm saying is they're limited."

Quickly swallowing my brags, I mumbled a lame, "Yeah, I know."

His left eyebrow shot up. He looked as if he were about to say something, but then, deciding against it, carried on tying my laces. The top of his hat was scarred and battered. I folded my arms, feeling exposed. I was going to have to watch what I said around him. He was sharp. Nothing escaped him.

"Want a cuppa?" Latif nodded towards a small green hut, no bigger than a garden shed. Outside, a line of black cabs stood snout to tail like pot-bellied pigs. The hut had the look of a time machine about it, and for a moment, I let myself believe that Latif was some kind of time traveller – a space cowboy – who was going to whisk me off around the universe, away from all my problems.

"What is this place?" I asked. "Some kind of pop-up cafe?"

"A cabbies' hut." His left eyebrow shot up again. "Nothing pop-up about it. It's been here for centuries. My mum eats here when she's on shift." We waited for a car to pass. "Jeannie, she runs the gaff, used to babysit me years ago, so I'm always welcome – with or without Mum. I'm mates with Ren, her son."

"So your mum's a cabbie?"

"Yeah. She's been doing the night shift for years. She gets all sorts in her cab after midnight: the trashed, the spaced-out, the loved-up and the lonely. They all pile in and spill their secrets. Mum says she's a chronicler of the human condition, or some cod like that." He took my elbow as we crossed the road. "She's got a book of short stories out of it, though. Beautiful, bleak, sad stories featuring losers. I swear she steals stories for a living. Ever heard of Harriet Hajjaj?"

I shook my head.

Latif pulled a slim, well-thumbed paperback from beneath his overalls. The cover featured a bird's-eye view of London at night. Its title was *The Nightingale and Other Stories*.

"Not bad for a story thief." He polished the cover on his overalls. "They're about the city at night. Have the same vibe as Raymond Carver. You know, sad, sparse, depressing. I'm in one, too." He flicked to the page; the title read 'Words Disappear at Dawn'.

"I thought you said she only wrote about losers." I smiled.

"Yeah, bubblehead. But every story needs a hero," he shot back with a grin.

As we walked towards the hut, Latif gave a group of men a mock salute. "*Salaam*, bruvs." They were huddled round the first cab in line, pulling on fags, chatting and fiddling with their smartphones. GoldRush Radio blabbed from the first cab. I recognised the voice of 'The Rottweiler' – Dad's favourite shock-jock.

"All right, Lazio FC," they said. Nobody bothered to look up.

"This bunch of professional blowhards worship the ground I walk on," Latif said, swinging his arm around the shoulder of a middle-aged guy in a biker's jacket.

"Yeah right, Lazio. Sure we do." The cabbie gave him a soft punch on the arm. "Have you heard the news?"

"What news?" Latif leaned into the semi-circle, tilting his head towards the cab so he could hear the radio.

"There's been a crash. One of them chartered trains has come off the tracks. News is patchy. The police haven't released many details yet. Sounds like a hold-up."

"What? A snatch job?" Latif asked.

I stepped back into the shadows.

"Yeah. Sounds like it," a bearded man in an anorak chipped in. "The train was full of stuck-up global girls from the Star Academy, heading home for Easter." He rubbed his thumb against his fingers. "Rich pickings."

Feeling Latif's eyes on me, I lowered my gaze, pretending to examine a splodge of chewing gum stamped into the shape of a four-leafed clover on the pavement. I hoped nobody had been kidnapped, I wouldn't wish that on my worst enemy — not even Coco.

"Trouble in Westminster, too. Our wire says it's a bomb scare," a cabbie with a pinched face said through a veil of cigarette smoke that did nothing to soften his skull-like features. "No offence, Latif, but it sounds like your mob are up to no good again."

"Offence taken, Dave," Latif muttered.

Although Latif's tone was cold, Dave treated his reply as a joke. His laughter rang out behind us as we walked towards the cafe.

Inside, the hut was tiny — a sandwich box of a room. Benches and Formica tables ran down three walls. A kitchenette filled the fourth. On the counter an old-fashioned tea urn stood huffing steam. Chelsea kit, posters and memorabilia covered the walls. In one corner a bearded man sat hunched over a plate of chips, shovelling in massive mouthfuls while flicking through *The Mirror*. A middle-aged woman with mashed-potato skin and ketchup-red hair was standing behind the counter reading a magazine.

"Hey, Lats. Help us with this, love. There's a holiday up for grabs. I've got to answer a few questions and think up a witty ending." She shoved a magazine under Latif's nose and pointed to the relevant bit. "Finish that. *All the world's...*"

"Going to hell in a handbag?" He tilted his head and scrutinised her, rubbing his chin with spindly fingers, as if assessing her ideal holiday destination. "I reckon hell's your kind of place, Jeannie. It's hot and full of bad boys."

Jeannie flicked at him with a grubby J-cloth. "No joking around, Lats. This is serious business." She shook her head. "No wonder your mum despairs. Everything's a joke to you, innit?" She handed him a pen with a chewed end. "Go on, have a go. There's a love."

Latif looked at the quiz while helping himself to a Kit Kat from a display on the counter. I hung behind him like a shadow.

"Same as usual?" Jeannie was already placing a chipped mug beneath the urn.

"Yeah. Make that two, Jeannie." A winning smile

guaranteed he'd get everything for free. "Has Mum been in tonight?"

"Not yet. She's late. The boys say there's all sorts of trouble out there tonight. Suppose the traffic's snarled up all over." She waved at the shaggy-haired bloke as he left and shouted, "See you, Geoff. Take care." He gave her a Border-terrier smile.

While they chatted and joked, I studied Latif: the street overalls, the keffiyeh, the cowboy hat and the book sticking out of his overalls pocket. Nothing about him added up to a nice neat whole. I desperately wanted to stick a label on him — *Civilian, Outcast, Geek, Goth, Skater, Street cleaner, Poet* — but I couldn't make him out at all.

"Jeannie, news if you want it," one of the cabbies shouted.

When Jeannie and Latif trooped out, I remained inside, moving closer to the door, straining my ears, desperate to hear the headlines. Despite missing the first half of the lead news item, I heard enough to catch the gist. Two girls had been kidnapped, as yet unnamed. This news shocked me. Assuming they were counting me as the other, the kidnap crew had actually taken a girl from my school. That was bad. Terrifying. Steadying myself against the wall, I let the news sink in, and tried to work out how it affected my situation. For now my parents must believe me kidnapped, which would buy me some time. A couple of deep breaths calmed my jittery nerves. At least they hadn't released my name.

First up, my appearance needed attention. Nipping behind the counter and over to the sink, I waited for the water to run hot before washing the smell of the horrible pervert from my skin. Then I pulled my hair back into a ponytail and wiped every trace of make-up from my face with a paper napkin. Taking a compact mirror from my bag, I flicked it open and assessed the results. Yeah. That was a definite improvement. I looked younger, less plastic, more like a civilian, which had to be a good thing. Pleased with my new look, I sat down at the table facing the door. Salt scattered the yellow Formica tabletop.

So what now?

Under the harsh light of the fluorescent strips, my plan to track down my birth mother seemed about as attainable as a dream. The incident down by the river had put me off night adventures, and my cluelessness about the real world was tragic. For a moment I thought about going back to my parents and resigning myself to my future.

My parents always got what they wanted in the end.

Why put off the inevitable?

But another, louder, more insistent voice in my head wouldn't hear of it. If I went back now, I would never forgive myself. I had a chance to change my life in so many ways, and I mustn't blow it. I had to get match tough. Once again the image of my mother in the hallway popped into my head – the memory that had haunted me every night for the last month. I checked my new look in the compact mirror once more. It was unreal how similar we looked. But I was glad – my face was my passport to my new world. I snapped the mirror shut. I had to find her. She held all the answers.

Well, an escape at least. My resolve strengthened. I had to discover the truth. The question was *how* I was going to do it. Not if…

Laughter from outside made me look up. Latif was ribbing the cabbie in the biker jacket, who took a playful swing at him. Latif dodged his fist, then, tipping his hat to the guy, headed back into the hut.

My next thought took me by surprise. Latif would be the perfect person to help me find my parents. He knew his way around the city and was totally at ease with lurking in the dark. I studied his loose-limbed coolness for a few seconds. Dream on. Why would someone like him help someone like me? But the idea seeded itself in my brain. I had to find a way…

I smiled when Latif entered the room and studied him with new interest.

"Beware of the builder's. It's like a blow to the head." He plonked two chipped mugs down onto the table, slopping tea over the yellow Formica. "Jeannie's tea is knock-out strong." His overalls swished as he sat down opposite. I couldn't help noticing his hands were soft, his nails clean. They didn't look like worker's hands.

"Thanks." I cradled the cup in my hands. I found the warmth against my palms comforting. The heat spread up my arms. I took a slurp and relaxed a little. I prayed he'd keep the banter coming, because right now jokes were better than questions.

And he did.

I sat back and let him chat away. I liked the way he spoke

about nothing in particular, cracked jokes and seemed totally uninterested in any of the usual stuff — parents, school and celebrities. I also loved the way he was behaving as if rescuing a girl under a railway bridge was just part of an ordinary day. I listened, nodded and smiled. Although I felt shy and out of my depth, there was a leapiness in my stomach and excitement ballooning up inside me. It was all so different from what I was used to.

After a while I asked casually, "What's the news on the train?"

"Two glob-girls have been kidnapped. The media's gone mad for it."

"Have they been named?"

"No names." His eyes pierced through me. "Those kidnap guys are getting real slick. Holding up the Bullet is smooth."

"I hate those kidnap guys," I said with a little too much feeling. "They're out of control. Those kidnap videos give me the creeps." My mouth was running away from me again. I stopped abruptly. My eyes slid towards the door, searching the night for a second or two. I shivered. It was dark out there.

"It's all about the money." He shrugged. "The girls' parents will pay. Then, boom, they'll go back to their safe little lives. Nobody's ever been murdered. It's a game."

"Great game."

My friend Georgina had been kidnapped on Christmas Eve the year before last. In the video, her kidnapper had stood at her side dressed in a Santa suit with a gun pressed to her head. A tinny version of 'In the Bleak Midwinter' had been playing in the background. Her parents had paid over a million pounds to get her back. Now another of my friends had been snatched. I shut my eyes and massaged my temples with the tips of my fingers. It could have been me. And Latif would have shrugged, wouldn't have cared. I was shocked to find this bothered me.

"You okay?" he asked.

"Yeah. Yeah." I stuttered. Quickly reminding myself that he was asking about the attack, I raised my head slowly and said, "No. Not really. Every time I close my eyes I see that creep. It's like his ugly mug has been tattooed beneath my eyelids."

"It's dodgy down by the river at night." Latif tilted his head and gave me a sideways look. "Why were you down there alone and that?"

I hesitated. My eyes slid towards the door again. Then I heard myself explaining that I'd decided to walk from Tate Britain to my friend's house on Royal Hospital Road because the river had looked so beautiful with the full moon glinting on its surface. Well, it was half-true, I thought, as I spun the story out.

"What was on at the Tate?"

"An opening," I said a fraction too late, praying he wouldn't ask the artist's name. I felt the full beam of his interest for a few seconds. He seemed to be going to ask another question, but decided against it.

I stirred two heaped teaspoons of sugar into my tea to hide a slight exhalation of breath.

"More tea with your sugar?" he joked.

I laughed a little too loudly. "I'm not allowed sugar usually."

"*Damn!*" he said. "Now *that's* what I call rebellion."

I took a gulp of the sugary liquid, cringing inwardly at my comment.

Latif slipped a cheap mobile from beneath his waterproofs. "I'll give Mum a bell. She'll give you a ride home." He held out the phone. "First you'd better call the feds. Report him. You know, so he can't try it again. Another girl might not be so lucky."

Home? Police? The words jolted me straight back to my dilemma. *The life-changer.* I stared at the phone but didn't take it. Once again I was overwhelmed by a desire to go home, curl up in my heart-shaped bed and fall asleep in front of my plasma TV with Bling, my Dalmatian. I pushed the thought to the back of my mind. I couldn't chicken out now.

I studied Latif for a few moments. That crooked smile again. Suddenly my earlier recklessness was back. It was a gamble. What the hell? I didn't make a habit of cosying up to strangers. But Latif seemed cool. He knew the city and seemed like the kind of guy who was up for adventure. Things would be a whole deal easier if I could hook him into my quest. Hope surged through me for a minute, then fizzled out. I frowned. It was going to take all my powers of persuasion.

"I can't go home." I met his eyes with unwavering resolve. "And I don't want the police involved."

Latif narrowed his eyes. "Why?" he asked after a few long seconds.

"I'm on the run, sort of," I said, keeping the details as vague as possible. I could feel a blush rising up my neck.

"What? Murdered your maid or something?" A hint of a smile twitched his lips.

"Is it that obvious?" I laughed, wanting to keep it light. "And I thought I was coming across so street."

"Yeah. About as street as a Chihuahua."

"Thanks a bunch!" I traced the wet rings left by my mug on the table. "Look, it's parent stuff. It's complicated."

"Why so secretive, *chica*?" Latif narrowed his eyes again. "Don't think it makes you seem mysterious because it don't. But if that's the way you want to roll…"

"I'm not trying to be mysterious." I shrugged a little too carelessly. I made a swift calculation about how much I should tell him. However friendly, he was a stranger, and a stranger who wasn't exactly a big fan of globals or celebrities, so the less he knew about my background for now the better. In a couple of hours, I would be named as one of the kidnapped girls, and if my parents thought me kidnapped there would be a massive reward – a million pounds at least. I studied him for a few more minutes. My guts were saying he was a good bloke, but even a saint might be tempted to hand me in for that kind of money. For that reason, I had to remain anonymous for the time being at least – until

I'd had a chance to work out whether I could trust him a hundred per cent.

"Honestly, I'm not trying to be mysterious," I repeated nervously, desperate to fill the silence.

He raised an eyebrow, but took the hint and eased off the interrogation gas.

The silence crackled with static.

I took a few more moments to work out my approach. I'd tell him half the story – the half that might win him round.

I cleared my throat. "I haven't told anyone this before."

Immediately I had his full attention. Lowering my gaze, I continued in a sad, small voice. "I'm adopted. I only found out recently." I paused for effect. "By mistake." Another long beat. Then, when he didn't speak, I carried on in an even softer voice. He leaned forwards to catch my words. My heart leapt. I was reeling him in. "It's an odd story. All I know is a woman showed up at our house a month ago, looking for me. I just happened to see her when my parents were hustling her off the premises. They never mentioned it, but since that night I've thought of nothing else. I'm trying to track her down. That was why I was down by the river."

I lapsed into silence.

He didn't fill it.

I looked up. His eyes lasered me.

I took a few seconds before continuing. "Since this mystery woman showed up, I've been waiting for the right moment to disappear. Tonight down by the Tate, everything fell into place. I knew that it was now or never. It's a quest,

I guess. I know that sounds cheesy, but I'm deadly serious about it. My parents are going to freak out when they discover I'm missing. They've probably called the police already. I hate them…" I tailed off, as if I had found it too painful to discuss. I was good at acting roles.

"No problem. It's your stuff. I get you, it's private." Latif shrugged, giving a good impression of being totally uninterested. But I could tell he was intrigued.

"It's just something I need to do."

"Find your own way." He gave me a look as if to say, "You haven't made a very good job of it so far."

I forced a sad little half-smile. "Up until the bridge, things had been going well. I was on a real high." Jeannie came back inside and started wiping down the counter, but I managed to hold his gaze. "Thanks again for helping me out."

"Pleasure, *chica*. All in a night's work."

"Is that where you work? Under that bridge?" I asked, wanting to shift the focus onto him. But as soon as the words left my mouth, I wanted to grab them back again.

"Yeah right! That's my office." A wry smile played at the corner of his mouth as he checked the clock on the wall. "Know what? I've got unfinished business back there so I'm going to head back. I've been staking the place out for days."

"Can I come?" I prayed my voice sounded casual.

"What, *you*?" He looked taken aback.

"Yeah. Why not?" I drew a squiggle in the spilt tea on the table with my finger. "I can't go home. I've got nowhere to go."

"Not my problem, Dasha."

"Okay." I stared at the squiggle, shaped it into a question mark. I wasn't sure how to play him. After a few seconds I stood up, zipped up my coat and shrugged my bag over my shoulder – all the while staring into the night. I met his gaze and said, "Seriously, thanks for rescuing me down by the river. It's been nice meeting you." I flashed him my best smile. "If not a little weird."

"Are you going home?"

"No way. I'd be nuts to go back. I'm on a mission." Then I quickly averted my eyes and looked out into the darkness, pretending to wipe away a tear. It was a pretty low-down trick to pull, but it was the if-all-else-fails part of my game plan. Playing parts was the one thing the Golds had schooled me well in. "Where's the nearest Tube?" I asked, voice trembling.

"'Sakes, Dasha. Don't be so ramshackle." He looked uneasy.

"Seriously. I'll cope. It's no big deal," I whispered.

He shook his head. "I know I'm gonna regret this..." He drummed his fingers on the table. "You up for a bit of after-hours work?" He smiled. "No fear, I'll protect you, bubblehead." He gulped down his last mouthful of tea. He seemed happier now there was a plan of action, and we were on the move again. "If you get freaked out, you gotta get back out there again. Soon as, get me?"

"Like when you fall off a horse?"

"Hell. Yeah! Just like that, bubblehead." His smile split open his face. "So you up for it or not?"

Without waiting for an answer, he was up and in the kitchen rooting around in the cupboard beneath the sink, getting under Jeannie's feet and making her curse. A few minutes later, he was back, clutching a black hoodie, a baseball cap, a pollution mask and a set of street cleaner's waterproofs, identical to the ones he was wearing. The logo on the jacket read *Westminster City Council*.

"Take these." He pushed the bundle of clothes into my hands. I took them reluctantly. The overalls were covered in mud and smelled of rubber and sweat. I wrinkled my nose.

Seeing my expression, he laughed and said, "If you wanna keep a low profile, *chica*, these are the real deal. They're essential night garms." He pointed to the label. "Nobody sees you, you know, *really* sees you. Not as *a real person*. You're a street cleaner. A loser. People cross the road to avoid you, scared they'll catch your bad luck. I'm not joking around. It's like a passport to a parallel world. Last month I painted a statue of Winston Churchill blue. Turned him into a Smurf. No questions asked."

I smiled. "He'd make a good Smurf."

"So? You up for it?"

I ran my finger across the Westminster logo, pretending to turn his offer over in my mind. He'd fallen into my trap. Mission accomplished. Hopefully I'd bought myself some time. Now all I had to do was persuade him to help me out, although I wasn't exactly holding my breath.

"Yeah. Why not?" I smiled.

He smiled back.

The overalls were stiff and rustled as I went to slip them on.

Latif put his hand on my arm. "Not in here," he said. "And leave that douchey bag with Jeannie."

"What? No way." I clutched my crocodile-skin bag to my chest.

"You're meant to be blending in, bubblehead! Check it!"

I smiled. "Suppose overalls don't rock with croc." I took out my cash card, shades, smartphone and a lipstick and stuffed them into the back pockets of my jeans before handing it over.

"First rule. Switch your mobile off. "

"It is, I swear. I turned it off so I wouldn't be bombarded by texts from the 'rentals."

"And the GPS?"

I nodded, but he checked anyway.

"Okay, *vamos, chica.*"

"Why do you speak in Spanish?"

He shrugged. "Why not?"

"Take care, Lats," Jeannie said as we headed out.

"Safe, Jeannie. Tell Mum and Ren to bell me when you see them."

"Righty-o!" she shouted after us.

Back on the streets, I slipped on the hoodie, followed by the waterproof overalls. They were big and bulky. But I was tall for my age, so I didn't have to roll the trousers up too much. Catching sight of my reflection in a shop window, I winced; I looked like a waterproofed Charlie Chaplin impersonator. Glamorous or what? A jogger passed without giving us a second look. He saw slouch kids who'd dropped out of school. That was when I understood Latif's point. We were trash. Instantly I was glad I was with him. He knew how to work the streets. My instinct to get him to help me grew stronger. I felt giddy with excitement, and I couldn't stop myself from grinning.

"So you don't work for the council?" I asked, catching a glimpse of our reflections again.

"Nah!" he said.

"But the overalls?" I pulled out the waterproof trouser legs and started to imitate the Chaplin walk, all heel-skittery and topple-back.

Latif laughed. "They're contraband. If a guy leaves them by his cart, I nab 'em. They're slick for undercover work. It's what nighters wear."

"Nighters?" I wrinkled my nose – that word again – I had no idea what it meant.

"You'll see. I bomb this city."

I slowed down.

"Not for real, bubblehead. Come on, let's get out of here."

"Sorry!" I muttered. "I'm feeling a bit edgy."

He shrugged as if to say, "That's to be expected," or that's how I read it, anyway.

Up ahead, a couple crossed the road. He nodded.

"See what I mean? We're toxic!"

And for the first time in my life, I felt invisible, anonymous, disguised, strangely liberated. I stared at a woman walking a labradoodle who didn't so much as glance in our direction. We were part of the street furniture. The recklessness was back – in spades. The night tingled with promise.

Bombing the Train

TEN minutes later, we were back under the railway bridge, standing in the shadows, staking things out – exactly what things, Latif wouldn't say. A chauffeur-driven limo swooshed past. My heart accelerated. A train rumbled overhead. Latif stared out into the darkness – completely still, but alert.

Across the road, behind high grey railings, a civilian train crawled to a stop, doused its lights.

"Bang on time," Latif whispered, more to himself than me.

The driver jumped down. His torch beam revealed a depot for trains. Watching him shrug on his overcoat, I was struck by how alone he looked. I shuddered, remembering how alone *I'd* felt only a few hours earlier. He stretched and started walking towards Victoria Station, his torch bobbing into the distance.

When the darkness had swallowed the driver up, Latif changed his focus. I followed his gaze. Attached to a six-foot security fence, a CCTV camera swivelled back and forth, watching over the sleeping trains. Gently clicking his fingers, Latif timed the speed of the camera's arc, like a jazz musician counting in the rest of his band. Then, as its steely eye rotated back again, he signalled to me to stay put and ran across the road, taking care to keep behind its surveillance curve, even though his keffiyeh covered his head and face, leaving only eye-slits.

I shoved my knuckles into my mouth. By my reckoning he had no more than twenty seconds to do whatever he had to do. I needn't have worried. In five, he was on the opposite pavement. In seven, he leapt up and slam-dunked the camera with his cowboy hat. Now sly-eye was no more threatening than a giant hatstand. Latif beckoned me over with a long, loose-armed gesture.

As I rushed after him, he leapt up onto a garden wall in front of a block of red-brick flats, and swung up into the branches of a tree overlooking the railway yard. From his surefootedness I could see that he'd taken this route many times before. I scrambled after him, my trainers skidding and scuffing across the silvered bark. Vertigo tingled my limbs, filling me with an urge to jump. I rested my cheek against the tree's rough trunk and hugged it tight.

"I'm rolling," Latif whispered, as he fixed a headtorch around his keffiyeh. "Keep lookout. Whistle if anyone shows up."

He edged along a wheezy branch until he could grasp the railway yard's spiky railings, and then, with one fluid movement, he vaulted down, landing panther-slick in the yard below. I heard the zip of his rucksack, followed by rustling. Peering into the darkness, I fleetingly thought Latif had grown translucent wings. But as my eyes grew accustomed to the gloom, I saw he was holding sheets of plastic. Next he took five aerosol cans from his rucksack and lined them up on the ground.

He switched the torch on.

Action stations.

With a can in each hand, Latif started shaking up the paint, waving his arms around, as if he were dancing to hardcore techno. The metal aerosol balls bashed out a minimal beat. The hiss of paint punctuated the night. He worked fast and efficiently, swapping stencils, juggling spray cans. The beam from his torch was a choppy disco ball.

When he had finished, Latif stood back to admire his work, and as his torch swung back and forth across the side of the train, I saw his graffiti in jump cuts. It featured a guy wearing a black and white keffiyeh and a pair of mirrored Aviators. He was some kind of freedom fighter, maybe. The image of a rioter throwing a homemade petrol bomb was reflected twice – once in each shade. Below the image, bright red lettering spelled something out in Arabic.

I had no idea what the words meant. I imagined it was some kind of call to arms, but I didn't care – it was totally cool. Switching on my smartphone, I took a photo. My mailbox was full of texts from my parents. I itched to open a few, but the control-freaks were history. I turned it off again.

A metallic crash made me jump and I nearly toppled from my perch, but it was only Latif rushing the fence. Hugging the tree trunk more tightly, I watched him scale the mesh quick and easy as Spider-Man.

"What do you think?" he asked, as we stood squashed

together in the fork of the tree. "I throw a piece up every day. I paint what's going on in the world as I see it. Good and bad. My moniker is Radical Witness."

"It's amazing. That writing's Arabic, right?" I whispered. "What does it say?"

"Brainpower not firepower." He made a freedom fighter's fist.

"Oh, my days, I'm a complete dim-bulb." I reddened. "So you're anti-violence?"

He shrugged. "I don't judge. I paint what I see."

"The petrol bomb made me think it was jihad or some kind of call to arms," I mumbled, hating the way I was coming across all hairspray and lipgloss.

"Yeah! You and every other doughnut. But that's my point. When people see Arabic graffiti they think the words must be inciting violence. I mean, give me a break… Sometimes I quote Sufi poetry, so beautiful it makes you want to cry. I use Arabic to mess with people's heads. The freedom fighter is my tag, but I change the words and what's reflected in his shades daily." He grabbed hold of a branch. "Don't get me started, coz we'll be here all night and we gotta ghost."

I could hardly watch as he swung out into the darkness and jumped soundlessly to the ground.

The birch tree glowed silver in the moonlight, its branches surrounding me like protective arms. I looked down; my legs tingled and my stomach leapt.

"Move it," Latif said, pointing out knotholes to support my feet.

I counted to three before scrambling down after him, glad of the thick work overalls. Then I scurried across the road and waited under the railway bridge once again. This dank place was getting a bit too familiar for my liking. With laserpoint precision Latif ran at the CCTV camera, strides lengthening as he grew closer until he finally leapt into the air and snatched back his hat. The steely eye stared down unblinking. Latif stood defiantly in its gaze and punched the air with a freedom fighter's fist. I tensed up, hoping nobody at Railway Control was watching. Latif enjoyed taking risks; I guessed that was all part of the buzz. Next minute, he was charging up the road yelling for me to keep up.

When we reached Chelsea Bridge I collapsed against its side, gasping for breath and giggling. This was all so new to me – so exciting. I shook my head, finding it hard to believe that I was out at night with a stranger, without guards or minders, just being carried along by adrenalin.

"That was trill," Latif said, hardly out of breath.

"What?" I spluttered. The sprint had blown my lungs to smithereens.

"Mental. A riot. Real!" His blue-green eyes shone in the moonlight.

"So that's what you do?" I straightened up.

"Yeah. Most nights."

"That's bombing nighter-style?" I smiled, picturing his paint bombs of words.

"Sure is, bubblehead… I bomb the city's furniture – trains, statues, walls and stuff. Have done for years.

That's what nighters do: we run, we tag, we outwit the police."

"Do you always tag at night?"

"Yeah. It's safer. These days you've gotta be quick, though. I've been busted a few times when I was a kid. That's why I take precautions." He pointed to the logo on his overalls. "Like I said, these garms make me look official." He shoved his hands into the pockets. "Appropriate the look of the state to do it over. Get me?"

"Official anarchy." I smiled.

"Truth!"

"But don't you get bored hanging around?"

"Nah. Adrenalin's addictive. Believe it!" He nodded in the direction of the train yard. "That'll be buffed by morning. It's crazed how quickly tags disappear. That's why Mum called my story 'Words Disappear at Dawn'."

The moonlight spangled the water into silvery rounds, like the ghostly lips of mermaids, coming up for air.

I shivered.

"Don't your parents mind…" I tailed off, seeing Latif's left eyebrow shoot upwards once again, and finished lamely, "you know, that you're out all night?"

"Nah. Mum's driving most nights and Dad…" He stopped mid-sentence.

A siren wailed – close by, heading our way.

Latif sucked air through his teeth. "Fed alert." He started unwinding his keffiyeh from around his face. Then, glancing over at me, he said, "Pull up your mask."

The mask smelled of peppermints.

I sped up. He grabbed my arm. "Slow it down. We're night workers, yeah? Pissed off. We don't hurry for nothin'. Check it!" He shoved his hat into his rucksack, followed by his keffiyeh. Then he pulled up his hoodie.

Blue neon flashed along the embankment. I counted two police cars. Latif glanced back towards the train depot.

"We've got fed action. Mirror me, Dash!" He slipped into a slow, loose-limbed, who-cares stride. "The train driver or security must've spied us."

Fear stiffened my limbs. I struggled to mimic his laidback look. More sirens wailed in the distance. Unease infected me. The police were all over the city like a rash. I glanced over at Latif. He shot me a grin. He didn't seem the least bit perturbed. In fact, he appeared to be relishing the buzz.

"All in a night's work," he said with a wink.

There was a hot-dog caravan on the south side of the bridge where a few cabbies were chatting, hands cupped around steaming cups of coffee. I kept my eyes lowered, praying they wouldn't think we looked suspicious. But they didn't give us a second glance, merely seeing night workers like themselves. Besides, they were too busy checking out the police action on the other side of the river. As we passed, I caught the word 'murder', in a strong Glaswegian accent.

We walked on down the road, the dark expanse of Battersea Park stretching out to our right. We'd only gone about fifty paces when Latif whispered, "You ready?"

And before I could ask for what, he'd picked me up by

the waist, as if we were ballroom dancing partners, and had lifted me up over the railings. I landed in a heap on a muddy patch of ground. As I scrambled to my feet Latif took a short run-up, clasped hold of the black spikes at the top of the railings, and vaulted over in one seamless movement, smooth and easy as a free runner.

"We'll jam here for now. Until the fed action simmers down." He set off into the darkness at a lope.

I scooted after him, heart thumping. We ran down through a wooded area, skirted the lake and then, keeping to the shady edges of moonlit lawns we headed toward the river. Daffodils starred the grass. All around shadows raced and shivered, whispered and rustled. I felt like they were ganging up on me. Suddenly Latif stopped and inclined his head; he appeared to be listening. After a few seconds, he said, "They're sending in the helis." A frown knitted his brow. "That's hardcore. Believe it."

"Are they after you?" I pushed the pollution mask up onto my head so I could breathe more easily. But he was already on the move so I didn't catch his answer.

The darkness closed in around me – squeezed me. Running for my life now, scenes from lost-in-the-wood horror films came floating back to me, transforming every sound, every shadow into something else, something scary. Twigs snapped under foot like rifle fire. Shadows stalked me. Up ahead, a gold sphere gleamed. Momentarily confused, I wondered if the moon had fallen from the sky. I blinked and saw a great gold Buddha.

The helicopter's clatter was closer now.

Latif shouted over his shoulder for me to run faster.

But I couldn't force my aching body to move up a gear, and the stiff overalls weren't helping either.

When we reached the Peace Pagoda, Latif raced up the steps towards the gleaming Buddha. From what I could remember from my rare visits to Battersea Park, there were four Buddhas in total, looking to the north, south, east and west. Thirteen steps later, I found myself standing on the pagoda's walkway gasping for breath, watching Latif vault up onto the Buddha's platform with ease.

"Come now!" He was stretching his arms down towards me. Clasping hold of his hands, I walked my feet up the slippery white side. Seconds later, I was standing next to him – all exposed, as if on a stage.

The Buddha was sitting cross-legged on a lotus flower, a golden leaf stretched up behind him. His face was kind and peaceful, and he was making a symbol with his fingers. I prayed it was a hopeful message, one that would keep us safe...

Downriver, helicopter lights strafed the sky.

A flock of frightened birds flew out of the park, silhouetted against the moon.

"Over here, Dash!" Latif whispered, slotting himself into a hidden space behind the Buddha. The gleaming lotus leaf gave him good cover. Without wasting a second, I scrambled onto the platform, touching the Buddha's arm for luck, before squeezing in beside Latif.

There was barely room for two.

"Squeezy, huh?" Latif whispered.

I gave him a searching look. He appeared totally unfazed.

A moment later, an engine's roar eclipsed the helicopter's metallic whir, and, peeping out, I saw a motorbike tearing along the river walkway. It was one of those low-slung bikes, which Hell's Angels ride – a Harley.

"What's he doing here?" Latif muttered.

But before I could ask who exactly 'he' was, the bike's headlamp was shining straight at our Buddha. For a couple of moments the Buddha blazed gold. I shrank back into our hidden space, heart thumping. Five parakeets shot out from under the pagoda's rafters, exploding into the night like bright green fireworks. I blinked. They looked as out of place as I felt. I heard the bike turn into the car park and skid to a halt. Sneaking a look, I saw a leathered hellhound sitting astride the Harley, revving the engine.

"Who's that?" I mouthed, eyes popping.

Latif edged closer. "Pest control from the dark side. Officially he shoots vermin, foxes mainly. Unofficially he…"

I strained to hear, but the rest of his sentence was swallowed up by the clatter of an unmarked helicopter as it flew over Chelsea Bridge and into the park. Seconds later, it was hovering above the car park, spotlighting the Harley in its beam.

The leathered biker saluted the pilot, cut the engine and dismounted. He was wearing a bush hat with fox brushes hanging from the rim. A rifle was slung over his left shoulder.

"Okay, Fred, let's hunt vermin." The pilot's voice boomed

from a speaker in the helicopter's cockpit. "Two suspects. One male. One female. We need them alive. Do you copy? Alive!"

"No way." My eyes widened. "I thought you said he hunted foxes."

"Officially."

And the way he said the word filled me with dread.

"What? They're after us?" My voice rose to a squeak.

Latif raised his index finger to his lips.

As I watched the hunter stride into the darkness, fear mushroomed up inside me. This all seemed totally irregular. The helicopter's lights swept across the park. Birds shot from its beam like arrows. Trees swayed back and forth, as if caught up in a tropical storm, their emerald-green leaves jitterbugging in its bluster. After a while, the pilot's robotic voice filled the park.

"I've got Nike trainers and an Adidas logo. Two suspects at coordinates A3-D12. I repeat, suspects are at coordinates A3-D12."

"That copter has X-ray vision," Latif whispered. "The temple's roof better block us — or else. Boom! We're ghosts!" Then seeing my look of terror, he added, "Don't vex. We're in deep cover. The infrared won't pick up our body heat in here. Chill."

With my forehead pressed against the cool, golden lotus leaf, I concentrated on bringing my temperature down. I was a penguin diving into freezing water. I was an Eskimo huddled in an igloo…

Latif jogged my elbow. An unmarked van had entered the park. It came to a halt next to the Harley. Two toughs jumped out, sauntered round to the back and unlocked the doors. A chill rose up from my guts. They had the look of the ex-SAS goons that Dad hired to protect us. Muscle. No rules. Mean. I'd spent my whole life being shadowed by them so I could spot them a mile off. As if to prove my point they shaped guns with their hands and pretended to shoot at the two teenagers Fred was marching across the grass. Arms pinned back, faces scrunched into screams, the two kids looked as if they thought their world was about to end.

Fred bundled the kids inside the van and slammed the doors shut. Then he waited while one of the goons spoke to someone on the van's radio. When he'd finished, they exchanged a few words. There appeared to be some kind of problem.

Moments later, the hunter turned on his heels and headed back into the park.

Only this time, he was walking our way.

As he approached the temple he signalled to the pilot. I shrank back into deep cover. I heard the helicopter fly over and take up position above the temple. A whirlwind rushed around the pagoda, making the bells clank madly, as if all four Buddhas were trying to ward off an evil force with ethereal music.

I glanced over at Latif. His face was expressionless, unreadable. I shut my eyes. CHOP. CHOP. CHOP. The blades churned my stomach and shredded my nerves.

Icy sweat beaded my back. My heart thumped against my ribcage.

After what felt like an eternity, the helicopter swept away. But the ensuing silence intensified my anxiety. Fred must be on the pagoda's walkway by now. I strained to hear some small sound of him. My breath was a full stop in my throat. A few more seconds passed, then I heard the flick of a lighter, followed by a deep inhalation. The tang of cigarette smoke tickled my nostrils. He began to walk around the temple, his footfalls sharp as pistol cracks. Time stretched taut, almost quivered. I found myself counting his footsteps. Thirty-seven gunshots later, he ran back down the steps.

I crumpled.

After one last tour of the park, the helicopter flew off up river. The van left at speed, red tail lights gleaming. Finally the hunter mounted his bike, revved the engine and shot out of the car park. His Harley gobbled up the walkway in one long wheelie.

Below the Radar

WE waited until the roar of the chopper had receded. Then we slid out from behind the Buddha. Standing on the platform, I stamped my feet, trying to get some feeling back into them. I took deep breaths, enjoying the fresh air – crisp and cold in my throat.

With the helicopter gone, I'd expected the park to be silent, but the undergrowth was alive with the rustle of spooked-out creatures. I peered into the darkness, scoping the shadows, half-expecting *The Hunter's Return.* The sequel.

"What was that about?" I asked. "Who were those guys?"

"Undercover feds. The clean-up squad. They pull in drunks, the homeless, taggers, outcasts. Anyone this government describes as scum." Latif rotated his neck until it clicked. "Unofficially, of course."

"What?" My mouth dropped open. "The government is *okay* with that?" I stamped my feet out more vigorously. "Those poor kids! They hadn't done anything wrong, had they?"

"Wrong time. Wrong place."

"That's it?" I was struggling to get a handle on things. "What do you mean?"

"The feds are after *me*, bubblehead." Latif shrugged. But I thought I heard fear catch in his throat. "My graffiti triggered the mayhem. Railway Control didn't relish the tease and called the feds."

"What? Really? That's how they go after taggers?" I asked, eyes wide as dinner plates.

"Truth, bubblehead! Two police cars stopped by the depot when we were crossing the bridge." Then, seeing my incredulous look, he added, "Believe it!"

"It was insane, though," I persisted, shaking my head, still stunned by what I'd just witnessed. "It was..." I searched for the word. "Disproportionate."

"Where have you been for the last decade, bubblehead? Another planet? These days, Dash, the feds pull you in for taking photos on the streets. Anything goes. Trust me! It's called zero tolerance." He tipped up the brim of his hat, setting his eyes on me for a few seconds, and then he jumped off the platform.

My gaze travelled to Millbank Tower, and the city's lights behind. It wasn't news to me, not really. I knew the government came down hard on civilian kids or the hood-rats, as Dad called them. His TV channels were always calling for zero tolerance. I guessed that was what zero tolerance looked like. I shivered. I had never really given it a shape. But now I'd seen it, I would never forget it. And I never wanted to see it again.

The Buddha's tranquil face gleamed in the moonlight, radiating peaceful vibes. I placed my fingertips on his hand, hoping to suck up good karma. But the chill was creeping up from my stomach again, seeping into every cell of my body, invading every particle of my being – a kind of sixth sense – irrational, maybe, suggesting that my parents were somehow involved. I started whispering a single mantra: "Please don't let Mum and Dad have anything to do with this. Please don't let..." I rubbed the top of my arms and shooed this crazy thought away.

Latif was already down by the river, leaning on the railings and staring out into the darkness. I was surprised to see the tide had gone out, leaving two pebble-dashed beaches stretching up from a glassy twist of river. Battersea Park was submerged in silence once again. The windows of the houses on the other side of the river were unlit.

There was a sizeable drop down from the platform, and I cursed Latif for leaving me stranded, but fearing he'd think me useless if I called him back, I grasped the thick perimeter pole and lowered myself down, landing in a mess of arms and legs. After picking myself up, I joined Latif riverside.

He was lost in his own world.

Resting my elbows against the red railings, I gave him a sideways glance. His face was as smooth as the river's surface. He appeared unruffled. Feeling my eyes on him, he turned and smiled.

"Dad said the government was getting tough on the small stuff – graffiti and that. But I didn't take any notice. The feds are always after taggers. We're soft targets. Even so, that was excessive." He picked up a twig from the walkway and dropped it over the railings. We watched it twist and turn as it fell to the riverbed. "I thought Dad was being paranoid. That's what he does for a living. Turns out he was right."

"What? He's paranoid for a living?" I said.

"In a way." Latif grinned. "He's paranoid about our freedoms and that. He's a lawyer — one of the good guys. He defends our rights and liberties and tries his best to stop this crookin' government taking them away. He's always on at me to watch out." Latif shook his head. "It's whack sending copters after taggers. But it's not unusual. Swear down! You can't do nothing these days. Soon they'll introduce curfews and that. And all we'll be able to do is stay home and watch television."

"Have you ever been caught?"

"A few near misses, and as I say, I was busted as a kid." He flashed a smile. "But that's the buzz." He shook his head again. "Too much craziness."

"Too much craziness." I repeated, still in a trance of disbelief.

Staring at the river, trying to gather my thoughts, I was unsure what to think. Too much craziness! *But why?* Was it really about Latif's graffiti? I couldn't help thinking there was more to it. For some reason, I found myself thinking about Dad's relationship with the chief of police. They were close; I knew that. But how close? I pictured the two of them laughing and joking together at GoldRush Image Inc's New Year's Eve party before disappearing into Dad's office for one of their private chats. Then there were the nights when the whirl of a helicopter landing on our helipad would wake me, and going to the window I'd see the chief of police emerging from the cockpit, moments before a ring of security swallowed him up, marching him across the lawn and into the house. Like a hood paying his respects to a Mafioso boss. I grimaced, tucking my hands under my armpits. They probably knew I was missing by now, so, I guessed, Dad would be holding crisis meetings with the chief of police. I pictured the policeman's Action Man face, courtesy of GoldRush Image Inc, nodding in agreement with Dad's every crazy demand.

My unease slid back.

"What are we going to do now?" I asked.

"You're joking?" Latif turned to face me. "*We're* doing nothing. You're going home and I'm keeping a low profile. You saw what happened to those kids, Dash. It isn't safe."

"But…"

"I'm gonna be straight with you, bubblehead." He gently pulled me round by my shoulders, and fixed me with a narrow-eyed look. "And you mustn't take it personal, yeah? I can't hang with you. You're not a nighter. You don't know the rules. You'll get us both nicked." He turned back to the river. "It's too risky with the feds crawling all over the city. That's why you're going home." His words dropped like stones onto the riverbed, smashing my hopes.

In a panic, I tried to think of alternatives.

Deep breaths. Okay. Okay. Think! I could revert to my old plan. No. No that was hopeless. Scarlet was as clueless about civilian life as I was — if not more so. We'd both been raised in the celebrity intensive-care bubble so hooking up with her would get me nowhere fast. I looked up at the luminous moon for inspiration.

It was then that it hit me, and with a force that took me by surprise: Latif's help was crucial for my mission. Without him I might as well give up and go back to the Golds. I knitted my brow.

So what now?

I had to find a way to stop him dumping me.

I glanced over at him. My hopes bombed.

His face was fixed in a steely mask.

"I can't go back," I said in a tiny voice. "Or else my life's going to get really dark."

"Not my problem." He shrugged. "You've picked a bad night for private adventures, Dash."

"Fine. But you have to help me out of here. You owe me that." I heard the sulky tone in my voice, and seeing him frown, I realised that I'd hit the wrong note.

"Like I'm going to leave you here, bubblehead. You'd probably die of fright." His tone was gruff. "But you need to stop whining or I just might. Trust me!"

I stared at the river. I'd run out of ideas.

"Getting emotional won't work this time. As soon as we're out of here, I'm giving Mum a bell and she'll take you home." His expression remained steely. "Accept it, Dasha. You're in too deep."

"You think I'm a real loser, don't you?" I forced a smile, realising I had to lighten up, ditch the spoilt brat routine.

"A liability, more like."

"Thanks a bunch!" I kept the smile blazing. On the inside I was scowling.

"Pleasure." He took a coiled rope from his rucksack.

"Snakes alive! Since when was cluelessness a hanging offence?"

"I wish," he said, but he was smiling again. "Tricks of the trade," he continued with a wink. "We'll be safe down on the riverbed. It's below the radar. Off the grid." There was a glint in his eyes.

"Radar? Grid? It's like being in a spy thriller." I grinned. The excitement of the adventure had him in its grip again. He was back onside. Better still, being off the grid was exactly where I wanted to be right now.

"Stay still. I'm gonna rope you down."

Latif tied one end of the rope around my waist in a simple pulley knot. I watched silently, my stomach contracting at the thought of a spot of amateur abseiling. He looped the other end around the rust-red safety railing, which ran along the top of the river wall, and said, "Walk your creepers down the side. It's easy."

"If you say so." I heard the wobble in my voice.

I climbed over the railings, and then, holding the bottom railing with both hands, I pressed my feet against the river wall, as if taking up position for a backstroke race. My stomach tumble-turned, and for a few seconds, I couldn't face pushing off into the darkness.

"Move it, Dash, or the tide will catch us," Latif hissed.

"See the chains running along the wall? Use them as footholds."

I grasped the rope and started to inch down. Although it burned my palms and cinched my waist, I carried on, desperate to prove to Latif that I wasn't a complete loser. Luckily the wall wasn't as steep as I'd anticipated, so, in a matter of seconds, the riverbed squelched beneath my trainers.

"What took you so long, bubblehead?" Latif threw his rucksack down onto the riverbed, followed by the rope. It slithered across the pebbles.

"Very funny," I said. The rope wriggled from my belly, like an umbilical cord, and in that instant, I saw myself through Latif's eyes — helpless as a newborn baby. I untied the rope.

No wonder he wants to lose me, I thought.

All of a sudden, I sensed the thick seaweedy air stir in the river basin and, looking up, I saw Latif swooping through the inky darkness. His body appeared fluid, elastic, but controlled — like a high diver spinning shapes. Except... Oh my God! There wasn't any water. I screwed up my eyes, hardly able to watch. He landed with a dull thud, rolled and jumped to his feet, easy as if he'd jumped off a bus.

"You scared the hell out of me," I hissed. "What are you trying to do? Kill yourself?"

"No, you're the spare part. Remember!"

I couldn't help smiling as I handed him the tangled rope. "That was awesome! Where did you learn to do that?"

"I jump London, Dasha. No sweat. I've been doing it for years." Latif coiled the rope lasso-style around his arm, took his hat and keffiyeh from his rucksack, before stuffing the rope back inside.

"Like in the adverts?'"

"Yeah. Something like that." He rolled his eyes. "Come on. The tide's on the turn. Keep close to the wall." He set his cowboy hat low on his head and strode off into the darkness. The riverbed smelled stale and salty, like a fisherman's pocket. There wasn't a whisper of breeze. Downriver, Chelsea Bridge's reflection blazed across the water's glassy surface, like a vast cathedral of dreams.

"How long have we got?" I asked.

"An hour max." His words drifted back, muffled by the clammy-fingered air.

We walked in silence, sidestepping Londoners' rubbish – a fridge without magnets or messages, a computer wiped of information and a headless doll. Buttons, glass, clay pipes and triangles of pottery scrunched underfoot.

The river wall shot up to the stars. We were in a secret, subterranean world, way below the sleeping city, safe for now. I searched the sky for a shooting star or some other lucky sign. But the constellations were cocooned in fuzzy orange neon. Only the big fat Michelin moon dazzled. I felt sad. Somewhere in the city my birth mother might be looking up at the same moon. Perhaps she was even thinking about me. I sighed and kicked a stone towards the water. *As if.* She'd be in bed, like the rest of London – that was if she even lived in London.

Maybe it was the silence or the full moon or thoughts of

my impossible quest, but my throat started constricting and suddenly I couldn't breathe. I clutched my throat with both hands, gulping at the night air.

Latif stopped. "Bubblehead, what's with the crazy breathing routine?" he asked, clearly exasperated. "Be easy, Dasha!" He turned on his heels and headed off.

I took a few more deep breaths before following him.

He was striding ahead now, shoulders hunched, hands sunk deep into his pockets, and, even though he was wearing workers' overalls, a cowboy hat and a keffiyeh, he looked super cool – an urban cowboy. I doubted that he'd ever had an identity crisis in his life. He just was Latif. Unique. Unconventional. Charismatic. So different from the blaggers and jetsetters I hung out with. He cared about things – the world and other stuff that mattered – which was probably why he hadn't got time for me.

"Wait!" I shouted, breaking into a run.

Latif stopped close to Chelsea Bridge.

When I reached him, he asked, "Are you okay?" His voice was gentle. It caught me off guard, and for a second, I considered telling him the whole truth – revealing my real identity, and asking him straight out for help. I studied his face in the glow cast by the lights on Chelsea Bridge. It was handsome, kind – almost serene. But his eyes glinted with cool amusement. I had to face facts. Latif thought I was a liability and wanted shot of me. He'd also made it clear that he thought the global super-rich were a complete waste of space. For that reason, I couldn't risk giving him the perfect excuse to send me back to the Golds and pick up a huge reward into the bargain.

"Yeah, I'm fine."

"So no more heavy-breathing routine, bubblehead," Latif cautioned gruffly. "We're ghosts. Silent. Get me?" He kicked a soggy tennis ball into the river.

I nodded and clamped my lips shut.

The foreshore became a narrow strip down by Battersea Power Station, its white chimneystacks stretching up to the heavens. Inside, I imagined a spaced-out Moon Goddess putting silvery lips to the white funnels and sucking stardust down from the night sky, getting wasted – just as Coco and the List would be doing round about now. Crammed into The Glitz, shouting shiny-eyed lies about how good, great, fantastic their lives were, their eyes roving, desperate for stardust.

We trudged on, our progress monitored by landing cranes that stood in the river like prehistoric wading birds – past the Toxic Waste Company and its mountain of yellow containers, past Fedex, past bleak industrial units, finally stopping twenty metres upriver from a huddle of houseboats, stranded on the riverbed by the tide. They were moored to a jetty. The American embassy squatted further down the river.

Latif gestured for me to hang back in the shadows, but seeing my alarm, he said, "*Tranquilo, chica.* It's not the Yanks you have to watch out for." He paused before adding cheekily, "It's the rats. They're king-size."

I watched him skulk over to the boats, silent as a moon shadow. Crouching down, he removed a pair of bolt cutters from his rucksack, and started cutting through a chain that attached a small dinghy to a yellow houseboat.

More tricks of the trade, I thought.

The water was edging closer. A rat scurried past, its tail slapping at the pebbles. I stepped back. Stones scuttled sideways. The riverbed was a scrabble of crabs. Squatting down, I studied them, amazed to find them living in the Thames.

Hearing a scraping sound, I looked up; Latif was dragging the dinghy towards me, like a funky, twenty-first-century Robinson Crusoe.

"Get in!"

He steadied the boat while I clambered aboard. He waited until I was seated before jumping in after me.

Latif rowed in silence, his brow furrowed. Every so often, he'd let out a puff of exertion. I could tell something was troubling him, but whenever I asked him if everything was okay, he shrugged me off.

The oars splashed against the water and finding their splish-splish soothing, I tipped my head back, and watched the planes gliding through the darkness at two-minute intervals, red lights blinking. Their reflections slid across the glassy surface of the river, like blips on a GPS grid. I let out a slow sigh of relief – if my parents had got their way, I'd be up there right now in their Learjet, heading for our private island in the Caribbean.

For a minute or two – out there on the river – I let myself believe that I'd slipped the moorings of my old life. But the tide was on the turn, and I could feel the swirling currents tugging at the boat, pulling it this way and that. I clasped the sides, terrified a dark, dangerous undertow might drag us under at any moment, and sweep us back downriver to GoldRush HQ. I started counting the dip and splash of the oars. Slowly my anxiety settled.

We were about halfway across the river when Latif leaned forward and asked, "Did you take photos of my tag?"

"Yeah, just one." I took my smartphone from my pocket and was about to turn it on when he hissed urgently, "Don't, Dasha."

I stared down at my mobile. My fingers twitched. I longed to see if the kidnap story was trending worldwide, find out who had been kidnapped for real. I hoped she was okay.

"Not now." There was something in his voice, which made me shove my phone back into my pocket without protesting.

A siren wailed. A blue light twirled on the embankment. We were about fifty metres from the shore.

"Not a word," he said.

I glimpsed the red letters of Dolphin Square once again.

My heart sank; I was more or less back where I had started.

So much for being on the run, I thought.

We came ashore by Westminster Boating Base. Its rickety pier was knee-deep in water. A line of tiny, beached sailboats lay on the mud like multicoloured seals. Latif jumped out and dragged the dinghy up onto a strip of stony ground, before helping me out. Then he pushed it back out into the river. I watched it bob and twist on the current. To our left a large blue fishing boat stood on the riverbed, its white prow towering above us, like a huge cresting wave. We walked over. There was a ladder on the river wall next to where the boat was anchored. Latif climbed up first. I followed, but the rungs were slimy, forcing me to take it slowly. Reaching the top, I held Latif's outstretched hands and stepped onto the deck. I did a double take. The boat was moored alongside an AstroTurf tennis court, which gleamed emerald in the moonlight. At one end, a pair of swans stood on the baseline, beak to beak, as if discussing tactics for a doubles match.

"Does anyone live here?" I asked, even though the boat was fenced off from the tennis compound by wire mesh. I cringed. Sometimes nerves made me ask questions to which I already knew the answers.

"Nah. Squatters did, but the feds evicted them months ago. You'll be safe here for a few nights, that's if you don't want to go home. Sleep on it. You'll probably think differently by the morning." He turned to leave.

"No, Latif!" I grabbed his arm and said urgently, "Please don't."

"I've told you, Dash. I'm not going back on my word. It's too complicated with a novice." But seeing my panicked face, he relented. "Okay. I'll stay with you tonight. One night only, special offer, so you can get some kip. I'll keep watch."

We exchanged a look, as surprised as each other by his

choice of words – keeping watch suggested some kind of war footing.

But war against what?

We let the moment pass.

It was a classic fisherman's tug, made of wood with a little wheelhouse on its prow. The door groaned open. It was warm inside and there were blankets piled up in the corner. I stared at the sailboats, bobbing off Westminster Boating Base's pier, their masts clinking and clanking. I turned the ship's wheel, my emotions spinning.

"So?" Latif said, as soon as he'd shut the door.

"So what?" I'd been dreading this question.

"What are you running from?" His turquoise eyes trapped me in their beam.

Immediately my mouth was full of marbles. "I told you I'm trying to track down my real mother. And…" My words came out thick and strange as if my tongue had been needled with anesthetic.

"And?" His gaze bored into me. "It's not my style to ask questions. Everyone's got a right to silence. But I get the feeling you're not being straight with me. You're a rubbish liar, bubblehead. So the truth, from now on – else I'm ghosting."

He took some worry beads from his overalls, and started working them across his knuckles. So he'd had his suspicions about my story all along. The clack of the beads was calming, and the way he made them dance across his knuckles mesmerised me.

He looked up when I didn't say anything. "I need to

know exactly what you're up to. The full picture, get me? Then I'll decide if I'm gonna help or not." He turned the full force of his gaze onto me. "You're hiding something, Dash. Swear down!"

I felt myself colouring up. The flush started at the base of my neck and spread across my cheeks. *The full picture?* I still wasn't up for mentioning my parents by name. Not yet. I didn't want him to leave me, not in the middle of the night. I promised myself I'd tell him everything in the morning, but for now I settled with more partial truths.

"It's big. Being adopted is only part of it." I spun the boat's wheel again. "My parents want me to be someone I'm not." The flush was hot and oppressive. "I need space to think things through," I added lamely. "Work out who I really am."

He just kept on staring, refusing to fill the silence, to help me out.

Turning the wheel again, I saw the whole scene as he would see it – *Rich Fake in Identity Crisis Shock*. I looked at him, sprawled across the boat's wooden panelling, so confident – so comfortable in his own skin.

I shook my head. "You wouldn't understand." My words came out soft, resigned. "Nobody does." But deep down, I believed that if I chose my moment carefully, Latif just might. I sighed softly. "I'll tell you everything in the morning, I promise. I'm too tired right now. Deal?"

He stretched his hand out. "Deal." Then again, that crooked smile.

His hand was warm while mine was reptile cold. As I shook his, I realised how much I wanted to talk to someone who wasn't in my parents' pocket.

I wrapped myself in a blanket, which Latif had found in a cupboard beneath the boat's wheel, and curled up on the floor. It was uncomfortable, but I was too exhausted to care.

I fell asleep to the clink and clank of masts, and dreamed I'd been captured and placed in chains.

Snakes and Ladders

I WOKE with a jump. Someone was shaking my shoulder. Still drowsy, I saw manga-huge eyes staring down at me. Thinking I must be dreaming, I closed my eyes again. Another shake — rougher this time, followed by a husky voice. "We've got to split. It'll be light soon."

I sat up, and when I saw Latif propped up against the boat's wheel, everything came back to me. Stuck in replay, the events of the previous night spooled through my head, scary as a horror flick. I hit the skip button and shot back into the present.

"You okay?" he asked.

"Why? So you can dump me?" I stood up, stretched and unkinked my spine.

The Thames was at high tide and the boat swayed uneasily beneath my feet.

"Don't give me a hard time, Dash. You know the rules." Latif was whittling a stick down to a point. Shavings scattered the floor like potato chips. He'd taken off his overalls and was wearing black skinny jeans, an orange T-shirt, and a charcoal-grey hoodie, plus his keffiyeh and his cowboy hat, of course.

"Whose rules? I thought you hated rules."

He tested the point with his thumb, then, seemingly pleased with his work, said, "Let's munch. There's a live cafe near here." He pressed the sharpened end of the stick against my forehead. "We've got a deal, remember?"

"Like you'd let me forget!" I batted the stick away.

This time he prodded the stick into my chest and spoke very slowly, as if talking to a naughty child. "I'm not promising anything, bubblehead." He gave me another prod. "You seriously cramp my style." And with that he fished a car-wing mirror from his rucksack and gave it a wipe on his keffiyeh, before attaching it to the whittled-down stick. Then he headed out onto the deck.

I stayed inside and started taking off my overalls, reluctantly, though, as if losing a protective skin. After I'd removed them I stood there for a few minutes, feeling exposed, like a soldier contemplating imminent combat without camouflage. I took a deep, calming breath, trying to psyche myself up for action.

Outside dawn glimmered.

Greys and mauves streaked the skyline.

A solitary seagull squawked.

It was that smudgy time of morning, that hazy hour tinged with sadness, emptiness and missed opportunity, about the time, I guessed, when I used to head home after a night's clubbing at the weekends when I was back from the Academy. Big Stevie would be at the wheel talking football while we cruised along the Embankment, the speedometer hovering at 100 miles per hour, safe in the knowledge that the police wouldn't dream of stopping a car with a GOLD number plate.

Watching a stretch limo streak past, I remembered how I'd found the early-morning journeys over the last month so emotional, how I would slump in the back seat, close to tears as I watched the city slide by, knowing that my birth mother was out there somewhere. I would picture her, as I'd glimpsed her that night, and I'd imagine a million different reunion scenarios. And every time Stevie stopped at traffic lights, I'd try the door in the hope that the central locking system might be switched off, never really believing it would be. When my moods were super-dark, I would wonder why she'd given me up.

"Psst. Quit dreaming, Dasha, and get over here."

Latif's whisper jumped me back to reality. He was crouching down at the rear of the boat, hacking through the security fence with his bolt cutters. I went over and stood behind him. The dewdrops flashed and flickered in the beam from his head torch, as if a kaleidoscope of tiny butterflies had landed on the fence. When he'd finished he held back a flap of mesh, and as I squeezed through, a dewdrop fell onto the nape of my neck, cold as an Eskimo's kiss. I shivered and pulled up my hood.

We waited by the gate to the tennis court compound for a convoy of sleek, black, chauffeur-driven Mercedes with tinted windows to swish past, and I found myself wondering if I might know the people inside. It could be Scarlet or any one of my friends. It felt good to be on the outside looking in for once. Fascinated, I watched my former life glide out of view.

The streets were empty – lonely somehow. Apart from us, only a few bleary-eyed night workers huddled at a bus stop, staring blankly into space.

"Illegals mostly," Latif said, following my gaze. "They put London back together again every night. Do Londoners' dirty work. This city would be a dump without them. But nobody gives them the time of day. They were probably doctors, teachers or poets back home before they had to escape because some deranged dictator wanted them dead."

"They look so sad," I whispered.

"So would you, if you had to clean up everybody's crap and were a million miles from home." His voice was clipped, impatient.

I kicked a stone into the gutter, hating his knack for making me feel small.

Up ahead, two girls were rummaging through a clothes-recycling bin, every so often holding up items of clothing that caught their eye. A spiky-haired girl was checking a denim jacket out for size while a short blonde was squeezing herself into a pair of jeans, wriggling her hips as she pulled them up over a pair of leggings. I couldn't take my eyes off them, finding it hard to believe that these girls were so poor that they had to scavenge through bins for clothes.

"Watch out, Dasha," Latif growled as I bumped into him.

Latif had stopped at the junction of two roads. He gestured for me to move closer to the black railings.

'What's up?" I asked nervously.

He didn't answer for a minute or two. Instead, he stuck his mirror-and-stick contraption out into the road.

"CCTV." His eyes flicked skywards.

"How come you didn't use the mirror last night?"

"I use it as a precaution when I'm sussing out new routes. Most places I've checked. Know which cameras are live and which aren't. It's a science."

He slowly rotated the mirror, so that – bit by bit – we glimpsed a smart stuccoed street with a church and a country-style pub. The leafy street was deserted apart from a magpie strutting down the central road markings. White houses rose up on either side like glaciers.

Uh oh, one for sorrow, I thought, surreptitiously saluting the magpie.

"See, there's a camera above the pub, another on the offy and one on the church's steeple." Latif rotated the mirror slowly. "Most of the houses are rigged too." He tsked. "Paranoids. This city is full of paranoids."

"Er, talking of paranoid." I nodded towards his mirror-and-stick. "You're a fine one to talk."

"Yeah, but I'm paranoid in a good way." He gave me that crooked smile again.

"Yeah. Right. Silly me. You channel good paranoia." I rolled my eyes.

He shrugged. "I hate the way there's CCTV everywhere silently filming us going about our everyday lives. It's nuts. That's why I dodge the cameras. It's an obsession." He paused. "I know this'll sound whack, but I believe that

CCTV cameras steal stuff from you. Spontaneity. Freedom. Your right to be different."

A smile twitched the corner of my mouth. "They haven't cramped your style yet!"

He shrugged. "Yeah! But I'm ahead of the game."

For a moment, I thought about telling him that I was a bit obsessive about stuff, too, that I micromanaged my world by counting – stars, steps, cars and magpies; that I wore lucky clothes, chanted calming words, repeated phrases and had a zillion bizarre rituals to help me get through life. But I couldn't bring myself to tell him. My stuff was small – superficial somehow, while his concerns were part of some bigger picture which I was only just starting to think about.

"Guess how many cameras there are in the UK?" Latif asked.

He changed direction, doubling back down the street that we'd just come up.

"A million?"

"Yeah right, and the rest." He held the mirror up, twisting it back and forth until he snagged my image. He grinned when I looked away. "Eight million last count, but there's probably more. We get caught on film at least three hundred times a day. We're the most watched country in the world. But nobody gives a damn."

"So? What's the big deal? You're fine as long as you don't break the law."

I liked the fact my parents' houses and apartments were protected by CCTV and state-of-the-art security. It made me feel safe. I pictured our mansion in the Billionaires' quarter: the watchtowers, the sentry box, the high walls and the cameras. It had better security than most prisons and, as my mother loved to boast, a better class of guard.

Latif looked at me as if I were a signed-up member of a crackpot, right-wing loony party. "Get real, Dasha..." He trailed off, shrugged his shoulders, as if to say, "What's the point? You know nothing." Then he stalked off, eyes skywards – searching for surveillance.

But Latif's words stayed with me, and got me thinking about how the paparazzi as well as civilians with mobiles were always trying to sneak photos of celebrities and globals to sell to newspapers or post on the Internet; how everything was filmed, photographed, documented and dissected; how nothing was private; how globals and celebrities were always watched, too.

We walked in silence as we crisscrossed the white-stuccoed grid of Georgian houses in a maddening game of snakes and ladders – two streets forwards, three streets back, as if Latif were determining our route by the throw of a dice.

"The houses are rigged because gangs go safari round here," he said, as we retraced our footsteps once again.

"Safari?"

"When gangs head out of the dead zones to crook the golden postcodes. Since the truce after the last lot of riots, the gangs stopped robbing their own. They hunt big game now. They've got a taste for it."

"What do you mean?"

"The gangs hit the rich now. Their true enemy."

I knew all about the robbing of rich neighbourhoods. A few weeks ago, a kid in a balaclava had robbed one of my mother's friends at knifepoint outside her house. They'd stolen a £50,000 Rolex, her £100,000 wedding ring and her £75,000 engagement ring. Combined haul – £225,000. Jackpot. I wanted to say how that sucked, but I bit my tongue. I was on a last warning. I had to be careful – or else I'd be history.

We walked on in silence.

After a while, we entered a street with a small parade of shops. Noticing a camera above a newsagent's, I hesitated.

"No film." Latif saluted the steely eye. "Joe tipped me off. It's a deterrent."

"Joe?"

"He owns the cafe I was talking about. It's at the end of the parade."

We'd only gone a few more paces when Latif stopped dead. I crashed into him.

"What the— Dash! That's *you*, isn't it?" He was staring at an info-stop. A large LED screen was playing out ten different news channels.

I gasped, hardly able to believe my eyes, merely whispered, "My God, that's me!"

A technicoloured patchwork of Dashas. My image repeated over and over like a series of Warhol paintings. And standing there in the street looking at my repeated selves, I had the strange sensation that I was more hologram than human.

Latif turned towards me, eyes wide as flying saucers.

Behind him, twenty Dashas smiled in unison.

I touched the GoldRush Media channel and it flicked to full screen — or, more accurately, my smiling face expanded to fill the whole screen.

Next up, photos of me as a little girl, opening Christmas presents, riding, blowing a kiss, swimming, skating and performing ballet. Fast forward. Recent clips showed me posing at a film premiere and a polo match. A montage of magazine covers came next, plotting out my life from a baby in a sequined romper-suit, right up to the last family photo shoot for *Celebrity!*

Well that's blown it, I thought, totally freaked-out by this impromptu slideshow, right in the middle of the street.

Breaking news scrolled along the bottom of the screens: **Dasha Gold Kidnapped.** Okay. So now it was official. I crossed my fingers, praying my parents wouldn't offer a reward. Fat chance! I tensed up when my worst fear slid across the screen: **Tarquin and Tamara Gold, owners of the GoldRush Image Inc, have offered a million-pound reward for information leading to their daughter's safe return.**

In a flash, my eyes were on Latif.

His face hardened. He clenched his fists.

I waited. My stomach fluttered with butterflies.

All he said was: "Swear down! I've been lurking with a goddamn Gold." A vein pulsed at his temple; apart from that his face was expressionless.

"I'm not a Gold. Remember!" I said firmly, wanting to

get a handle on the situation, sensing things were about to spiral out of control.

His aquamarines fixed me for a few moments, as if he were skim-reading my genetic code, trying to work out how many of my parents' crazy chromosomes I had inherited.

"Your dad's scum, Dash. He's Mafioso. The ultimate predator."

"I know," I said simply. "That's why I'm running."

Latif stared at me with narrow-eyed scepticism. "Why should I believe you?" His eyes narrowed some more. "Go on, Miss Gold. Tell me. It's not like you've been straight with me so far, is it?" His voice was like a slow, angry handclap.

"I haven't lied to you, though," I said in a small, guilty voice.

"Yeah! Right! But you've left out some big, ugly biog details. Like the fact your dad is the most powerful media mogul in the world. That your dad – not the government – runs this country. That he owns the prime minister and the police." His voice crackled with anger. "That he's screwed us."

"That's not strictly true," I mumbled unconvincingly.

For a moment I stared at the LED screen, taken aback by his outburst. It was so out of character, so unlike the laid-back Latif that I had grown used to.

"Isn't it?"

I met his gaze. His eyes glittered dark like anthracite. And I couldn't help wondering why he hated the Golds so much. But, of course, I knew, really. He saw my dad as some kind of Godfather figure who got whatever he wanted through bribes, threats and his control of the media. And he wasn't far wrong.

"Yeah right, Dash. Anyone with half a brain knows that this muppet prime minister and his millionaire Cabinet wouldn't be in power without your dad's support. That's why politicians suck up to him. My dad says he's the power behind the throne. The kingmaker." He glared at me. "I can't believe you're the Dark Lord's daughter. 'Sakes, Dash, why didn't you tell me?"

"I'm not his daughter." I repeated even more firmly. "How many times do I have to tell you? *I'm adopted.*"

"That's not the point. You're still family." Latif raised his hand when I tried to cut in. "Not by blood, maybe. But the Golds raised you. You grew up a Gold. No denying that. You've lived the deluxe life for time. You're a global, for God's sake. You're so damn privileged; I couldn't even begin to imagine your lifestyle. Wouldn't want to." The vein at his temple throbbed angrily.

"They hijacked my life," I whispered.

"Whatever." His eyes slid toward the info wall. "Your dad's hijacked this country. That's all I care about." He turned back to face me and fixed me with a cold stare. "Not you. Not your life. Not your dramas."

Boom! Boom! Boom! I recoiled three times, as if he'd struck me. Then I leaned against the iron shutters of the Food and Wine store, all punched out. The cold seeped through my jacket. I shivered.

On screen, footage showed me with my parents at home in

our art deco hallway with its truck-sized chandelier, Tamara de Lempicka paintings, and Jeff Koons' shiny, supersized red heart. We were greeting guests at GoldRush's annual New Year's Eve party. I cringed on the inside as I watched myself shaking hands with a pop star, the PM, an oligarch, a prince and a hot, hot, hot Hollywood star. Great! That was all I needed. Guilty, your Honour. On all counts.

"It's all about you, Dasha Gold, isn't it?" His eyes remained fixed on the screens.

"What is?" I frowned.

He turned towards me. His eyes looked flinty grey in the lamplight. "The shock and awe routine in the park – the helis, the guy on the Harley, the heavies – the whole lot of it *was all about you.* Not me." All the warmth had drained from his voice. "Those kids were hauled in because your parents were looking for you."

"You don't know that for sure," I mumbled without conviction.

"Don't I?" His face was more serious than I'd ever seen it.

I couldn't meet his eye, dreading what he was about to say next.

"The police must've pinged your smartphone when you switched it on, bubblehead. That's why they were onto us so quickly." He stared into the middle distance for a few seconds. "I should've guessed there was something up and dumped you down by the river." His eyes fixed on me. "You should've told me the truth."

I stared down at the pavement. He was right. I should

have put him in the picture. I'd wanted to, but I'd been too scared of losing him. But I couldn't have told him that. And it was too late now.

"Sorry," I whispered.

When he didn't say anything, I glanced up. His face was steely, apart from the popping vein. He was never going to forgive me. I propped myself up against the metal shutters of Food and Wine.

"I'm sorry." I repeated louder this time.

His eyes flashed with anger. "Didn't it cross your mind that your parents would get every cop in London – good or bad – involved?" He tapped his index finger to his temple. "That they just might call in favours from everyone who owes them. 'Sakes, Dasha! You don't have to be Einstein to work out what happened back there in the park. It was all about your parents trying to get their precious daughter back. They think you've been kidnapped, dim-bulb. Remember!" He spoke in a slow sarcastic voice, as if talking to the stupidest person alive.

"Yeah. I knew they'd search for me." I couldn't look him in the eye. "But not like that. With the guy on the Harley, thugs and stuff." I shivered. Thinking back, I remembered how I had wondered whether my parents might be involved, and how I'd pushed this terrifying thought to the back of my mind.

"What did you think it'd be like? A frickin' murder mystery? This is the real world, Dasha." He looked as if he wanted to throttle me. "'Sakes! I could've been banged up in that van. Swear down! You're one selfish girl. Self-obsessed."

He kicked the tyre of a parked car. "Like your parents."

"What? No way!" My mouth gaped open. "Like how?"

"Like, you'll stop at nothing to get what you want." His words were blunt as a mallet. "Lie. Tell half-truths. Manipulate." Each word was like a blow to my skull.

"And what do I want?" I whispered.

"Some effing muppet to escort you round London. Your own personal walking, talking satnav, because, Dasha Gold, you can't survive without your army of slaves, guards, maids and servants." His clenched and unclenched his fists. "But you can count me out. I won't be anyone's slave. Especially not yours."

His words stung. I lowered my eyes. Still I could feel his gaze lasering me.

"I got you out of trouble, Dasha. I saved your miserable skin, and when you were feeling scared, I looked after you. I took you tagging to stop you dwelling on stuff." He shook his head. "You used me, Dasha, even though you knew the dangers. Admit it."

"It wasn't like that. I was frightened. I wasn't thinking straight. I wasn't thinking at all." My words came out in a guilty rush.

"Admit it! My safety never figured in your scheming, did it?"

I stared at the info-screen. Latif was right on all counts. I hadn't got the energy to pretend otherwise. I let out a small sigh, slumped a little more inside.

He turned to leave.

Although I knew it was hopeless, I grabbed his arm, and said, "Please, Latif, don't go! You promised to listen to my side of the story. We had a deal, remember?"

"That was then." He stood stock-still, hunched and angry.

"You've got to hear me out."

"Really?" He spun round. His face was furious. "Go on. It better be good."

The severity of his tone made me stumble over my words. "I... I... you're not being fair. I was going to tell you everything. All about this." I gestured at the LED screen. "Over breakfast. That was the deal we made on the boat."

"You should've told me direct." He was still looking at me, as if he'd like to throttle me. "Back at Jeannie's."

I stumbled on. "I didn't tell you earlier because I thought you'd dump me if you knew who my parents were or..." My eyes flicked towards the screen. The word *reward* was crawling along the bottom.

He saw it too. "Or what?" He must've seen guilt register in my face. "No way? You thought I'd hand you in for cash?" His laugh was bitter as a Siberian wind. "I'll tell you something for free. I wouldn't take your dad's money even if I was down and out and living on the streets."

I slid down the shutters onto my haunches and put my head in my hands.

It was over. I'd blown my only chance.

"That's the problem with you globals. All you care about is money and power. I despise your lot."

"So do I," I whispered.

He towered over me, angry and unforgiving.

Stillness surrounded us, pressing in on me, crushing my heart.

"Don't you get it?" I looked up. "I hate them too."

His eyes bored into me. He didn't speak.

I continued, tripping over my words as I spoke. "That's why I'm running. If I hadn't escaped, I'd be on my parents' Caribbean island right now having an extreme makeover. GoldRush has state-of-the-art operating theatres on the island. It's where globals go to get fixed secretly, away from the press." I was struggling to hold back my tears. "Dad was going to operate on me. He was going to make me picture perfect." I could barely say the words. "Enhance me."

"What? Change you completely? Knife you?"

"Yes. *Knife me!*"

"Why?" He was visibly shocked.

"I was going to become the new face of GoldRush on my seventeenth birthday, my next birthday, but for that he said he had to..." I bit my lip, remembering Dad's words. "Refashion me. Remodel me. He has developed all these procedures to transform me into his beauty ideal." I shook my head wearily. "That's why I had to escape."

"I don't get it." Latif's eyes scanned me. "You're beautiful just the way you are." And the way he said it, in such an unschmaltzy way, so matter-of-fact — it almost took my breath away.

"Thanks," I mumbled. "My parents think my face isn't luxe enough for a global brand."

"Luxe? That's for handbags, shoes and that. Not faces."

"We're a brand — not a family. Go figure…"

"That's insane."

"Try telling Dad that. The brand is his priority. He doesn't love me because I'm his daughter. To him I'm a franchise girl. A brand baby. That's why I'm important to him. He's even trademarked my name."

His thick eyebrows furrowed into an arrow. "For real? Like the ultimate product?"

"It's the truth. What kind of dad would force his daughter to have surgery when he knows she doesn't want it? That's not love as I see it. I hate him."

"Why would he do that?" He shook his head.

"Dad is always pushing frontiers. That's what makes him tick. It's an addiction. He wants to take TV to the limit, cosmetic surgery to the limit and image-making to the limit. The people he loves are there to help him get what he wants." I frowned, trying to recall Dad's creepy phrases. "I'm some kind of prototype. It's complicated. You know he made all his money in cosmetic surgery, don't you?"

"Yeah. That's how he financed his media empire."

"Exactly. Anyway, he's been researching the concept of beauty for decades. Since way before I was born. He's developed a formula for idealised beauty, and has drawn up some crazy blueprint. I don't really know the details. It's all very hush-hush. He's been waiting for the technology to catch up. And now GoldRush has the know-how he was going to…" A chill rose up my back. My fingers were freezing, and touching them to my face, I made icy indentations in my cheeks. "Make my face fit the brand." Another of Dad's horrible expressions popped into my head. "He wanted to transform me into a living logo."

"But logos never change. They're timeless." Latif looked puzzled.

"He's found a way, or so he says."

Seeing his frown deepen, I added, "I don't really understand everything completely. He was going to customise me, like some kind of avatar, which he could play in his global power games."

I saw the hardness in his eyes dissolve. "So that's where you fit into his plans for world domination. The guy's a psycho."

"What do you expect? He's spent half his life stabbing knives into people."

He shook his head. "How the hell did a frickin' face doctor get to be so powerful?"

"It's Dad's crazy world. We just live in it."

"*Basta!*" He held up his hand. "Don't depress me, Dash."

He looked so bleak, so unlike Latif, that I was overtaken by an urge to make him smile. If he was going to dump me, I needed to see that crooked smile one more time, because that was how I wanted to remember him. *Not like this...*

"Want a sneak preview of my future?" I didn't wait for his reply. "Dad was going to take fat from my bum and graft it onto my lips so they'd look plumper, more kissable." I trout-pouted. "Which means I'd be talking out of my arse for real. For ever. Amen!"

"Amen!" A slow smile spread across his face. "I guess that explains the crap celebrities spout."

My heart leapt. The smile was back.

I pointed to my trainers. "He's already botoxed my feet to stop them smelling. My armpits, too. And these little beauties..." I fluttered my eyelashes, "have been fertilised so they'll grow real lush."

"My life, *chica*! You're some kind of mutant." He stepped away, as if I were contagious.

I laughed.

Behind him, Mum's botoxed lips were goldfishing.

"Mum can't feel her lips when she kisses Dad. How sexy is that?"

Latif tsked. "Women like your mum give me the spooks."

"And she can predict cold weather with her boobs. Her implants get *sooo* cold. She never gets it wrong. Now that's a skill."

"Too much information." He held up both hands this time.

"My parents thought I was being a difficult teenager. That I'd grow out of it. But the more I thought about Dad's crazy procedures, the angrier I became. I didn't want my parents to decide how I should look. I didn't want them to choose my clothes, and I really, really didn't want Dad to remodel my face. I mean, Dad's got terrible taste in everything. It's insane." I moved closer to the screens. "Imagine ending up looking like that. They've got made-for-media faces. Mum looks fab on TV, in photos, on film, but in real life she looks weird. Her features are way too big." I turned to look at Latif. "You should see her after the ops. She's bruised and battered. Broken almost, like she's been beaten up by a gang." I screwed up my face. "She looks like she's crying blood. It's so gross." I let out a long, sad sigh. "Every girl at the Star Academy would eat their own head to swap places with me." I shrugged. "But, you know what? I just want to make myself up as I go along."

"As it should be." Latif tipped up the brim of his hat. "That's what I do."

"Yeah. Right. On second thoughts. Maybe it's not such a good idea." I smiled, but I was serious again in an instant. "You've got to believe me. I don't want this. Imagine waking up every morning and seeing a stranger looking out of the mirror, being shocked by your own reflection. How weird would that be? That's why I'm running. I want out. My real mother offers me an escape from my parents' psycho world. A different life. That's why I want to track her down." I took a deep breath. It was crunch time. "But I can't do it by myself." My words trembled on the air.

I tapped the screen. Banks of news channels flicked back. They were all running my story.

Fifteen pairs of parental eyes lasered me. "Anyway, whatever... I need to get out of here." I pointed at the screens. "Things are getting a bit too Big Brother for my liking."

Latif didn't make a move.

"So what are you going to do?" I murmured.

He was leaning against the lamppost, like a private eye in a film noir settling in for a stake-out. He took a long few minutes and then he asked, "Where to, Miss Gold? Your satnav awaits instructions!"

"Really?" My heart was a roaring supersonic jet.

"Really?" he imitated my silly little voice.

"So you'll help me find my real mother?"

"I wouldn't have said it if I didn't mean it, bubblehead."

"No way!" I wanted to whirl and twirl, and shout for joy.

"Believe it! You deserve better than those two psychos."

"But I don't want to put you in any danger."

"Yeah, right! It's a bit late for that. Have you got an address?"

"Only for the adoption agency." I smiled.

I opened my locket and took out the tiny piece of paper. I handed it to him. The address was written in pixie-small, spidery writing.

"FuturePerfect?" he raised an eyebrow.

"Okay, okay. I didn't choose the name, but I'm pretty sure it's the place." Sensing he was about to ask more questions, I added quickly, "I don't want to go into it right now."

"It's in Buckinghamshire." He handed back the address. "Looks like we're going country. We'll have to jump a train." Clocking my face, he said, "What? No way. You've never been on a civilian train before. Seriously? Welcome to the real world, Dash!" He started walking towards Fat Joe's cafe.

"Is it safe?" I hung back.

"Yeah. Joe's sound. Does the best fry-up in London."

He waited for me to catch up, then, pulling down my hood so only the tip of my nose was showing, he said, "We're going to get a couple of fried egg sarnies, and then, mystery girl, you've got more explaining to do."

Fat Joe's was a huff of steam. Huddles of workers were tucking into full English breakfasts. Most were flicking through newspapers, laughing and chatting.

"Are you insane, Latif? I can't go in there." I grabbed his arm as he went to open the door. "They're all reading papers. My face will be on every front page. It's suicide."

Cupping his hands, he squinted through the glass, and said, "Yeah, you'd better stay outside. I'll get us a takeaway."

He was already inside before I had chance to protest. A wafting scent of bacon escaped as the door closed behind him. It smelled really good. My stomach grumbled. I moved closer to the window, my nose almost touching the glass. Fat Joe greeted Latif warmly, and from where I was standing, looking in, every gesture seemed conspiratorial – Fat Joe's raised eyebrow; the way he wiped his hands down the front of his apron; the way he slowly took the pencil from behind his ear, wet it with the tip of his tongue before scribbling furiously in his order pad as Latif spoke; most suspiciously, the way they shook hands a few minutes later. I froze. Questions bubbled and squeaked: had they sealed some kind of deal, agreed to turn me in, to split the cash?

'Fessing Up

HALF an hour later, I was eating a fried egg sarnie with chips on a scrubby bit of land by a railway bridge that was scrawled with tags. The egg oozed fat as my teeth sank into the bread, just the way I liked it. I tried to remember the last time I'd eaten carbs. It seemed like a lifetime ago. Winners don't do carbs. That's what Mum says, anyway.

The chips tasted of my new life.

Stretched out before me was a complicated cross section of railway tracks. I guessed they were part of Victoria Station. Directly ahead, Battersea Power Station's four white chimneys stabbed the sky like a giant upturned table. So close again, although we'd been walking for hours. I frowned. London was playing tricks on me, throwing landmarks into the mix where they shouldn't be.

On a wall overlooking the tracks, a billboard advertising my parents' prime-time show pictured them on a sofa, giving soft-focus smiles. I turned my back, but still I could feel their eyes burning holes between my shoulder blades. I rolled my shoulders, trying to shrug off their gaze. My parents were everywhere – staring down from billboards, ranting on the radio, glaring at me from TV screens. It was almost as if they were hiding behind every corner waiting to ambush me.

A train slid south.

A noise startled me. It was only Latif returning with newspapers. "You're front-page news, Dash!" He handed me a copy of *GoldRush Image News*, my parents' free newspaper. I took it and started flicking through, desperate to see how my story was shaping up.

Big, bold, brassy headlines screamed:

Kidnappers Go For Gold!
Golden Girl Snatched!

I rolled my eyes. "Original, huh?"

Inside a scaremonger headline bellowed: ***Lock Up Your Daughters!*** A photo of yours truly peeped out from beneath; my radiant ten-year-old smile was guaranteed to melt hearts. Next to mine was an even prettier photo of Coco.

I put my hand to my mouth. "They've taken Coco. For real."

Reading on, I discovered that the police had lost Coco's kidnappers on the outskirts of Crunch Town. A shiver crept up my spine. I imagined masked men holding her captive in a squalid tower block in London's scariest dead zone. I pictured her alone in a room with blacked-out windows, her peroxide hair shining in the dark, like a shimmery halo.

"Poor Coco," I said. "She'll die of fright if she's in Crunch Town." My stomach clenched up when I said the name of the place. Photos from news stories flashed through my head. Crunch Town was hell on earth.

"And you wouldn't?" His eyebrow was at full tilt.

"Very funny," I said, scanning the report. "The kidnappers were really organised. They had a fleet of getaway motorbikes. The police followed dummy vehicles."

"These guys are professionals. They know what they're doing. They'd probably been planning the raid ever since the Bullet Company started chartering trains to the super-rich. That stirs up envy big time. Believe it!"

Latif started skimming through another copy. Every so often he'd read out embarrassing titbits, a smile playing at the corner of his mouth. "Golden Girl Grabbed. For the Love of Gold Find Our Princess. As Good as Gold…"

"Cut it out, Latif! It's all gas. I've told you already, they don't give a toss. I'm just a… what's Dad's gummy phrase?" I wrinkled my nose. "A brand-booster. Yeah. That's it. He only cares about the brand, I promise. End of story." I stabbed at a studio shot of my parents with a neon fingernail. "They probably see this as good publicity."

He grimaced. "Truth!"

"Don't laugh, I swear they're only hunting me down because I'm the brand's future."

"But what about your past?" His eyes travelled over a doublespread of photos showing my luxe life. My stomach knotted some more. I knew what was coming. "Did you love all this?" He waved his hand across the photos. "The yachts, the houses, the parties, being famous. Rah! It's crazy." He shook his head. "It's unreal. 'Sakes, Dash, how many houses do you own? You live everywhere and nowhere all at once. You're stateless." He gave me one of his narrow-eyed looks, not one of my favourites. "So did you enjoy being a Gold? A global?"

I averted my eyes.

"The truth, Dash. No bullshit for once."

"Yeah. Sort of…" I mumbled.

"Sort of?" His aqua eyes bored into me.

"Okay. You're going to hate me for this." The confession caught in my throat. I took a deep breath. "Okay! Okay! I 'fess up." My arm gestures were getting wild and nervous. "I loved the whole lifestyle. It was fun. I loved the clothes, the holidays, meeting stars, having stylists and an army of maids. I got caught up in the glittery whirlwind. I spangled-out… Who wouldn't?"

He shrugged.

"'Sakes, Latif. The air must be really pure up there." I folded my arms. "So, if my parents offered you an art show on GoldRush TV, you'd turn it down?"

"Yeah! My art is authentic. TV would kill it. Make it mainstream."

"For real?"

"For real. I hate sell-outs and fakes. I'm not interested in money and fame — it spoils the good stuff."

"Yeah. I know," I whispered.

"So you bought into all their rubbish? Even the surgery?"

I flushed, furious that he'd asked me that question. I studied his face for a few seconds. I shrugged inwardly. He was always going to see me as a rich kid and a fake. *Whatever.*

I felt too exhausted to lie. I took a deep breath and started.

"Okay. You're *really* going to hate me for this. Until recently I wanted to be the face of GoldRush. The truth is I couldn't wait for my makeover. I wanted to be picture perfect." I couldn't meet his eye. "I was shallow. A total fake. Satisfied now?"

A smile flickered at the corner of his mouth.

"Then a few months back, I found out how rad the surgery was going to be. Until then my parents hadn't been totally straight with me. I was like, 'You're *not* doing that to me, psychos! No way.' But Dad said it was time to give back to the brand. He was like, 'You've enjoyed the lifestyle. Now it's payback time.' That's when I realised all this came at a price." I waved my hand over the photos. "Nothing was for free. When I rebelled, Dad made it clear the brand came first." I shook my head sadly.

"Your dad's real shady." He sucked air through his teeth. "That's rank."

"It was horrible. I felt so lonely. Unloved. And then my birth mother turned up that night like some kind of guardian angel. That's when I started dreaming of escape."

"What happened that night?"

This was the easy bit – I'd been dying to talk to someone about it. It had been a struggle keeping it secret for so long. I took my time, revelling in the details: the fight with my stylists, the hoaxed security alarm and the scene in the hallway. My voice wobbled with emotion as I described my shock at seeing this beautiful, mystery woman – my mother

– in the hallway as my parents were having her thrown out of the building.

"Did you confront the Golds?"

"Are you mad?"

"For real? So you've never spoken to them about her?"

"No way. I didn't want to put them on their guard. I was worried they'd up my security. I decided to play the long game."

"What did you do?"

"I hit the Internet. Dad had mentioned the name of the agency, so I looked it up straight away. It was a strange site. Minimal. All it had was the name of the agency and the address. Nothing else. Apart from the slogan: 'Ultimate Childcraft: Unlocking the Mystery of Your Child's Potential.' It was weird. Like a riddle or a clue. I haven't got any proof, but I don't think the circumstances surrounding my adoption are legit."

"What makes you say that?"

"They paid to adopt me. Probably thousands. Anyway it was a commercial transaction. That's not legal, is it?"

"Thousands?" A smile twitched the corner of his mouth. "That much? What did you do next?"

"I started trawling adoption sites, forums and chatrooms. I sat at the computer for hours trying to figure things out. I went deeper and deeper until it felt like I'd searched the furthest corners of the net. For days, I didn't find out anything relevant. Then one night I was messaging a girl called 'Pawnqueen' in a chatroom and she seemed to know all about FuturePerfect. We struck up a relationship. Pawnqueen is a global, too, and her story's similar to mine. She put me in the picture. FuturePerfect arranges for super-rich couples to adopt the baby of their dreams. Couples choose their child based on its genetic profile. Wish-list babies."

"Yeah right, Dash. So you've got gold-plated genes. You're letting your imagination run away with you."

"No, hear me out. Pawnqueen says FuturePerfect sells babies with the genetic make-up to match the couple's special requirements. So let's say you want a tennis champion, a maths genius, a model or a total egghead – that's what you get. Pawnqueen's parents wanted a chess champion, and she is one. FuturePerfect offers babies with superior genes. They'll only take babies on if they are genetically 'advanced'."

"But Pawnqueen could be a nut. She could be making the whole thing up."

"I believe her. Her parents have told her all about her adoption. They were proud their ambitions for her had worked out, that she'd grown into the champion they had always wanted. I don't really know how it works, but I think they profile and vet the birth parents. Then they map the babies' DNA with a microchip. Get a full genetic profile and match it to prospective parents' wish lists. That way the couples get the baby they want. No nasty surprises. The whole thing is pretty sci-fi."

"Dash, rule number one. Don't believe everything you read."

"Do you really think my dad would go through normal channels?"

He still looked doubtful.

"Okay. How dodgy is this? You can't access FuturePerfect's site on the normal Internet. There's another invisible, shadowy web, the dark web, where illegal stuff goes on. It's a haven for cybercrims who traffic everything. You know, the buying and selling of guns, drugs, women, tasers and *me!*" My voice rose to a squeak.

"You accessed the dark web?" he asked dubiously.

"No way. I can't access that. You need special software. It's for crims, gangsters and villains."

"And the police," he said grimly.

"That figures." I juggled my phone from hand to hand. "The chief of police probably did the deal." It was a joke, but my tone was bleak. "The truth is my parents bought me, preordered with specific requirements."

"So why's he knifing you?" Latif said dubiously.

"There's always room for improvement, I guess. He chose the best raw material to work with, like a potter works with quality clay — you know, hair colour, height, frame, eye colour, skin — and now he's going to create his ideal. He sees himself as an artist. He spends hours in art galleries, studying portraits of beautiful women. I'm going to be his masterpiece."

"That's capo criminal!"

I raised an eyebrow as if to say, "When has that ever stopped my dad?"

"More to the point, Dash, you've got no proof." His voice was impatient again. "Dash, you've got to get real. Deal with the facts. Are you trying to tell me you're a superior being?"

"Okay. Okay. But my real mum's the only person who knows the truth. That's why I have to find her. I need answers. I need to find out who I really am. It's driving me nuts."

He laughed. "Now that's a fact."

It was a good sign that he was joking around again. "So you're still up for it?" I said, taking advantage.

"Here, give me your phone."

When I handed it to him, he removed the SIM card with a paperclip, and then, before I could stop him, he had ground it beneath his heel and thrown it onto the railway tracks.

"Hey, what the hell are you doing?" I snatched my phone back. "That's my life."

"I thought you wanted a new life."

"But my photos and…" I tailed off when I saw his eyebrow shoot up again. "Not of me… my dog and stuff." I shrugged. "Memories."

"You can't be sentimental, Dash."

"So I'm going to be a person with no past, like a spy." I smiled. "I could get used to that."

"Invisible. That's what you've got to be."

Two trains trundled off.

"You still up for it?" I whispered again, dreading his reply.

"Killer!" He was already heading for the streets.

The sun was up. Daylight. Bright. Exposing.

Eyes Everywhere

EUSTON Station. Rush hour. A grimy hangar of a space clotted with commuters. Latif coasted the perimeter, checking for CCTV. I kept close – his shadow. Our reflections in shop windows showed two lurkers: caps down, hoods up, scowling, skulking, avoiding eye contact.

After we'd completed one full circuit, Latif headed into the centre of the concourse, weaving through the crowds, finally coming to a halt when he reached a Paperchase kiosk, where he pretended to browse for cards. I stopped, too, wondering if he'd lost his mind. *Get Well Soon.* The card-stand swivelled with a creak. *GOOD LUCK.*

You said it, I thought, tracing the outline of a four-leaf clover, wishing I could absorb luck by osmosis. But Latif's eyes were looking beyond the cards, checking out the cameras' sight lines. I imagined them intersecting the space like a complicated mathematical diagram, which illustrated the blatantly obvious point – *there's nowhere to hide, suckers!* Not an atom of unfilmed air. Not a millimetre of unsurveyed space. Instantly my mind pictured our images shooting along underground cables, faster than a Tube train, swooshing up into some cavernous bunker where we'd slink ghostly across monitors watched by jobsworths with puffy Burger King skin. Creepy. I pulled my hood down a fraction further.

A station announcement droned that CCTV cameras were watching the station for safety management.

"Don't look up," Latif hissed, anticipating my reaction.

Fighting the urge, I fixed my gaze to the floor, focusing on footwear: ballet pumps, trainers, high-tops, wedges…

Then we were off again, ducking the invisible sight lines like a couple of jewel thieves dodging security lasers. We stopped by the Britannia pub and crouched down. The acrid smell of piss and disinfectant blasted my nostrils.

"Blind spot." His eyes flicked towards the CCTV cameras. "And we've got an awesome view of the star attraction."

For the first time since we'd entered the station, I registered the huge news screen next to the departure boards, and seeing my goofy face staring down, muttered, "'Sakes. Give me a break."

Bold red headlines screamed: ***Kidnap Terror!*** as footage of me posing with my parents at the Oscars played out; mother and daughter decked out in diamonds, smiling and blowing kisses. Commuters were staring up at the news board like zombies, desperate for fresh gore. I buried my head in my hands and whispered, "This is totally weird. It feels like the whole world is looking at me. I mean, looking *for* me."

"Chill, Dash. People are looking for *that*." Latif pointed to the shiny, happy person on screen. "Not a grunge-ball." He turned towards me with a wry smile. "People only see what they expect. And they don't expect to see you without the gloss. Honest. Check it. Nobody's giving you a second look."

"Great, so now I'm invisible," I muttered, pinching myself to check I still existed. Because crouching there, looking up at my larger-than-life, glamorous TV self, I felt like a ghost. I put my hands up to my mouth, palms cupped, and breathed into them, enjoying the sensation of my warm breath on my skin.

Okay, Dash, don't panic. You're still alive. I exhaled again, wanting to reassure myself once more.

"You okay?" He squeezed my arm.

"Take a wild guess." I shot him an angry look. "Watching my life flashing by up there is creeping me out big time. All the photos and praise, it's like an obituary, isn't it? I feel like I'm dead." I shuddered, shifted my gaze. "And these crazy dudes are freaking me out." I nodded towards the rubberneckers, staring up at the news screen. "They remind me of those weirdoes who gawp at car crashes…" I broke off as an unsettling thought struck me. Each and every one of those crazy losers had assimilated my image, processed it and stored it away in some dark cranial nook where it would remain lodged, like a ticking bomb, until a glimpse of my chin or nose would detonate it. Kepow! Game over!

"No way!" Latif muttered. *"That's all I need."*

Looking up quickly, I couldn't believe my eyes. Latif was on screen. Despite his masked face, I recognised him instantly. The CCTV footage showed him giving a freedom fighter's fist to the camera down by the train depot. Luckily, apart from the cowboy hat, which was stowed away in his rucksack, he looked like any other hood-rat. I crossed my fingers. As far as I could see there was no way of recognising him. Then the headline flashed up: **Goldrush Image Inc Exclusive: The Kidnapper's Identity Revealed.**

What? For real? But how? I watched through splayed fingers as the yellow ticker tape crawled across the screen, like a poisonous spider.

Latif Hajjaj has been named by police in the Dasha Gold abduction case. His motives are so far unclear. Although police sources believe Latif Hajjaj is a lone wolf, they haven't ruled out that he may have connections to a terrorist cell. There are as yet unsubstantiated reports that Dasha Gold's kidnap may have links to a wider terrorist plot.

I was totally confused. His face had been covered, so how had they got his name? Weirder still, how had they linked him to me? I thought he moved in the shadows. A panic switch in my head clicked to on, then maxed out.

Next up, grainy CCTV footage showed two figures running down a street at night. It had to be us because the taller of the two was wearing a cowboy hat. But there was something odd about it. The taller figure hadn't got Latif's loose-limbed gait. The camera zoomed in to reveal a gun. We exchanged a grim look. The figure in the cowboy hat and keffiyeh was pushing the gun into the smaller figure's back. Latif removed his keffiyeh and shoved it into his rucksack. Then I noticed more discrepancies; the girl in the film was wearing the same outfit as I'd been wearing on the train – sparkly top, high heels and a Dior bag bumping at her hip, not overalls. And she was struggling.

"That footage is too good for CCTV," he growled. "Go figure."

My head started to spin. I moved closer to Latif, shrinking into my hood.

Grainy footage showed the Latif lookalike forcing the girl onto a motorbike. Then he jumped on behind and they shot off down the road.

Latif's eyes never moved from the screen.

I started scanning the station nervously. The news package cut back to the shot of Latif punching the air in slo-mo by the train depot. The keffiyeh wrapped around his face knee-jerked prejudice. Then the graffiti that he'd painted on the train hit the screen. The freedom fighter with images of rioting kids reflected in his glasses menaced. The Arabic lettering exploded off the screen like a homemade bomb. *Boom! Guilty!* This was followed by generic shots of soldiers training in a dusty camp somewhere in North Africa. The ticker tape read: **Gun Mad Graffiti Artist Holidays in Terrorist Boot Camp.** A personal photo of Latif, posing in the style of Andy Warhol's Double Elvis ended the news item. In less than two minutes my parents had turned Latif into a terrorist.

"Your parents are scum," Latif hissed. "They've made this up. Totally concocted the story. They're setting me up."

"I know," I whispered, scanning the station. "But how did they get your name so quickly?"

"Facebook, I guess, even though I deactivated my account years ago. That's where they got the Elvis photo. I posted my early graffiti there too." He was working the worry beads across his knuckles. "I exist on the net. That's enough."

It was then I saw the thug.

"We've got to go, Latif!" I tugged at his sleeve. "Over there!" I flicked my eyes towards a man, not unlike Big Stevie, dressed in a bomber jacket and Timberland boots. He was pushing through the commuters talking into a hands-free.

"Okay, goon alert! Stay cool." We stood up slowly. "Don't run. These guys are like dogs; start running and they'll give chase."

I hurried after him, skipping a few steps to keep level.

"Cut it out," he said, eyes fixed straight ahead. "You'll draw attention to us."

A few paces later, he glanced over his shoulder. I couldn't stop myself from mirroring him. The goon was talking into his walkie-talkie and he was looking in our direction. He sped up. Something had triggered his interest. The guy broke into a run.

"Okay. He's got peepers on us. We need out of CCTV range and fast." Now Latif was running. "Look for spaces," he shouted.

I tore after him and for a few strides we ran in sync, but in a matter of seconds, he was streaking ahead, even though I was running flat-out. I hadn't got his knack for searching out spaces.

"Wait!" I screamed, pumping my arms harder in a desperate attempt to generate more speed as we ran past fast food outlets, florists and sandwich bars.

Latif was slowing down. I glanced back; the goon was still coming. Latif fetched something out of his rucksack's side pocket and gestured for me to move to my left. As I got out of the way, he dipped down and bowled a handful of marbles along the concourse. They rattled past like balls in a pinball machine.

When I caught up with him, Latif winked and said, "If it was good enough for the Sidney Street anarchists… Low-tech never fails."

I hadn't a clue what he was talking about, but looking over my shoulder, I saw the bomber-jacketed goon was lying beneath a day-trip of ladies, his Timberland boots kicking out at the passing snaffle-bit loafers.

Latif was already charging down an empty gangway towards platforms one, two and three. I kept my eyes peeled for guards, but luckily the barriers were unmanned. When Latif reached the platforms, he turned right and sprinted for the fire exit. With one swift movement, he pushed down the metal safety bar and flung open the double door. Turning round, he yelled for me to run faster. His words hissed towards me with fire-hose intensity.

Outside, a street colonised by lap-dancing clubs and tacky bookstores. Latif ran across a busy road, dodging traffic, I followed with my heart in my mouth. Then we were hurtling down sooty-sided streets. My knees knocked together and I nearly fell. We tore into a housing estate. A moped zipped past in the twisty labyrinth of walkways. Still running but on my last legs, I trailed Latif through a graveyard marooned between a road and railway tracks, down a flight of steps into a maze of redbrick Victorian hospital buildings, spiked with Gothic towers. Finally Latif stopped by a line of trolleys piled high with laundry bags and disappeared into an outhouse. I hesitated in the doorway. The labels on the bags read: *For incineration only.*

"Come on, Dash!" Latif said as he squeezed between gridlocked trolleys. At the far end, an incinerator glowed. The small room was sweltering. Slipping in behind a row of trolleys lined up against the back wall, I followed Latif's lead by gripping the mesh with both hands and pulling myself up so my feet were a few inches off the ground. When we heard footsteps pounding past, we exchanged a look; it confirmed what we knew already, that we'd been spotted on CCTV, which could only mean one thing – *people were watching.*

After a short while, I heard running footsteps again. They were returning.

They slowed.

Stopped.

A devil dog clamped my heart in its jaws.

They started up again. One, two, three… I guessed the goon from the station was approaching our hideout. I imagined his bulk filling the doorframe, his big slaphead ballooning up from his neck like a bubblegum blow. I held my breath. The mesh cut into my fingers. Sweat beaded my temples. Time folded in on itself. Suddenly the crash of trolleys split open the silence. A gruff voice shouted something in an Eastern European language.

Another clash of metal out-jangled my nerves.

Out of nowhere, a second voice, clipped with authority barked, "Excuse me, sir. Can I see your ID tag, please? This is medical waste. Are you authorised to be here?"

A grunt, followed by one set of footsteps retreating rapidly.

We waited until we heard the second set of footsteps heading off, before slipping out from behind the trolleys. My hands were moulded into claws from clinging to the mesh; I slowly stretched out my sore fingers.

After a few minutes we crept out and sprinted in the opposite direction.

Beyond the hospital gates, there was a drab industrial park, full of elephant-grey buildings, blowing out stale air through metal pipes. We ran in silence. Every so often I'd glance over my shoulder. Nobody, apart from a bag lady pushing a pram piled high with junk. We raced on along bleak, desolate roads towards the empty steel basket of a gas tower, its grid reminding me of a giant cat's cradle, then down onto a canal path, quiet and gloomy; a no-go area, forgotten London. The canal water was brown and stagnant. Petrol rainbows smeared the surface. Beer bottles bobbed. As I hurtled along the towpath, loose paving stones splashed filthy water over my trainers. *SLOW!* warned white lettering across the path before each low canal bridge. I sped up.

After a while, Latif stopped under a bridge, which stretched for about thirty metres along the canal. It was gloomy and smelled of mausoleums, but the shadows offered good cover and an excellent view in both directions. Latif squatted down and, picking up a few flat stones, started skimming them one after the other. He didn't say a word, simply watched the stones bounce and skid across the water.

Placing my hands on my knees, I took a few minutes to catch my breath.

"I'm really sorry," I said as soon as I could speak without puffing. "Making out you're a terrorist is low even for them."

Latif remained silent. He was leaning back, knees bent, as if on a skateboard, fine-tuning his posture. As I waited for him to speak, I noticed the stone that he was holding between his thumb and fingers was smooth and brown – the same colour as his skin. And all I could think was: *Please don't dump me now.*

"So you don't think it's true." His aquamarines fixed on me.

"What?"

"That I'm a lone wolf. That I've spent time in a terrorist training camp."

"Are you nuts?" My laughter bounced off the water and echoed around the curve of the bridge. "My family *is* television. I know what my parents do and it's ugly. 'Sakes, Latif, they make up the news most of the time. Reality's too boring or it doesn't play right, so they spice it up. Guess what Mum's favourite phrase is? 'Make it happen.'" I shrugged. "That's code for 'make it up'. Right now, my parents want me back and they'll do anything to *make that happen.*"

"That dope is dirty. It sticks. I'll never clear my name now. Never."

"Yeah. I know." I tailed off, wishing I could think of something positive to say.

He skimmed another stone, but didn't speak.

"Look, Latif, I know you think I'm clueless, but I can identify faked CCTV footage and generic news images of a terrorist training camp. No trouble. I've spent hours in edits with Mum and Dad so I know the score. That's where they construct the lies. They don't care if they ruin lives. They don't care about anyone, except their brand." I shrugged. "They'd probably kill for ratings."

"Truth!" He shaped a gun with his fingers and put it to his temple. "They've sure as hell killed my rep."

"Don't be stupid." I squeezed his arm, desperately trying to think of something a little less lame to say.

"So you don't think gap-year jihad's my style?" There was a hint of a smile.

"Yeah! Right!" I rolled my eyes. "You spend your nights tagging Arabic graffiti. What's so sinister about that? You're cool. Different. And those headcases are using that against you."

"We've gifted them a great story. A ratings winner. Tragedy sells, Dash. Kidnapped glob-girl. Heartbroken parents. Throw a terrorist into the mix. Boom! Suddenly it's explosive." Latif depth-charged a rock. "They're making it up as they go along." Our reflections shattered into a million pieces. Our faces swam back into focus bit by bit.

"But how did they connect us? In the CCTV footage they're pumping out, the girl impersonating me wasn't wearing overalls. She's in heels and carrying a handbag." I spoke slowly, trying to work things out as I went along. "So they can't have seen recent footage of us together."

"They've worked out we were both near the depot around the same time. They're running with that. They need a fall guy, and I'll do. Wrong time. Wrong place. Lucky me!"

"I'm so sorry," I repeated dismally. I could picture my parents fleshing out the storyboard, working out the most sensational angle – the one that would hook viewers in. "Framing you is…" I tailed off. No word in the English language was bad enough to describe their behaviour.

"If they think you're with me they have to discredit me."

An uneasy silence followed.

When he turned to look at me his eyes were burning with anger, which gave them a hard edge, like a newly-cut jewel. "Your parents have to explain your disappearance somehow. They can't say you've run away coz that'll make them look bad, so they've decided to fit me up. I'm half-Lebanese. I tag in Arabic." He shrugged. "That doesn't take much spinning, doctor." He stretched out his hand. "Lone wolf, self-starter and enemy of the state number one. Pleased to meet you."

I didn't take his hand. I wasn't in the mood for jokes. Instead I batted his hand away and picked up a stone.

"I guess that's Dad's speciality." I jiggled the stone in my hand. "Stitching things together. Stitching people up." I chucked the stone into the canal. Smack! It hit the water like a big, bold exclamation mark. THE END! "We can't even go to the police. They're *so* involved in this. They must've seen us on CCTV in the station and tipped off my parents, and that's why the goon showed up."

"Total connectivity. Believe it!"

"Do they think I'm kidnapped?"

He shrugged. "What do you think?"

I dropped another stone into the canal and watched the ripples radiate out and vanish. This was big. And we had no one to turn to.

"Sooo." I stretched the word out, not wanting to ask the next question. "What are we going to do now?" My question echoed around the bridge's curve. When I looked up he was taking his spray cans out of his bag. My heart jumped. His doomy expression had dissolved into a broad smile.

"We're gonna reframe the story."

My eyes widened. "How?" I made a square with my fingers and thumbs, and viewing him through it, said, "Easier said than done."

"Your parents want a scalp – *mine*. But they ain't going to get it. Baba will sort it, no problem. *Inshallah!*"

"Baba?"

"Dad. He'll run rings round your folks and he'll enjoy the fight. I'm gonna have to keep below the radar. Avoid getting into an arrest situation."

He was throwing up his piece as he spoke. First up, the template of the freedom fighter. This time his Aviators reflected banks of plasma screens. Across the screens he blasted the words: **DON'T BELIEVE THE LIES!** in Arabic and English.

When he'd finished he pulled his cheap mobile from the back pocket of his paint-spattered jeans.

"I thought you said no phones."

"It's pay-as-you-go. Can't be traced to me." He punched in a number.

"Who are you calling? Your dad?"

"Nah! My parents' mobiles will be slammed." Seeing my puzzled look, he tugged his ear. "The feds will be listening in. They'll have spooks tailing Mum's cab most likely." He put his hand up to stop my chat.

"Ren. Yeah. It's deep, fam. I need a ride. Links at the sushi, yeah?" He finished the call without saying goodbye and tossed his mobile into the canal. Clocking my expectant look, he filled in the gaps. "Ren's Jeannie's son. We've been bros for time. I'm hoping Mum's got word to Jeannie."

He took a roll of masking tape from his rucksack. "Catch, Dash!" he said, throwing it over. I missed and as I scrambled after it, he said, "Cover up any logos on your garms. Hundred per cent the police have the info on your runners." He winked. "De-brand or die."

I tore off strips of masking tape with my teeth before sticking them over the Nike logos on my trainers – front, side and back. By the time I'd finished, there wasn't much trainer left.

"Won't it look weird?" I asked, as I smoothed the tape over both heels.

"Nah. This look is cool with the anti-capitalist crew. A DJ did it and now lots of people rock it." He adjusted his face coverings, sealing himself off from the world.

I examined my feet dubiously. They looked like miniature Egyptian mummies.

"What else, Dash?" He ran an expert eye over my outfit. "Your jeans. Sort it!"

I pulled my trackie top down over the label.

Latif started walking off. "Let's creep. It helps me spin."

"Spin?"

"Think, bubblehead!"

He set off down the canal at a brisk walk, deep in thought, past brightly painted houseboats moored up at a New Age hippy outpost, past a ragged line of ducks that took off in fright, past neglected barges.

"So you've got money and that?" he asked.

"What do you think? I'm a Gold, for Chrissakes. Why?"

"Case the going gets tough."

"Like it hasn't already." I bit my lip, working out the best way to broach a subject, which would definitely make things get a whole deal tougher. I dreaded a negative response.

Just say it, Dash, I thought, *you have to know one way or the other.* But I felt uneasy.

I cleared my throat. "Are you still up for finding my real mother?" The words tumbled out in a rush.

"Don't push it, Dasha Gold." But there was a smile in his voice.

"You're still up for it? Despite everything?"

"Yeah. You deserve better than those muppets."

"Really?" My voice shot up an octave. "I don't want to get you in any deeper."

"As if…" He gave me that sideways look. "It don't get much deeper than this, Dash."

I stuck my tongue out. "But don't say I didn't warn you. Dad holds all the cards and the house always wins."

"Yeah. But he doesn't know London like I do. The police keep clear of Crunch Town unless something serious is kicking off. They can't touch me out there." He pretended to flick dust off his shoulder. "It's another world out east."

My heart sank. Crunch Town was the last place on earth I wanted to go. We headed up some crumbling steps and into a rundown estate.

"So what now?" I asked, all smiles. "I've got twenty on me and my cash card."

"That's it? I thought you were rolling in it." He tsked. "Using an ATM's risky. Your dad's probably stopped your card. But in Crunch Town we'll have flight time."

"Flight time?"

"Time to scarper." His voice crackled with excitement. "So, Miss Gold, we'd better go see if we've got the Midas touch."

He held out his hand and we bumped knuckles. Seeing my ring, he whistled and then he took hold of my hand, lifting it up so he could get a better look. An electric current shot up my arm. "Now that could get us out of trouble." The ring was white gold with a diamond inset. "That's serious bling. It must've cost a stack."

"Eight thousand pounds. Vulgar, innit?" I joked.

"Eight k!" He whistled. "That would sort our jaunt, no problem. Cover favours, bribes and that. You okay to flog it?" he asked as we walked through the estate.

"No. I couldn't. It has huge sentimental value for me." I clutched the ring to my chest. "It's a present from Mummy dearest." I eased the ring off my finger and gave it to him. "Only joking. Take it. They're blood diamonds. People died because of them. They're ugly diamonds for ugly people."

I liked the irony of using a gift from my fake mum to fund my quest to track down my real mum. There was something deeply satisfying about the trade-off.

Breathless

THE sushi bar was a dive; a row of converted garages with makeshift rooms flung up one on top of the other – all higgledy-piggledy and chaotic, which gave the place the look of a favela dwelling.

"This place never sleeps. It's live. Open-DJ spots. Karaoke. Gambling out back." Latif walked under a sagging awning and sat down at one of the tables. Ashtrays piled high with cigarette butts cluttered the table. A scattering of ash dusted the surface. Latif wrote his name in bubble letters with a long, elegant finger. Then he wiped it out.

Although the bar's metal safety shutters were pulled halfway down, a group of Japanese workers ducked under and trooped over to the bar. All were wearing uniforms.

Night shifters, I thought.

A few moments later, an explosion of colour whooshed from beneath the shutters as a gang of clubbers emerged, blinking. I watched them walk off down the street, chattering manically.

"What about the police?" I looked around nervously.

"The feds? What about them?" Latif shrugged, eyes fixed on the entry to the dead-end street, more out of habit than anxiety. "The street's blind and the club's off the radar."

"Blind?"

"No cameras. Want a beer?" he asked, rooting around in the back pocket of his jeans for change.

"Yes, please."

I slouched down into the chair. Yeah. A beer was exactly what I needed to take the edge off things. Everything about me was jittery: my mind, my hands and my nerves.

As Latif mooched across to the vending machines, I wondered how he managed to keep so cool. Whatever. He fired a handful of coins into the slot. Zap. Zap. Zap. The rows of silver beer cans lined up in the vending machine made me think of robots preparing for battle. He drummed his fingers against the machine, but I couldn't decipher the tune. After a few seconds he kicked the bottom when it refused to give up its booty. Two cans clattered down. He walked back over and handed me a beer. The cans gave a satisfactory *pish* when we eased back the ring pulls.

Latif watched the street, shrugging off my attempts at conversation. I guessed he wanted quiet time. His vibe wasn't doomy, though, more contemplative. Taking the hint, I scouted the cul-de-sac for CCTV. He was right about the cameras. There weren't any. I took a long swig of beer and rotated my neck, trying to ease the tension in my shoulders. Nothing doing. I was wired.

Inside, whacked-out staff were propping up the bar. They were watching a Japanese game show and knocking back shots of sake. Nobody in the bar showed the slightest interest in us. We could have been in a seedy back street somewhere in Tokyo – thousands of miles away from the media storm.

A cab turned into the cul-de-sac and trundled towards us with a throaty gurgle. My stomach clenched.

The cab slowed.

Stopped.

Latif drained his can, stood up and gave a mock salute.

At the wheel sat a Japanese guy who was smiling at us. When he rolled down the window I noticed he was styled like Elvis. His quiff was immaculate. "Respect, bruv."

Latif leaned into the cab. "*Salaam*, bruv. I owe you big time."

They bumped fists.

"No worries, fam. This is deep. You've stirred up a commotion. You're trending worldwide on Twitter and I was like, "Sakes, either he's lost it big time or there's more to it.' But I know there's always more to it when the feds are involved. Anyway, when you called, I was like, 'Jesus walks, he's safe.' I picked up Yukiko and came straight over."

"Rah! It's all gone crazy!" Latif said. "Nothing Baba can't handle. *Inshallah.*"

He opened the door and I climbed in.

Inside sat a Japanese girl with vibrant splashes of vermillion pink in her hair and swooping black make-up. She was wearing a Victorian-style maid's outfit matched with black and white striped tights and Dr Martens. The pocket of her white, crisp apron was stuffed with cosmetics and hairbrushes. I recognised the style as GothLoli, a subculture in Japan.

"Hi, I'm Dasha," I whispered, slightly taken aback by the flamboyance of our new allies.

The girl stretched out a delicate hand. "Hi, I'm Yukiko. This is bonkers, innit?"

I nodded stiffly. When we shook hands Yukiko said, "I know what you're thinking. Don't panic. I'm the distraction. We'll look like crazy tourists with me in the back, innit?"

"So that's your excuse for hitching a ride in my road movie, Yukiko!" Latif said as he ducked into the cab. He pulled down the bucket seat and sat directly behind Ren. Once settled, he sprawled out his legs. "Starlets are so pushy these days."

"I wouldn't have missed this for the world, Lats." Yukiko kissed him on both cheeks. "Anyways, you'd better be nice to me, because I've got garms in here to save your skinny arse." She patted a large sports bag, which lay at her feet.

"You blackmailing me, Yuks?"

"Could be." She unzipped the bag and pulled out a scarlet piece of parachute fabric. "It's your choice."

"Where to?" Ren asked. "East?" We were already hurtling down the road. "We need to ghost. There are bare loads of bully vans all over."

"Yeah. East." Latif swivelled round on his seat and pushed back the plastic partition. "We're gonna lie low while the media's roaring."

"I can't believe those muppets broadcast that photo of you posing as Elvis to grub your good name. That shot rocked, fam." Ren kissed his knuckles and punched his fist towards a black and white photo of Elvis, which was stuck to the dashboard.

"Believe it!" Latif poked his head through the partition.

"How come they were on you so quickly?"

"Facebook, I guess. Even though I deactivated my account years ago. That info's always out there. The algorithm squad must've sussed it."

"That sucks. I guess few people tag in Arabic," Ren said.

"And you did that cool graffiti for the youth project in south London," Yukiko said. "There was press about that."

Latif shrugged. "Has Mum spoken to Jeannie?"

"Yeah. She stopped by the cafe as soon as the TV started blagging. Your dad's on it already. She says keep calm. Don't panic." Ren laughed. "As if my main soldier's gonna freak out."

"As if... Get Jeannie to tell Mum everything's under control."

Control? My eyes opened wide. If this was control I'd hate to see things when they got messy. I almost said as much, but decided against it. For some reason, I sensed it would be better to let the conversation come to me rather than seek it out. It was just a feeling.

"So what's going on, cuz?" Ren was eyeing me with suspicion in the rear-view mirror. I shifted uncomfortably in my seat. "The real story?"

"We were IDed on CCTV at Euston, and boom, an ugly started tailing us. We lost him in the hospital. The feds are on it for once. With massive help from GoldRush Image Inc…"

"We haven't got time for this," Yukiko cut in brusquely.

She turned to face me and said, "You're obviously not kidnapped, so what's your game?"

"Game?" I blinked.

"Is this some kind of publicity stunt?" She got straight to the point. Her tone was no-nonsense *"I want to know what you're up to."* She emphasised each word, treating me like some kind of moron. "We don't want you doing Lats over, that's all."

My jaw dropped open. I glanced over at Latif, wanting backup.

"Straight-up, guys, she's running," he said. "She's got personal reasons, so back off. I know what I'm doing. It's cool."

Ren and Yukiko shot each other a doubtful look.

"No really… It's the truth. I want out. I promise," I flustered. The knot in my stomach had shifted to my chest and I was finding it difficult to breathe.

"Don't blame you. But why?" Ren's tone was sceptical.

I exchanged another look with Latif.

"Tell them." He shrugged. "Ren's adopted. He'll understand."

"What?" Ren and Yukiko chorused in unison. *"You're adopted?"* Yukiko's eyes popped wide.

"Yes. I'm adopted." I fidgeted in my seat, reluctant to discuss something so private with strangers, and not very friendly strangers at that. "Latif is going to help me find my birth mother. The Golds aren't my real parents. Strictly no blood ties." I enjoyed using my parents' surname. It gave me distance, almost made me believe that I'd finally escaped their world. "That's why I'm on the run."

"You're joking me? You ain't a twenty-four-carat Gold." Ren swivelled round in his seat so he could get a better look at me. "You're skin and bone, like the rest of us."

Yukiko's eyes looked as if they might explode out of her head. "You ain't real Gold," she repeated, as if she'd lost the power to think for herself.

"That's a twist I wasn't expecting." Ren shook his head in disbelief. "So you ain't got their rotten blood in your veins."

"Not a drop."

"Totally unreal." He checked me out in the rear-view mirror again.

"She's bona fide, fam. Trust me!" Latif said.

"That's crazed." His eyes flicked to the mirror once more. Yukiko kept on staring at me, eyes wide.

"So you're adopted?" I asked Ren cautiously.

A balloon was expanding in my chest.

"Yeah, Jeannie's my adoptive mum. I was in care for years until I was shipped out to her. I lucked in – Jeannie's seriously cool." His eyes fixed me. "She couldn't effing believe she had a Gold in her cafe drinking tea right under her nose. She's pissed off she didn't recognise you." He laughed. "Especially as she reads every celeb site going and thinks she's an expert. Up until last night, she claimed she could spot a celebrity at fifty metres."

"Poor old Jeannie. She'll never forgive me for that." Latif chuckled.

"Yeah. You'd better watch out, bruv. You're never too old to get a beat-down from your auntie. She's banned you from the caff!"

I waited for the laughter to die down before asking: "Have you met your real parents, Ren?"

"Yeah! First time a few years back. But it was a real so-what moment. No chemistry. No connection. All that junk people spout. I guess making small talk with complete strangers ain't really my thing. Get me?"

I didn't. But I didn't say so. Instead I asked, "What are they like?"

"They're okay. Just didn't click, that's all. Trouble was my expectations were sky high." He gestured up to the heavens. "You know what they say about meeting your heroes. Meeting your birth parents is a bit like that. A let-down. That's how it rolled for me."

My disappointment must have shown because he added, "Everyone's scenario is different. Dad's a crim, not exactly father-figure material. But he's pretty handy if you want something on the grey."

"Grey?"

"Hookie. Stolen goods…"

"What about your mum?"

"She makes great sushi and is mad about Japanese tradition." He opened the glove compartment. A dozen red balls with bearded faces fell out. "Mum gives me a Daruma doll most times I see her. They're meant to be lucky. She's really into them."

I flinched as I watched his good luck tumble to the floor. "Do you see them much?"

"You bet. If I want a new plasma." Then, seeing my horrified look, he added, "No seriously, I see them quite a bit these days. Now I've got to know them better they crack me up. I'm getting pretty good at Japanese as well. I feel like I've inherited a whole new story, culture and that. Dad might be real hard, but they both respect old-time Japanese traditions. I like that about them. It's... what's that word? Quaint, innit? And the sushi round there is awesome."

"Why were you adopted?"

He shrugged. "Life was bad back then."

"And you never wanted to live with them? You know, after you'd got to know them better?"

"I couldn't have done that to Jeannie. She was there for me. It would've broken her heart."

"Ren, the heartbreaker. Give it a rest." Latif rolled his eyes.

I took a deep breath, steeling myself for the killer question. Then I let the air out of my nose slowly and asked, "Are you glad you found them?"

"You make it sound like I was lost before." His eyes fixed me in the mirror.

"You know what I mean..." I held my breath.

"Yeah, of course. They make me who I am. The hookie video games, the knock-off Adidas trainers, the Nike trackies and that. Without all that I'd be nothing." He winked. "Seriously, though, anyone's gotta be better than those two clowns who raised you."

Rattled, I turned and looked out of the window – a million questions spinning through my head. What if my real mother turned out to be dodgy? What if meeting her was a complete let-down? Never in a million years had I considered *that*.

But Ren and his parents had worked things out. I traced the lifeline on my left palm. At least Dad had searched out and paid for the best, I reassured myself. That much I knew. Dad was a control freak. He never left anything to chance – a characteristic that I usually detested, but which, in this instance, might work in my favour. I doubted Dad would have adopted a baby, especially one he was going to groom to be the face of his beloved brand, without doing extensive research into the parents' background.

"I guess we better get you disguised," Yukiko said. She scooped a bundle of hoodies, hats, T-shirts and long, swishy swathes of brightly-coloured fabric from her bag and dumped them in a heap on the floor. "Take your pick. I'm thinking renegade refusenik. Edgy."

"Don't use that word, Yuks." Latif shuddered. "You sound like a middle-aged TV exec."

He picked out a purple and gold tracksuit top and, holding it up, gave Yukiko one of his narrow-eyed stares, and said, "Looks like you're trying to pimp me up, Yuks." He slipped the trackie top over his orange T-shirt. Next up, he swapped his black and white keffiyeh for a length of dark blue cloth decorated with loud yellow, orange and red African print. He wrapped this flashy fabric around his hair and neck, concealing most of his face in the process. He pushed it down so he could speak. As an afterthought, he tied a bright red length of parachute silk around his shoulders. "In case of an emergency landing." He flashed a smile.

His transformation was dramatic. Nothing matched, but as soon as he'd shrugged himself into the ensemble, it looked cool, and made me wonder why I'd ever doubted his choices in the first place.

"I'm done," he said. "What do you reckon, Style Queen?"

Yukiko narrowed her eyes. "That you've taken it to the max." She pinned the corners of his makeshift red cloak together with a star-shaped Che Guevara badge, somehow fashioning a hood from the fabric.

Latif grabbed an England shirt and shoved it into his rucksack. "In case the going gets *real tough*." He winked at Yukiko. "The feds would never expect to see me in a footy shirt."

I remained silent, wondering if his outfit was an elaborate hoax. Everything about his look was seriously at odds with any ideas I had about going undercover. There was nothing covert or discreet about it. Perhaps his plan was to dazzle our enemies into submission.

"You're gonna need a pay-as-you-go." Yukiko produced a cheap throwaway phone from the sports bag and handed it to Latif. "It's brand new. I've put twenty on it."

"Safe, Yuks." Latif pocketed it.

"Don't call me again, yeah?" Ren shouted from up front. "There's a chance the feds'll slam my phone."

"Yeah. I know." Latif swivelled round and started chatting

to Ren. This time I caught very little of what was said. They were speaking fast and low so their words ran into one another, punctuated every so often by my name. From what I could work out, they were discussing events since I'd crashed into Latif's life. I strained to hear, desperate to know his thoughts, but I could only pick out about one word in five.

I stared down at the heap of clothes on the floor, looking for inspiration. Nothing really grabbed me. Everything was so bright, so look-at-me. I picked out an oversized green hoodie. On the front *Counterculture* was spelled out in the style of the Coca-Cola logo. It swamped me when I slipped it on, but I liked the way the hood swallowed up my face. Then I took a length of orange silk and wrapped it over my jeans sarong-style. I wanted to make a bold statement. This, after all, was the new me!

Yukiko took a few minutes to size up my new look. Then she took a blond wig from her bag and asked, "Fancy wigging out? I'll cut it short. You know, like Jean Seberg in the classic on-the-run movie, *Breathless*. Blond, boyish, gamine." Clocking my face, she laughed. "No need to worry, golden girl. I style pop promos and magazine shoots when I'm not disguising runaways."

"Go for it!" I said, sensing that Yukiko's makeover was going to be a whole deal cooler and a whole lot less painful than the one my parents had been planning.

Yukiko placed the wig on my head, expertly tucking up my real hair as she did so. Then she took a pair of scissors from her apron and started cutting into the wig. She worked quickly and deftly, unfazed by the bumpiness of the ride. I shut my eyes, terrified the scissors were going to stab into one of my eyes at any moment.

Her questions came as fast as the snip of her scissors, so fast, in fact, I hardly had time to answer.

"Do you have stylists?"

"Yeah."

"How many?"

"Oh, you know, a few. A team."

"Wow! And they choose your style?"

"Yeah, mostly. But recently I'd been trying to do things my way. Express myself. That's when the trouble started. The clashes. My parents want me to look a certain way for the brand, and I was getting more, like, 'No thanks.' Things started getting real testy."

"'Sakes, I'd rather die than let those clowns dress me."

I laughed. "Yeah. Tell me about it. I lived the shame."

"No offence. But I'd love to be a stylist to someone rich, famous and clueless. They could become my project. I could mould them."

I opened my eyes. "What? Like me?"

She smiled and carried on snipping.

I found Yukiko's obsession with my global life unnerving. As she grilled me, I could feel myself shrinking away from her, my replies becoming softer and softer until finally I was merely nodding, as if she'd cut my tongue out by mistake. A flush rose up my neck, inflaming my face.

Outside, the affluence of Islington ebbed away to stale

suburban streets, which in turn gave way to crumbling houses with boarded-up windows and shrugging timbers — grim, sour, forgotten places.

The rundown streets were worlds away from the secure billion-pound neighbourhood where my parents and their friends lived. Instead of trim, tree-lined avenues, high gates and state-of-the-art security systems, there were filthy streets, haphazard houses and shuttered shop-fronts blasted with graffiti. Instead of mown lawns, mini-golf and swimming pools, there were scrubby gardens sprouting tents and improvised sheds. Tower blocks cast long, gloomy shadows over the neighbourhood.

Yukiko clicked her fingers to attract Latif's attention. "Hand over your magic mirror, Lats, so Dasha can check out her new style."

I took the mirror and stared into it.

A stranger looked back.

Yukiko had cut the wig into a boyish blond crop.

My freedom haircut.

I checked it out from various angles. It was going to take some getting used to, but it worked.

"Now you look the part," Yukiko said, casting a critical eye over her masterpiece. "Just don't go getting Latif shot, okay?" Then seeing my blank look, she added, "You know like in the movie."

"As if..." I joked, half-heartedly.

"Hey Lats, check out your new-look runaway," Yukiko said. "She's hot!"

"Good girl gone bad!" he said with a grin. "Looks like you're ready for Crunch Town, Dash."

My eyes widened. So we *were* going there. It wasn't a wind-up. I gulped. As far as I knew, the only time a global ended up in Crunch Town was if they'd been kidnapped. It was where the kidnap crews, drug-dealers and murderers lived. It was a seriously scary place. Coco was already there, probably imprisoned in a dismal tower block. I shivered.

"Do we have to go there?" I asked, chewing my lip.

"We need money. I told you, we don't have a choice."

Latif took an aerosol can from his rucksack and started shaking it. Then he sprayed paint onto the little finger of his right hand, followed by his index finger. The paint was the same colour red as the parachute silk. I guessed he was putting the finishing touches to his outfit.

"What's that for?" I asked.

"It's a gang thing," was all he said as he blew on his fingers.

When they were dry, he handed me a blue scarf decorated with skulls and crossbones, which he'd extracted from the bottom of the heap. I looked at it uncertainly.

"Cover your face with it," he said. "Because, where we're heading, it's *faceless*."

I wrapped the scarf over the wig and around the bottom half of my face, then I pulled up my hood and put on my D&G shades. They masked my fear.

"Aaaw! You've only gone and ruined the look," Yukiko grouched.

"Tough!" Latif put on his reflector Aviators. Then he

adjusted the African print scarf. "We won't attract trouble if we're bundled." He handed Yukiko his cowboy hat. "Keep this safe for me, Yuks. Don't go selling it on eBay or I'll be after you." He was a cooler version of the guy in his graffiti. Yukiko and I were reflected in his Aviators. We looked like extras in a pop video. Behind his mirrors, he must have been scanning my outfit because he said, "Your bracelet's got to go."

"But…" I trailed off. Resistance was hopeless.

Looking down at my identity bracelet, I traced my middle finger over my name, which was engraved on the silver tag. It had been a sixteenth birthday present. Each charm represented something individual to me: a stiletto shoe, a D for Dasha, a four-leaf clover, a lipstick, a camera… I slowly undid the clasp. The charms clanked when I took it off. For a couple of seconds, I jiggled it in the palm of my hand. Removing my identity bracelet felt final somehow. I opened the window.

"Goodbye, Dasha Gold," I whispered as I flung it into the road.

"You okay for money?" Ren asked.

"Not for cash. We need to shift this on the grey." Latif dug deep into the back pocket of his jeans, pulled out my ring and held it up. "I don't want to risk an ATM. Most likely the feds will have frozen Dasha's account."

"Ice, ice baby!" Ren whistled when Latif handed him the ring. "Talk to Zayan. He'll set up a trade tonight with Chuka, one of my dad's lieutenants."

"Where?"

"At Café des Espices. Be tough with Chuka, yeah? He tries to beat everyone down but he ain't gonna see jewels like that unless he goes crookin' Bond Street."

He pulled over. "This is as far as I can take you. Luck, fam."

I shrank back into the seat. Crunch Town was the last place on earth I wanted to go right now. Even though the sun was out, the street looked squalid and wretched. A gust of wind whisked a crisp packet up into the air. A chocolate wrapper whirled up, up, up to join it. They flashed blue and red, like two dragonflies in a courtship dance.

"Wait up, Dash." Yukiko had picked out a length of turquoise parachute silk, which she fashioned into a hooded cape. "I want to ramp up your disguise."

Yukiko kissed Latif on the cheek. Then, she gave my cape one last tweak. She squeezed my shoulders. "Latif will look after you. Act as if you own the place. Stay blessed."

Ren and Latif bumped fists.

"Come on, Dash!" Latif took my hand.

Again, an electric pulse shot up my arm, almost stopped my heart. The synapses in my brain exploded with a dizzying swoop of happy chemicals. Endorphins rushed my bloodstream. I was floating on air. I held Latif's hand tightly; scared I might drift away.

Latif pulled his face covering up over his mouth and nose.

As I was getting out, Ren banged on the partition. He smiled encouragingly and shouted, "Luck! Remember, Dasha, blood's thicker than botox."

Crunch Town

THE streets were empty apart from gangs of kids bundled up in hoodies, padded coats, balaclavas and shades. Most drifted back and forth as purposeless as tumbleweed while others propped up corners selling drugs. Everyone was wearing masks. Latif was right. Crunch Town was faceless. It gave me the creeps.

"This place is scary," I said.

"It's camera-free so it's the safest place right now." Latif flicked his worry beads across his knuckles.

Nothing about this place looked safe to me – not the hooded figures, not the boarded-up houses, not the burned-out cars.

Also, the way Latif kept looking over his shoulder cranked up my fear. My panicky thoughts chimed with the clack of his worry beads.

Please let things be okay. Please let things be okay.

I walked in the road, avoiding the cracked paving stones; there were too many possibilities for bad luck.

"Step up, Dasha," he hissed.

He was walking briskly, his red cape billowing out behind him – the only splash of colour in this washed-out, gutted grimespace.

Terrific, I thought. *Nothing like blending in.* Catching up with him, I asked, "Aren't we a bit flash?"

"Stop fretting," he said. "Creatives dress like this."

"Creatives?"

"Art crews. That's what the gangs call us. They suck up graffiti. So they leave us alone most times. Trust me."

"Gangs?" I asked, checking out the kids on the corners.

"Yeah. The Headhunters, the Asset Strippers and the Rogue Traders. And I don't mean the city scum who come round your dad's for dinner. These guys are hardcore. The Headhunters kidnap. The Asset Strippers rob. The Rogue Traders deal drugs and sell swag on the grey. After the last crash the gangs renamed themselves. That's when the game changed. It became all about kidnapping, ransoms and sorties into the golden postcodes. They turned their beef on the rich. You lot."

"How can I tell who's in a gang? Who's a Headhunter?" My voice was barely more than a squeak. I tried to mimic Latif's rolling stride, suddenly terrified that my walk or posture might mark me out as a global.

He shrugged. "You can't."

"Fabulous," I muttered.

To avoid looking at the hoodies mooching around, I focused on the graffiti scrawled across the shutters of long-since abandoned shops. On one shutter a fat cat in a business suit was curled up on a bed of cash smoking a cigar. On another a policeman was arresting a teddy bear. Another piece read: **Capitalism Screwed the 99%!**

We entered a street that was busier than the rest. The focus was a makeshift checkpoint on a traffic island. Sentries sat in armchairs, chatting. Masked kids whizzed around on bikes with child-sized wheels. In nearby houses people watched the road from upstairs windows. Metal flashed.

Guns, I thought, averting my eyes. I pulled the swathe of blue parachute silk a little tighter around my face. It felt like a shroud.

"Those kids are so young," I said, watching the kids on the bikes.

"The tinies? They run messages for the commanders, keep lookout and smuggle the swag into Crunch Town through the mall's foundations."

He nodded towards a six-foot security fence. Beyond it, I glimpsed the grid of a half-finished shopping mall. Hooded figures manned the scaffolding. They were keeping watch, like soldiers up in the ramparts. They communicated with gang members on ground level with a complex system of whistles, trills and whoops.

Latif let out a long low whistle. I nearly jumped out of my skin.

One of the tinies pedalled over and skidded to halt in front of Latif.

"*Salaam*, cuz." Latif handed the kid a twenty-pound note. "What's the news?"

The tiny flashed a smile from behind his Spider-Man mask.

Great, I thought, as I watched my only note disappear into the kid's pocket.

"You throwing up pieces today, cuz?"

"If you're lucky."

Another toothy smile.

"Be safe, bro. Word is the feds is coming in tonight. That they're gonna go medieval. Tanks, copters, hoses. The works, yeah? We saw a copter morning time. It zipped before the soldiers got sights on it. Shame, coz otherwise..." He twirled his finger in a downward motion, and then he made a *boof* sound. "Best place to be is the souks. Trust me!"

"Safe. Stay blessed, cuz."

They bumped fists. A sharp whistle sent the tiny pedalling back to the checkpoint. Latif left the road and headed down a scrubby path towards the security fence. He slipped under using a well-used crawl space. I followed. Inside was a vast building site: acres of exposed girders, empty retail units, peeling billboards and flapping plastic. Across a billboard advertising the defunct mall someone had scrawled the words: ASHES TO ASHES. BOOM TO BUST! My eyes were drawn to a weather-beaten billboard hyping my parents' prime-time Saturday show. They were posing like a pair of glamorous gangsters. The brand's catchphrase: *Goldrush Image turns your dreams into reality!* arced above them. The word 'dreams' had been crossed out and replaced with 'nightmares'. The graffiti underneath read: **The Game is Rigged. Only Suckers Play by the Rules.**

As we set off, whistles echoed around the site. Looking up, I saw hoodies silhouetted against the blue sky. They were scoping us out. A wave of panic whooshed through my body. Latif slowly raised his red fingers. The whistles died down. Seeing me staring at his fingers, he explained, "Red fingers mark you out as one of them. A Crunch Towner." He shrugged. "It's the code. It guarantees the gangs'll leave us alone." But the way his head kept swivelling round suggested that it wasn't a done deal.

Up ahead a group of masked kids popped up from beneath the perimeter fence. They formed a chain and started passing boxes through the gap. All were wearing gloves despite the warm spring day. When they had finished, they raced off, laden down with the goods, vanishing into the mall's foundations.

"Was that stuff stolen?"

Latif nodded. "They bring the swag through here because there are bare ways out, tunnels, scaffolding and that. The feds don't follow them in here, in case they get jumped. The gangs call this place customs. The guys up there." He nodded skywards. "They're the customs officers."

"And you think that's okay?"

"They've got nothing." He shrugged. "I don't roll with them. I don't judge them. They go where the money is. There's nothing left here…" He turned to look at me. "Anyway, what do you know about anything? The rich – your people – screwed the poor. You created Crunch Town. Turned the east into junk spaces and prairies."

A sharp clanging rang out. Our heads snapped skywards. Up in the rookeries, the lookouts were banging the scaffolding poles with iron bars. The sound echoed around the empty retail units. Immediately everyone started running for cover.

Latif grabbed hold of my arm and we sprinted towards the scaffolding.

"Go," Latif shouted as he lifted me onto the ladder.

Once we were up on the scaffolding planks we raced along the gangways, climbing from level to level by rickety ladders until we were way above the treetops. Then, as abruptly as it started, the clanging stopped. A deep silence settled over the site. It was as if everyone was holding their breath. The only sound was a slight whir of metallic wings. I scanned the sky. Then I saw it. A tiny bird, no bigger than a man's hand. A bird-bot. As it skimmed through the air, filming everything, it glittered in the sunlight. I exchanged a grim look with Latif. We both knew who'd sent it. I'd heard Dad talk about bird-bots. They were cutting edge spy-craft. He owned one. He described it as the ultimate executive toy.

A guy coughed. The bird-bot circled slowly and started flying towards our section of scaffolding. I looked down, terrified the bird-bot might identify me by taking a biometric reading of my iris. Despite being bundled, I wasn't going to take any risks. As the bird flew closer, the kids pelted it with bricks, hollering whenever they got a direct hit. But the robot remained airborne. I steadied myself against the scaffolding. The bird started flying straight towards us. I stared at my feet. The whirring filled my head like a ticking bomb. I shut my eyes. *Tick. Tick. Tick.* A clang. The whirring stopped. A stadium roar. Opening my eyes, I saw the bird-bot fall to the ground in a shimmer of metallic confetti.

"*Vamos!*" Latif was halfway down the gangway already, heading for the ladders.

Five minutes later, we climbed down from the skywalks and picked our way through the ruined retail space. We left the site by crawling back under the perimeter fence into Crunch Town proper. The place lived up to all my fears.

It was a bruised and bombed-out area. The streets were lined with deadbeat, dilapidated houses. Most were squatted by families. All had rickety extensions, front and back, as if the houses were mutating and growing extra limbs. Sheds and garages were doubling as crashpads. A traffic roundabout mushroomed with brightly coloured tents. In a churchyard gravestones were being used to hang out washing. We passed a block of flats where yards had been turned into pop-up cafes or illicit drinking dens. People sat around chatting, playing cards and smoking. Makeshift barbecues sizzled.

There was hardly any traffic; no delivery vans, no Chelsea tractors, no taxis. Every now and then a clapped-out car chugged past. Frequently the hiss of bicycle spokes startled me as we walked in silence.

We skirted round a chained-up, long-abandoned supermarket. The car park was chock-a-block with makeshift houses made from cardboard boxes, strips of corrugated iron and supermarket trolleys. Families were camping out in cars, belongings spilling out from the boots. Daffodils bloomed in a tyre which doubled as a flowerpot.

Wherever we walked, we were watched. Kids monitored us from street corners, women stared from windows hung with bedsheets and guys checked us out from souped-up cars with tinted windows. I checked my disguise was still in place.

All of a sudden the throb of music filled the air. I glanced over my shoulder. A gleaming black SUV was manoeuvring along the litter-strewn road. It slowed. A guy wearing a pollution mask, mirrored shades and a cap pulled down over his eyes was leaning out of the back window, banging a gloved hand against the door.

"Yo! Where you at, graffiti-boy?" the guy in the back shouted.

Latif raised his red fingers. "Throwing up pieces, bruv."

The gloved hand kept on banging. My heart echoed its beat.

Everything's okay. Everything's okay.

The driver nodded, but didn't return the signal.

My heartbeat quickened.

Latif repeated the salute. The driver slammed the horn. My heart was in my mouth. The guy in the passenger seat shouted, "On your way, bruv!"

As I watched the SUV drive away at speed, I asked, "Who the hell were they?"

"Headhunters." His voice sounded tight.

An image of Coco kidnapped, bundled and tied-up in the SUV's boot flashed into my head. My fingers twitched nervously in my pockets. "Will you spray my fingers in case I get lost?" I whispered.

"You won't," he said. Nevertheless he gently took my

trembling, outstretched hand and started spraying my fingers. The paint was cold against my skin. As I watched my fingers turn red, I found myself praying that the police had found Coco, and she was back with her parents.

We carried on walking through flyblown streets, lined with derelict lock-ups and work units that hadn't seen work in a long time. Neither of us spoke.

Up ahead, a guy in white overalls, sunglasses, black balaclava and monkey boots – all splashed with paint – was coming towards us. By the look of him he was a Creative.

"A brother!" Latif raised his red fingers.

I rolled up my sleeve so mine were visible, too.

The guy lifted his arm to return Latif's greeting. That was when I saw the barbed-wire tattoo circling his wrist. This sight acted like an adrenalin shot. He was from my dad's security detail. He was one of the Golden Knights. And, oh my God, he was reaching into his deep overalls pockets. Without thinking, I jumped in front of Latif, shouting, "He's one of Dad's." Metal flashed. "He's got a gun." I screamed, my arms and legs stretched out in a star jump of blue parachute silk.

Then Latif was yanking me into a narrow street. The man's footsteps pounded the pavement behind us. There was a crack. The air swished. A bullet rushed past me. *Smash!* A camper van's rear window shattered into a thousand shards. Another bullet ripped through a garage door. A third sank deep into an abandoned sofa. The bullets flew after Latif as he zigzagged down the street, using free-running tricks to outwit his assassin. But the bullets kept on tracking him, missing him by seconds, as he vaulted over the bonnets of burned-out cars, bins and an abandoned wardrobe. Trailing after him, my heart pounding in my chest, like a wrecking ball, all I could think was: *Dad wants Latif dead. D. E. A. D.*

Halfway down the street, Latif vaulted over a recycling bin and, crouching down behind it, out of sight, he waited until I'd run past, before pushing the bin into the hit man's path.

I ran on for a few paces, but hearing only one set of running footsteps behind me, I glanced back. The street was empty apart from the assassin.

"*LATIF!*" I screamed.

His name echoed back off the shuttered garages.

It was as if he'd vanished off the face of the earth.

I screamed his name again.

The hit man had stopped shooting, but that meant he was running faster. My brain was shutting down. Without Latif at my side, I couldn't think straight. I knew I had to keep on running. *But where to?* Up ahead, a block of flats loomed. Checking the street for Latif again, my foot landed in a pothole; I stumbled, falling forwards. The goon was on me in seconds. He clamped my neck in a rock-hard grip, pinching my tendons. Then he viced my neck in the crook of his arm, lifting me off the ground. My arms and legs windmilled uselessly. Fighting back tears, I tried to shout Latif's name again, but the goon's grip was squeezing my windpipe so hard, nothing came out. The hit man ripped the scarf from my face and, taking a white cloth from his pocket with a gloved hand, muttered, "Sleep well, Dasha Gold!"

I recognised the voice beneath the balaclava immediately.

"Stevie!" I choked. "Don't!"

"Sweet dreams, Dash," he said, as he placed the cloth over my mouth.

It was cold, moist and suffocating.

A sweet, sickly whiff hit me and, guessing I had less than thirty seconds to go before I went under, I summoned up my last ounce of strength and kicked down on Stevie's kneecaps, before ramming my elbows into his ribs. He grunted, but didn't relax his grip. The cloth felt soft against my skin. Now the smell was overpowering. I held my breath. The world was swimming in and out of focus. Suddenly everything was warm and fuzzy.

Up above, the sky was Caribbean blue. I was floating on my back in the warm, warm ocean. A bird of paradise took off from its perch, swooping above me in a burst of red, purple and gold plumage — *and trainers?* The bird had feet, was running through the air. *Bam!* Two trainers hit Stevie's shoulders with such force that he was thrown across the street. Then the road was rushing up towards me. *Smack!* I crumpled on impact, but my body was so relaxed that I hardly felt any pain; it was as if the drug had caused me to grow a new, bouncy layer of skin, a magical shock absorber. I embraced the pavement like a long-lost friend. Schoomed out, I lay there counting stars.

Next thing I knew, Latif was pulling me up. But my

rubbery legs gave way and I slumped back down onto the road, as if filleted of bone.

"Latif? Shwhere didshh you go?" My speech was slurred, as if someone were holding my tongue. "I missshhed you. I looossht…"

Before I could finish, Latif was shaking me by my shoulders. I groaned. All I wanted to do was sink back down onto the road and sleep. *Slap!* Then my face was stinging and Latif was shouting, "Get up, Dash." I shrank from him. "Can you hear me?" He slapped me again. His face was millimetres away. "Dash, snap out of it. Breathe!" He demonstrated by taking long, deep breaths. I mimicked him. And as things began to come back into focus, I gulped down more air. The fug in my head began to clear. That was when I saw Stevie start crawling towards his gun.

"Run!" Latif shouted, pulling me to my feet.

Next up I heard the click, click, click of his gun being reloaded.

The sound snapped me into flight mode. The terror switch in my head flicked on. Panic pumped up to ten. I channelled all my thoughts into the act of running. My legs were bionic. They were made of metal, not jelly. They would carry me out of danger. We tore down the street towards the brutal-looking tower block. Latif was running at my side shouting instructions, like a personal trainer, demanding I run — *faster, faster, faster.* We sprinted through the tower block's car park, taking cover behind burned-out cars and skips piled high with rubbish. Entering the block, we raced up a concrete stairwell and along an unlit gangway. The smell of drains hung in the air. Broken glass scrunched underfoot. Another set of stairs. Another gangway. At the far end, a bundled gang moved to block our way. *No!* They had guns, too. The stairwell rang with Stevie's footsteps. No way back. We were trapped. The horror soundtrack in my head maxed out. Its feedback vibrated my guts. One of the hooded figures flashed a spotlight. Caught in its beam, Latif raised two red fingers. The guy with the flashlight spotlit his own, and shouted. "You okay, bruv?"

"Undercover feds after us, bruv!" Latif shouted.

The gang surged forwards in a wave of padded jackets, swallowed us up for a moment, before racing off. Another shot rang out. Latif pushed me to the ground. I heard the bullet ricochet off a wall, followed by a blood-curdling scream as one of the bundled guys took a bullet. An angry roar went up from his friends. A few gathered round him while the rest chased Big Stevie down the stairwell.

I steadied myself against the railings and gasped for air. My lungs were shredded. I took deep breaths. In. Out.

Down below, the gang was chasing Stevie across scrubby wasteland. Latif stood silently watching the drama unfold. A shot. Stevie roared with pain, clasped his hands to his thigh, and staggered behind a row of garages, dragging his leg. The gang ran after him. Another shot.

"Is he dead?" I whispered.

Latif didn't answer.

"That was Stevie. He's one of Dad's security detail."

I steadied myself against the railings. "My minder."

"That figures." Latif's voice was quiet but full of rage. "Regular feds don't head into Crunch Town without backup. And when they do, they arrive in tanks and copters."

"The barbed-wire tattoo around his wrist alerted me. All Dad's Golden Knights have one."

When Latif turned towards me, I saw myself reflected twice in his sunglasses — small and scared. "You said your parents would stop at nothing to get you back." His bundled face gave nothing away. "Now we know that includes blowing me away. For real." He kicked an empty Coke can down the gangway.

"I think I'm going to puke," I leaned over the railings and retched. The phrase "Sleep well, Dasha Gold!" hissed around my head. I retched again. Straightening up, I whispered, "I can't believe Dad sent Stevie to shoot you. To kill you!" My voice wobbled. "That he really truly wants you dead." I blinked back tears. "And it's all my fault."

"It's not *your* fault." He squeezed my shoulder. "Come on, Dash. We need to get out of here. There might be others." He started walking off.

I hurried after him. Catching sight of our reflections in a cracked window, I asked, "How did he find us? I mean we're bundled and everything."

"I don't know. All our garms are new on…" He shook his head. "It beats me." I felt his eyes travelling up and down my body. I shrank from his gaze. Then he tsked. "That bird-bot must've got a biometric of your iris." He stared out over the wasteland, tsked again." Nah. The Golds couldn't have got him over here that quick. Your minder was scouting Crunch Town on a tip or a hunch. Most likely they guessed I'd head here." He unclipped his cape. "Ditch the silk." He let his cape drift down.

We watched the silk twist and turn in the breeze until it finally came to rest on the pathway like a pool of blood. Mine landed next to it, like a shimmering tear.

I pulled down the green hood of my trackie, withdrawing into it like a tortoise retreating into its shell.

We headed out of the tower block, past a parade of battered shops and into a children's playground. Latif climbed up a ladder and scrambled into a playhouse. I followed.

"I'm rinsed after that," he said. "We'll hang here until nightfall."

He took up position by the window.

It was already getting dark. The sky was shot through with pink. A talent-show wannabe warbled on a prime-time show in the distance.

I lay on the floor, eyes shut, saying nothing – desperately wishing I could put my thoughts on hold. But the silence was overstimulating my brain. Suddenly my mind's eye was a giant cinemascope, which was replaying the chase over and over again. Stevie, the gangs, Crunch Town... Then in close-up, Stevie's lips were moving behind his black balaclava, and his face was millimetres from mine: *'Sleep well, Dasha Gold!'*

I shivered. Stevie, my shadow, was dead.

The gunshot rang out in my head. I put my hands over my ears, and scrunched my eyes up more tightly. Weirdly, even though he had never been my favourite person, and he had been on a mission to hurt Latif, I wished the gang hadn't killed him. My mixed feelings took me by surprise. Stevie had been there for me twenty-four/seven, and now he was gone. Bang! The gunshot rang out in my head again, and like a starting gun at the beginning of a hundred-metre sprint, it set the horrible images racing through my head once more.

And as it got darker outside these terrifying images only burned more brightly.

Night fell.

We headed into the darkness.

Blood Diamonds

WE melted into the night, two more shadows, shifting through the estate. The place was even more terrifying after dark. Shouts, catcalls and whistles rang out from gangways. A dog barked. My heart fluttered at every sound. When we turned into an unlit gangway, glowing cigarette tips studded the darkness. My heart leapt. Latif switched course to avoid the gang.

Back on the streets again, two garishly painted cars raced towards us, headlights dazzling, sound systems booming. Twisting round to escape their glare, I saw my shadow thrown up onto a building – a cowering figure, hiding my eyes as if I'd witnessed an atomic explosion.

"Gangs race junk cars for stupid money," Latif shouted while we waited on the pavement for the cars to pass. "They pimp them and race them till they crash and burn."

The cars U-turned and screeched back. A dragon spewed fire on the purple car's side. On the red, Pegasus swooped in a rush of winged blue.

As soon as the coast was clear, we hurried into a hustle of narrow streets. Only a few streetlights were lit. From the shadows hisses of, "Hashish, hashish," reached us, like the click of press cameras. A few guys confronted us with staring eyes. But Latif kept it friendly with a brief: "Not for me, mate."

About twenty minutes later, we entered a bustling street. I stopped in my tracks. After the gloomy backstreets, this place buzzed with light and chatter. Market stalls lined one side of the road, stacked high with fruit and vegetables; candles stuck in pumpkins threw a flickering light. The rip-off merchants had colonised the other side, their tables piled with fake brands: smartphones, tablets, bikes, perfume and the latest fashions. Boys selling knock-off cigarettes weaved through the crowds. Everyone was shouting. A stall selling hair extensions caught my eye. The wonky sign read: **Slebrity & global scalps**. I'd heard stories about gangs hacking off women's hair to sell on the black market. I'd never taken them seriously, though. I rubbed a strand between thumb and finger. It was real. I shivered.

The houses in the street were in bad shape. Some were tagged with graffiti. Most had been converted into rough-and-ready restaurants, cafes, clubs and dive bars, serving up food from all around the globe: Moroccan, Indian, Lebanese, Russian. The smell of spices hung in the air. Chinese lanterns strung across the street at intervals cast a red glow. A DJ was playing salsa records from an upstairs window. Hastily-assembled snack shacks buzzed with punters. It was a midnight feast of a place. My stomach grumbled.

But there was something wrong in this otherwise welcoming scene. At first I couldn't put my finger on it. Then it hit me. Everybody — men, women, kids — was bundled. Even the elderly men playing chess outside a Turkish coffee house were wearing hoodies.

A little girl ran over with a collection of headscarves, shouting, "Please Mister, please Mister." Latif picked out a green one with a red geometric design and handed the kid a fiver. Seeing the flash of money, restaurant touts suddenly surrounded us. All were gesticulating madly and tugging us towards their restaurants. Latif shrugged off offers of 'half-price Turkish', ''licious Thai curry' and 'the best ever kebabs in the world'. Instead he walked over to a Lebanese restaurant. I recognised one of Latif's tags on the front of the house. He greeted the restaurant owner in Arabic and they kissed three times on the cheeks. After a hurried discussion, they walked through the restaurant and out into the garden at the back.

We sat down on leather poufs at a low mosaic table lit by a candle stuck into a beer bottle. I scoped the shadows nervously. I noticed that the walls separating the gardens had been knocked through, freeing up space to grow vegetables. Kids were playing tag, chasing in and out of the light like moths.

"Will we be safe here?" I asked.

Latif handed me the green headscarf. "Yeah. But cover your head – Arab style."

He began working the beads over his knuckles, watching the shadows. "Back here's a special place, huh? The restaurant owners clubbed together and turned the gardens into allotments. They grow veg for their restaurants. The supermarkets moved out years ago. No great loss. Although Crunch Towners have been ghettoised, they're turning things round. Cool, huh?"

The Lebanese guy (who had introduced himself as Zayan) came out with a tray laden with dishes. It was a meze of tabbouleh, hummus, salad and pitta bread. "Enjoy!" he said, placing the dishes on the table.

My stomach rumbled in anticipation. Latif tucked in, tearing off strips of pitta and scooping up dollops of hummus and tabbouleh. I followed his lead.

"This is good," I said between chews, pointing at the food enthusiastically. Suddenly eating seemed more important than anything else. The stars were bright as jewels. I stared up at them. I was all chased out.

They exchanged a few more words in Arabic. Then Zayan headed back inside.

"The stars are amazing," I said.

"Less neon pollution in this barrio. Folks can't afford the electric." Latif scooped up more hummus. "See the Plough." He pointed out the constellation. "We still call those stars by their Arabic names: Alkaid, Mizar, Alioth and Megrez... We Arabs were ahead in the astronomy game."

Zayan whistled from the doorway.

"We're rolling." Latif snapped into action mode.

He took the ring from his pocket and placed it in the palm of his hand. The candlelight caught the diamonds and spangled them. "Chuka's on his way. He'll take the ring off us, if he rates the jewels." He closed his fist around it. "No questions asked."

Latif's eyes searched the garden. I followed suit, uncertain what I was looking for. The darkness pressed in on us.

The candle spat and crackled in the silence. Suddenly a thickset guy emerged from the shadows and walked over to our table. He was wearing a coat with a fur-lined hood, zipped up to his nose. His shades were reflectors. Zayan greeted him warmly and introduced Latif. When they shook hands, the stranger said, "My associates call me Chuka. You know Ren, innit?"

"Yeah. He's fam."

The guy studied us both. The candle's flame was reflected in his shades, giving him fire for eyes. "Got the cargo?" he asked, after a few long minutes.

Latif held the ring between thumb and finger; the diamonds glinted. He took a few seconds before handing it over.

Chuka whistled when he held the ring up to the naked flame. Lifting his sunglasses for a moment, he ran a hawk eye over the jewels. His smile revealed two rows of silver-capped teeth. "This cargo's live, bruv! Whaddya want? A grand?"

"Two grand," Latif countered, poker-faced. "Face value's eight. You won't get better without ram-raiding De Beers, bruv."

"But you're in a hurry, bruv."

The candlelight danced in their reflectors. Neither smiled.

Latif held his hand out for the ring. "Not that much of a hurry."

Chuka held the ring closer to the flame, running his tongue along his lower lip as he watched the diamonds sparkle.

"One thousand five hundred or the deal's off."

Latif leaned forwards, palms on the table, and repeated his final offer. His breath made the flame flicker.

"You win, bruv." Chuka closed his fist around the ring. "I'll sort the paper."

He took a crumpled brown envelope from his coat's inside pocket and, sliding out a wedge of fifty-pound notes, started counting them out beneath the table. I counted with him. When he reached the agreed amount, he shuffled the notes into a pile and placed them on the table.

"Go ahead. Check the paperwork." He pushed the money towards Latif. Then he slipped the ring into the envelope and returned the package to his inside pocket. After he'd double-checked the amount, Latif stuffed the notes into the front pocket of his jeans. "Good to do business with you, bruv." He held out his hand. "Till next time."

Chuka shook his outstretched hand. "Yeah, next time soon." Then he vanished back into the shadows, leaving as mysteriously as he had arrived.

"Time to shoot with the loot." Latif scraped back his chair.

We exited through the garden without saying goodbye to Zayan. The market was packing up. All was chaos and noise. People were shouting for loved ones. Mothers screamed for children. Husbands shouted for wives. Punters were hurrying home while market stallholders shoved their wares into bags. The vibe in the street had changed. A buzz of fear energised the market. Everyone kept glancing up at the sky, jostling and shoving as they left. I searched the skies, but saw nothing but stars and inky blackness.

Latif stopped at a table where a guy was packing away stolen tablets. None were in boxes or packaged. "These untraceable, bruv?" The guy glanced up, but carried on cramming the merch into a sportsbag.

"Yeah. False IP included." Latif picked the cheapest, peeled a few notes off the wedge and paid. We'd only gone about halfway down the street when a low, vibrating throb cut through the market's din. Although I still couldn't see lights in the sky, I recognised the unmistakable sound. Helicopters. The shout went up in a jangle of languages. Panic swelled the street. Latif started pushing through the crowds with greater urgency. I tucked in behind him, grabbing hold of his trackie, scared that I might lose him in the mayhem.

Latif took out his phone and punched in a number. He spoke for about thirty seconds. The only word I caught was 'ambassador'. After he'd finished he tossed the phone into a pile of empty boxes. Then we headed into the side streets where we picked up speed. A battalion of balaclava-heads ran past shouting instructions to each other. I noticed some had shotguns slung over their shoulders. At intervals they stopped to set off fireworks or flares. A rocket sputtered upwards, exploding in a kaleidoscope of red and orange.

After about five minutes, we turned into a dingy street where an underground club bellowed urban beats. Outside, clubbers were smoking and dissing the avian police. Across from the club there was a dodgy-looking mini-cab firm. Latif was walking towards it.

"What are you doing?" I whispered.

"What does it look like? Getting a ride out of here, dim-bulb." His eyes flicked heavenwards. "They're looking for people on foot, doughnut. Not cars."

"But what if they shop us?" I peered into the office through a grimy window, trying to suss out the cabbies, who were playing a rowdy game of cards.

"Got a better idea?"

I kicked at a stone, looked daggers.

"Bubblehead, these guys are illegals. They want the police in their life like they want a gun to their head. They'd be bounced back to their countries quicker than you can say 'asylum seeker'. These guys care nothing about the news and that. They don't give a damn about you! I'm not saying it's safe. But we don't have much choice."

Homemade rockets sputtered up towards the advancing helicopters. Still, the noose of light inched closer. The police had Crunch Town in a stranglehold.

Another group ran past. McDonalds brown paper bags with eyeholes cut out covered their heads and faces. The upside down golden M was a W for war. At the bottom the McDonald's logo bellowed: *GOING THAT EXTRA MILE.* The gang looked like they intended to do just that.

I took a deep breath. "Okay. Let's go."

"No names," was all he said as he went inside.

From the street I watched Latif haggle with a tall African guy. A flurry of hand gestures later, they reached a deal and high-fived. I hung back as they walked over to a beaten-up, silver ghost Mercedes. Another battalion of hoodies ran past.

"Over here, babe. We're in the Benzo." Latif beckoned me over. "Load up!"

I slid onto the back seat. He squeezed in beside me and draped his arm across my shoulders. "You okay, babe?" It was only then that I got his game. We were lovers, not kids on the run. I rested my head on his shoulder, shut my eyes – I could play that role. Easy. I moved closer, soaking up his body warmth. Slowly my jitters calmed down.

"Let's get out of here, brother." Latif slapped the back of the passenger seat. "And pump them tunes up loud. Them helis are doing my head in."

"Sure thing, boss." The minicab driver looked up at the sky. "Avian flu, bruv. *Tsk!*" He sucked air through his teeth. "They're deadly." He cranked up the stereo. Grime blasted out.

The cabbie checked me out in the rear-view mirror. I rolled down the window and inhaled the cool night air. The helicopter lights strobed the sky, searching out the main actors. The runaways. Us.

Suddenly our cab was centre stage, spotlit in the helicopter's beam. Despite the blaring music, I heard the helicopter lose height. The minicab driver floored the accelerator, jumped a red light and swung a right. I crashed against the door. My hands white-knuckled the driver's seat. The helicopter continued flying into Crunch Town. I coughed, attempting to hide a rapid exhalation of air.

"Hey girl, *tranquilo*. What would they want with us?"

The driver stared at me in the rear-view mirror.

I averted my eyes.

Up ahead, hoodies were standing at a checkpoint, hurling bottles at two police cars, which were speeding towards Crunch Town, blue lights twirling. A storm of bottles glittered in the headlights. Minutes later, both police cars were spinning out of control. The hoodies cheered.

I watched the helicopters through the rear window. Hatches open, lights trained down on the policemen swinging down on hoists, like deadly spiders. Kids lasered the helicopters from tower blocks, green bars of light stabbing at the sky like witchy fingers. The helicopters' lights searched them out. My stomach clenched. Innocent people were going to get hurt tonight. And it was all my fault. I started praying that no one would get injured or arrested. It was the only thing I could think to do.

"Sorry, mate, which street do you want in Mayfair?"

"Drop us outside the cinema, bruv."

"Mayfair?" I shot Latif a what-the-hell-are-we-going-to-the-centre-of-town-for look. He counterpunched with a winning smile before relaxing back into the seat, his eyes fixed on the streets, his head bobbing to the stark, gritty beat.

Media Circus

I KNEW the restaurant well. Anyone who was anyone did. High Table was a favourite with stars and politicians – a face place. Located in a narrow townhouse in Mayfair, it was the restaurant of choice for celebrities who wanted to get snapped. It was impossible to get a table unless you were *someone* and you never left without dropping five hundred pounds.

Latif was doing his stake-out thing; silent and secretive, frowning whenever I asked him what we were doing standing fifty metres away from the most exclusive restaurant in London, like a pair of freaky autograph hunters – watching and waiting, for what? I really had no idea. I looked at my watch. I couldn't for the life of me work out how hanging around here could help us get to FuturePerfect, especially as this was my parents' weekday restaurant of choice, which meant they were due to turn up at any minute. Brilliant. Genius. Perhaps we were going to hitch a lift with them.

"You know this is my parents' favourite restaurant, don't you, brainiac?" I couldn't keep the panic from my voice. "They eat here most nights and it's a dead cert they'll come here if there's a crisis. It's the place to be seen. Show the world you're coping. Put on a brave face."

"For real?" This revelation seemed to genuinely surprise him.

"Take a wild guess why." I nodded towards the thronging paparazzi. "Just the place for PR-hungry psychos."

"Might work in our favour," he replied, a little too breezily.

"Like how? Come on, talk to me, Latif. Why are we here?" I asked. "My parents are about to show, and guess what? I'd rather not be here, if that's okay by you."

He shrugged. "Tough. It's the only way out."

"That's really reassuring. I know you have to keep your enemies close, but this is ridiculous…"

"Don't get stabby, Dash. We're safer here than anywhere else right now. It's the last place on earth anyone would expect to see us. And we have the perfect cover." He pointed to a ramshackle group of women who'd just arrived. They were holding homemade posters plastered with photos of yours truly cut from newspapers. Across the top, messages were spelled out in a jumble of capital letters and joined-up writing. The most popular read: *For the* **LOVE of** *Gold* **Give Dasha** *back* and **We** *feel* **Your** *PAIN.* Studying this ragbag of women, I knew they felt everybody's pain. They were attracted to grief like bloodsucking bugs. They gorged on others' pain, especially celebrity pain, because somehow it gave their life meaning, and made them feel less sorry about their own existence. Kidnap gawpers. Pain hunters. Losers. I shrugged inwardly. But who was I to judge? At least they weren't stalking one set of parents while looking for the other set. That had to put me right up there with the sobbing loons for Fruitcake of the Year award. That really was *something else.*

We pushed further into the crowds from where I watched hyped-up paparazzi jockeying for position. It was a busy night even for High Table. My heart sank when I saw the head waiter fussing over my parents' favourite table, setting out my dad's preferred wine glasses and lighting the candles. Now there was no doubt in my mind. My parents were about to show. I imagined my mother and her stylists discussing what she should wear as the mother of a kidnapped child; calculating how many diamonds she could sport without looking heartless; rejecting fur in case she appeared callous; deciding whether black was too funereal or a flash of a red Louboutin sole too gory.

"Braniac!" I hissed, then repeated it louder, to make sure he could hear me above the wailers. "This place is heaving with weirdos. I want out of here, okay?"

"See you, then." Latif carried on staring straight ahead, his eyes fixed on the maelstrom of activity front of house. I followed his gaze, trying to second-guess him. Perhaps he was waiting for this ambassador character he'd mentioned on the phone back in Crunch Town. Perhaps he was a friend of Latif's dad.

Glossy women with shiny manes posed with stick-insect arms resting on hips as they popped fake smiles for the cameras. Valets snapped open limo doors, fussing over celebrity diners as they helped them out, before whisking their cars down into the restaurant's underground car park. A half-moon of paparazzi shouted, "Over here, love," whenever female flesh tottered from a limo.

I grimaced, remembering nights at High Table, how Dad would slyly check out the punters, and say, "Full of faces tonight. Gorgeous now. With a little help from the maestro." He'd wink and crunch his knuckles like a cartoon villain.

A shout went up. The weirdos surged forwards. The paparazzi raised their cameras and took aim. Leggy girls from a soap opera were giggling and flashing their perma-tan thighs. Latif gave a piercing wolf whistle. I shot him a look as if to say: "Have you gone completely nuts?"

But he simply said, "Hold that sound. I'll be back in fifteen minutes." He shoved his rucksack into my hands and disappeared into the crowd.

I stood there bereft, close to tears, only half listening to the paparazzi cries of: "This way, darling!" "Smile for Daddy!" and "More leg, sweetheart!" I was feeling so strung out, I hardly registered a black stretch with tinted windows glide up to the restaurant, until suddenly all was shouting and noise. An explosion of flashes engulfed the Golds. They dazzled. Exquisitely turned out, they stood motionless for a few minutes, glassy-eyed, soaking up the flashes like vampires sucking up blood, recharging their sense of self and satisfying their fame fix. Then, feeling alive once again, they struck poses and sparkled. A tear glittered in the corner of my mother's eye – a crocodile tear to match her handbag.

I moved closer. I had to hear her every lying word. Years as a chat-show presenter ensured my mother's delivery was perfectly pitched. Clear and crisp, so she would be heard above the wailing harpies, but quavery, too, so her words would tug at heartstrings.

"She's our princess. Our angel. Our life. Without her we are *nothing*. So please, please, if anyone has any information pick up the phone." She made a phone gesture with diamond-encrusted fingers. "Do the right thing. Make our family whole again. We believe in you – *the public*." She stretched out her arms to the sobbing women. "You are our only hope. And we choose hope over fear."

Her soap-opera delivery triggered a low, mournful sound from the women. Some sobbed as if they'd lost their own child. When she'd finished, she wiped away a shimmering tear from her cheek. There was no denying she was a good actress. My father was scouring the crowd. I slid behind a tall woman in an extravagant hat and looked down at the pavement. Despite my blond wig, I felt exposed. Dad was good with faces.

A cheer went up. My parents were on the move. They posed for one more set of photos in the foyer before the maître d' whisked them upstairs to their usual seat.

Swept up in the tsunami of celebrity, the staff hurried to restore normality. They ferried away the flowers, candles and oriental blankets that had made up the sumptuous backdrop for the Golds' 'impromptu' press conference. Meanwhile the paparazzi rushed back to their SUVs where they started uploading photos onto their laptops, emailing them across to picture desks in a desperate race to secure a media splash. Horns were sounding from further down the street. Engines revved impatiently. Self-important people, unaccustomed to waiting, were demanding immediate attention. A valet stepped onto the red carpet and whistled for the next car in line. Something familiar about the sound made me look up, double take. *Latif?* Despite the slicked-back hair, which gave him the appearance of a Middle Eastern Elvis, and the maroon valet uniform, which gave him the look of an air steward, there was no mistaking him. Latif was standing front of house, beckoning on the next car in line.

A steel grey Mercedes with blacked-out windows smooched up. Slick-quick, Latif opened the door and gave a shallow bow. Out stepped a grey fox wearing an impeccable suit and a smart-arse smile. The Italian ambassador — a total sleazeball.

Not so smart now, I thought, when he handed Latif his keys. Moments later, Latif was behind the wheel.

Skirting the crowd, I watched Latif drive the car down into the garage and shoot out the other side. I scooted after him; the red tail lights guided me for a few seconds, and then he swung a left and he was gone. Brainsnap. Where had he said to meet? Had he? No, he hadn't. I sped up. Then, remembering Latif's rules, I reined myself back; terrified I'd already drawn attention to myself.

Don't blow it. Don't blow it, I thought, turning left into the street and scouring its length for the silver car. No sign of it. It was like he'd performed another vanishing trick. Keeping my eyes fixed in front of me, I carried on down the road. The end of the street loomed. Still no sign. Then I saw the

Merc tucked behind a black Range Rover; it gleamed in the moonlight. It was all I could do to stop myself from breaking into a run, but I checked the impulse. When I reached the car I tapped on the tinted window. It zizzed down slowly. For an instant, I imagined eyeballing a mafia heavy. Instead I was greeted by Latif's crooked smile.

"The ambassador sends his compliments…" He jerked his thumb toward the rear seats. "You'd better take the back. I'm your chauffeur for tonight. Next stop FuturePerfect, milady."

Sliding onto the back seat, I inhaled the familiar smell of expensive leather upholstery. Latif pulled away from the kerb and we shot off down the road. The borrowed uniform lay discarded at my feet.

"What the…?" I laughed, giddy with excitement.

"This boss motor is a diplomat's car." Latif stroked the dashboard. "D plates give us top-notch immunity. The feds can't touch us. But you know all about that, don't you, milady?" Seeing me frown, he laughed. "Smile, Miss Gold, we have the perfect getaway car."

"Can't they track it?"

"Not tonight. The ambassador was using it for pleasure, and that's strictly against the rules, especially without a driver. He's switched the GPS tracker off so we're off the radar until he realises his car's gone MIA. That gives us three or four hours' head start." He grinned. "Dash it all, Dasha. I think we've only gorn and done it again," he said in an upper-crusty voice.

I smiled and slid down in my seat. A getaway car just like in the movies. Green Park slid by on one side, jazzy hotels on the other. I snuggled into the soft leather seat as we whooshed through London, finally on our way to the sci-fi-sounding FuturePerfect. I wound down the window and watched the houses flick past. I imagined London mapped out like a Monopoly Board: Green Park, Baker Street and Park Lane. Collect two hundred pounds when you pass go. The tang of petrol filled my nostrils.

"So? How did you pull that off?" I asked, high on car fumes and escape.

"My friend works as a valet. He's told tales of the Italian ambassador and his nocturnal habits."

"Yeah. Dad knows him. He creeps me out. He's always hitting on women. He even tried it on with some of my friends."

"The sleazeball's in there most nights with an assortment of chicks on his arm. Never his wife. We always joked that his car would make a smart getaway car. And here we are." He thumped the steering wheel. "I made Hassan an offer he couldn't refuse: two hundred pounds for his skanky uniform. Another two hundred if he zips it." He mimed a zip across his lips.

"You were robbed," I joked. Then I asked more seriously, "Has he seen the news?" I clamped my lips together, but couldn't stop myself from blurting out, "He won't tip the police off, will he?"

"Nah. We go way back. Some of us have *real* friends, Dash.

Not just airheads and flunkies." Seeing me frown, he added, "We've got wheels. That's all that matters." He turned on the radio and fiddled with the tuner until he found a station playing back-to-back mash-ups. "Sit tight, *chica*. We're gonna mash it up, pirate style."

The oncoming headlights dazzled me. I pictured my parents' phoney faces illuminated by the paparazzi flashbulbs. I shivered.

"Mum's tears creeped me out. Not bad for a vampire, huh?"

"Yeah. The Golds are good. I'll give them that. Professional blag artists. The whole world believes they actually care."

"Once upon a time our ickle, lickle princess was kidnapped." I mimicked my mother's TV voice. "She's our world. Our angel. All we want is our golden girl back." Anger sharpened my delivery. "That's why we've set our goons onto her. That's why we're hunting her down like a dog. That's why we'll knife her when we get our hands on her. That's why we want to make her into someone else. *Chop. Chop. Chop.*"

"Girl, that's one virtuoso impersonation."

"Years of practice." I leaned forwards and turned the music up. "I don't want to think about those freaks any more. I hate them. They're history."

We swooped up onto a motorway. Danger Mouse's 'Encore' pumped up loud. I glanced over at the speedometer and seeing the needle was hovering at 80 miles per hour, shouted, "Won't we get stopped?"

"Nah. I told you: diplomatic immunity. We'd be arrested if we *didn't* bash the speed limit." He floored the accelerator and the car purred towards 100 miles per hour. "Shame I haven't got a test," he shouted.

"*But...*" I made a gesture with my hands as if to say, "But you're driving."

"Joyride only. Speed's my thing." He laughed. "Don't freak, *chica*. I've been driving Mum's cab off-road since I was old enough to reach the pedals."

I settled back into the luxurious leather seats. So here I was in a stolen diplomat's car, being chauffeured by a speed freak without a licence. So what? I shrugged inwardly. In the twisted scheme of the Golds' universe this wasn't such a big deal.

Nodding my head to the music, I studied Latif. He must have felt my eyes on him because I saw him flash one of his sideways smiles in the rear-view mirror. Something melted inside. And as we flew into the darkness, I felt happier than I'd ever felt before. I wished we could keep driving into the night for ever. But unease crept back.

My eyes lasered the darkness. Since being on the run, the helter-skelter heart-race of the chase had swept me along so completely that I hadn't had time to think things through. I pressed my hand against the cool window glass, as if reaching out to touch a ghost. Hopefully I would meet my birth mother soon. I still couldn't quite believe it.

A quiver of *what ifs* shot straight into my heart. What if she acted like a stranger? What if we had nothing to say to each other? What if we hated each other on sight? What if we didn't have an instant bond?

I shook my head and shooed these thoughts away.

My mother had come to find me. I must hold onto that thought.

We were driving along country lanes now. Catseyes spangled a gleaming path. A lush canopy of bright spring green leaves blocked out the stars.

"We're here," Latif said.

I glanced at the car clock. It was almost midnight.

With the engine off, the car was a dark hushed space. He parked up on a grass verge about one hundred metres up from an imposing spiked gate. Behind it, a large house loomed. Dark and unfriendly-looking, it made me think of a Victorian loony bin. A high perimeter wall snaked around the grounds.

As Latif put on a pair of leather gloves, he said, "I'm going in over the wall." I reached to open the door; he leaned back and placed his gloved hand on my wrist. "I'm going in alone." When I started to protest, he shrugged. "You can't come, bubblehead." His voice was firm. "It's way too risky."

I fronted cool. On the inside I was fuming. It was my story. My mother. My life.

I focused my thoughts; I had to tell him how I felt. But by the time I'd ordered my words, he'd already slipped on a pollution mask, wrapped his scarf around his head and was halfway out the door. As an afterthought, he poked his head back into the car and said, "Don't chat up any locals." And with that he was gone.

As I watched the darkness engulf him, I was overwhelmed by an urge to run after him. I took deep breaths. *Be brave.* I clicked on the central locking system. *Be brave.* I ducked down as oncoming headlights razored the darkness, strafing the inside of the car. *Be brave.* Terrified, I sank down onto the backseat.

Moments later, tap, tap, tap. Then I saw a silhouette outside the blacked-out window.

I froze.

Tap, Tap. Tap.

I slid down to the floor.

"It's only me, Dash!"

I melted. Waves of relief swept through me as I switched off the central locking system with trembling fingers and opened the door. A rush of country air, clean and tangy, caught in my throat.

He slid in, started the car and said, "We need to hide the motor."

He drove along the road to a field. I guessed he must have checked it out already because the gate was open. The wheels sank deep into the grass when we drove in. He parked up behind the hedge and cut the engine and the headlights.

Before he had a chance to cold-shoulder me, I said, "I'm coming with you, Latif. *This is my life!*"

Without waiting for a reply, I jumped out of the car, slamming the door on him.

He got out slowly. Then he rested his elbows on the car roof and stared at me. He took a few minutes before he spoke. "I'd be breaking all the rules, bubblehead, but I guess it's your identity we're chasing." He shook his head, as if he couldn't believe he'd broken his number-one rule. Don't burden yourself with losers. "But if we get caught, you're on your own. Believe it!" But his voice had a smile in it.

"Very funny." I stuck my tongue out.

"You're in luck." He was already loping across the muddy field. "I've scouted a tree for beginners, dim-bulb."

I smiled, although I didn't believe him.

Identity Theft

LATIF shone his torch along the perimeter wall. Coils of barbed wire ran along the top, glinting like sharks' teeth in its beam. Watching the light skid back and forth, I began to wish I'd stayed in the car. He handed me the head torch and I strapped it on. We walked over to a stout, gnarled, old oak tree. I ran my hands across the rough bark, searching for holds.

"Action, bubblehead." He shone his torch into my face. "We're not at a village fete."

"Okay. Okay." I muttered. "I was just…"

"Hands there…" He spotlit the grabholds. I looked up at the tree, its branches stretching up to the stars. There had to be a way. Next thing I knew, Latif was shunting me up so I could reach the hold. The bark was chunky and strong like oversized Lego pieces; it gave me good grip. Then, with Latif pointing out grabholds and guiding my feet into footholds, I clambered into the tree's fork. Latif climbed up after me in seconds. Once in the fork he tested the strength of the branches. They stretched over the wall.

He went first, walking along the branch swiftly and gracefully, arms out, as if on a high wire. A second later, he swung down, landing on the grass with a light thud. No sweat.

He whistled.

The sound I'd been dreading. It was my turn to walk the plank.

Edging forwards, a vertigo-tingle hypersensitised my feet, connecting me to the branch, as if by a magnetic force. Below, barbed wire coils rose and fell in steely waves. I inched forwards, gripping hold of branches for support. Baby steps.

An owl hooted. I froze.

"I can't do this, Latif," I whispered.

The branch swayed a little beneath my feet. Quivers shot up my legs. My knees were caving in. I glanced over my shoulder. The fork was metres away. No way back.

"Jump, Dash." He stretched his arms up. "I'll catch you."

I crouched down slowly, keeping my eyes fixed straight ahead, until I was sitting astride the branch. The tingling sensation sizzled my fingers and toes. The grass was a long way down. Latif looked spindly, like a stickman. I shut my eyes. I lifted my leg over the branch and lowered myself down.

I dangled in space.

Vertigo whizzing.

The sweat on my hands slipped my grip.

"I've got you!" he hissed.

Not exactly, I thought, looking down at his outstretched arms. They looked light years away. My grip was giving way millimetre by millimetre.

"It's all about trust, Dash. Let go. Trust me!"

I fell into his arms.

We tumbled to the ground. The grass was wet. His cheek was warm against mine. His arms closed around me. He smelled musky. I moved closer, sucking up his body heat. Straightaway, he unhooked himself from my clasp and stood up. The cold from the earth seeped into my body.

"See?" He pulled me to my feet. "You need to trust me, Dasha Gold."

"I do," I whispered.

But he was already on the move.

I switched off the head torch before chasing after him.

We kept to the shadows, avoiding the moon-drenched lawns. A twig cracked underfoot. My brain snapped back into the moment. I focused on the house. There was a single light on in a downstairs window, which gave the house the look of a guard dog snoozing with one eye open.

We crept closer. The watchman, a heavy-set guy with craggy features, was sitting at a table in the lit room, hunched over a Pot Noodle. I took his slouched body language to be a good sign. His shoes lay discarded under the table. His socks were odd colours. He looked like he'd settled down for the evening. Latif gave me the thumbs up and we retreated behind a yew bush.

"He's in kickback mode," Latif whispered. "It's just a matter of time."

As we waited, country smells hit me: damp grass mixed with cow dung; wafts of hawthorn blossom spliced with pine. The latter reminded me of the Diptyque candles that Mum ordered the maids to light by the hundred every night.

The temperature had bombed. I rubbed the tops of my arms and studied the stars. They were pinprick-sharp in the countryside. I couldn't remember many of the constellations Latif had named earlier, so I reordered the stars into my own spangly patterns: a dragon, a dolphin and a dazzle of fireflies.

After a short while, the security guard strolled into the kitchen and switched on the kettle. He stretched, walked over to the open window and stared out into the darkness, retreating when the kettle's whistle screeched into the garden like a steam train. He made a mug of tea, wringing out the tea bag with asbestos fingers before chucking it into the sink and adding a dash of milk. Then he headed back into his den where he sprawled out on a shrugging sofa in front of the TV.

The night watchman punched a number into his mobile. I heard him say: "Hello, babe," in that leisurely way which suggested he was on for a good long gossip. His voice was heavily-accented. I guessed he was Eastern European. Latif took his torch from his rucksack. Then he gave me the thumbs-up sign again.

Time to move.

Keeping to the shadows, we skirted the house, scouting for possible entry points.

It was a large sprawl of a building. The front was shipshape, posh and polished, while the rear looked shabby and unkempt. As far as I could make out, everything looked secure around the front and sides. The rear of the house was a different story, though. The tatty backyard looked as if it hadn't been entered for decades. My eyes followed the beam from Latif's torch as it swept around the yard. In one corner, there was a mower and a wheelbarrow stacked high with junk. In another, there was a mess of pipes, poles, planks and dustsheets, abandoned by builders. Latif went over to the builders' debris and started poking about. Something copper gleamed in the torchlight. He picked up a short length of pipe and pressed it to his cheek thoughtfully, before slipping it into his pocket.

He swung his torch around the yard again. The downstairs windows were shuttered from the inside, making access impossible. A jumble of outbuildings ran up one side. Kennel. Coalhouse. Washhouse. Next up he shone his torch along the yard's perimeter wall and across the back of the house. He flicked the beam back and forth between the wall and the closest upstairs window, sizing up the gap. I guessed it was about a metre and a half. I could tell by the expression on his face that he was ordering this space into some kind of climbing apparatus. Even so, I could hardly watch as he vaulted from one outhouse to the next – up, up, UP – easy as if he were wearing spring-heeled boots. Then he moved stealthily along the wall, stopping about a metre away from where it joined the house. When he strapped the headtorch on, my anxiety escalated. I watched through splayed fingers as he leapt into the night. For a moment his body was bunched up like a spring. My heart rocketed. Seconds later, he landed on the window's ledge, surefooted as a cat.

He wedged his gloved fingers into a small gap at the top of the sash window and pushed down. After a few failed attempts, he changed tactics and started punching out one of the small square glass panes with his gloved fist. Each thud shot into the night like an explosion. After a couple more thumps, the pane splintered.

A tinkle of glass rang out.

I counted to twenty.

Nobody came.

He reached his arm through the jagged hole and rammed back the window's rusty catch. The sash window slid up with a groan. He ducked sideways across the sill and disappeared.

I waited.

The moon burst out from behind a huge black cloud. I shrank back into the shadows. A hooded, wide-eyed freak was staring out at me from a downstairs window. I jumped back. But it was only my reflection. Then the shutters folded back and Latif reappeared. He turned the window lock and opened the window. A few minutes later, I was scrambling over the sill and down into the room.

Inside, a smart state-of-the-art meeting room. A host of angelic babies were smiling down from the walls, making me think of churches in Italy where fat-faced cherubs look down at tourists from domed-ceilings. A slogan, which arced across the wall in a rainbow of colours, read, ULTIMATE CHILDCRAFT: Unlocking the Mystery of your Child's Potential.

My stomach clenched.

The distant cackle of TV.

The burble of lovers' chat.

Latif crept across the room.

I followed; his less stealthy shadow.

The door creaked open, the sound of arthritic joints.

Outside, a corridor of squeaky floorboards — a country house's in-built burglar alarm — separated us from the front hallway and the watchman's room. Latif crossed the space in seven graceful leaps, glancing back when he reached the stairs, as if to say: "What's keeping you, Dasha?" I tiptoed after him, my heart hammering each time a floorboard creaked beneath my feet.

Crouching down behind the banisters, we listened to the night watchman chatting. Laughter and whispered promises. Minutes ticked by. The TV clowned around in the background. A grandfather clock tutted out seconds. My heartbeat boomed.

Please let Latif's plan work.

It seemed like hours before the night watchman finally hung up, sat back and turned up the television.

Latif glided across the parquet-floored hall. He paused in the doorway while the watchman switched channels, before moving stealthily to the sofa. Without hesitation, he took the copper piping from his pocket and pressed it against the watchman's neck, just below his hairline. The man froze momentarily. Then he started trembling and pleading with Latif in broken English.

"You won't get hurt if you do what I say," Latif said in

a monotone voice. "I want the keys to the office and the password to the main computer."

The guard remained silent.

"The keys?" Latif gave the piping a nudge.

"Okay. Okay," the guard muttered. "I do what you ask. The keys is on my belt." He fumbled to unclip the key ring, all thumbs. He flinched as he handed over the keys.

"Which one?" Latif jiggled the key ring in front of the man's nose.

The man pointed to the largest key.

"You sure about that?" Latif applied more pressure.

"I sw-swear." Stuttering this time, "D-d-do what you likes." Sobs glued the words to the roof of his mouth. "L-listen, b-b-boss. I'm nothin'. I hate this job. It pays n-nothin'. Do what you want. It makes no d-difference to me."

He tried to shrug off the gun muzzle.

I averted my eyes, finding it difficult to watch Latif playing the hard guy.

"The password?" Latif gave the piping another nudge.

"Swipe cards." He pointed to a glass cabinet in the hallway. "No password needed."

"For the main computer?"

He nodded. "Show me keys, boss."

Latif held up the keys.

"That one." He pointed to the smallest key on the chain and then back to the cabinet. "Mrs Haslett-Hines is the boss lady. That the card you need."

"Thanks, bruv," Latif took five hundred pounds from his pocket with his free hand and waved it in front of the guy's nose. "Payment," he said.

"What? You serious, boss?"

"Yeah. I'm serious. When's your shift end?"

"Saturday evening."

"This is the deal. Don't call the feds."

"Sure. Whatever. I told you. I don't care. You're the boss."

"I trust you, brother. But in case you come over all law-abiding and decide to make that call, I want you to know one of my crew's watching this place and you don't want to mess with him. Get me?"

The guard nodded wearily.

"Give me your mobile."

"Anything you say, boss." The guard handed over his smartphone.

Latif pocketed it and took the coiled rope from his rucksack. "Sorry, bruv, I've got to tie you up." He wound the rope around the man's wrists and tied it securely. Then he fashioned his paint-splattered rag into a blindfold and placed it over the guy's eyes. "I'm going to put the cash in the freezer so the police don't find it, think you're in on this. Or else you'll be doing time."

Latif went into the kitchen and hid the money in the freezer compartment. Returning with a grubby tea towel, he asked, "Where's the office?"

"Go down the hall. Turn left. You'll know you're in the right place because it look real good. Velvet paper and that.

You want the big green door. You can't miss it. Security code is 1322."

"Sorry about this, man," Latif repeated. And I could tell from his tone that he meant it. "Enjoy the cash. Sometime soon you'll understand. When it all unravels." Latif tied the tea towel over the watchman's mouth. "It'll look more authentic."

"Whatever, man." The cloth muffled his words.

Latif unlocked the cabinet where the swipe cards were kept, and took Haslett-Hines's security tag from its nail. The photo showed a smartly dressed businesswoman in her fifties.

We followed the corridor round. A fire door. Beyond that, posh became deluxe. Loud, swirling wallpaper kaleidoscoped my vision. Reaching the door, Latif zapped in the code and inserted the key, twitched it back and forth, but it wouldn't turn. Sweat beaded his temples. He took the key out, blew on it and eased it back into the lock until it clicked, then, with a quick flick of his wrist, he turned it until the door groaned open.

The air was heavy with the scent of lilies. Glass cabinets lined one side, which gave the room the feel of a pharmacy. Expensive art hung from the other two. When I shone the torch over the walls, I recognised a Damien Hirst spot painting.

Latif made straight for the computer. I followed. Then we both huddled round the screen. My heart jumped when Latif turned the computer on. The machine requested a password, and I held my breath as Latif swiped the card across the screen. Panic balled my throat. A red light flicking on and off in the corner of the screen quickened my pulse, but a few minutes later a big bug-eyed baby floated up out of the blue background and onto the screen. The red light stopped flashing. My heartbeat slowed.

Latif went into the finder window. He typed in the name Gold. Nothing. The files were numbered, not named.

"Any ideas?"

My mind froze.

"Significant numbers the Golds use. Phone passwords?" he hissed.

Brainfreeze. My mind was blank. "I don't know. I can't think. No, nothing," I gabbled, pressing my fingers against my temples.

"Come on, Dash. I need you to beam yourself down to planet earth."

I gripped the table. Shut my eyes. Nothing. *Come on, Dash, Get your brain in gear. Think! Think!* My mind remained a blank. And then a number flashed into my head. 9614. It was the number my birth mother had shouted out in the hall. I heard it clearly, as if she were standing right next to me. It was worth a try. "Baby 9614," I whispered, my fingers crossed.

He tapped the number in. The time arrow rotated. Kepow! My file sprung up. He clicked onto it.

I checked my parents' personal details and gave Latif the thumbs up. He took a data-stick from his pocket and saved the Gold file onto it.

"Shoot, Dash. I'll catch you up." He handed the data-stick to me. As I closed my hand around it, a jolt of electricity shot up my arm. My heart rate spiked.

"Still here?" he said, as he finished shutting down the computer.

We headed back to the front door. Tacky thriller music was blaring from the television. The escalating orchestral chords ramped up my anxiety. Convinced I heard footsteps from the security guard's room, I glanced back, heart thumping. But the night watchman was still sitting there – exactly as Latif had left him. He must have sensed our presence because he shouted, "Good luck!" A muffled sound, but the meaning was clear.

Latif quickly drew back the bolts and turned the keys.

"Sorry, mate," he shouted.

Then he walked out into the night. I knew playing the hard guy wasn't his style. He hurled the watchman's mobile into the bushes.

The Real Deal

"BINGO!" Latif slid into the driver's seat. He slammed the car door, unwrapped the scarf covering his head, pulled off the pollution mask and took the tablet out of his rucksack. He took a few minutes to set it up and then passed it to me. His hair was crazy with static, like candy floss.

I sat completely still for a few minutes staring down at the data-stick, cupped in the palm of my hand. I couldn't believe such life-changing information was stored inside. Latif frowned.

"What are you waiting for?"

I clenched my fist around the data-stick.

My secret world lay inside.

"Whatever!" Latif sounded weary, as if he'd had enough of being given the runaround by a spoilt brat.

"Sorry!" I whispered. "I need to do this in my own time."

Latif started the car, swung a U-turn and rocketed back down the lane. Then he turned the music up full blast, making conversation impossible. The data-stick was burning a hole in my hand. Still I didn't put it into the slot. I wanted the music off. I wanted peace and quiet. I wanted to hear myself think. The blaring music was a wall of sound, locking us into different worlds. As I closed my fist around the stick, hundreds of questions bombarded me. Why had my birth mother given me up? Was it money? Circumstance? I squeezed it tighter. The answers lay inside. I took a deep breath.

Dope! Put it in. What have you got to lose? My fingertips tingled as I pushed the data-stick into the slot. The file showed up on the screen. Baby 9614. It was weird to be defined by a number, like the latest model of a smartphone. I tapped my finger on the file nervously, as if knocking on a secret door into a parallel world; a fantasy world that I'd been constructing for the last few weeks. *My perfect life…*

I could hardly breathe. FuturePerfect's logo and mission statement spun into view: **UNLOCKING YOUR CHILD'S POTENTIAL…** followed by the contents page.

BABY 9614

I	**DNA PROFILE**
II	**BIOLOGICAL PARENTS**
III	**ADOPTIVE PARENTS**
IV	**SPECIFIED REQUIREMENTS**
V	**CONTRACT**

My eyes travelled down the options. Where to start?

I touched the adoptive parents heading first; wanting to double-check this was my file. Up came the Golds' details. I swiped the screen and the next page came into view. The Golds stared out. A glossy PR shot. But I knew enough about them to last me a lifetime. I returned to the menu. Now for what really mattered.

Okay, Dash. Be brave. My finger trembled as I tapped onto the biological parents heading. *Parents?* Up until now I hadn't given my real father much thought. I held my breath.

In a flash, a beautiful face popped up – a young woman's. Although the photo had been taken sixteen years ago, I was certain she was the woman who I'd glimpsed in the hallway. *My real mother.* The crackle of connection electrified me, as if every cell in my body had lit up in recognition. I took a few moments to trace the outline of her face with my fingertips. Wow! It had to be my birth mother. We shared so many features: jet-black hair, thick eyebrows and intense green eyes. Spellbound, I scrutinised her face – a face that I'd conjured up a billion, perhaps a zillion times over the past month, which now I had the chance to study in detail. She was even more beautiful than I had remembered. She looked sad, though. This gave me hope. For in her sadness, I saw the possibility of a happy reunion.

Underneath the photo, my mother's name – MAXINE TAYLOR – was typed in capital letters. Her birth date was 3November. She was a Scorpio. I quickly did the calculations; she would be thirty-eight this year. Her status was single mother; a graduate. I swiped to the next page.

A photo of a young man with dark, curly hair, beard and piercing blue eyes stared out at me. My father. I took a few minutes to examine his face. It was kind and open somehow. His name was Zac Cable-Smith. I read on. *Kepow!* His status jumped off the page and punched me right between the eyes. *Father dead.* My jaw dropped open.

On the next page, there were more detailed profiles of my parents. I read on. According to the file, my father had studied at Oxford where he had received a first-class degree in Philosophy, Politics and Economics. He had died in a motorcycle accident a month before I was born. My mother had also been an outstanding student, having received a first-class degree from Oxford in English. Both had IQs of over 150. I flicked back to the photo of my dad. He had a smooth look about him – dapper, I supposed. His style was retro smart. He was wearing a sharp suit and a thin black tie. I had his nose and his smile.

Flicking between the two photos, I tried to picture them together back before he died. Had they been happy? In love? Had they wanted a baby? Me? Had my dad even known of my existence? I bit my lip. My life had been tragic right from the very start. I wiped away a tear. That was when the killer question hooked itself into my brain like a burr: why had my mother given me up for adoption when I was the one person who would remind her of Zac? I stared into the oncoming headlights. Perhaps that was why.

I gave their medical history a miss, swiping instead to the sections detailing the Golds' special requirements. My eyes widened. My parents' shopping list covered two pages, and took the form of a catalogue of desired physical attributes and traits. Physical attributes wanted: female, straight dark hair, emerald eyes, slim, size eight, high cheekbones, porcelain skin, heart-shaped face, small nose, wide smile, height five foot nine inches, compact ears, curly eyelashes, narrow feet and so on and so on. It seemed no detail was too small. There were also sections on talents, mental skills, traits, IQ and longevity. FuturePerfect guaranteed all the babies on their books would be free from disease, addictions, mental health problems and abnormal genes. Snakes alive! By the looks of things, I was going to live until I was about 130. I shivered.

I clicked onto Baby 9614, heart catapulting,

A baby.

ME.

Pink arms grabbing at handfuls of air, plump legs kicking. There was no mistaking that scowling face. Underneath the photo, a sketchy description: Female. Dark hair. Green eyes. Seven pounds. *That was all* — as impersonal as a missing person's bulletin. But there I was in glorious technicolour.

I bit my lip.

Typed above my baby photo was the name – Sadie Taylor.

My real name, I thought, saying it under my breath as I ran my finger beneath the name like a child reading the words for the first time. "Sadie Taylor," I whispered again, trying it out for size… It sounded strange – so un-*ME*.

Okay, now I had to get my head round the science. My stomach churned as I swiped to my DNA profile. The science zizzed my head. I narrowed my eyes as I tried to decode the pages of data, complicated charts, multicoloured diagrams and graphs. Sheez! I had never imagined that I was this complex. It was like a unique barcode of my genetic building blocks. Although I found it difficult to decipher the data, from what I could work out, my DNA had been mapped, analysed and shown to prospective couples, and by some trick of fate, my data had matched the Golds' creepy checklist.

I slumped back in my seat and took a few minutes to stare into the darkness, trying to order the facts surrounding my adoption and make sense of them. One thing was clear; it was far from a straightforward adoption. It was darker, more sci-fi...

I clicked on the last section – the contract. Pages and pages of legalese followed. Skimming through, I noted the terms of the adoption agreement were laid down here as well as a four-page confidentiality clause. I didn't have to read the small print. I knew the deal already. The Golds had paid off Maxine – my real mother – so she'd never come looking for me. Cash for anonymity. I smiled. For once Dad's attempt to buy someone had failed. She had come back to look for me. Fact.

I swiped to the last page and took a few minutes to study Maxine's signature. It was large and loopy like mine. Her address had been updated three times. My heart skittered. Finally I had her address. I started dancing around to the music. Opening the window, I stuck my head out into the cold night air and whooped at the stars. My whoops rushed away behind us.

"Bad news, then?" Latif was smiling.

"I've got her address." I shouted over the music. "It's been updated."

"So where we heading, Dash?" He turned the music down.

"North London, Archway."

"Sassy. Is it up to date?"

"I don't know." I swiped back to the change of dates. "She last updated her address…" I quickly did the calculations in my head, "four years ago. It looks like they update addresses every five years. She was due to update next year. Just before my eighteenth birthday."

He fixed his eyes on me. "So what's the story?"

"Okay, don't laugh, the Golds chose me for my superior genes." A smile twitched the corner of his mouth. "I said no laughing. Advanced genes, I believe is the technical term. They paid through the nose for my amazing physical attributes, talent and my razor-sharp brain."

"They were robbed." He gave me one of his sideways looks. "I've seen no evidence of advanced genes so far, bubblehead."

"I do a great job of keeping my genius secret." I smiled.

"So how does it work? The science?" Unlike me, Latif was keen on facts.

"Okay. From what I can work out, FuturePerfect mapped my DNA with a microchip. My genetic information was shown to prospective clients, couples wanting to adopt. And being born lucky, my DNA data matched the Golds' creepy wish list."

"So this microchip reading gives couples an amazing preview?"

"Exactly." I said, slipping into a smooth PR pitch. "FuturePerfect unlocked the mystery of my personality."

"What mystery, bubblehead?"

I stuck my tongue out at him. "It's really weirding me out. They bought me like they would a luxury holiday. I'm a freakin' barcode baby."

Latif shrugged. "If the technology is out there, it's going to happen, whatever. That's human nature. Bespoke babies for the super-rich; it's a no-brainer. They've got the money, and they expect to get exactly what they want. No surprises. They want to control every part of their lives. Even the make-up of their children so they'll rule the world, too."

I stared out into the darkness. Of course, it made perfect sense. A complete control freak like my dad was always looking for ways to lower the odds; to take chance out of the equation so he got exactly what he wanted. His child was the future of his beloved brand. He wasn't going to gamble on that. I wiped away a tear.

Latif looked over. His eyes were pooled with light from the oncoming traffic. "You can't change what's done, Dash. You've gotta move on. All you can do is change yourself. Be the best you can. That's what being human is. And you're doing that."

"I guess," I whispered, swiping back to the photos of my birth parents, my fingers leaving damp prints on the screen. Maxine looked so young and lost. As I stared at the info-screen I couldn't help thinking how crazy it was to be reading such personal information from a stolen document, in a stolen car, driven by a cool stranger, who I'd met little more than twenty-four hours ago under a bridge. Things couldn't get much crazier than that.

Beams from the approaching cars swept across Latif's face; gliding over his features, smoothing out his skin. He looked so serene, so handsome, so composed. I punched his arm lightly. "Thanks, Latif. I could never have done this without you."

"Truth!"

"Do you know what the worst thing is? With these genes I'm going to live for ever."

"Now that's real dread."

He switched stations, just as a news bulletin announced: "Terrorist steals diplomat's car for audacious getaway. Dasha Gold on board."

"'Sakes, they're onto us already." He sucked air through his teeth. "It's too risky to park up near your mum's so we'll have to ditch the car in the Edgelands. Feds shouldn't find it in that broke barrio for time. And we can grab a few hours sleep in…" He trailed off and turned the radio up. His face became hard. "No way! They're interviewing Baba."

His dad's voice filled the car. "This media circus is absurd. A witch-hunt. My boy is an A-grade student. An exceptional artist. He lives for his graffiti. Perhaps some of his work is provocative. But that doesn't make him a terrorist. In fact, he hates extremism of any kind. He uses his work to comment on society. Other graffiti artists are seen as celebrities and sell their work to Hollywood superstars. What's the difference? My boy speaks out, since when has that been a crime?"

"What about the abducted girl?" a reporter asked.

"Abducted? Do you believe she's with him against

her will? He is a charming boy. I imagine she is enjoying his company…"

Boos from the assembled crowd drowned out his last words.

I smiled at Latif and mouthed, "Are they out of their minds?"

"Mrs Hajjaj, have you got anything to add?" the reporter asked.

"I would like to read a poem by Martin Niemöller." Latif's mother cleared her throat and waited for the crowd to simmer down.

"First they came for the communists,
and I did not speak out because I was not a communist.
Then they came for the socialists,
and I did not speak out because I was not a socialist;
Then they came for the trade unionists,
and I did not speak out because I was not a trade unionist:
Then they came for me,
and there was no one left to speak for me."

Latif's parents' voices flew from the radio like starbursts of hope in a mad world.

"Your dad'll get you off," I whispered.

"*Inshallah.*" Latif smiled.

As Good As Dead

WHEN the bulb blinked on in the motel room, a cockroach scuttled under a dark-stained wardrobe. I hesitated in the dooway. The room was gloomy as a funeral parlour. Two single beds with moth-eaten blankets were lined up like coffins. I pictured my epitaph scratched across one of the headboards.

GREW UP PLASTIC.
Melted in the heat of the chase.

Latif crossed the room and drew the frayed brown curtains, shutting out the pink neon lights, which wiggled and shimmied with the promise of GIRLS, GIRLS, GIRLS! I turned on the TV and started flicking through the channels. Most stations were running repeats on us, even though it was the middle of the night.

"We're rolling on every channel." I stopped on GoldRush TV, sucked into watching another package featuring my perfect life. "Don't look now, Latif. It's the return of the zombie." I sat down on one of the beds as hundreds of shiny, happy, attention-seeking Dashas smiled from the screen, trying their best to tempt me back to the ranks of the glamorous undead. I couldn't take my eyes off them – totally transfixed by my other saccharine self. "It's weird." I searched for a way to describe the experience. "A total brainsnap. Like I'm watching a tacky tribute to myself."

My gaze remained fixed on the screen. And as I studied my former self, everything else melted away. I couldn't relate to that person. She had nothing to do with me. She was an alien, a sparkle-fairy. Since the train crash, I felt as if I'd shed that glossy skin and a tougher one had grown back. I had outgrown that girl and her world. That was why I could never return.

After the montage, the programme went back to the studio. "That's all I need." I pulled a face. "Screen time with the Dark Lord and his apprentice."

"What the hell are those two comedians up to now?" Latif tsked, sucking air through his teeth.

My parents were sitting on a red velvet sofa in a studio lit by thousands of candles. Girls from the Star Academy wearing T-shirts with *We Want Dasha Home!* slogans emblazoned across the front were holding candles with my name stencilled onto the side.

"Practising the dark arts?" I exchanged a baffled look with Latif. "Search me!"

My parents were perfectly turned out for the roles of high priest and priestess of doom. They were both immaculately dressed in black. My mother's dress was Chanel, this season's haute couture, of course. It had cost close to £100,000. Her diamond necklace rocked in at £500,000. The candlelight softened my mother's taut face. Her freshly curled hair extensions shone and slithered like a nest of serpents. Ultra-bright white teeth glittered when she spoke. She adopted her tragic face. "This has been a tough and tearful time. But thanks to your support we are finding a way through these desperate days. Going through the photos and footage, talking to friends and family, and reading all your wonderful messages has given us immense strength. Tonight we want to share our favourite moments."

"Sick bucket, please." I ignored the amused glint in Latif's eye.

"We are counting on your positive energy to help us bring Dasha back." She trailed off. My dad squeezed her hand encouragingly. "We ask you to offer up your thoughts, prayers and positive vibes. Let's feel your good vibrations."

"So that's their game." Latif clacked his worry beads across his knuckles. "Suck up everything good and positive in the world and turn it into black magic."

"I told you they were vampires." A shiver crept up my spine.

The show was called 'A Vigil for Dasha Gold', and promised a mishmash of celebrity tributes, interviews with my friends, my parents' favourite Dasha stories, clips and, weirdest of all, prayers. The prayers took me by surprise.

"Let us pray," my father said.

I rolled my eyes. Dad famously claimed that he didn't 'do' God. As far as I knew he thought he *was* God.

The studio audience chanted the prayers in a mesmerising murmur. For those at home, the words rolled along the bottom of the screen like a karaoke machine. I imagined hundreds and thousands of viewers whispering the prayers in their sitting rooms. I shifted uneasily. The effect was more seance than prayer meeting; as if my parents were trying to conjure up my spirit live on TV.

"I'm not dead." I shook my fist at the TV.

Another clip montage started rolling. Prayers and thoughts texted in by viewers whizzed across the screen.

A loud heartbeat boomed. Up came a scan image of a baby in the womb. My mother cradled her stomach.

My mouth fell open. "Oh no. That's too much."

The heartbeat boomed out from the sound system. It was hypnotic.

She waited for the beats to subside, before saying as an introduction to a montage: "From the very beginning Dasha was loved…"

The opening shots showed me crawling around in a gold lamé romper-suit. The song was Robbie Williams' 'Angels'. Not one of my favourites.

"*Basta!*" Latif made a zapping gesture with his thumb. "I want to see if there are any visuals on my parents' interview. Eyeball something that matters," he added with that lopsided smile.

I stuck my tongue out at him.

But before I had time to switch channels, breaking news flashed up on screen. His face darkened. My eyes locked onto the TV. A presenter was reporting live from a leafy suburban street. "I'm standing outside Latif Hajjaj's parents' home in Kensal Rise, west London. Minutes ago, armed police stormed the building on a warrant issued from the Home Office. Mr and Mrs Hajajj will be held under the Prevention of Terrorism Act. Mr Hajjaj is a lawyer who has made it his life's work to defend terrorists and terrorist activity. A police spokeswoman has informed the press that the police are investigating claims that Latif Hajjaj and his parents are part of a coordinated network of cells, planning a series of outrages in London. Dasha Gold and Coco York's kidnappings are thought to be the first of many attacks on London and Londoners."

Live footage showed police in riot gear leading Latif's parents from their house in handcuffs. His father was wearing striped pyjamas while his mother was in jogging pants and a faded T-shirt with the slogan *PEACE & LOVE*. Men in white forensic suits, carrying computers sealed in plastic bags, brought up the rear.

"Tell me this isn't happening," Latif groaned, flicking his worry beads. "This is totally insane."

The police van's doors slammed shut and then it screeched off in a blur of blue strobe.

Then my parents were on screen again.

"Beats me how you've put up with those clowns for so long. My parents are worth a million of them." Latif slumped forwards. All the defiance and finger-to-the-world cockiness had disappeared. I wanted to put my arms around him and tell him that everything would be okay. But I kept quiet. Anything I said would sound hollow. My chest was constricting. Everything was my fault. If Latif hadn't rescued me from that creep, he'd still be a nighter, a tagger and a free spirit. Instead the world believed he was a monster. I placed the heel of my hand against my forehead. How had that happened?

On screen Latif punched a freedom fighter's fist at the CCTV camera down by the train depot. His grainy image punched again and again, sometimes in slo-mo, sometimes in real time. Meanwhile a reporter went hard on the terrorist angle.

Minutes passed, the only sound my parents blabbing big, vivid lies that would stick in people's minds. Propping myself up on my elbow, I studied Latif – or, more precisely, the two Latifs in the room: the on-screen Latif, fired up with rebellion, and, in contrast, the real-life Latif, who looked smaller somehow, crushed.

I slid down onto the floor beside him. "Don't let their lies get to you, Latif."

"The world believes this crap." He flicked his worry beads angrily. "Get real, Dash. I'm as good as dead." He jumped to his feet, walked over to the window and peered out from behind the curtains. "They've arrested my parents, for Chrissakes."

"But none of this is real." I flapped my hands in the direction of the TV. "It's make-believe. We've got to do something." But my mind was blank. I tapped my fingertips against my temples, desperately trying to crank it back to life. "We could go to a rival TV channel. Explain this terrorist blab is all lies." I didn't say it with any conviction.

"Yeah right. Like that's really going to work. The Golds have created a slamming story. That's what people want, Dash." His voice was emotionless, resigned. "Even if you held a press conference saying it was all bollocks, your dad would pay an expert to explain that I'd brainwashed you. That this is a classic case of Stockholm syndrome and you'd fallen in love with your kidnapper. That you're the twenty-first-century Patty Hearst – posh girl gone bad. Dash, you know how it works. Your parents will undermine you as a credible witness." He paused. "But thanks, anyway."

I gave a weak smile. And as I stared at the television screen, I struggled to straighten stuff out in my head. The trouble was everything seemed so unreal. I looked around. Even reality, the two of us hiding out in a fleapit motel on the run, felt unreal! Bonkers! As for the stuff on television, which was shaping up like a Hollywood blockbuster; that was beyond bonkers. Yet, *that* was the story people believed. It was as if our television personas had lives of their own, like avatars – dreamed up by my parents to act out their crazy game of cat and mouse. I watched the TV miserably; I was beginning to lose my grip on reality.

My finger hovered over the off button on the remote. I wanted everything to stop. I wanted to turn the Golds' world off. But their lies were out there. They'd been pumping their version of the truth into thousands of homes for the last twenty-four hours, poisoning everyone's minds against Latif. We couldn't counter the untruths or press rewind. I felt as if we were in a video game which we couldn't exit,

and the levels kept on getting harder. That was our problem
— well, one of them.

"What are we going to do now?" I asked.

"The plan remains the same." He took the tablet out
of his rucksack and hunched over it as he logged onto the
wi-fi.

"I'm so sorry for...

He put his hand up. "Forget it. Dad'll be out in no time.
He'll smash it. But right now we've gotta get our swagger
back. Boom, I'm connected. What's your mum's name?
Address?"

"Maxine Taylor, eighty-eight Orchard Road."

He tapped away on the keys for a few minutes. Then
whistled. "The electoral register says she still lives there."

"Result!" I jumped to my feet and fizzed around
the room.

I looked over his shoulder as he entered her address
on Google Earth. It was nothing much: a grotty-looking
semi-detached house. My eyes fixed on a trampoline in the
back garden. My heart lurched. That could only mean one
thing. There was another child, maybe children. An ugly
grub of jealousy wriggled in the pit of my stomach. Other
children had never figured in my fantasies.

The Golds were promising exciting new revelations.
"Stay tuned," my mother purred as they went into the break.

"Thanks, but no thanks!" I headed into the bathroom,
shut the door and leaned against it. Space, that's what
I needed right now, room to breathe. I wanted to shake the

Golds out of my life for good. But they were everywhere, always invading my life. The only Gold-free zone was Crunch Town. At least pirate radio ruled in the junk spaces.

When the naked bulb snapped on, a cockroach skidded across the greasy linoleum. I turned on the taps to drown out the TV. Catching sight of my reflection in the mirror above the basin, I did a double take. The blond wig took me by surprise. I studied myself in the glass. Despite it appearing as if I hadn't had a good night's sleep in weeks, I looked cool, like a heroine in a quirky independent film – a girl making herself up as she went along…

"Tomorrow," I whispered to the glass.

Drawing closer, I wondered whether my mother would recognise me in a flash, whether we would click immediately like lost pieces of a puzzle. I splashed cold water onto my face and watched a single droplet trickle down my left cheek. For all I knew, my mother might not recognise me at all. I buried my face in a mouldy-smelling towel.

"Dash? Your friend Coco has been released." Latif knocked softly on the door. "It's breaking news."

"Really? When?" I rushed from the bathroom. "Did her parents pay the ransom?"

"Allegedly a covert police operation freed her."

"That's brilliant news," I said. "I hope she's okay."

Coco looked angelic in a simple, chic, white tunic-dress. She was talking my parents through her ordeal: the abduction, the imprisonment and the dramatic rescue. I stood in the doorway while I listened to her story.

When she'd finished, my mother asked gently, "Do you have a message for Dasha's kidnapper?"

Latif and I exchanged a grim look.

The camera zoomed in.

Coco batted her eyelashes. Her glitter make-up sparkled.

"Please let Dasha go. She knows nothing about politics. She's an innocent."

I rolled my eyes.

"So were you and Dasha close?" my mother asked.

The camera zoomed in even closer.

"I loved Dasha like a sister. We were besties." Coco gave a curtain-call smile. "We were inseparable."

My mouth dropped open. "News to me!"

"She's been bought. Keep up, dim-bulb. They've…"

Footsteps on the stairs caused him to tail off.

We exchanged a look.

The Golds were signing off. "The prayers will continue through the night. Keep your vigil. Goodnight. God bless. Keep praying."

Latif glided across the room. He turned off the television before taking up position by the door.

The footsteps stopped outside.

A barrage of questions went off in my head. Was it the police? Was the game up? Had the guy in the lobby called the cops? Surely not. We'd picked this dump precisely because it was the only motel on the strip without a television in the foyer. Even better, the guy on the desk had been so bonged-out he hardly knew what time of day it was.

The knock, when it came, was soft.

"Yeah?" Latif's voice remained calm.

"Turn the TV down, yeah?" He spoke slowly. "It's late, man. Guests are complaining."

"It's off, bruv."

The steps retreated.

"They have other guests?" I whispered.

"Girls turning tricks. Civilians down on their luck." He walked over to the window. "Turn off the light." He drew back the curtain a crack and watched the street.

"But why would they care?"

"Exactly. We'd better shoot."

The footsteps returned. Another knock.

"Got a ciggy? I'll swap a couple for some weed. Come on, bruv. Open the door."

Immediately I pictured a tough from CID piling in as soon as Latif unlocked the door. I slid under the covers and pulled the blankets up to my nose.

"Don't!" I mouthed.

Too late! Latif had already wrapped himself up in a blanket and was opening the door. The guy's bloodshot eyes goggled. He steadied himself on the doorjamb, peered at Latif, and slurred, "Hey man, cool outfit. You scared the hell out of me. Got a cigarette?"

"Sorry. Don't smoke, bruv." He shook his head when the guy offered him a lump of black wrapped in cling film. "Not for me, bruv. But you could do me a favour." He pressed a fifty-pound note into the guy's hand. "Bell me if anyone asks after us. Our parents aren't cool about this – us." He jagged his thumb back towards me. "Don't exactly approve, know what I'm saying? My dad's a cop. His mind's so small I could use it in a pea-shooting contest. So it'd be good if you'd buzz up, if anyone comes looking."

Eyes half-covered by hooded eyelids, the guy peered into the unlit room. Not that there was much to see as I was lying in bed with the blanket pulled right up to the tip of my nose, scared that he might recognise me even in his drugged-up fug.

"Anything you say, man." I heard him walking unsteadily back down the corridor. About halfway down, he stopped and said, "Oh yeah. Two brick shithouses with walkie-talkies were checking the flophouses across the road. They had the look of feds. Probably an immigration swoop, innit?"

"Thanks mate." Latif shut the door.

"Time to road it," he hissed, wedging the window open with the fire extinguisher.

Moments later, we were heading down the fire escape like a couple of stray cats.

Tooled Up

LEAVING the main drag of strip joints, sex shops and motels behind, we headed down a dimly lit street lined with ramshackle B&Bs and hostels. We walked in silence apart from the click, click, click of car-door handles. We were in the Edgelands, a strange twilight zone on the fringe of the city. Here, everything was low rent.

"TWOC time," Latif said in explanation.

"TWOC?"

"Police speak for Taking Without Owner's Consent." He swore under his breath when a bashed-up Mini refused to open.

"What?"

"Borrowing, bubblehead."

I laughed.

He continued pulling the door handles as we walked. Meanwhile, I examined the formerly well-to-do family houses, which were seedy and rundown now, and by the looks of things, rented out by the room. We traipsed up and down streets for what seemed like hours until finally — open sesame — we were inside a grimy white van. Taking the metal cutters from his rucksack, Latif reached down and started fiddling about under the steering wheel. I kept my eyes on the street as instructed, watching for goons. There were piles of clothes and blankets in the back. The van was a tip. Someone had been sleeping rough in it by the looks of things.

"What are you doing?" I glanced over.

"Hot-wiring the engine." I heard the snip of wires.

"'Sakes! This is insane." I kept my eyes fixed on the street

"Come on. Come on," he growled when the engine wouldn't start.

Before long, he swung the van out into the road and accelerated.

"TDA," he said.

"Two Dumb Assholes?"

"Sounds about right."

"Tried Died Attempting?"

"Nah. For real. Taking and Driving Away."

"*Boring!*" I rolled my eyes.

"Right. See how boring you find this." He floored the accelerator pedal.

Immediately we were roller-coasting through the empty, early-morning streets. I gripped the seat, eyes half-closed as we flew over speed bumps, screeched round corners and hurtled down the centre of the road, hoovering up the white markings. An empty bottle in the back rattled from side to side. The van smelled of fags and booze. After a while, Latif slowed down.

"We don't want to get pulled," he said in explanation. "See if there's an *A to Z* in the glove compartment, Dash. Satnav's too risky. We might be GPSed."

"Do you think they're onto us?" I asked as I rummaged through the junk in the glove compartment, poking around until I found a pocket-sized *A to Z* wedged under an empty beer can and scrunched-up crisp packets.

"No way. They shouldn't find the security guy until Saturday evening when his shift ends. Those zero-hours guys work crazy long shifts."

"What about the guy at the hostel? Do you think the men he described were police?"

"Nah. More like his skunk paranoia. That dude was flying. 'Hey bruv, there was, like, a guy out there. He had feathers in his hair...'"

His dope drawl made me laugh.

All at once his tone changed. "But we'll stake your mum's house out before you make a move. Check there's no action from the feds."

The laughter died in my throat.

When I'd found Orchard Road on the map, I handed him the *A to Z* and pointed out the coordinates. The van swerved as he checked it out.

"Got eyes on it," he said, passing the book back.

"Euggh. I can't believe the driver keeps his socks in the glove compartment. That's so skanky." I prodded a thick brown sock with the *A to Z*. There was something hidden inside. I removed it gingerly, took a sharp breath in. "Latif, there's a gun hidden in this sock." I could barely say the words.

We exchanged a look.

I held it as far away from me as possible.

Latif's eyes flicked towards his rucksack.

Without saying a word, I unzipped it and slid the gun inside, next to his spray cans. Neither of us spoke; we were both too stunned by our silent agreement that a gun was necessary.

After a few minutes I asked, "Have you ever used one?"

"Of course not, bubblehead. What do you take me for? Some kind of gangster?"

He turned the music up. Conversation over.

I sat back, gripping the seat. In a couple of hours I'd be outside Maxine Taylor's house – my birth mother's home. It still felt unreal, but for some reason, knowing her name made things feel more real. It proved she wasn't a figment of my imagination. I whispered it. This action cemented my belief.

Watching the houses glide by, I pictured my mother, as she looked in the photo in my file, staring out of upstairs windows. A tingling sensation swept through my body in waves. It was so close now...

I started rehearsing possible opening lines, icebreakers. As usual, the exercise overwhelmed me. What was there to say? Everything seemed trite, stupid or too emotional. It didn't help that I was so keyed up my mind wouldn't settle. Flit, flit, flit went my thoughts. I was on edge too. I couldn't stop fidgeting. I opened the window, switched the radio station, pulled down the sun visor, checked myself in the mirror, put on lipstick, pouted, smiled, frowned. Should I wear the wig?

My frown deepened. I was tempted, but, no, this had to be the time for truth. No disguises. No fakery.

I slowly removed the wig and stuffed it into Latif's rucksack next to the gun. For a moment I was the old Dasha again – unsure of myself; it was as if the wig had given me an invincible aura. I fixed my reflection with a steely stare. Shape up. Get a grip. I combed my hair out with my fingers. I looked like a total soap-dodger. I cursed the fact that we'd had to leave the motel before I'd had time to make myself look human.

"It's mental." I pulled a screwball face. "I'm about to meet my real mother and I feel like I'm going on a date. How weird is that?" I studied my face in the mirror. "Sheez! I've got to act natural. Be myself. Whatever that means." I struck a few more poses. "It sounds so easy, doesn't it? Like it's a definite thing. *ME. MYSELF. I.*" I squinted at my reflection, took a deep breath. "I don't think I can go through with this, Latif."

"Stop chirping, Dash. Picasso painted himself at the age of eighteen. It's called 'Yo, Picasso. I am Picasso.' It's awesome. He exudes total self-belief. When you meet your mum you need to think, *Yo, Dasha.* And believe it!"

"Yo, Dasha?" I raised an eyebrow.

"That's my advice. Take it or leave it."

I shut my eyes. Thoughts about the meeting with my mother were too huge for me to deal with right now. They pressed at the edges of my brain and made my skull ache. I cradled the top of my head, pushed the explosive mix of feelings back down into some dark, secret place.

Bang! Next minute I was lurching forwards, the seatbelt snapped me back. Latif cursed as the van swerved into the midde of the road.

"What's going on, Latif?" I screamed. "Pull over."

He carried on driving.

"What happened, Latif? Did you fall asleep?" I grabbed his arm. "Pull over, now."

The van's wing mirror was shattered.

Oh no, I thought, *seven years' bad luck.*

He slowed down. "I must've nodded off for a second. I clipped a lorry back there." He blinked his eyes. "I'm rinsed, Dash."

"Clipped? Hit, more like. Sheez, Latif! Talk about a lucky escape." I did a rough calculation. "You haven't slept for about forty-five hours." I squeezed his arm. "You need to get some sleep. We both do. I'm shattered too." He carried on driving. "I'm serious, Latif. Pull over or you're going to kill us."

"I hear you. I hear you," he said. "There's a place up here where we can stop. The warriors won't mind."

"*Warriors?*"

"Eco." He gave me a sly smile. "Don't vex, Dash."

I rolled my eyes.

Frowning a little, he said, "You're right. We gotta be sharp for the next episode. And if you're lucky you might get to scrub up." He sniffed the air. "Which wouldn't be such a bad thing."

I laughed and mouthed, "My hero."

After about ten minutes, he pulled into a derelict petrol station. Two camper vans were parked up, curtains drawn. Brightly coloured tents bubbled the forecourt. Pairs of trainers were lined up outside each tent like guard dogs. Everyone was sleeping, apart from a freckle-faced boy with purple hair, who waved us through a gap in the security fence. Banners with eco messages were tied to the mesh: **I ♥ the planet. Green is the new black. THERE'S NO PLANET B.** The petrol pumps had been boxed in with hardboard, and were shaped like teepees. Murals of totem poles adorned them. A hammock hung between two petrol pumps. Grass sprouted up through the concrete. Creepers in huge blue pots climbed around the station's struts. The red **TEXACO** sign now read **TEXANO**.

We parked up, facing the exit. "In case we need to leave in a hurry," Latif said, getting out of the van. He mooched over to the purple-haired boy, hands sunk deep into his pockets. I was glad to see he was wearing his face coverings. They chatted for a while, and from their pointing and gesturing, I guessed that they were discussing the graffiti sprayed across the boarded-up service station.

When Latif came back, he hoiked his rucksack off the seat. "I'm going to throw up a piece. Payment for our stay," he said to my raised eyebrow. "And Jake says you can have a shower." He pointed to the car wash.

"Seriously?" I asked, not sure what to believe. "In the…" I stopped when I saw the glint in his eyes.

"Nah. Bubblehead. They've rigged up facilities round the back. A shower and that."

Jake came over with towel and soap, which Latif passed through the window, before heading over to the garage.

The shower room was basic. The water was cold and little more than a trickle, but I didn't care – it just felt good to wash away the grime and sweat from the chase. The smell of the chemical toilet turned my stomach.

When I came back out, Latif had finished his tag and was back in the van. This time the freedom fighter's aviators reflected a polar bear stranded on an iceberg. Underneath he'd written **ICED**.

"Iced? Like cold?" I asked as I got back into the van.

"Nah. Iced, like slang for killed. Jake wanted an eco message. He's going to look out for us while we sleep." Latif settled back into his seat, pulling the material from his face coverings down over his eyes.

I climbed into the back of the van and straightened out the grubby blankets. They were thin and threadbare, but I could have slept anywhere. I curled up like a dog in its basket and fell asleep in minutes.

When Latif shook me awake a few hours later, I saw squares of cobalt blue sky through the van's windows. I rubbed my eyes.

"Yo, Dasha!" he said with a wink. "It's time to hit the road."

Maxine Taylor

ORCHARD Road was a quiet, leafy street – quite possibly a nosey-parker street before the repossessions set in. Tatty, tumbledown houses lined the right-hand side of the road. A scraggy, wooded area sloped away to the left. It wasn't a no-go area yet, but I had the feeling that it was sinking fast. I counted eight trashed *For Sale* signs. Although I couldn't help thinking that the gardens, wild and unkempt, gave the street a romantic air.

Barely breathing, I pressed my nose to the window as we cruised down the street, swerving potholes and roadworks, checking out my mother's house like a couple of hit men. Eyes fastened to it, I twisted round as we drove past, not wanting to let the place out of my sight for a single second.

"Act normal, bubblehead!" Latif said. "If you know what that means."

"This isn't a normal situation," I protested.

"All the more reason." I could hear exasperation in his voice.

My mother's house was, I guessed, in civilian terms, family-sized with a tidy garden. Nondescript. It was painted white with blue guttering, door, windows and trim. There was nothing special about the house – no fast cars parked up, no security. Dull and undistinguished, it didn't square with the place I had imagined my mother would live, which would be all cottagey and clad with ivy – a kid's picture-book house.

Latif swung a U-turn at the bottom of the road and we coasted past the house again, and then up to the Station Pub on Archway Road, where we parked up. As we got out of the van, a fox, eyes burning as orange as its brush, left off scavenging through a pile of bin bags, before slinking down a muddy dog-walkers' path.

"Spies approach sideways on," Latif said, heading after the fox.

"What's the plan?" I asked when we reached a disused railway track. I checked my watch; it was twelve-thirty.

"Stake the house out. Check there's no fed action." His eyes scoured the shadows. "Make sure there are no uglies hanging around. You can head in when I'm sure the coast is clear."

His use of the word *you* jolted me right back into the present. Soon I'd be entering my mother's house – *alone*.

We walked along the gritted track for about two hundred metres, before climbing up a wooded slope. We hid behind a stack of recently felled timber, a little way up from my mother's house. There was nobody about. Bluebells sprawled across the slope and a silver birch gleamed in the pearly rays of the spring sunshine. The shuttered house gave the impression of a place with secrets. I dug my nails into my palm. The trouble was, the biggest secret was standing right outside.

My nails jabbed deeper into my skin. Watching my

mother's house like a snoop ramped up my anxiety. Was it okay to turn up uninvited? Would she be pleased to see me? Would she slam the door in my face? If only things had been different, and I could have let her know…

"Psst."

When I looked around, Latif had vanished.

"Up here." His disembodied voice whispered from a powder-puff of blossom.

I climbed up into the cherry tree and peered out. We had a partial view of the front of the house and the alleyway next to it.

Two vans drew up. One parked up on the street and the second reversed into the alleyway. The logo on the van read THAMES WATER. Four men got out, went round to the back of the vans and started unloading pneumatic drills. We exchanged a look. Now I looked closer, I could see there were pools of water on the road. The pipes must have burst. The *stram-stram-stram* of the drills set my teeth on edge. Latif shouted something about Victorian water systems, I wasn't exactly sure what, because his words were lost in the drilling.

The front door opened and a woman came out. My gut jumped an affirmative, although it was impossible to get a positive identification from this distance as she was wearing an anorak with the hood up. A little girl skipped alongside, her hands clamped over her ears. Jealousy overwhelmed me. That girl had my life. I started to climb down.

Latif placed his hand on my shoulder. "The workmen might recognise you, Dash. Don't blow it."

I shook his hand from my arm as I watched Maxine drive off in a bashed-up old Renault.

Furious with him, I picked at ivy tendrils; the larger stems were thick and strong, they gripped the trunk like claws. My nails were broken and my neon varnish chipped. Latif sat silently, thinking, I guessed. I imagined this is what he did when he was staking out his graffiti spots.

The track was a dog-walking superhighway; two Border terriers, a sheepdog, a Labrador, a Jack Russell, a King Charles and a sausage dog. Counting the dogs calmed me down. Occasionally a breeze got up, sending flurries of blossom to the ground like confetti. A mother with two small children came down the rail track in a bright bubble of chatter. Watching this happy family scene set a slideshow whirring in my head, flashing up vivid snapshots of a life that never was: trips to the seaside, Christmases and my first, tottering steps towards my mother's open arms.

I shut my eyes, closed the album.

It was nearly time for everything to be resolved.

My mother returned. She took armfuls of bags from the boot and then she shepherded my half-sister inside.

Latif rolled his eyes. "Typical. Your mum's been popping tags."

I ignored him. The door slammed behind them. The shuttered windows gave nothing away.

About ten minutes later, Thames Water drove off.

Bang! An explosive cocktail of emotions was fizzing through my veins with such intensity that I felt as if I might spontaneously combust. I clenched and unclenched my fists, as if they were valves with which I could release the pressure building up inside me. But the waves of excitement and fear kept on colliding.

"Can I go in?" I mouthed. As far as I could see there was nothing suspicious in the street – no cops parked up, no goons on the prowl, no surveillance. Fingers crossed, we were in the clear.

He nodded. "I'll whistle if I see anything out of sync." He whistled, the sound of a nightingale, sharp and shrill. "If you hear that sound, it's time to leave."

I nodded, but didn't move. The woman with all the answers lived right over there. And that scared the hell out of me.

"Go on then! Roll."

Still, I didn't move.

Latif squeezed my arm. "Dash, she's going to love you."

"But…"

He put a finger to his lips. "You'll never know if you don't get over there right now and find out." He gave me a gentle push. "Go. Get out of here, bubblehead. I haven't become public enemy number one so you can hang out in trees looking tragic. Truth!"

"But what if…"

"Cut the 'what ifs', Dash," he hissed. "You were sure about everything until now. She's your mother. And you're right, she's the only person in the world right now who can save you from those comedians. She looks cool. Kind. Like you."

"Yeah. I know." I smiled half-heartedly. "It's going to be awesome."

"And if you don't get out of here, I'm gone. Believe it!" He winked. That crooked smile again. "Now go."

I slid down from the tree and crept through the undergrowth. When I drew level with my mother's house, I took a few seconds to collect my thoughts, before scooting across the road – heart pounding. My stomach jack-in-a-boxed as the latch on the little green gate squeaked open. Then I started up the path, hesitantly, as if I were playing grandmother's footsteps.

The bell ding-donged around the house, sad and portentous.

Nothing.

I rang again. The shuttered house remained silent.

Third time lucky, I thought, pressing the bell again, long and hard this time, belligerent even – overcompensating for how anxious I was feeling inside.

The skip of footsteps – light and breezy.

My heart skipped too. Don't peek. Don't peek. But the anticipation was too much. I pushed the letterbox open a fraction with my fingertips and was about to peep when I heard bolts being drawn back one by one. The door opened a crack. A girl peered out; her eyes level with the security chain. My hopes crashed down into my trainers.

"Yes?" Brattish.

"Is your mother in?" I could hardly form the words as I scanned the girl's pouty face for family resemblances.

Jealousy ripped through me. How come she got to live with our mum?

"What do you want?" She didn't draw back the chain.

"I'd like to speak to your mother if she's in." A heartbeat hesitation. "I'm Sadie. I need to talk to your mother urgently. She'll know what it's about." I thought I saw a glimmer of recognition in my half-sister's eyes. "*I'm Sadie,*" I repeated so she wouldn't forget.

She drew back the chain, the door edged open.

A rush of stale air.

"This way."

So much for the tearful reunion on the doorstep, I thought bitterly, as I followed the little stranger through a dingy hallway and into the sitting room.

"Wait here while I go and get her. She's upstairs." The girl disappeared.

I heard my half-sister shouting, "*Mum,*" as she climbed the stairs. Again I felt a twist of jealousy in my stomach.

A sitting room of sorts.

A dump.

Dustsheets covered the furniture as if my mother were redecorating, except there was no smell of paint. Cardboard boxes were stacked at the far end of the room while an oriental screen dotted with turquoise hummingbirds blocked a closed door leading to another room. The windows were shuttered with wooden doors and the walls were bare.

Without natural light the gloomy room felt claustrophobic.

Sheez, I thought, *is my mother some kind of vampire?*

I wanted to open the shutters, but decided against it. I was a guest, after all.

There was stuff all over the floor – plastic bottles, rolls of masking tape and cable wire. A mess.

A smoke alarm blinked an evil red eye.

There were framed photos in one of the boxes. I walked over and studied a Polaroid of my mother, posing in sunglasses, a cigarette balanced between her fingers, like a movie star from the 1960s. She was wearing a little black dress and she looked so sophisticated. I picked up the frame and looked more closely, searching out similarities. We had the same heart-shaped face, pale complexion, green eyes and black hair. The features worked better on my mother, though. I sighed. One day I might look like her, if the Golds quit controlling me.

My gaze strayed to a wedding photo. My mother was standing arm in arm with an ordinary-looking man, my stepdad, I guessed, outside a scruffy urban church. He looked uncomfortable in his cheap, ill-fitting suit, while she was stunning in a sequined flapper dress. She had a faraway look in her eyes, as if troubled by secret thoughts.

The rest were family shots: a whole life in photos – Halloween, Christmas and happy holiday snaps – the life I should have had.

All of a sudden the room felt hot, oppressive, threatening even. I steadied myself against the mantelpiece and took a few deep breaths, trying to space out the butterflies in my stomach. A scraping sound from the next room startled me.

I straightened up slowly and crept towards the screen.

The lights went out.

I froze.

For a few moments, I stood there, rooted to the spot, my eyes wide as saucers, seaching the darkness while my ears, like antennae, scanned the house for the slightest sound.

Whispers.

A heavy tread, followed by the tick-tack-tack of high heels.

Then a light went on in the hall. Immediately I started groping my way towards the strip of light beneath the door. In seconds I was turning the handle, but it wouldn't budge. My first instinct was to shout for help, but not wanting to appear rude at best and insane at worst, I took a deep breath instead.

Hold it together, Dash. Stay cool.

"Hello? Hello? Is there anyone out there?" In the pitch black, my voice came out lispy and spectral. A slither of fear.

"Keep calm. It's okay," a man shouted.

The doorknob jagged in my hand as the handle turned from the other side.

The clack of heels from down the hallway kick-started my heart.

"Stand back." The male voice came again. "We're going to force the door." The orders were delivered with clipped authority. It calmed my nerves.

I backed away, taking refuge behind the sofa, eyes wide, peeping over the top like a cartoon character in a fix. I jumped when the guy rammed his shoulder against the door. The impact shuddered the glass in the window frames.

With the second thud, the door swung open and a man came crashing into the room.

"Dasha?" His SUV-sized silhouette filled the doorway. "You okay?"

I stood up hesitantly. Who was this man? My stepfather? My mother's boyfriend? From my first impression he seemed much bigger than the guy in the photo, but before I could get a better look at him, he backed out.

It was then I saw her.

My mother.

She looked so beautiful standing there, pooled in light.

An emotional fusebox blew in my head.

Although her face was in shadow, I recognised her instantly. She was dressed from head to toe in black – skirt, jumper and T-bar heels – apart from a white shirt with a round collar. The effect was stunning, but subdued – almost nun-like. Around her neck was a chain with a silver cross. Raising it to her lips, she kissed it, and murmured something, which I didn't catch. She appeared to be praying. Instantly my thoughts went back to the candlelit vigil on TV, and I started to feel uneasy. Had the whole world gone nuts for praying?

My mother lifted her head. The spookiness of our likeness made my stomach jump. Something shifted inside me. A shiver of recognition shot up my spine. A crackle of connection tingled every millimetre of my skin. Her emerald eyes flashed in the light as she searched me out in the gloom. Then they fixed me.

"Dasha?"

"Mum?" My voice was tiny, as if I were speaking from the bottom of the world.

Then she was rushing towards me with a click, click of shoes, and next second she was scooping me up in her arms. I enjoyed the sensation of letting go – of being swept up in the moment. I sank into her arms as they closed around me. She pressed my head to her chest. Our hearts were beating in time. For a moment it was as if two had become one. I felt as if I'd found the missing part of the jigsaw. My blood fizzed. As she stroked my hair, she said: "Dasha. Thank God. We've been out of our minds with worry. It's over. We're here now, angel. You're safe. Everything is going to be okay."

We? Why was she using the royal we? I looked around the room. It was empty. The bald guy had disappeared. Who was he, anyway? Something was niggling. Something didn't feel right.

"Thank God, you're safe. Alive. We were terrified. We thought you were dead."

Alive? Terrified? Dead? Nothing was playing out how I'd imagined it would. Over the last month, I had conjured up thousands of reunion scenarios, but none were anywhere near as bizarre as the one unfolding right now. The power cut, the jammed door, the strange man, my half-sister, and now my mother acting weirdly. I felt wrong-footed, unbalanced. In the rush of it all I had lost my bearings. I wriggled free and was about to say: "What do you mean *we* thought you were *dead*?" when I realised my mum had probably been watching the wall-to-wall news coverage of my kidnap. My heart sank. I didn't want to go into all that now. The lies. The kidnap. That was going to take some explaining. I stepped away, wanting space to breathe. I was suffocating.

"Dasha? Are you okay?'

"Yeah, sort of," I said, massaging my temples with my fingertips, trying to unscramble my thoughts.

"You're all over the news, Dasha. The whole of Britain is obsessed by your story. To be honest, I can't believe my own eyes. You! Here!" She pressed her earlobe nervously as she spoke. "One minute I'm watching a news item on TV about your kidnap. The next you're here. It's too much! It's amazing. *You — here like this.*"

"I guess," I said, desperately wanting to bring it back to the things that mattered. "I mean, yes, it's amazing…"

"A miracle." Her words gushed over mine. "I've been glued to the news ever since you went missing. I was petrified something awful was going to happen to you. And then the doorbell goes and Lily comes upstairs and says someone called Sadie's here to see me. But she's looking at me strangely, and then she comes right out with it: 'Mum, it's the girl from the news. The missing girl.' That's when I knew for sure that my beautiful baby Sadie is Dasha Gold. I'd always had my suspicions, but now it was fact. I almost fainted on the spot. I couldn't believe my baby girl was here. Out of the blue. Like some kind of angel."

I took a deep breath, pressing my fingertips against my temples, trying to work out a way to manage the situation. I had come here for the truth, for answers. The lies could wait. The media storm, the kidnap and the chase weren't important. They weren't even real. They'd been invented by the Golds.

"I don't want to talk about the kidnap." My voice sounded strange, distant somehow. "Not right now."

"Oh, I'm sorry. Of course you don't, my poor baby. It must have been terrifying for you. Such an ordeal." She beckoned me with small hand movements. "Come here, Dasha. I want to check you're for real. That I'm not dreaming."

Instead of going over, I crossed to the other side of the room, wanting to put distance between us. The dark space seemed to stretch all the way back to the moment when she had given me up for adoption. It represented my mother's years of absence.

A look of confusion scudded across her face.

I cleared my throat, the sound of a marble hitting the floor. "I want to take things more slowly, Mum. I've got so many questions."

"Okay. Okay." She held up her hands and backed off. "We'll take things more slowly, if that's what you want. It's just you… here… it's hard to get to grips with. To believe…" She lost momentum and tailed off sadly. She walked over to the standing lamp and switched it on. "Sorry about the lights. A fuse blew. Everything's gone haywire since the pipes burst." When she turned back, she was smiling and appeared less agitated. "That's better!" she said. "Now I can really see you."

Her eyes travelled across my face, taking in every feature. When she smiled I noticed the lines around her eyes wrinkled up. Fascinated, I studied her more closely. In my world, adult's faces were as taut and smooth as masks. Plastic. They didn't register emotion. I loved the way the lines around Maxine's face and mouth highlighted her smile, authenticating the emotion somehow.

"It's uncanny! You look so much like me." She smiled again. "Totally uncanny!" Her wrinkles made her easy to read. She was genuinely pleased to see me.

"I know," I mumbled, relaxing a little. "Spooky, isn't it?"

We carried on studying each other for a little longer, and then my mother murmured, "The truth is, Dasha, there hasn't been a single day since I gave you up for adoption that I haven't thought about you. I've missed you every day. Every night. Every minute." She wiped a tear from the corner of her left eye. "You are always in my thoughts. My beautiful baby daughter."

I pictured my mother handing her baby daughter over to a nurse, who would in turn hand me over to the Golds in an elaborate and expensive game of pass the parcel. I clenched my fists; I could feel a dark, furious force rising up from my gut.

I would have been so tiny, so fragile and so totally helpless. Something clicked, but in a bad way. Boom! And every negative emotion I'd experienced since my mother had showed up at my parents' house ripped through me, like a storm twister. All the anger, resentment and doubt exploded somewhere deep inside me. But my fury sharpened my thought processes so everything fell away, apart from the one question that mattered: "Why did you abandon me?"

My mother flinched. "I didn't abandon you," she said gently. "Not in my heart."

"Like hell. Mother goes MIA for sixteen years. If that's not abandoning me, I don't know what is." My voice trembled with emotion.

She was walking towards me, arms wide, as if another hug would solve everything. My chest constricted because the idea of touching my mother right now felt about as natural as hugging a stranger. I stepped back. My legs pressed against the sofa. Not this. Not now. Next minute my mother's arms folded around me. This time it didn't feel right. The stiffness of the embrace jarred. Our bones knocked and stuttered against each other. *We didn't fit.*

I pushed her away.

"What's wrong, Dasha?" Pain flashed in her eyes.

"Just answer my question." It was as if I couldn't carry any more. I couldn't live for another second without knowing the answer to this one question. "I need to know why you *abandoned* me?"

"I didn't abandon you." My mother's eyes took on the faraway look, which I'd seen in her wedding photo. She seemed to be retreating into her own world.

"That's how it feels."

"I gave you up for adoption, Dasha. It was complicated."

"Yeah. Right. You didn't give me up. You sold me. I've seen the files."

She wouldn't meet my eyes.

"You signed me up to FuturePerfect, had my genes

mapped and then you sold me to the Golds. How could you do that?" I glared at her. "Was it for the money?

"No, I did it because I had to. You've got to understand, Dasha. I was young, broke and without a future. It's hard being a civilian with no options. I didn't want that for you. I wanted to give you a better life. The agency said your parents were beautiful, wealthy people, who would give you a wonderful home. They promised me that you'd have a global lifestyle. That you'd be one of the one per cent."

"Big deal." I fixed her with a steely look, enjoying her discomfort. "I still don't get it. Why did you sell me to a pair of psychos? How could you be so cruel? How could you care so little?"

"It wasn't like that."

"What was it like?"

Maxine sank down into an armchair. "I want you to hear the whole story. Then, hopefully, you'll understand how complicated things really were."

She took a few moments to gather her thoughts, as if sifting through various versions of her story, deciding on which would best suit. But once she got going she spoke quickly and fluently, as though she'd rehearsed the story in her head a million times, polishing it with each retelling. She was a good storyteller, too, knowing what elements to play up or embellish, weaving a web of words with which to ensnare her daughter, shaping it into a fairytale, reeling me in.

My mother stressed I had been a wanted baby, a love child, a happy mistake. She described how she had loved being pregnant with me. "Every moment. Every second. Every nanosecond." She made as if she were measuring out the smallest unit of time with her fingers. "It was the happiest time of my life. It was a magical eight months." Tears welled up as she explained how I'd been so special to both her and Zac, curled up deep inside her belly — no bigger than a fingernail with a tiny beating heart. She touched her tummy and smiled. "Yes, you were very special to us. We wanted you to rule the world." She went on to describe how the summer of her pregnancy had been so hot and sticky that she and Zac used to lie out in the garden at night to keep cool, looking up at the stars while thinking up names and speculating on which features and characteristics their baby would inherit. "But no matter what, we'd always give you Zac's smile."

I smiled.

"And you know what, Dasha? You've got his smile."

My smile widened.

My mother paused as if she were remembering those treasured moments. Then she let out a small sigh, before going on to recount how they'd cooed over the ultrasound, marvelled over their beautiful fairy-child floating in her own magical world. With a dreamy look in her eyes, she explained how they'd play music for me and how they'd even compiled my very own top ten *in utero* hits.

I was hooked. I'd been a wanted child. My parents had adored me. They had loved me to pieces. They thought I was special. It was as if she had cut a knot of anger in my stomach. I slowly began to relax.

My mother took my hand. This time I was smiling. All my earlier resentment and anger had receded. The connection was warm, real. It fizzed.

"This is the hard bit. I need you to try and put yourself in my shoes."

I tensed. I knew what was coming.

My mother squeezed my hand. "You ready?"

I nodded as we sat down on the sofa, still holding hands.

She took a deep breath before going on to describe the events of that terrible night. How Zac had nipped out to pick up an Indian takeaway on his motorcycle. Her panic when he hadn't come home. The police phone call that confirmed her worst fears. The emptiness. The sadness. The infinite nothingness of a world without Zac.

She wiped a tear from the corner of her eye. "And then there was you." She sniffed back sobs. "I'd just finished university and I knew I wouldn't cope. Single. Home alone with a baby. I had no funds. This wasn't the life I'd dreamed of — I wanted the world." She stared down at the floor. "I wanted a life."

I withdrew my hand from hers. "You had a life — *me*."

My mother looked down at her empty hand. "If only it had been that easy. You've got to understand. The man I loved — your father — had just been killed. I was a mess. It was far too late for an abortion. I was saddled with crippling student debt. I needed space. Looking after a baby would have driven me over the edge. You have to believe me — giving you up was the hardest decision I have ever made.

The hardest thing I have ever had to do. No mother wants to give up her child, and you were such a beautiful baby when you arrived. You've got to understand. It was the only way." She leaned forwards and fixed me with a pleading look. "Please understand. I had no choice."

"Yes, you did." I jumped up and walked across the room.

"I'm sorry, Dasha. I was young. I wish I could go back and change things, but I can't. All I can do is pray we can work things out. That you can find it in your heart to forgive me."

"Forgive you?" I spun round angrily. "Just like that?"

"Yes. Sometimes things are tough. Complicated. That's life. You'll find out soon enough." My mother stood up and held out her arms tentatively. "Give me a chance. Don't hate me. I want to make things up to you."

"Is that why you came to the Golds' house?"

A look of surprise crossed her face. She smiled. "Yes. I was looking for you. I wanted to see you. I had to know if you were my baby." There was something so warm, so genuine in her voice that I wanted to forgive her immediately.

Once again I could feel myself getting whooshed away on a sea of emotion. I pulled back. I had to ride the wave. I mustn't go under, not yet. I still had some detective work to do.

"But why did you sign up to FuturePerfect?"

"Really? You want to go into that?"

"Yes, I want to understand everything."

She pressed her earlobe nervously. "Okay, if you're sure." She looked reluctant to go into it, but glancing up and seeing my take-no-prisoners expression, she continued hesitantly.

"I'd heard rumours about this adoption agency, which guaranteed that kids who were on their books would get the best chances in life. A global lifestyle, if you will. There was one catch; they would only take on kids with advanced genes. Which meant, in order to get your baby signed up, you had to agree to all kinds of tests. Your child's DNA had to be screened for illness and mapped for intelligence, longevity, physical characteristics and a million other things. The agency wanted quality kids for their rich clients. They'd spotted a gap in the market; globals didn't want scrapheap kids – their words, not mine. By sequencing a child's genetic code FuturePerfect gave wealthy couples, who were prepared to pay for FuturePerfect's services, the chance to choose their kid's genetic make-up. They could read the code like a book, put their money on a winner." She shrugged. "I thought it offered a solution for both of us. I would get money to continue my education, pay off my student loans and get my life on track, while you would get an unbelievable start in life as well as the stability that I couldn't provide. Things were rough for civilians. No jobs. No prospects. I had no bank of Mummy and Daddy to fall back on. I didn't want to end up living in Crunch Town. FuturePerfect offered me a way out. Once you were on FuturePerfect's books things started happening really fast. Not in a million years did I think your DNA profile would be accepted, let alone snapped up. But to my amazement they found a match for you immediately. Apparently your DNA profile fitted the Golds' wish list exactly. The whole process was anonymous. Top secret. Although recently,

I had begun to suspect you were my daughter. We look so similar, for starters. I could almost feel the chemistry through the television."

"So that's why you came looking for me?"

"Yes. I wanted to make amends. The truth is I had regretted my decision to give you up for adoption instantly. But I had signed legal documents with a terrifying confidentiality clause. I'd taken a vow of secrecy. There was no hope of getting you back... Please don't judge me."

Suddenly Latif's words came into my head: *Don't judge.* That was when I knew I had to climb into my mother's skin and try to understand things from her point of view.

I folded my arms and fixed my mother with a cool stare as I considered my options. I could leave in a huff, go back to the psychos, lose myself in the celebrity bubble. But was that what I really wanted? Alternatively, we could try and work things out, see what happened. Okay, things hadn't turned out exactly how I'd wanted. But I'd conjured up a fairytale happy-ever-after ending. I'd constructed a perfect mother and a perfect love, neither of which could have survived a minute in the real world. I unfolded my arms. I had to give my mother a chance. At least we were here together. That was a start. That's what I'd always wanted. And my mother was lovely, smiley and genuinely happy to see me – a bit sad, fragile. But life hadn't been kind.

"It's great to be here with you, Mum," I said sheepishly. "Sorry about acting like a complete idiot and giving you a hard time."

"No problem." Her face lit up.

"The whole situation threw me. I've spent so long thinking about…" My arms windmilled. "What you'd be like. What this would be like. You know, the first meeting and stuff. I just freaked when it became real. Sometimes things just don't work out the way you expect."

"So you're saying I'm a disappointment?" A mischievous smile played around my mother's mouth. "That I didn't live up to expectations?"

"No, no, that's not what I meant," I said, walking towards her. I was smiling, too. We shared the same sense of humour. We embraced again, and this time it wasn't so bumpy and unnatural. We could work it out – it would just take time. I could feel tears welling up. Life was messy. I started sobbing.

"Ssh. Take it easy." My mother was stroking my hair. "I'm here for you now. We'll sort everything out. We've got each other."

I smiled through my tears. This time her use of 'we' sounded right.

"Is everything going to be okay, Mum?

"Yes, Dasha. We're going to do great."

I hugged her tight.

"It must have been terrifying for you, angel. It's all okay now. Dad's on his way. He's been with the PM. He's outside with the police."

"Dad?" I pushed her away. "I thought you said he was dead."

Lights, Camera, Action

MOMENTS later.

Dazzling light.

I squinted up into the glare.

A spotlight had risen above the Chinese screen, fixing us to the spot.

"What's going on?" I demanded, trying to wriggle from my mother's grip.

"It's okay, darling." My mother clamped her hand to the back of my head, pressing my face into her chest. "Ssssh. Don't cry. There's no need to worry any more." She was stroking my hair. "We're here now. It's all over, angel." My mother was speaking loudly, as if auditioning for a part. "Dad's coming."

I pushed her away.

Footsteps in the hall.

"What's going on?" I repeated, trying to look beyond the dazzling light.

The Chinese screen was concertinaed now and the second door was open, revealing a spacious conservatory, and as my eyes became more accustomed to the glare, I saw shadows, which slowly morphed into men, dressed in black, like mime artists. Two were holding television lights while a third was operating a camera and a fourth thrust a furry sound-boom in my direction. Despite the heat from the television lights, I felt chilled to the bone.

From the hallway a whiff of 'Treachery' – my *other mother's* signature perfume – reached me. Followed by the tick-tack-tack of heels. A moment later, Tamara Gold sailed into the room while Maxine edged back towards the door, as if they were connected by an elaborate pulley system. My mouth gaped open. Two mothers dressed identically: one receding, the other advancing. A double vision moment. A second later, Dad marched into the room and greeted me with an oil-slick smile.

"Hello, Dash," he said, slipping his arm around his wife's waist. "So what kept you?" He smiled. A slash of perfect white.

They stood there like a couple of swank-pots enjoying my surprise. How the hell had they got here so quickly? Had they cracked time travel, too? Under the television lights my parents appeared like Hollywood stars posing on the red carpet – all composure and gloss. Meanwhile I gawked and twitched like a talent-show hopeful, waiting for the judges to rip me to pieces.

Each second seemed a year apart.

"You shouldn't have taken us on, precious," Dad said with an amused sneer. "What were you thinking?"

"Thinking straight for once. For myself."

"And look where that's got you." His eyes glinted with amusement, but he was looking at me with intense interest, as if he were seeing a whole new side to me.

"What the freak are you two doing here, anyway?"

"Don't sound so surprised, Dasha." Tamara arched a perfectly plucked eyebrow. "Did you really think we wouldn't work out your little scheme, that we'd let you go without a fight? You underestimate us, Dasha – my little ingrate. We came in with the Thames Water chaps." Hardboiled eyes. Pupils big as snooker balls. She'd been taking stuff, which always made her mean.

"How did you know I was looking for Maxine?"

"Credit where credit's due, Dash." Dad was still lasering me with his intense look. "You gave us a real headache. To start with we hadn't a clue what your game was. We couldn't think why you'd take off with a hooligan. When we saw the CCTV footage of you two together, we couldn't work out the connection. We had no idea how you could have met someone so *street*." He spat the word from his mouth, as if he feared it might give him an ulcer. "It took time to get the authority to access your electronic footprint, but once we had permission it was a breeze. Nothing in your recent search history on Google, Facebook postings or emails, although fascinating, gave us any clues. We checked right back. It's only when we accessed the academy's computer system that we finally discovered your little obsession. Your attempts to access FuturePerfect's site, your research into adoption and your nightly chats on forums."

"Is nothing private?"

"Nope. Not these days. The breakthrough came in the early hours of this morning. The police missed you at FuturePerfect, but we figured you'd head here. And here you are." A smarmy smile stretched his lips.

"Anyway, we've got a few matters to straighten up, haven't we, darling? Make things right." Tamara held my gaze for a moment before locking eyes with Maxine. "And the sooner you discover the truth about your *birth* mother, the sooner we can get on with our lives."

Blanking the Golds, I turned to Maxine and said, "What's she talking about, Mum?"

Maxine was staring at the floor.

"It is time to come clean, Maxine." Tamara Gold glided towards her. "Time to let Dasha know what a truly tragic human being you are."

Maxine shrank away, clamping her hands over her ears. Tamara batted them away and snatched a concealed earpiece from behind Maxine's ear. She held it up with a flourish. "You haven't been totally straight with your daughter, have you?" she said, as she removed a hidden mike from beneath the lapel of Maxine's jacket.

"No way!" I glared at Maxine. "Seriously? Were you taking directions from these psychos?"

One mother looked mortified, the other looked triumphant, while my father rocked back and forth on his heels, enjoying the show.

"Of course she was. We stage-managed the whole scene." Dad raised his eyes to the winking red light of the smoke alarm.

I followed his gaze. "What? Secret cameras?" I frowned. "But why?"

"A little safety precaution. Viewers love a happy ending. A family reunion."

I still didn't get it. "Why would you shoot a reunion with me and Maxine?" I frowned. "There's nothing in it for you."

But even as I spoke, seeing the two women standing side by side, my parents' game became clear. Both mothers were styled in the same way. This meant they could construct a totally different scene in the edit. All it would take was a few clever cutaways, some creative editing and some extra filming with Tamara, and then, abracadabra! One similarly styled mother would morph into the other. The black suit, the white collar, distinctive T-bar shoes and the crucifixes: all these identical elements could be intercut and spliced together, allowing the conjuring trick to take place.

"Think about it, Dasha. I will become Maxine in the edit." Tamara clicked her fingers. "Simple as that. We are filming a Gold reunion. We came here to create our version of events."

"As usual," I snapped, and then, turning back to Maxine, I asked, "So was *everything* staged?" Even as I asked, the memory of her pressing her earlobe flashed into my head.

Maxine refused to look me in the eye, shifting her weight from foot to foot.

"Time to tell Dasha the truth, Maxine." My father moved closer, invading her space. She looked up at him pleadingly. Still she didn't speak.

Tamara filled the silence, relishing the opportunity to explain the tacky truth. "We needed certain shots, you know, something that visually said 'happy ever after' as well as a few key phrases and pick-ups so it would work in the edit. We almost captured the whole scene with the first hug, but you freaked out before we got the complete script in the bag."

"So you turned the most important moment of my life into a soap opera. Fabulous." I glared at my so-called parents. "No wonder I'm on the run."

Then I turned my sights on Maxine. "Why did you agree to go along with them?"

"Why did you play the game, Maxine? Your daughter wants to know," Dad needled, as he and Tamara moved towards her in a pincer movement. Maxine retreated, pressing against the wall in a star shape, as if pinned to it by their stares. She reminded me of a beautiful butterfly on display in a speciman cabinet. When she didn't speak, Dad replied on her behalf.

"Money, of course, and, like a true professional, Maxine delivered."

My mouth dropped open. "No way." For a few seconds, I was lost for words. Shell-shocked. When I continued, my tone was sharp. "For money?" Anger was bubbling up inside me like a toxic gas. My hands clenched and unclenched, but my fury kept escalating, and then, boom, I exploded. "Abandoning me – or should I say selling me – as a baby was rubbish. But not half as rubbish as playing the loving mother, while hamming it up for the cameras, so you'd get another big fat pay-off." Tears were streaming down my face. I wiped them away angrily. "'Sakes, you're as bad as them. What about all that stuff you spouted? About how you loved being pregnant with me. How it was the happiest time of your life. The most magical eight months." I sniffed back sobs. "Was that all fake?"

"Padding," Tamara chipped in, her smile wide and vacant as a ballroom dancer's. "We told Maxine to get emotional. We needed her to soften you up, win you round. We needed to film a second hug with the line about Dad and the police. The money shot."

"What did they pay you?"

Maxine wouldn't meet my gaze. She wiped away a tear.

"Half a million pounds, a makeover and a duplex in Dubai," Tamara replied on Maxine's behalf, only too happy to fill me in.

"Is that what I'm worth to you?" My voice was tight. "Tell me, Mum."

Her face crumpled.

Dad towered over her. "Go on, Maxine." He moved closer, casting a shadow across her face. "Tell her." She cowered away, as if he'd raised his hand to hit her.

"You're a Gold. You're worth billions." Maxine's voice was little more than a whisper. "I gave you up for adoption so you could have a better chance in life. Most kids would do anything to be a celebrity. *To be you.* Don't throw it all away. For what? To be anonymous. It is worse than a death sentence. Believe me."

"What Maxine is trying to say is that you're an ungrateful little wretch," Dad said, taking control again.

"Shut up!" I snapped. "Get your nose out of my life, Dad.

I want to hear what Maxine has to say. *Not you.*" I focused on Maxine, eyes drilling into her. Unlike my parents, her face gave away her emotions. She looked defeated. "I still don't get it. Why would you take their money? Why would you betray your own daughter?"

Maxine stumbled on. "Your parents have given you an amazing life. They want you back. Take it from me – you wouldn't want to be in my life. My luck ran out. I'm at the end of the line, broke and broken. You must make the most of your good luck." Her words sounded scripted; there was something hollow about her delivery.

"Good luck?" I scrunched up my face sceptically. "Do you really believe that?"

"Yes." She shifted uneasily, still trapped in Dad's stare.

"What's wrong with you?" I shook my head miserably.

"I'm sorry, Dasha." Maxine was shrinking into herself, her body language was becoming more and more closed. "I'm going to make the most of this opportunity. You should go back to the Golds and make the most of yours. Please try and understand. This is what I want now." I still had the feeling she was speaking lines.

"It seems you keep on showing up at the wrong time in her life, Dash." Dad was enjoying himself. "Isn't that right, Maxine?"

"Dasha, please. It's too late to fix things." Maxine's words were small and broken, the sound of a snail's shell crushed underfoot. She had no power to stand up to my dad. The trouble was *nobody* did.

I stared at the floorboards. Maxine was as rubbish as everyone else in my life, apart from Latif. I toed one of the plastic bottles lying at my feet, tears rolling down my cheeks. A skull and crossbones, which was printed on the label, rocked back and forth. I felt like it was hexing me.

A thought flashed in the fug of my sadness. "Why did you turn up at my parents' house, if you didn't want to see me again?" I asked, lifting my gaze.

Her eyes flicked up to my father. Irritation slid across his smooth face. My stomach tightened.

"Blackmail. What else?" he said quickly. "We paid her off and sent her packing."

I remembered the police cars outside our house.

"You're lying, Dad. I overheard you and Mum talking. You didn't give her money. The police handled it."

"She was demanding money, Dash." He cracked his knuckles.

"Is that the truth?" I asked Maxine urgently. "I know he's lying. This is your chance to make things right, Mum. I don't care about the rest – the money, the adoption, tonight – just tell me what happened that night in Dad's study." The Golds were crowding her out. "Please do this one thing for me, Mum." I was shouting. "*Stand up to them.*"

Maxine stood frozen to the spot for a second or two, and then, using the wall to pull herself up to her full height, she started talking in a rush. "I love you, Dasha. It's never been about the money. I promise." There was grit in her voice now. "That night in his study, Mr Gold said there would be terrible consequences if I broke our contract. He said they would take Lily away. Put her in a foster home. That I would go to jail for being an imposter."

My father was shouting for backup.

Maxine raised her voice. "I promise it wasn't about the money. I came to the house because I wanted to see you. Say sorry. Nothing can change that. I played their game because I had no choice. Everything I said about being pregnant with you, about Zac, about our love for you was true. I wasn't faking, I promise. I love you."

I ran over to my mother and flung my arms around her as the man who I'd initially thought was my stepfather stormed into the room.

"They forced me. Blackmai—" The goon's hand was over her mouth. My father's hands gripped my shoulders and he was pulling me back. I kept hold of my mother's hand until they wrenched us apart. "No, Mum!" I screamed as the heavy marched her towards the door. She shouted something, but his huge hand smothered her words. It sounded like "I love you," again but I couldn't be sure.

Next moment, Maxine was gone.

My heart was constricting. I imagined it brown and shrivelled, walnut-sized. I couldn't look at the Golds. Those vampires had sucked me dry. I hated them.

"Quite the drama, eh?" Dad said, with a smile. "You should have stuck with us, precious."

"You blackmailed her. That's the pits," I whispered, all punched out.

"Maxine was merely saying what she knew you wanted to hear to ease her money-grabbing conscience. Believe what you want, but she made it very clear to us that she doesn't want you in her life."

"But you do?" I looked daggers. "Lucky me!"

"So?" Tamara asked pointedly.

"So, what?" I balled my fists, scanning the room for an escape route. The TV crew was in the conservatory. The slaphead was guarding the door. The windows were shuttered. There wasn't a hope in hell of making a break for it.

"What's this about, Dash? Why are you so angry with us?" Tamara asked. "Is it because we didn't tell you that you were adopted? Is that why you ran away?" She was looking at me as if she actually cared. "Darling, we were trying to do the best for you, I promise. We took advice from experts. We were going to tell you everything when you were eighteen. That's normal procedure." Tamara had slipped into her smooth, brisk chat-show voice.

"Normal procedure? You screened my DNA and you bought me like a must-have accessory. Then you trademarked my name. That's not normal." My gestures were getting stabby. "It's not just the adoption. It's everything. Finding out about my mother is only part of it. I'd had my doubts ever since I realised the extent of the procedures, and then, when I realised you were going to force me to have surgery even though you knew I was dead set against it, that's when I wanted out big time. Why would you want to change me, anyway? How do you think that makes me feel? Beautiful?

Loved? No, I feel like trash. A disappointment. A loser. I don't understand why you can't you love me for who I am."

"Of course we love you…"

"Yeah. Right," I snapped. "Why would you want to change me if you loved me? Parents are meant to love their children. *Whatever.* The fact you don't breaks my heart."

The room was spinning now. I put my head in my hands. I didn't want them to see how upset I was.

"Come on, Dash. We love you very much. We'd do anything for you." Tamara's tone was conciliatory. She came over and, crouching down beside me, took my hand and squeezed it reassuringly. "Dad is going to turn you into a superstar. On your birthday we'll launch you as the face of the brand. Next stop – global fame. Every girl's dream. After you've had the procedures your life will be super-fabulous, I promise. Every girl at the Star Academy would kill to be in your shoes."

"You still don't get it, do you? I don't want to be the face of the brand! I don't want to be famous or a superstar. I just want you to love me for who I am. But you're not capable of doing that because you only care about the freaking brand." My hand gestures were getting wild. "You're both screwy. Your world is twisted. Everything you value is wrong." I clasped my hands to stop them windmilling. "That's why I want to get out of the celebrity bubble."

"To live like a civilian?" Dad exchanged an amused look with Tamara. "How very noble."

"Yeah, right. Make a joke of it. As usual." I wanted to smash their smug heads together.

"We only want to do what's best for you," Dad said.

"Tough! Because I'm going to do my own thing. Find my own way without you dictating everything. I'm sick of having my life run by a couple of control freaks."

"All teenagers resent their parents at some point." Tamara was in TV mode again, sympathetic and reasonable. "Think they know best. It's a phase you have to go through. But in ten years' time, you'll look back and thank us, I promise."

"It's not a phase. It's what I believe. Hanging out with Latif has helped me see things more clearly. He's a million times better than you and your lies. He thinks you're fakes. That your world is shallow. False." I spoke slowly and calmly, ramming each point home.

"Of course," Dad said patiently. "That must be why lover boy accepted our bribes and agreed to help us. That's why he brought you here. You were too shallow for his tastes." His words were like a blow to the head. "One phone call. Total time to change his mind: five minutes."

"What?"

A terrifying emptiness engulfed me.

"You heard."

"No way." Words tumbled out in a panic. "Latif wouldn't do that. He's not a sell-out. I don't believe you. He's just not like that." Despite my forthright words, doubt nagged at the back of my mind.

"Is that so?" He raised a perfectly shaped eyebrow.

"I know you're lying," I whispered, clutching at my throat. I could barely breathe.

"Everyone has a price, Dash," Dad said. "I thought you'd know that by now."

"He wouldn't hand me in for money," I whispered. "It's not his style."

"Why are we here if he didn't tip us off? Think about it." His tone was triumphant. "I said we figured it out, but in fact, we were told"

A long pause while I tried to work things out. But my brain had logged out.

Sensing victory, Tamara said, "Dasha, wake up. He betrayed you, darling."

I collapsed down onto the sofa. My world was broken. Maxine's rejection had been hard enough to take, but Latif's as well? That was too much. To think I'd believed that Latif was the one person in my life who didn't have a price tag. A tear trickled down my cheek. He'd seemed so completely genuine. But now I realised that he was the biggest fake of them all.

"Is that really true?" I whispered. "Please, for once, I want the truth." As soon as the words left my mouth, I wondered why I'd bothered.

"People let you down, baby. That's life."

What a cow, I thought, eyes smarting. She might as well have gouged her three-inch heels into my eye sockets — it would have been less painful.

But something niggled. Something didn't ring true. For starters, how could Latif have tipped them off? I'd been with him twenty-four/seven, more or less.

"So what was his price?" I asked dubiously. "The million-pound reward?"

"He didn't do it for the money. Come on, Dash, surely you know him better than that. He had a far more *honourable demand*." Dad paused for effect. "Latif's price? His parents' freedom."

I took a sharp breath in, remembering Latif's anguished expression as he'd watched the police arresting his parents on the television. That was when everything fell into place. Latif must have called my parents from the motel bedroom when I was in the bathroom.

Dad wasn't bluffing.

I slumped further back into the sofa. My world tilted. I felt as if I were falling into a dark, dark place from which there would be no escape.

A place without hope.

"Where's Latif now?" I whispered, blinking back tears.

"At present jihad-boy is helping the police with their enquiries. He'll be facing charges of kidnap and terrorism, looking at years behind bars." He flicked a speck of fluff from his suit with manicured fingernails. "But all is not lost for my favourite hood-rat. Luckily I have the ear of the prime minister, so I am in a position to broker a deal."

"But I thought the *deal* was delivering *me* in return for his parents' freedom."

"Well, that's the impression we gave Latif. But you know how things change. The truth of the matter is that his freedom is in your hands…" His smile glittered with malice.

"His future rests with you, Dash."

I felt sick with guilt. I couldn't blame Latif for betraying me. After all, it was thanks to me that his parents had been arrested in the first place. And now he was in prison, too. I pictured him sitting alone in his cell in regulation prison duds.

"So you double-crossed him?"

"Of course. But you can make things right."

"What do you want?" I spoke robotically. "A happy ending? The Golds reunited?"

"You've got the picture, princess."

My gaze shifted to the crew. They were setting up angles for the shots. "So what's '*the story*'?" I made speech marks with my fingers as I sneered the words.

"Look around you. What do you see?" Tamara asked.

"A dump. Two power-crazy psychos."

"Try harder, Dasha." Dad swept his hand around the room, drawing my attention to the bottles and wires. "A bomb factory. Your prison. Latif's lair. We've filmed most of the story already. We've got shots of you holed-up in here, banging on the door and shouting for help. Then there's your rescue and the emotional reunion with your mother – *Tamara*. It's not going to win any awards, but with careful editing we can transmit it, if necessary." He rubbed his palms together. "Now that's a cracking story, don't you think?"

"So why shoot another?"

"We want a slicker version. The real thing. Emotional truth."

"But it'll be acted out."

"Exactly. *Cinéma-vérite.*"

"So if I do it, you'll let him go?"

"You have my word." He said it with about as much conviction as a shop assistant saying, "Have a nice day!"

"For what it's worth." I picked up a length of wire from the sofa — part of Latif's supposed bomb paraphernalia — and twisted it around my fingers. "Happy endings, huh?" I whispered, staring into Dad's highly polished shoes; my face, reflected twice over, was long and gloomy, like a reluctant guest viewed through a spy-hole. "So you promise that Latif can go back to his old life?"

"Not exactly. He'll be tried. Found guilty. Sentenced to years in prison."

"*What?*" I raised my eyes slowly and fixed him with a ferocious stare. "What sort of deal is that?"

"The public wants to see justice done. Good triumph over evil…"

"Yeah, whatever!" I snapped. "Get to the point."

"After he's been convicted and the furore has died down, I will see that Latif receives a new identity. He will gain his freedom, on the condition that he lives abroad and never returns to England. Disappears."

"You're too kind. That's no life."

"It's the only deal I can broker with the prime minister. There's massive public pressure to lock him up and throw away the key. For ever. Amen."

I twisted the cable around my thumb and watched the tip turn purple.

"It's not much of a get-out-of-jail card, is it?" I eyeballed them both.

"It's the only one on offer."

I stared into middle distance. Empty. Defeated.

A mournful trilling from outside filled the silence. The bird sounded as sad as I felt. There it was again. A jolt of electricity shot through my body.

Meeting my father's gaze, I said, "Okay. I'll do it." Although my face was expressionless, my brain was in overdrive.

My parents were bluffing.

The whistle. Latif was outside.

I had to escape.

But how?

"I knew you'd see sense." Dad clicked his fingers at the director. "Get ready to roll the cameras."

My mother clapped her hands and shouted for make-up. Instantly the room was filled with a gossip of hair and make-up artists dressed in white overalls, who rushed around the Golds, as if they were Formula One cars in a pit stop. All was chatter and noise. Except for me, who sat perfectly still – the eye of the fragrant storm that whirled around me.

"Can I have make-up too, please?" I asked, stalling for time.

"You're a hostage, darling," Tamara said, catching my eye in the mirror. "You need to look rough. You're fine as you are."

"Thanks a bunch!" I said, giving her the evils.

I leaned down and picked up one of the bottles from the floor. "So what's this for?" I unscrewed the lid and sniffed the liquid; an acrid smell caught in my throat and made me cough. "Heavy duty!" I spluttered.

"Careful, Dasha!" Tamara warned. "It's sulphuric acid. You know how Dad loves to wind up the health and safety department."

"Terrorist paraphernalia. Brilliant touch, don't you think?" Dad's eyes were shut as a make-up artist applied powder to his face.

"Genius!" I said sarcastically, picking up a second bottle. I unscrewed the cap. Then holding one in each hand like loaded pistols, I stood up and said calmly, "It's show time, folks."

The Golds swivelled round to face me, their eyes wide and crazy. The make-up artists dropped their brushes, twittered and flitted behind the screen.

"Okay guys, I'm out of here. Get back unless you want your faces burned off." My eyes flicked around the room, holding eye contact with each one of them for a second, so they knew there were no exceptions.

My mother was backing up behind the screen with her hands over his face, shouting, "No, my face is my life!"

Dad slid behind the screen, one hand raised, as if he were trying to hide his face from a paparazzo. The television crew had already retreated into the shadows at the first sign of trouble. The heavy edged towards me.

"I'm not joking. Get behind the screen. Now."

He kept on coming forward, eyes fixed on me, trying to psych me out.

I held his gaze. "Behind the screen. Now!" I repeated.

Next thing I knew he was lunging towards me. Without missing a beat, I threw the acid. And as the clear liquid looped towards him in a glistening arc, I spun round and ran from the room, slamming the door on his roar of pain.

The hallway was empty. Upstairs TV people were crowding onto the landing. When one guy started down the stairs, I shouted, "It's acid. It'll take your face off. Stay back. Don't come any closer."

Keeping the bottle trained on the staircase, I opened the front door, took the heavy, metal key from the old-fashioned lock and backed out, like a cowboy leaving a saloon after a ruck. Once outside, I pushed the key into the lock. I could hear people rushing down the stairs and across the hall. My hands were trembling. The key jammed. I shoved it further into the lock and twisted, putting all my strength behind it, until I heard a click. Then I left it in the lock.

Next minute, I was running down the path, shouting for Latif.

I stopped in my tracks.

A man in a motorcycle helmet was sitting astride a bike in the alley next to the house, revving the engine. A goon? I looked around desperately searching out an escape route. Where the hell was Latif? The guy on the bike looked my way.

"Latif?" I shouted, peering into the fading light. I tried to pick out the cherry tree in the copse.

The goon lifted his visor. "Over here, Dash." He revved

the engine and headed out into the road.

Immediately, I was racing down the path. As the gate slammed behind me, I saw security guards piling out of the back garden and running down the alleyway towards us.

"Security's onto us!" I shouted, scrambling up behind Latif.

Latif waited until he felt my arms tighten around his waist before accelerating. The bike reared up. I clung on. Then we were shooting across Orchard Road. We mounted the pavement with a jolt, next minute we were careering down through the trees. When we hit the track, a grit-cloud kicked up behind us like a genie escaping its bottle.

Alley Cats

THE bike ploughed along the disused railway track. I clung to Latif, my arms wrapped around his waist. The warmth from his body reassured me; it helped me understand that this was real – that I wasn't dreaming. Latif. The bike. Escape. They were all real. I tightened my grip. He hadn't betrayed me. He cared. I tipped my head back and looked at the sky. My hair streamed behind me. A cool rush of air sandblasted my face. My blood was charged. Despite everything, I had never felt so alive.

Suddenly the bike's wing mirrors were ablaze with light. I swivelled around. A jeep was chasing us down. Its headlamps dazzled. In a panic, I shouted for Latif to go faster, but our bike was making heavy work of the dirt track. I tensed up. No, that wasn't it. Latif was slowing down.

"What are you doing?" I screamed as we came to halt.

Latif was shouting something. But the engine's roar swallowed up his words. I only caught the word – 'GUN!' After that everything started happening in slo-mo. He kicked down the bike rest, dismounted, took the gun from his pocket, knelt down, took aim, fired. But the jeep kept on hurtling towards us, headlamps glaring and bullying in the gloaming while we remained frozen to the spot. Moments later, a loud bang as the front tyre exploded. Then the jeep swerved off the track, crashing into a tree in a mangle of metal and spinning wheels.

Stunned, I stared at the wreckage. Without saying a word, Latif jumped back on the bike and we were racing along the track again. After about seventy-five metres, he decelerated and, leaving the track, manoeuvred the bike down a steep siding towards a road, which ran parallel to the railway track. The back wheel skidded and dragged in the undergrowth. And as we slalomed between trees, I pressed my face into Latif's hoodie, shielding my face from low-hanging branches, which snagged at my clothes.

When we hit the road, we raced through quiet suburban streets. High-rise security gates. Fortressed houses. Bigwig residences. Security cameras swivelled at every entrance. Switching off the headlamp, Latif accelerated into the blurry twilight, stopping at neither traffic junctions nor lights, tearing through the sleepy 'burbs like an avenging angel, leaning into corners so tightly that on occasions the bike was almost parallel with the road. I clung on. Every now and then I checked over my shoulder. At least we'd lost our pursuers. Slowly my nerves steadied.

After a short while, we approached a busy high street. Latif cut the speed and flicked the lights back on. A young crowd was spilling out of bars and pubs onto the pavements where they stood around drinking, chatting and laughing. As Latif wove through the dawdling traffic, bubbles of tipsy chatter reached me and I found myself wishing more than anything in the world that we could join them, relax and grab a beer – *do something normal,* put the chase on pause for an hour or two.

Latif turned right by a Starbucks into a street lined with shabby business premises. He parked up in the forecourt of a printing shop; kicked down the bike rest and cut the engine.

"We're ditching the bike."

I noticed his hands were trembling.

We left the bike with the key in the ignition, lights on full beam – screaming out to be stolen. He set off at such a pace, I had to break into a run to catch up with him. We had only gone a few metres down the road when he pulled me into a doorway and said, "Lose the hoodie." Reaching into his rucksack, he handed me my wig. "Hide your locks."

I slipped out of the hoodie and was about to tie it round my waist when Latif took it off me. It was a warm night for the time of year, but even so I could feel my skin goosebumping. I rubbed the top of my arms as I watched Latif wipe our fingerprints from the gun with it. Then he headed over to a line of recycling bins.

I placed the wig on my head. Then, crouching down by the side of a parked car, I twisted the wing mirror towards me and made a few adjustments, tucking up stray wisps of my hair, and adding a slash of red lipstick to complete the look. Instantly I felt camouflaged when I saw my 'fugee-self staring back.

The clank of metal against the bottles made me glance up. Latif was already walking back; he looked as if a weight had been lifted from his shoulders. In fact, he appeared to have his swagger back.

"How do I look?" I stared straight into his eyes. "Would you recognise me?"

He narrowed his eyes. "Nah. You're masked!"

I hid my disappoinment.

You're on the run, idiot. Looking hot isn't top priority. But still I felt crushed.

He put on the England shirt, which he'd taken from Yukiko's bag as a last resort, and strode off, pulling a white baseball cap down over his eyes as he went.

"What now?" I asked.

He gave me that sideways glance. The one I hated. "What do you think, bubblehead? Getting the hell off the streets. This barrio will be a hotspot in no time."

I looked up at the sky, I couldn't see any helicopters, but I could sense them. The air was charged. My skin prickled with fear.

Back on the high street, we pushed through clusters of happy punters with booze-pink cheeks. All was noise and jostle. Everywhere I looked, dangly gold earrings, sparkly eyeshadow and ironed hair. An undercurrent of violence rippled, but had yet to make waves. We kept to the most crowded parts of the pavement, trying our best to blend in. Latif led the way, mumbling, "Sorry, mate," every time he knocked an elbow or jogged someone's drink. I fixed my eyes on the pavement.

"What happened back there?" Latif asked, as we left

the crowds behind. "Were the Golds there?

"They arrived in the Thames Water vans, or so they said."

"I knew it was bad when a heavy came out and started nosing around. I jumped him when he walked under the tree. Knocked him out."

"Was that his bike?" I searched Latif's face for signs of a fight.

"Yeah. I borrowed it."

A siren wailed. His eyes darted back and forth, checking the shadows. Up ahead there was a bus station and a railway bridge. Beyond that, Finsbury Park Bowling Alley's neon sign flashed. Latif took my arm.

"Fancy bowling?"

I held back, unsure if I had understood his drift. "What? Are you mad?" I asked, goggle-eyed.

"Never more serious." He had his arm around my waist now, and was guiding me towards the bowling alley.

"Screwball. This is suicide." I muttered, heart pounding like a pneumatic drill.

"And staying on the streets isn't?" He glanced up at the sky.

I heard the clatter of helicopter blades in the distance.

He squeezed my arm. "Ten pin is our best chance. Truth!"

A screech of girls on a hen night was keeping things lively in the queue. An array of headboppers – glittery stars, red hearts and bumblebees – bobbed and clacked as the hens huddled round a girl wearing a flashing *Bride-to-Be* sash and a tiara with a veil attached. She had a pack of ten cards fanned out in her hand with which she was rating boys in the queue. After a confab with her hens, she pulled out SEVEN: DREAM BOY. An auburn-haired Scot laughed and gave a deep bow.

Latif pulled his cap down further.

They turned in our direction. My heart lurched. Latif was next.

I cringed at the attention, terrified one of them might recognise him, but he didn't seem phased, instead he was playing along with them. The girls clustered round the cards whispering scores. There seemed to be some kind of disagreement. Finally the bride-to-be held up an EIGHT. The verdict read: TOTAL HUNK!

"Thank you, ladies," Latif said with a twinkle in his eye. The bride-to-be smiled, and then looking over at me mischievously, she asked, "Is he with you?" Without waiting for an answer, she raised her veil, and scooped Latif underneath it. A pang of jealousy stabbed.

As they approached the cashier, the security guy went to lift the veil, but the bride-to-be batted his hand away playfully, and giggle-whispered, "Hey, hands off! He's mine."

Latif pushed money for both of them under the partition, and they swished through. The rest of the girls followed with a clack of deely boppers. My palms were sweating as I pushed the twenty-pound note towards the cashier, but he was gawping at the hens. I headed after them, heart racing.

Once we were inside, Latif took me by the hand. "Come on. We need shoes."

"Hand in our trainers?" I turned to face him. "What if the police show up?"

"We'll scoot. Shoes, bubblehead, are shoes." He adjusted his cap so it completely shadowed his face.

We couldn't have picked a noisier place on earth. Music blared, skittles crashed and balls thundered down the bowling lanes. Even better, the hen party provided the perfect diversion. Their raucousness demanded attention, drawing everyone into their orbit. They had to be noticed. I could have hugged the whole giggling whoop of them.

As I watched Latif trade our trainers for bowling shoes, all I could think was: *We're on the run. And we're handing in our trainers? What kind of cuckoo plan is that?* Brilliant! I slumped back against the wall, adrenalin gone. What was the point of dragging the chase out? We were going to get caught sooner or later. It was just a matter of time. Three days. Twenty-four hours. Thirty minutes. For all I knew, police in riot gear were lined up outside the bowling alley right now, awaiting orders to storm in.

When Latif handed me my bowling shoes, he said, "Think about it, bubblehead. These beauties work on two levels: first up, camouflage; second up, warning – if we see someone out of regulation shoes we know we're in trouble. Get me?"

"Okay. Okay. I get it. You're not mad."

As we made our way over to the bowling lanes, he said, "It's Saturday night, Dash. You're meant to be having fun. Smile. Pretend you're in Premium, Minted or somewhere swanky, if that helps."

I frowned. Was Latif always going to see me as a global, a fake and a class tourist? My brow furrowed some more. *Whatever.* I felt his eyes on me.

He leaned down and whispered, "I'm serious, smile." His breath was warm against my cheek. "Just hang on my every word! As usual."

I smiled.

"Hold that smile." His eyes flicked towards the bar. "I could murder a beer." He fished a note out and tsked. "But a fifty's flash."

"I'll go." I held out my hand. "I'm better disguised."

His eyebrow shot up. "You sure, bubblehead?"

"'Sakes, Latif. I've just outwitted the Dark Lord and his apprentice. I think I can get us a drink." I rolled my eyes. "Anyway, I haven't road-tested the wig yet."

He pressed the note into my hand. "Kill it!" He cracked a heart-stopping smile.

The bar was heaving. I checked out the punters and headed for a section rammed with scruffy-looking boys. Elbowing my way into the crush, I caught a glimpse of my blond self in the mirror behind the bar. The transformation from teenage dirtbag to presentable human being was spectacular. In the low lights, my skin looked dewy, my crop was standout and my lips were lush. Ready for action! I turned my attentions on the barman. He was serving a boy a little further down the bar. I fixed him with a stare and smiled. He returned my smile. My stomach lurched; I knew I would be next.

The barman came over.

"Two Becks," I shouted across the bar.

The barman leaned forwards, pointing at his ear.

"Two Becks," I shouted, louder this time.

He gave me the thumbs up and headed over to the fridge, took out two bottles and removed the tops with a bottle-opener attached to a chain on his belt. I watched him exchange a few words with a pretty red-headed girl. They both looked my way. I smiled. The girl nudged him in the ribs and went back to her customer.

He slid two beers across the bar. When I pushed the fifty-pound note into his hand, he whistled, and held it up to the light to check it wasn't a fake.

My heart raced as he went over to the till and rang up my beers. I kept on smiling; fronting it was the only option.

"Who are you with?"

My heart skipped a beat. "Friends... girlfriends." I nodded in the direction of the hen party.

"The next two are on the house." He pressed the change into my hand with a grin.

"Thanks," I mouthed.

"Looks like you pulled," Latif said when I handed him his beer. He took a swig from the bottle, never once taking his eyes off the room.

I shrugged. "He's not my type." I placed the chilled bottle against my cheek and took in the scene. Latif was standing with one hand thrust into his pocket, bobbing his head to the beat while his eyes flitted across the crowd. He was giving everyone the once-over from the shoes up. All regulation.

Genius. I took a sip of beer. My shoulders relaxed a notch. Another sip. My spine unkinked a fraction. I started bobbing my head to the music, too. Latif nodded towards an empty booth. As we walked over, I saw Latif lift a mobile from the hen party's table while the girls were celebrating a strike. As soon as we sat down in the booth he tapped 1, 2, 3, 4 in as the security code.

"What the..."

He raised his hand. "Keep watch, Dash."

The code worked, and he quickly started texting someone on the stolen phone.

"How did you know the code?"

"Most common one by a long shot."

In minutes, he'd finished, and was heading back over to the girls' table. As he checked to see whether our lane was free, he casually replaced the phone. No sweat.

"Mission accomplished," he said with a wink when he returned to the booth. "We'll be out of here in thirty."

"What? How?"

"I took the liberty of texting a friend. Sent. Deleted. Job done."

"Who? Ren?"

"Nah. Decca. She's an old school friend." He looked at my watch. "We're linking outside in half an hour."

The next swig of beer was the best of my life.

He took my arm. "It's time to knock some pins."

While Latif kept watch, I entered our names into the electronic scorer as Zac and Max, even though Latif had told me to keep them random. I prayed my parents' names would bring us luck. I took another swig of beer and chased away the doomy images of police preparing to storm the building. The music rocked my head; pins crashed down and punters whooped madly when they got a strike, as if they'd just won a rollover lottery. Letting my eyes travel around the hall again, I understood why we were here; anyone over twenty-three – the Golds' heavies, for example – would look like relics. I checked out the punters – regulation shoes as far as the eye could see.

"Be very scared!" I picked up a yellow bowling ball, testing its weight. "I'm a professional."

"No way!" Latif's eyes stopped roving the room. "Don't tell me you've got your own private bowling lanes."

"Yeah. Next to the swimming pool and Dad's art collection."

He rolled his eyes.

I sized up the pins, took four steps, the last morphing into a skip, and released the ball. Three skittles fell. My next took out four more. Watching the machine sweep away the skittles, something snapped inside me. Only a few hours earlier my dreams had been swept away uncerimonously – just like the skittles.

Latif chose a black ball and stood a little way back from the line, eyes narrowed, as if he were working out the physics of his throw. Then he took three measured steps, bending his knees on the fourth as he released the ball. He bowled a pole-straight ball. Eight skittles fell. The two remaining skittles were an arm-stretch apart. He turned, smiling. "Damn, a split." He hooked his next ball down the lane, but only one skittle fell. "Your turn, Dash." Already his eyes were looking beyond me, scoping the joint.

I picked up a ball and bowled it down with force. The stabbing anger was back, shooting up from the pit of my stomach. My relationship with Maxine was history – over before it had even begun. The ball bounced into the gutter. Totally over. The second ended up in the gutter, too. I sank down onto my haunches. I hoped they weren't going to slam her in jail.

Latif stopped mid-stride. "You know the deal. When I bowl, you keep lookout." His eyes flicked around the room.

"Sorry. Everything came flooding back..." I tailed off.

His eyes fixed me for the first time since we'd entered the bowing alley. "You okay?"

"Not really."

"Was Maxine there?"

"Yes."

"And she was pleased to see you?"

"Yeah. She was pleased to see me." I laughed bitterly. "She'd done a deal with my parents. Traded me in for an appartment in Dubai and a stack of cash." I stood up slowly.

"She traded you. Just like that? Classy!"

"No, the Golds had put pressure on her to do the deal. They'd blackmailed her." I raised my beer bottle. "But she fought back in the end. To Maxine!" I took a swig. "Get this – they threatened to put her in prison and take her child away…" I trailed off; my words were getting smudgy with tears.

"I'm sorry, Dash. Life's a bitch."

"You said it!"

"And the Golds? What was their game?"

"The usual. Trying to save face. Sabotaging people's lives. Constructing a happy ending for the brand…" I screwed up my face as if I'd sucked on a lemon. "They had a camera crew there, of course." I took another swig of beer, and even though I didn't relish going over the events, I knew I had to put Latif in the picture. Forcing myself to remember the nightmare scenario, I ran through the bare bones of my ordeal; explaining how my parents had staged and filmed the reunion so they could keep their rotten lies alive – two identikit mothers, hidden cameras and a happy family reunion. "Priceless, eh?"

"Seriously mental."

"They said you'd sold me out." I could feel the pain all over again. "That they'd bribed you to go along with their plans."

"Did you believe them?" His aquamarines fixed me.

"Guilty." I bit my lip.

"That's never going to happen, bubblehead. As if I'd take orders from those clowns. I could've walked away when you were in the house. Cut my losses. But for some insane reason, I couldn't leave you in there. If you hadn't come out, I was going to drive the bike through the conservatory window round the back. A bit James Bond for my style, but sometimes you have to make allowances…"

He took his turn at bowling. All the skittles fell, except for one; it wobbled, but remained standing.

I knew I had to tell Latif the rest: how my parents had framed him, how he'd go to prison if they tracked him down, how bad things were for him. But as I watched the steel jaws knock over the solitary skittle, I couldn't find the words.

He must have sensed something because he asked, "That bad?"

"The truth?"

He nodded.

"Seriously bad." I let my eyes slide around the room. "They've totally stitched you up. They rigged up the room to look like a bomb factory. Dad said you'd be sentenced for kidnapping and terrorist offences. Although he also said that you would be given a new identity after the trial. He'd arranged for you to be released on the quiet, after the storm had died down. But you'd have to live abroad."

"What, like an exile?"

He whacked down a ball angrily. Ten men fell. A strike. He turned triumphantly, and was about to whoop when his face froze. "We've got heavies in the house. Don't panic. Bowl."

My eyes scanned the floor for rogue footwear.

A pair of Timberlands was checking out the bar area.

Cowboy boots barged into the toilets.

Black Dr. Martens headed downstairs.

"Bowl, screwball," Latif growled.

I went through the motions. One skittle fell. Out of the corner of my eye, I saw Timberlands was questioning the barman who shrugged in a Gallic style. Meanwhile Dr. Martens was running back up the steps and Cowboy boots was slowly checking the lanes. I noticed they were scanning punters from the floor up. They were on the shoe tip, too.

"Go for it, Dash," Latif hissed.

I started walking towards the lane unsteadily. Cowboy boots was halfway down the bowling lanes.

Control! Control! I thought as I measured out my steps. My heart was gunning it and I could hardly breathe so that when I went to bowl, I totally mistimed my throw. I watched the ball bounce into the gutter. I couldn't bear to turn round.

A hand grabbed my shoulder.

My stomach lurched.

It was Latif. "They've gone. We need to get the hell out of here."

"What? Now?"

"No. Keep bowling." He picked up a ball. "No panicky moves. We'll leave at a leisurely pace."

When we finished our frames, Latif strolled over to the counter to reclaim our trainers. His fluid gait gave no hint of tension. Heart galloping, I followed. The guy took an age. Twice he glanced over at me. I fidgeted. I'd seen him talking to the man in cowboy boots only moments earlier. For all I knew, they might have been discussing our shoe sizes. I stared down at my glittery socks. I found it weird that so many strangers knew the smallest details of my life, details I couldn't give a rat's arse about. I did my best to look casual, but sitting there in my socks, I felt strangely exposed. In my head, we were already caught.

Tracker

OUTSIDE. Chaos. Everywhere.

Kids were gawping as if they'd walked onto the set of their favourite cop show. A frisson twitched the crowd as they jostled for a ringside view of the action, hoping for a bit of post-pub entertainment – an arrest, a drugs bust, a shoot-out, even. Parked up in the high street under the railway bridge a fleet of police vans stood empty – spooky as pirate ships.

Latif pushed a way through the boozy hangers-on gathered on the pavement outside the bowling alley. I slid in behind him, grabbing a handful of football shirt so we wouldn't get separated. He stopped a little way back from the road. I squeezed in next to him.

A policewoman was striding towards us, shouting into a megaphone: "Move along now, folks. Haven't you got homes to go to? For your own safety, please go home."

The policewoman was looking my way. "You." I stared down at my trainers. "Haven't you got somewhere to go?" I kept my eyes lowered. Fear mushroomed up from my stomach. Time slowed down. My heart hammered. I waited, expecting the policewoman to handcuff me at any moment and haul me over to the vans. But she'd already moved on down the line, repeating the same orders, which fell on deaf ears. A story was unravelling, and the crowd weren't going to miss it for the world.

"What's up?" a bloke with a nose piercing asked the policewoman. "I heard that religious nut was spotted round here. Some bloke said he's got a belt of explosives and had a gun to that chick's head. Boom!"

The policewoman ignored him, repeating robotically: "Move along now, people. Time to go home."

Suddenly there were shouts. Then policemen charged out into the high street. They formed a line and began advancing at a steady jog, shields thrust forwards. The crowd taunted them with shouts of "Filth!" while boys in hoodies chucked cans and bottles. Huddling close to Latif, I buried my head in his shirt and shut my eyes. I didn't have a good feeling about this, not at all. The stamp of boots reverberated in my ears.

Moments later, the pounding footsteps stopped.

Silence, except for the swish and rustle of protective clothing. I pictured the police taking up position. A volley of bangs rang out. The crowd cheered. I looked up quickly. A flotilla of red tail lights was disappearing up the high street. More doors slammed shut, followed by the screech of vehicles leaving at speed.

The crowd pushed forwards. Two peel-heads were shovelling a way through the crowd like a couple of digger-trucks. One was shouting into a walkie-talkie, something about "MI5", "a motorbike", "Hackney Marshes". I caught words, not meaning, until the guy shouted to his mate. "Suspects traced. All systems go. The bowling alley tip-off was a dud."

Within minutes, the rest of the police vans tore off.

I exchanged a look with Latif, but we kept our heads down.

At least the traffic was on the move again. Cars were crawling past the bowling alley, stopping and starting as the traffic lights changed from red to green. Petrol-heads and speed freaks were honking their horns impatiently as the traffic crept forwards – making no headway. The lights changed back to red and the cars ground to a halt.

"Come on. Our ride's here," Latif shouted over the hoots. Taking my arm, he shoved a way through the crowd, and then, stepping off the pavement into the road, we walked quickly down the waiting queue of traffic. The next thing I knew, he was opening the rear door of a clapped-out Ford, which couldn't have cost the owner much more than a fiver on eBay. He pushed me inside. A dark-haired girl was at the wheel. Latif jumped into the passenger seat, leaned over and kissed her on the cheek.

"Hey Decca. Let's get the hell out of here."

The lights remained red. The girl hammered the horn. "Jeez, Latif. What the hell's going on? I've been mad worried. Your mobile's dead. Your parents have been arrested." She squeezed his arm. "Are you okay?"

"Yeah. Decent."

The dark-haired girl was staring at me in the rear-view mirror. "You didn't say *she'd* be here." Her look was unfriendly. "What's the deal with her, anyway?"

I hated being talked about as if I were a piece of lost luggage. But I kept quiet. Latif could sort this. I'd only mess things up if I spoke. What's more, I really wasn't sure what the deal was...

"Dec, it's a long story. Anyway 'she' has a name – it's Dasha."

I smiled at the dark-haired girl. "Hiya." My voice came out perky and insincere, like a PR girl warming up for her pitch.

Decca held my gaze; she neither smiled nor said hello. She had a mass of tangled dark hair, sculpted cheekbones and blue eyes that reminded me of the ocean. The lights turned green. Decca crunched the gear stick into first and released the handbrake. Only then did she liberate me from her gaze.

"Decca," Latif snapped. "Cut the ice queen routine. She's cool, all right? Don't vex me. I've got enough rubbish going down without you chirping." He fiddled with the radio dial, trying to get reception. A disembodied voice shouted something about a dangerous terrorist before dissolving into static. "Next you'll be believing that blab." He shaped a gun with his fingers and put it to Decca's head, shouting in psycho-pidgin English. "Drive, you bitch of a son. Drive!" They were laughing now. He wiggled his fingers against her temple. "So tell me, Dex – you fother mucker – did you at any point believe the lies?"

She reached over and squeezed his leg, but avoided

eye contact. "As if… as if I'd believe that nonsense. *Latif — the terrorist.* Give me a break."

"Dex, you're looking guilty," he teased. "Come on, let's see your face. I want the truth." He wiggled his finger-gun at her temple again. "The truth, Dex. The truth."

Decca laughed. "Once or twice. You would've. Jeez, Lats! They've stitched you up like a kipper. I mean, have you seen the stuff they're broadcasting? It's so totally realistic. I didn't know what to think."

Latif pulled his gun-fingers away from her head. "Yeah, I know." His voice had lost its bounce. He put his fingers to his own temple. "Boom!"

Decca pulled his arm down. "Save it for TV." He laughed. I envied the way that they were so easy with each other. She knew how to make him laugh. Damn it!

Decca made eye contact with me in the rear-view mirror again, only this time she smiled, and said, "Hello, I'm Decca. I feel like I know you already. Your life story at least."

I rolled my eyes. "Don't believe the hype."

"I'm Latif's oldest friend. That's why I so couldn't believe this rub on the news. But then he gets crazy sometimes, so I thought maybe he'd flipped big time. What else was I meant to think?"

"Did you speak to Ren?" Latif asked.

"Yeah, thank God. The day your story hit the headers, he creeped me in his cab outside college. Put me in the picture."

"Yeah, I told him to get in touch. No phones?"

"Strictly no phones. He was scared his mobile was

slammed so we sorted out a system. It was so totally spy-cool. He'd wait in the taxi rank outside Tate Britain at four p.m. each day. If he wanted to speak to me, he'd be wearing his red Hawaiian shirt. If I needed to speak to him, I'd head over to the Tate from college and wait till he was head of the rank, flag him and we'd go for a spin. He always kept stuff real vague whenever we met. Cheeky nerd doesn't trust me." Decca held up a mobile. "He gave me this pay-as-you-go. Instructions were to text Yukiko when you made contact." She passed him the phone. "The message is: *2 xtra tckts 4 rad gig*."

"What does that mean?" I asked

"Two extra passengers on board."

"Tune the radio, Dex. It's doing my head in," Latif said, as he texted Yukiko.

The car swerved back and forth as she turned the dial.

"'Sakes, Lats, are you sure you want to hear it?" She slid into a plummy TV anchor accent. "Latif Hajjaj is a threat to national security. I repeat, a threat to national security. The police are appealing for information from the public. Meanwhile lock up your children. I repeat, lock up your children." We burst out laughing. It was all too absurd.

Decca looked over at Latif. "Seriously. Are you okay?"

"Yeah, fine. Never been better. Come on, Dec. I've got a freakin' price on my head. My parents are in prison. If the feds catch me they'll probably cut off my balls. And that's if I'm lucky," he said, kicking the radio. It crackled into life. A man with a sock in his mouth was shouting up from the bottom of a well. I heard my name, muffled, distant.

"You didn't tell anyone where you were going, did you?" Latif's voice was stretched tight like an elastic band.

"Yeah, as if."

From the bottom of the well, a phrase floated into the car – the words were fractured and fuzzy, making it difficult to decipher. Something about the chase going live. Some mention of 'Tracker'. Latif must've heard something similar because he asked, "What do they mean by the chase is going live?" He hunched down closer to the radio.

The radio slid to static. White noise. My nerves jangled. Something wasn't right with that phrase. How could the chase go live, unless... unless... unless – Decca had grassed us up. I pushed the thought away. That was impossible. Decca was Latif's oldest friend...

A siren wailed behind us.

I willed Decca to put her foot down. Watching the speedometer hover at forty, my suspicions edged back, louder, more insistent this time. Maybe Decca was going to trade us in for the reward money, become an overnight star, sell her story. Sure, Decca appeared genuine enough. Something niggled. I didn't trust her. Our eyes met in the rear-view mirror again. There was a stony quality that reminded me of my father. I looked away. Nothing would surprise me.

"You haven't heard?" asked Decca. Taking our silence as a negative, she continued. "They – that's your parents, by the way, Dasha – are making a monster reality show called *Tracker*."

"What, like a huge game show?" Latif asked.

"Exactly. GoldRush has networked London's CCTV onto the web, so when *Tracker* goes live tonight, the public can log on and surf every street in London. Your parents are dressing it up as a deluxe *Crime Watch* when in reality it's the mother of all game shows; a real-live thriller and a cop show rolled into one. There are cash prizes for sightings, and a whacking million for information that leads to Latif's arrest. It's a game of cat and mouse citywide. And your parents are hosting the whole jackass jamboree. GoldRush's coverage of your story has aced every show ever made. It's like the best real-life soap opera ever. Lost little rich girl kidnapped by dishy terrorist. Female columnists can't get enough of you, Latif. Swoon! Swoon! They've seriously got the hots for you. Crazy, eh?"

"Great!" I said bitterly. My parents had upped the game. London was the set. We were the hunted. This was *Big Brother* for real. "And the government is okay with it?" I asked, even though I knew the answer.

"You bet! Even the PM has endorsed the show," Decca said.

Dad had often talked about the Metropolitan Police's CCTV network and joked about its connectivity, how he dreamed of using it for a reality crime show. That was when I remembered the trial runs in Northampton, which used the police's CCTV cameras. My parents had been working on the idea of networking CCTV for some time. They had created a top-secret development division.

Even so, networking all of London's CCTV cameras would be a difficult trick to pull off at such short notice. But knowing Dad, he'd probably had everything in place for months – awaiting his moment. Now with my kidnap and the alleged threat of a terrorist attack, he wouldn't have any problem getting the authorisations required at the highest level.

A chill crept up my back. I couldn't believe my escape had given him the excuse to implement his grand plan. How ironic was that!

I pictured Dad in private meetings with the chief of police and the prime minister – how he would argue that *Tracker* was in the public interest, how it was the best way to find his precious daughter, that it was the only way to keep London safe from an attack. They were both so thick with my dad, so stupidly scared of him, that they wouldn't have raised any objections, anyway.

The chill spread through my body. He had probably been pushing to implement his all-singing, all-dancing chase show from the moment he thought I'd been kidnapped.

"So how does it work?" Latif asked.

"The CCTV feeds – you know, the footage you see police monitoring in movies. Dasha's parents have networked up to ninety-five per cent of them so when *Tracker* is transmitting live, anyone, anywhere can tune in, tap in a postcode and monitor their 'hood or any place else in London. That's the idea, anyway. That's what I understand from the trailers."

"Yeah. That sounds about right. Dad's been developing

this concept for ages. He's just been waiting for the right time to put it into action. It seems like I'm the excuse for his hunt 'em down show, guys. He'll have had teams of people working on this twenty-four/seven. So when was *Tracker* announced?"

"This evening. That's when they started trailing the show. You're not going to like this, but *Tracker's* going to be epic. The whole world is hooked on your story. The kidnap is all anyone's been talking about since Dash did her vanishing act. You're superstars. Hollywood's bidding for the rights. Lats, you're a legend. There are websites devoted to you."

"Just what I've always wanted." He put his feet up on the dashboard, totally gloomed out.

"Come on, you're hotter than the hottest hottie in Hottiewood."

"That'll be really helpful when I'm in jail."

"Get with the programme, Lats. I'm seeing cameras in your cell and twenty-four/seven coverage. GoldRush TV is probably working up the idea right now: you in the exercise yard, you doing pull-ups in your cell, you reading Sufi poetry in the prison library. TV gold."

"Shut it, Decca. Sounds like you've signed up already."

"Only joking," she said with a wink.

"Don't. I've had a humour bypass."

"Everyone's real jumpy. I mean we've seen your bomb factory and everything. Although I did think that was a bit much." Decca giggled. "I can't believe I thought you'd flipped for real." She squeezed his arm. "God. Am I glad to see you again! The last few days have been a living nightmare."

Latif grunted, half-smiled. "Seriously, though, Decca is there a way out?"

She turned to look at him. "You want the truth, right?" The radio was hissing and spitting. "Not that I can see."

A pause, eerie as the silence before a bomb blast.

Latif fiddled with the tuner. He swore under his breath. The radio wheezed. He turned the dial some more. A pirate radio boomed. A phone-in. A sonata. More screeching static. A syrupy ballad. A hyped-up presenter on GoldRush Radio signed off his show by saying: "Don't forget. *Tracker* goes live at midnight. Why don't you stay up and bag yourself a million?"

I checked my watch. "That's in an hour. Midnight's a weird time to air a live show, isn't it?"

"Less traffic. More chance for people to get involved," Decca said.

Latif drummed his fingers on the dashboard. "What's the playlist? Swerve the city? Go country? Jed would take us in. He's sound." None of these options were said with conviction. It was as if he were merely thinking out loud.

"I don't reckon we'll get out of London, if they've networked all the CCTV cameras," Decca said.

"It's way too risky," I agreed.

"There must be blind spots." The drumming of his fingers on the dashboard became more insistent. "It's impossible to network all the CCTV cameras in London in under fifty hours – to make it a real slick operation. Even if they've bribed the feds and are piggybacking on the police's network of cameras there must be blind spots. Believe it!" He sounded more cheerful. "The question is where?"

"Crunch Town?" I said with unusual enthusiasm.

"There's a ring of steel around Crunch Town," Decca said. "The police are stopping people getting in and out."

"Another junk space, then?" Latif said grimly.

"I think we should go back to mine. Log onto the *Tracker* site and see if we can find a safe route out of town to..." Decca tailed off.

"To where?" I whispered. My question hung in the air.

"If only Dad wasn't banged up." Latif rapped his forehead with his knuckles. "There must be someone out there who isn't in your parents' pockets, Dash. Who's brave enough to speak out?"

I pictured the guests arriving at GoldRush Image Inc's New Year's party and shook my head miserably. "Nope. He's got most of them sewn up."

"In more ways than one. And the rest are too scared to speak out or stand up to him." Latif was trawling the airwaves again. "Don't depress me. I need to think."

"It's an outrage!" The words floated out of the aural snowstorm like bright orange lifeboats. Latif slid the dial on the radio a fraction. *A dissenting voice?* I held my breath; scared I might waft the words back into the staticky squall. I thought I heard the words 'human rights'. Then, clear as a bell, a female voice cut through the static. "*Tracker* is a fiasco for human rights. An absolute outrage."

"Freedom Radio!" Latif punched the air. "Dad had his own show on Freedom a few years back." A slow smile spread across his face. "That's Chitra Azmi. She heads up Freedom. She knows Dad. She was born to kick ass."

"Do you reckon she could help us get our story out there?" But even as I spoke, I knew my plan was a non-starter. Dad would have the station blocked as soon as it started broadcasting the truth. Freedom Radio was a media minnow. Dad would eat Chitra Azmi for breakfast.

"I wish. There are probably about three people listening." He held up three fingers. "*Us.*"

"Great!" I growled.

"But it's good to know there are still a few sane people out there," Decca said.

"Silence, *chicas.*" Latif held his hand up. "We've got some thinking to do."

I watched the city slide by. Despite the late hour, lights were burning in most houses. I pictured people settling down to watch *Tracker* on TV, or hunched over computers – each and every one of them dreaming of becoming a millionaire by morning. I drummed my fingers against the window. I couldn't hack the silence. Without conversation to distract me, black thoughts had taken control again. Bitching. Scaremongering. Shouting the odds. I blew on the window with misty breath, drew a hangman, smudged it out.

Up ahead, GoldRush Towers loomed like two massive fingers flicking a V sign at us. I knew that Dad held all the cards. Anyone that mattered was on his side.

"What? You've sold me out?" Latif's angry words jumped me back to reality.

"I'm sorry. I need the money for my college fees."

Decca might as well have lobbed a hand grenade onto the back seat of the car. Silence. I imagined the fuse burning, waiting for the blast.

After a few seconds, Latif said, "Yeah right. Nice one, Dex."

"I've been told to take you straight to GoldRush Towers." Her voice was emotionless.

"Come on, Decca, cut the crap. I'm not in the mood."

Above a helicopter was dipping down low.

"That's the police." Decca's voice was deadpan.

"This better be a joke, right?" Latif kicked the dashboard. I slid across the backseat and squeezed the door handle, ready to jump.

Peals of laughter. The glint in Decca's eyes was back. "Just kidding around. Honestly, you two were being so glum I thought I'd liven things up. You can't problem-solve when you're gloomy – your brain slows down. FACT!"

"Jesus, Dex," Latif growled. "Don't be funny all your life."

"Give us a break, guys. Did you really think Dex would give up her midnight runners?"

We all laughed. Laughter helped. We relaxed a little.

"Okay, guys. We're here."

Ghosts in the Machine

LATIF and Decca were messing around; arm in arm, stumbling as if they'd had a few too many beers. I knew they were pretending for the CCTV cameras, on the off chance that *Tracker* was up and running, but when I tried to follow suit, I became camera shy. Even though *Tracker* was scheduled to start at midnight, I couldn't shake the idea that wannabe millionaires could be tapping in postcodes and searching London streets on their smartphones and computers. I imagined Pimlico residents spying on their streets, like neighbourhood snoops. I tensed up even more.

The other two had stopped outside a rundown house at the far end of the street that we'd parked up in. A lopsided sign read *PimPlico Arts*. Someone had added the extra bright pink P with a spray can. In other circumstances I might've laughed, but right now I was too busy trying to calm my escalating panic. I took a deep breath.

Keep cool! One foot in front of the other… each step felt as ungainly as an astronaut's on the moon.

By the time I reached the house, Latif and Decca were already inside. The house throbbed to a techno beat. I crept in. A room scattered with found objects – a weather vane, driftwood and black railings hung about with string. Canvases were propped haphazardly along one wall. The only furniture was a saggy sofa draped with tie-dye throws. A clay obelisk stood in one corner surrounded by scrunched-up beer cans. A kiln stood in the opposite corner, large-mouthed and hungry.

Despite the raging techno, Decca placed her finger to her lips before heading into the hallway and up the stairs. We tiptoed after her.

Decca's bedroom was crammed with canvases, too. Pages pulled from newspapers from the last few days were stuck across one wall. I stopped dead – creeped out, stunned, as if I'd stepped into a stalker's lair. The cuttings shared one common feature – yours truly. Weirdest of all, a freshly finished oil painting stood on an easel in the middle of the room. My face filled the canvas. Bathed in light from the paparazzi flashbulbs at some premiere or other, there was something spooked-out, otherwordly about it.

"I look like a ghost." I moved closer. "This is insane." I fixed Decca with a curious look. "Why would you want to paint me?"

"Because you're a superstar, doll. Live with it!" Decca switched on her laptop. "I chose that shot because you look lost. Disconnected. Haunted. Like the others." She gestured around the room.

"Wow," I whispered, barely moving my lips.

The other canvasses showed women with sad faces transfixed by TV; each held a remote, which they pointed at loved ones – kids, husbands, lovers – as if they desperately wanted to turn off their demands.

Latif walked over to a mirror propped up on a chest of drawers. There were twenty or so beer mats tucked into its frame. Each mat pictured Latif wrapped up bandit style. Bloodthirsty capitals bellowed: **WANTED! DEAD OR ALIVE**, like a poster from a cheesy old Western.

"Suppose that's every geezer's idea of fame," he said, staring at them, hands thrust deep into his pockets. His eyes appeared grey in the mirror. A flash. He winced. "Cut it out, Dex! I've had enough of photos for a lifetime."

"Hey, Lats. It's my pension plan." She took another. "Have a heart."

The music stopped. We exchanged a look. In the ensuing silence my heart banged out the techno beat. Upstairs a door opened.

"Hey Decca, you wanna come up and play *Tracker*? It's going to be wild."

Footsteps descending.

Decca scooted across the room, opened the door and stuck her head out. "Hey Ralph, how's it going?"

"I'm about to do some tracking. Wanna join me?" His voice had a nails-on-blackboard quality about it.

Decca stepped out into the corridor, closing the door behind her. "Are you mad? Latif's our mate, for God's sake."

"*Your* mate – and *I'm broke.*"

"'Sakes, Ralph. Since when has it been okay to hunt people down on TV? What's wrong with you and the whole freakin' world? You're all sick in the head. Anyway, I've got to finish a canvas for college."

"Suit yourself."

Footsteps retreating.

"Night." She rolled her eyes as she shut the door. "Loser. Home alone as usual."

Latif turned on the television and started channel-hopping, transfixed like the women in Decca's paintings. He stopped when he saw a title sequence showing two kids in silhouette viewed through telescopic gun sights. Thriller music blared as the title *Tracker* spun into view.

"This is it," he murmured.

My parents were sitting in a studio on an orange sofa. Two massive photos of Latif and me provided the backdrop. Superimposed across the images were the words – **Beauty and the Beast**. Video jockeys dressed in white boiler suits stood at mixing desks with rows and rows of controls, twiddling knobs. They were cutting together visuals of London landmarks, streetscapes, police snatch squads and gangs of bounty hunters captured from London's network of CCTV cameras. The video jockeys were projecting the images onto huge screens, synching the montages to spooky electronic audio.

A drum roll hushed the audience.

"Welcome to *Tracker*," Dad announced solemnly. "Tonight we are showcasing a new tracking system, which allows you – the public – to play detective. We are relying on you to bring Latif Hajjaj to justice. You are our eyes." He stood up and walked towards the audience. He was holding a silver-tipped cane, which he was twirling like a bandmaster. Then, silver-haired and silver-tongued, he set about seducing the viewers with a silky preamble.

It was pretty much as we'd predicted. The Golds had networked all the police CCTV cameras, as well as those belonging to private companies, covering a vast area from central London right the way out to the M25. Through networking the cameras, this cutting-edge technology could bring London's *A to Z* of streets into everybody's homes, and allowed anyone with a computer, tablet or smartphone to log on, tap in a postcode and monitor every street in London, more or less.

His slick sales pitch was persuasive. He explained how this game-changing technology was a force for good in society, how it would keep London's streets safe and crime-free. Not just tonight, but every night, and every day too. "Just imagine if you could check your kid was safe as she walked to school or monitor Granny when she totters to the shops. This technology will be vital both in times of national crisis and as we go about our day-to-day lives."

He ended with a call to arms: "So log on. Get tracking. Time is running out for Dasha. *Dasha needs you.*" Lies came easily to him, as toxic as the poison that his teams of surgeons injected into celebrity faces. "Together we must make sure Latif Hajjaj has nowhere to hide. Spin through *Tracker*'s street-finder app, pick a street and pray you strike lucky."

He started reeling off names of London streets at top speed, as if he were calling bingo numbers. He pointed his silver-topped cane into the audience. "Pick a street, any street." The studio audience yelled out hundreds of names. "You, the woman in red... Rupert Street, you say? How can we recognise it? By the Duke of York pub?"

Zap! The VJs conjured up the street in nanoseconds. "Where do you live?" he asked a woman wearing a twinset. They switched to the cameras in her street. She squealed when she saw her son and daughter rush to the window and wave. "All you need to access *Tracker* is a smartphone, tablet or a computer. Log in, and you will have London at your fingertips."

Dressed in black, my parents were like two poisonous spiders, sitting at the centre of an invisible web, waiting for us to fly into one of its invisible strands.

"Blast off!" Decca's fingers galloped across her laptop's keyboards. "Come on. Come on." She drummed the table. "'Sakes! There's monster traffic. I can't log on."

I prayed the grid would crash.

On the television screen a montage of scenes from earlier was rolling: shots of the so-called bomb factory, my freak-out, the rescue and a slickly edited 'happy family' moment, showing my tearful reunion with Maxine, which had been expertly cut together so it looked as if I were being reunited with Tamara. If I hadn't actually been there, I would have been fooled. The package finished with a stuntman wearing a black and white keffiyeh, exploding into the conservatory on a motorcycle in a blizzard of glass. My parents' version of events spun as truth.

A reporter was standing outside the alleged bomb factory talking to camera. "Tamara and Tarquin Gold are in shock. They are still reeling after Latif Hajjaj thwarted a rescue attempt, dramatically snatching Dasha Gold back from right beneath their noses. The police have carried out a thorough search of the premises. Martyr videos, weapons and bomb-making materials have been retrieved. The evidence points to a network of terrorist cells. Reports suggest the kidnappings are the first of many planned outrages against so-called degenerate Western values. Tomorrow Latif Hajjaj's parents will be charged with masterminding a series of attacks on London. The police are stepping up security."

"These clowns kill me," Latif muttered.

Next up, Dad announced they were going live to Downing Street to hear from the prime minister, and then we were in Number 10. The prime minister was at his most statesmanlike. Speaking directly to camera, he locked eyes with the nation and said gravely, "Latif Hajjaj is a threat to democracy, to liberty and to Londoners. That's why you must log onto *Tracker* and hunt him down. Be vigilant. Today it is Dasha. Tomorrow it could be your child. So get tracking. Together we can cleanse society of terrorism and make London a safer place. We will never give in to terrorism in any form."

My heart stopped. Dad had pulled it off. He had managed to network the CCTV cameras and roll out the surveillance state – all in the name of entertainment. And by a weird twist of fate I had given him the opportunity.

He'd conjured up my kidnap, a lone wolf and a terrorist threat to convince people that they must come together to fight a terrible evil. He'd brainwashed the nation into chasing down make-believe villains.

A sappy photo of me flashed up. A smile flickered across Latif's face. "To think I'm risking my neck for *that*..."

I stuck my tongue out at him.

As they went to the commercial break, my parents chimed, "A million pounds goes to anyone who gives us information leading to Latif's arrest. Change your life by changing our lives. Remember, it pays to play. Dasha's counting on you." In the office behind the studio the phones lit up.

"See what I mean? *Tracker*'s turning crimewatching into a game, and that sucks," Decca growled. "'Sakes, next he'll be dishing out loyalty cards, luxury yachts and kill-all-you-want vouchers."

"Tonight's like a pilot for *Tracker*. If he catches us, then he'll argue that *Tracker* should be kept in place as a weekly show. I know what angle they'll use." I impersonated Mum's voice. "It's all about making crime-fighting fun. Edgy. *Tracker* is Sherlock Holmes for the media-savvy generation."

Latif laughed. "Media-sappy generation, more like."

"Man, this laptop's slow!" Decca tapped her fingers frantically on the table. "Come on. Come on. I can't get connected to the 'street search'." She scraped back her chair and began pacing up and down the room. "There must be monster traffic."

Latif took his tablet out of his rucksack. "Wait up, *chicas*,

I'm going to be good at this. Don't forget monitoring CCTV cameras is my specialty. So with the help of *Tracker's* eyes, I should have an exit plan in zero time." He hunched over the unregistered tablet, logging onto *Tracker* under some fake identity – as God knew who...

"At last your paranoia has a practical use!" Decca joked. "Hey, what about finding some likely suspects, a few red herrings to get them off our trail?"

"Throw a few ghosts into the machine? Sounds like a plan," Latif agreed.

"What? Text in fake sightings?" I shivered, wishing we didn't have to stoop to my parents' level.

I went over to Decca's laptop and as I watched the rainbow-coloured wheel rotate on the computer screen, part of me wished it would keep spinning for ever. I didn't want to get people arrested or find out how hopeless our situation was on street level. But when I touched the trackpad, *Tracker's* 'street search' spun into view. "We're up and running," I whispered.

Decca shunted me off the chair and ran through the registration process using a false name, address and email. Ignacio someone or other. More voodoo-finger tapping, and then she shouted, "Bingo! Let's do it, baby." Within seconds, she was calling up London streets, shaking her head ever more gloomily with every click. "Take a look at this. It's a nightmare out there. Police everywhere, roadblocks and vigilantes."

Latif stood behind Decca, resting his elbows on her shoulders while he watched the screen. I hovered close by.

After she'd called up a random selection of streets, he tsked. "The feds mean business." Then he sat down on the bed and started checking street views on his tablet.

"Oh no, I can't believe it!" I hissed, pointing at the television. A split screen revealed two streets. In one street, two kids were walking along, eyes glued to their smartphones. In the second, policemen in full riot gear were piling out of vans. The split screens dissolved into one when the policemen entered the street where the kids were walking and started shadowing them. The kids were oblivious to the danger.

Tracker went back to a split-screen frame. This time the right-hand screen showed the Golds sitting in the studio while the live CCTV feed rolled on the left-hand screen. The studio audience went nuts; clapping, screaming and jumping about like lunatics. I watched through splayed fingers as the police arrested the kids, snapped their wrists into handcuffs and bundled them into a waiting police van. Tamara Gold could hardly contain her excitement. "Hold the line, Clare from Camden. The police will be IDing the suspects shortly." I couldn't deny it: the Golds had a natural flare for stagecraft.

As if taking their cue from Tamara Gold, two policemen disappeared into the van. Immediately the Golds started a bloodthirsty countdown, "Three, two, one, ZERO…" Tamara pressed her studio earpiece with her fingertips. "We have negative identification. Better luck next time. Keep watching. Keep calling. Keep sourcing suspects. One hundred pounds will be coming your way, Clare from Camden, for playing the game." With a smile she turned to her husband, who took up the refrain.

"False alarm, sleuths! *Keep on tracking. Keep crowd-scanning. Keep calling.*" Then he started urging people to get out into the parks and places unwatched by CCTV. "We're relying on you to fill in the gaps. Search out the dark, unfilmed spaces with your smartphones. Crunch Towners, this is your chance to get rich."

My unease ramped up. The idea of being hunted down in Crunch Town terrified me.

"Had any luck, Lats? 'Sakes, look at these losers." Decca clicked onto a selection of streets near Victoria Station. At each location people were prowling around, chasing down likely suspects. Most were checking *Tracker*, eyes glued to smartphones or taking calls from friends who were scouring the CCTV network on computers at home. All had a cash-hungry gleam in their eyes. My skin crawled. Bounty hunters. Panic cramped my stomach. Between them, my parents, the police and the vigilantes, they had the city on lockdown.

"This isn't television. This is video gaming live and raw." Latif looked up from his tablet, eyes dark and furious. "And we're at the top level."

A SWAT unit leapt from a police van on Westbourne Grove. They were following up a tip-off from Natasha Barrington in Notting Hill. A glinting snake of shields slithered down the street, swallowing the kids up, like a reinforced python. The girl was wearing a green hoodie similar to the one I'd been wearing back at Maxine's house. The boy was wearing a keffiyeh. I frowned. The kids bore a striking resemblance to us – well, our clothes, at least.

"Spot the difference! Looks like they're using actors to keep the suspense up." I rubbed my eyes; it was unsettling to watch a nation chasing down phantoms.

The VJs were spinning through hundreds of viewers' sightings, cranking the music up to fever pitch.

"What are you going to do?" Decca tapped in a W12 postcode. Footage of people milling about on Shepherd's Bush Green came up on screen. "It's crazy out there. You'll be caught right away."

"Truth!" Latif was tapping away manically. "I'm checking the parks." His eyes widened. "'Sakes, Holland Park is on helicam. They've got copters filming unmonitored spaces, and the footage is connected to the grid. There's no CCTV in Crunch Town, but getting there is risky. The route is camera-heavy."

"Could we hole up here for now?" I said without enthusiasm.

"What about…?" Latif raised his eyes upwards, indicating Ralph.

"Never leaves his room. So he shouldn't be a problem. Gus, on the other hand, is. He's mostly round Frankie's. But when he's here, he's in and out of my room like a freakin' yo-yo."

"Do you trust him?"

Decca shrugged. "If money's involved – no. And if

there's a sniff of celebrity – absolutely not."

I was poking around a walk-in wardrobe stuffed full of canvases. "This could be our new home. Not sure about the wow fact—" I broke off when I heard Dad announce smoothly, "Coming up after the break, we'll bring you the last sighting of the terrorist scum and our angel. Sleuths, stay tuned."

"No way." I sat down on the bed and slumped back against the pillows, praying they hadn't sourced footage of us since our escape from Orchard Road. I shut my eyes, lying corpse-like through car ads and celebrity-endorsed tat, until the *Tracker* theme tune blasted out once again.

Propping myself up onto my elbow, I let out a zizz of disbelief. Two generic kids were standing in a crowd outside Finsbury Park Bowling Alley, so far so ordinary, except for the red arrow pulsing above their heads. A minute later, spooky déjà vu, as I watched two kids, the taller of the two in an England shirt and a baseball cap, push through the crowd, step out into the road, walk quickly past a queue of cars waiting for the lights to change and get into Decca's Ford. All the while the red arrow bobbed above us like a wicked aura. They zoomed in on the registration. Zoom, zoom, zoom, like something out of a spy movie.

I pulled off the wig. "Now what?" I whispered. My stress levels were sky high. I felt as if I were about to explode.

"We need an exit plan. Believe it! They'll trace your registration to this house in seconds, if they haven't already." Latif was checking routes, brow furrowed. "It's crazed out there. I reckon the sewer network's our best chance right now." Clocking our horrified faces, he added, "I'm serious. We've got less than zero minutes to get out of here and nowhere to go. Think about it."

"Chill, Lats." Decca grabbed his arm as he stormed past. "Ignacio gave me the car when he went back to Argentina. It's registered in his name, at his address; the insurance and tax are in his name, too, so it can't be traced to me. I never use this address for official stuff. I don't want to blow the squat."

"Yeah. But it's on the streets. It's been seen. So it won't take long to track. We've got minutes. Not hours." He took off the England shirt and flung it onto the bed. He adjusted his purple and gold trackie, immediately looking more at ease. "It'll take them no time to trace our route back here by cross-referencing the CCTV footage. So it's the sewers for def. Dex, check for manholes in the streets nearby." He was pacing the room, hands linked behind his head. "We need to enter the sewers at a blind spot. Can you think of any manholes on the Lillington Gardens estate?"

I was freaking now. "But there are rats in the sewers, aren't there? The size of dogs."

"Any better ideas?" he asked, without looking over.

On screen, my parents were building up to Latif's alleged jihad video. "Stay tuned if you want to find out what turned an A-grade student into a 'soldier'..." Then they broke for adverts.

As the thriller music rolled, the pay-as-you-go phone that

Yukiko had given to Decca beeped. He read the text out loud: "Links at 1.00 everything is going to be all right."

Decca rolled her eyes. "Great, Ren. What the hell does that mean? Is that his idea of a joke?"

"It's coded," Latif said, rereading the text. "What's the time, Dex?"

"Quarter to one."

"We've got fifteen minutes to solve it so the meeting place must be close by and known to us." Latif continued pacing, muttering the text under his breath: "Everything is going to be all right. Everything is going to be all right…"

For some reason, the phrase seemed familiar. I racked my brain. After a few seconds, Decca whooped and shouted, "I've got it!"

We looked at her expectantly.

"It's Martin Creed's installation." Decca slapped her hand to her forehead. "That's where I used to meet Ren most times," she said, as she quickly called up one of the CCTV camera feeds outside Tate Britain. I joined them at the computer. Sure enough, the white neon tubes spelt out: EVERYTHING IS GOING TO BE ALRIGHT. I smiled bitterly, remembering how I'd walked past it on the night of the train crash. Back then, I had interpreted the sign as a good omen. It seemed like an age ago, so much had happened since then – so much bad stuff had gone down. Now two empty cabs were parked up in the taxi rank outside Tate Britain – nothing out of the ordinary.

We exchanged looks, shrugged. No eureka moment.

The laptop clock hit five to one.

"Sewers it is, then," Latif said.

"No, no, look!" I pointed at the computer screen. "Both registration numbers are masked. And there's someone inside."

The door of the first cab was slowly opening, a figure climbed out.

"It's Ren," Decca shouted, as a Japanese Elvis lookalike emerged. Yukiko followed. She was dressed in a black maxi dress and a veiled bonnet. She glided from the cab like a Victorian ghost. Minutes later, the door of the second cab opened and out clambered Jeannie. All three stretched, as if they'd woken from a long sleep. Then they moved into a huddle, exchanging a few words before fanning out, each choosing one of the three CCTV cameras monitoring the entrance. When they were within range, they took rocks from their pockets and threw them at the cameras. Both Yukiko and Ren hit their targets with their first shot. Jeannie missed. Seeming to mutter under her breath, she fished another rock from her pocket and tried again. ZAP. The connection went dead. Decca checked the other camera feeds; both crackled white noise.

"*Blinding!*" Latif said, with a wink.

"Please, God, let everything be all right," I whispered.

Decca was clicking through nearby streets. "Yeah, but we've got a major problem. The CCTV on the way over there is still operational. Our route's live."

"How long will it take to get there?" I asked nervously.

"Ten minutes by foot, five by car." Decca clacked her

tongue as she double-checked the route. "We'd better take the car. Too many bounty hunters."

On the TV screen, my parents were trying to keep calm as events took a turn for the unexpected. Both wore fixed smiles. Both pressed their earpieces as they listened to the producer's brief on the situation. Their stretched expressions gave nothing away. My father was the first to speak. The camera zoomed in. "We are receiving accounts of cabs coming into the city from the suburbs. Initial reports suggest cabbies have turned out in support of our campaign to find Dasha." The relief was visible on his face.

We turned to look at each other. What the hell was going on?

CCTV feeds showed cabbies heading in from the suburbs, taking over the streets like a revolutionary army. But the Golds continued to praise the cabbies' public-spirited action.

A flustered newsreader was stumbling over her words as she tried to deal with the breaking news, and manage the claims and counterclaims in a way that would keep the Golds ahead of the game.

"A growing number of taxis are heading into central London, in an as yet unexplained phenomenon. We go live to Janet Drake in central London."

"Thank you, Natalie. As you can see, the centre of London is thronging with taxis. The cabbies are out in force in a show of solidarity for the Golds, and they will be helping in the search. A short while ago, I was speaking to a London

cabbie who told me that they supported the Golds and—"
Suddenly the reporter was ambushed by a rowdy group
of cabbies. A middle-aged man with a goatee grabbed the
mike.

"Don't believe her claptrap. We are staging a protest
over the imprisonment of fellow cabbie – Mrs Hajjaj – and
the illegal treatment of her family. Our aim is to disrupt
Tracker, and cause chaos throughout London by disabling
the CCTV." Obviously enjoying himself, he cranked up the
volume. "ARE YOU LISTENING, PRIME MINISTER?
LONDON CABBIES ARE REVOLTING!"

His cabbies-in-crime laughed and gave the thumbs up
to the camera. Then they handed back the mike and made
a beeline for their cabs. I noticed their registration numbers
were covered up.

A shaky-looking Janet Drake stuttered. "We have received
unsubstantiated reports that cab drivers are knocking
out CCTV cameras. Back to you in the studio, Natalie
Provost…"

The first images showing cabbies disabling CCTV
cameras flashed up. We punched the air in unison. The
Golds' smiles vanished. Their initial hopes had been dashed
live on screen. Disappointment clouded their faces. Dad
was cracking his knuckles. A breaking news crawler stated:
Cabbies Invade the City.

I smiled. The control-freaks were losing control.

"Awesome." Latif punched the air. "Cabbies kick ass.
That's rad! Believe it! *Vamos, chicas.*" He was already by the

door. He grabbed three coats from a rack: a parka for me, a duffle for Decca, a military overcoat for himself. More layers. Another disguise. He slid the tablet into his pocket.

"What happens if someone recognises Decca's car?" I asked without moving.

"And we've got a choice?" Decca had already picked up the car keys from her desk and was heading for the door.

Footsteps on the stairs turned us into statues. The bathroom door slammed shut. Decca's eyes flashed with relief. "We've only got a few minutes before that geek's back at his computer." She placed her finger to her lips. Latif raised an eyebrow, his expression said: "For Chrissakes, Decca, tell us something we don't know."

We were just about to leave when the toilet flushed.

We exchanged an anxious look.

Decca pressed the keys into Latif's hand. "Go!" she hissed. "I'll watch *Tracker* with nerd-boy. Keep him distracted." She pushed us out of the door.

We left as the prime minister was declaring a state of emergency. From what I could gather, soldiers had been drafted into London to guard sensitive government buildings, banks and global brands.

State of Emergency

OUTSIDE, the air was thick and hot, as if the city had been stuffed into a plastic bag. Latif set the pace. Casual. Eyes down. Slouching. I followed. In my head, every step we took was being freeze-framed by millions on a mission to identify us. After what seemed like a lifetime, we reached the car. Inside, cool turned to jittery panic. The key wouldn't go into the ignition. The car started, stalled. Then it spluttered into life.

We took for ever down Tachbrook Street, past Pimlico Tube station, all shuttered up for the night, and into Lupus Street. That was when I saw a guy in a leather blouson and trackie bottoms clock our registration number. Alarm bells started ringing in my head.

"He's onto us," I screamed, before he'd even started running.

Latif accelerated, hitting fifty as the traffic lights on Vauxhall Bridge Road changed from green to red. Two vigilantes stepped out into the road, shining torches into our eyes. He floored the accelerator, jumped the lights and skidded across Vauxhall Bridge Road before steaming through another set, narrowly missing a bollard, as we swung hard left into a tree-lined road, which ran parallel to the Thames. The clapped-out piece of junk juddered and stuttered. Latif put his foot down. "'Sakes, the engine's about to die," he shouted. Trees with gnarled fists punched at the moon.

When we turned right into a road I saw the Embankment up ahead, Latif stamped down on the accelerator, as if crushing a cockroach underfoot. The car lurched forward.

"We're back in business, Dash!" he said, as the car picked up speed. Through the rear window, I saw bounty hunters wheel into view like ravenous birds following a plough. They were holding up their smartphones, arms stretched towards us like antennae, giving the impression that we were being chased by monstrous all-seeing bugs.

A tailskid onto the Embankment sent us spinning through a figure of eight. I crashed against the door. Meanwhile Latif's arms tied themselves in knots as he tried to handle the steering wheel. We were hurtling towards the Embankment wall.

"Latif!" I screamed, my guts liquid fear.

He pulled the steering wheel down hard left and we veered back into the centre of the road. My stomach slid back. Police lights strobed the petrol-blue sky. Sirens screeched. The Tate's taxicab rank was a sprint away.

Headlamps filled the wing mirrors. Turning round, I saw black cabs slowly approaching in double file. In fact, they were closing in from both directions. All had their *for hire* lights on. They stopped about fifty metres either side of Tate Britain, providing a ten-deep security cordon. Only a daredevil rider could have jumped over this barrier of bumper-to-bumper cabs.

"Bail!" Latif shouted, as the car spun to a halt.

We leapt out and raced over to Ren's cab. Yukiko held the door open and we tumbled in. She hugged us both.

"How you doing, bruv?" Ren said

"Decent," Latif replied.

"'Sakes, I never thought we'd pull it off." Yukiko's eyes flashed with excitement beneath her veil. "Let's go!" she shouted, banging the partition.

Ren was hunched over the radio, listening to the Taxi Wire, a digital radio station for cabbies. "We've smashed it, seven thousand cabbies have turned out tonight, and we've disabled bare loads of CCTV." He slid the perspex partition back. "The police are telling cabbies to go home. They're threatening to arrest us. I'd like to see them try. There'll be a riot."

"Join the club, fam."

They bumped fists. "Believe it!"

The cabs were on the move again, a steady stream of black to our right, jockeying for position, like racing cars on the grid. Ren stuck his arm out of the window and made a slow circular motion. A cabbie gave way and Ren pulled out. At once we were camouflaged, becoming one more black cab in a carefully choreographed citywide invasion. Jeannie slotted into the stream of cabs two vehicles behind. Moments later, a gang of bounty hunters rushed from a side street onto the Embankment. They stopped in their tracks, completely bewildered by the queues of cabs jamming this stretch of road. A few started running alongside the cabs, faces pushed up against the windows, trying to see if we — *the hunted* — were inside.

The slow procession of cabs reminded me of state funerals. I tried to shut down my gloomy thoughts. But Yukiko wasn't exactly helping; sitting there in her widow's weeds, like an angel of death.

She reached into her bag and took out Latif's cowboy hat.

He put it on, setting it low on his head. "Thanks, Yuks." His eyes glinted as he tipped up the brim.

A gunshot rang out.

"Are they shooting at us?" I shouted in a panic.

Latif craned his neck to get a better view as he scoured the skyline. "Keep close to the kerb, Ren. They've got snipers up on the roof of MI5." He opened the window, and poked his head out a fraction. "Relax! They're firing warning shots."

His words did nothing to ease my nerves. "Yeah, right!"

Another shot rang out, followed by the squeal of brakes. A cab on the other side of the road crashed into the river wall; the bonnet concertinaed.

"See! I told you," I screamed, ducking down. "It's like the Wild West out there."

"Be easy, Dash. He's firing into the air." His gaze remained fixed on MI5. "The cabbie must've taken his eyes off the road."

The cabs closed ranks, slotting seamlessly into the empty space, and then we all continued to glide into the night, as if we were part of a slick, synchronised dance routine. I allowed myself to relax. We were well concealed. I imagined the TV screens back in the studio showing streets chock-a-block with black cabs. It crossed my mind that we had a real chance of escaping. If only we had a plan…

Latif was hunched over his tablet.

"What now? Are we heading out of London?" I asked, trying to keep the anxiety from my voice.

"No way," Latif said, eyes glued to the screen. "Not with this craziness."

"Agreed, fam. We'd never get out. The M25 is locked down. Road blocks and that." Ren said.

"What about Crunch Town? No cameras, and bare loads of junk spaces to hide out in."

"Feds have sealed it off. It's a military operation."

Latif sucked air through his teeth. "The way over could get heavy. There's live CCTV on the most direct route. But I'll check roads on *Tracker* as we go. Is that a plan?"

"One of your dad's lawyer friends said we should take you to the Lebanese embassy. Make it a diplomatic issue, that way they can't do a cover-up. The embassy will give you immunity. They can do deals, bruv. Get you out the country and that."

"Wanna bet?" Latif said bleakly. "Suppose it's closer." He didn't look convinced.

"Come on. Come on!" Ren drummed his fingers on the steering wheel when he had to give way to cabs filtering off Lambeth Bridge.

The same bridge, I suddenly realised, that I'd followed the skater kids across only two days earlier. I let out a slow exhalation of breath. It felt like an age ago – a different time almost, a more reasonable time, when the streets weren't full of bounty hunters, when snipers were something you heard about on the news, when a state of emergency was something that only happened in far-flung, military dictatorships.

When London wasn't on lockdown.

Helicopters were zipping over central London, their lights shaping crosses in the darkness. But I knew the helicopters were merely the visible bits of spy craft – that drones and satellites were up there, too. All of which were searching the streets for the slightest sign of us. An invisible, high-tech network that was perpetually monitoring London, which tonight – I couldn't stop myself from smiling – had been completely outclassed by the cabbies' very low-tech revolt. From above, I reckoned, the cabs must look like moving targets in a video game, thousands of black blips, each one indistinguishable from the next. Even better, we'd outwitted *Tracker*, for now…

On the streets, people were flagging down cabs: a smartly dressed couple, a Muslim family, the mother in a hijab, and a group of teenagers who looked as if they were about to go out clubbing. Unlike the bounty hunters, they weren't walking along with their heads down, eyes glued to their phones. They didn't appear to be playing *Tracker*.

"What's going on?" I asked.

"The cabbies've been broadcasting messages on Freedom Radio. They're asking people to show solidarity with the Hajjajs, by taking to the streets and hailing a cab. We billed it as a free ride for justice, liberty and freedom of speech and that. We tweeted details too. Hashtagged the hell out of it: #justice, #freedom, #fasciststate."

"#Latifheartthrob," Yukiko said with a wink.

"That's how it started, anyway. It's probably trending on Twitter by now, and the networks must've picked it up," Ren said. "The wire's saying Trafalgar Square and Whitehall are rammed with cabs. A flash mob has formed around Eros in Piccadilly Circus demanding justice for Latif. They're holding candles and singing: 'All You Need is Love'."

"Spare me." Latif rolled his eyes.

I began to feel calmer. The world hadn't gone mad. Well, not completely. I crossed my fingers. Perhaps things weren't so bad after all.

Another shot rang out.

We searched the darkness.

"Up there!" I heard someone scream from outside.

"There are snipers on rooftops all over," Latif said, squinting up at the skyline. "Not just government buildings and that."

"Squaddie alert," Ren growled.

A convoy of army vehicles was rolling slowly towards us in double file. A water cannon brought up the rear.

The cabs in front were turning to the right and to the left, red brake lights flaring up. Ren banged a left and followed the cabs down a residential road.

We hadn't been driving for long when Ren started cursing. "Police checkpoint ahead." He was slowing down. "Must've been a trap."

Two police vans blocked the road. I saw a look of panic cross Latif's face. My blood froze. The police had flagged down three cabs already and were forcing the drivers out at gunpoint. My heart rate spiked. The cabs behind started reversing at speed.

Ren swore under his breath. His gaze flicked from the police in front to the cabs behind. There was a look of grim determination on his face as he grasped the back of the passenger seat, hit the accelerator and put the cab into reverse.

Flak-jacketed police with guns were running down the road. An officer was shouting commands into his walkie-talkie. A helicopter hovered overhead. Two soldiers were leaning out. They were pointing automatic guns down into the street. I desperately searched for an escape route, but the police had closed off all exits. I exchanged a bleak look with Latif. We were as good as captured. He stretched over and squeezed my hand. We had run out of luck.

"Time for plan B," Yukiko said.

She gestured for us to lift our feet. Consumed by panic, I watched her pull up the matting.

"A smuggle-hole? Nice work, Ren," Latif said.

He crouched down to help Yukiko pull back a trap door.

"Told you my folks are only good for one thing," Ren said. His eyes were focused on the road behind, his arm hooked around the back of the passenger seat. "And that's smuggling hookie goods. They customised my cab. Neat, huh?"

I half-scrambled, half-tumbled into our hiding place as

the cab tore backwards. He braked violently, and I nearly shot out again.

"Move it. An ugly's heading our way and he's got a gun."

Latif handed Yukiko his tablet and his hat. She slipped them into her bag. Latif slid in beside me. There was barely room for both of us. Yukiko swiftly replaced the trapdoor and the matting. Ren brought the cab to a halt.

We corpsed it.

The judder of the engine swayed our shallow grave.

Ren cut the engine.

The silence was even more unbearable.

Darkness shrouded us.

Smothered us.

Petrol fumes burned my nose and throat.

I heard a policeman order Ren out of the cab. His tone wasn't friendly.

Another barked, "Spread them."

A patting sound followed as one of the policeman frisked Ren while a second searched the front of the cab: "So you think you're the King?" The policeman sneered. An image of Ren's quiff flashed into my head. My mind placed a gun at his temple.

"Think again. You're not fit to kiss Elvis's feet, hear me?"

Next up, I heard the smack of a police baton against flesh.

The passenger door opened with a snap.

I shut my eyes.

"Good evening, gentleman," Yukiko said.

"Stay in the cab, madam," one of the policemen advised.

"What's going on? Why you hitting my cabman?" she asked, in a hesitant English-as-a-second-language manner. "Please don't hurt him. He's been so gentleman to me. Promised me a free ride and everything. Very kind man. In Tokyo this wouldn't go."

One of the policemen laughed. "Hey, Joel, we've hooked ourselves a vampire."

"Pull up your veil," Joel said in a clipped tone.

"Excuse me, sir?"

"Pull up the veil, fright-fest, and get out of the cab."

Minutes later, the tread of boots in the cab above us.

Our tomb shook again.

I lay there motionless.

The darkness was super-charged.

Every cell in my body was vibrating with fear.

I held my breath as the policeman stamped the floor. He kicked the base of the passenger seat before climbing out and walking round to the rear. "Keys," he ordered.

The keys jangled when Ren handed them over. The click of the key turning back and forth in the lock made my heart stop-start... stop-start.

"Get over here," the soldier bellowed.

Another sickening thud, followed by a choking sound as Ren tried to catch his breath.

I pictured him bent double, puking his guts up as blood streamed from his nose. Yukiko was begging the policeman to stop. Her pleas turned to a whimper when the policeman hit Ren again. I took a shallow breath, appalled to realise that I was using Ren's groans as a cover. The air was sour.

Our smuggle-hole rocked as Ren staggered to the rear, using his cab for support. I winced. He was obviously in a bad way.

"I'm warning you, Elvis. Tonight we've got powers to act exactly as we please, so if you don't open this boot by the count of five, you're going down for a very long time. *Capice?*"

Latif took my hand.

I prayed to every god I knew.

Please don't let him arrest Ren. Please don't let us be discovered. Please don't...

"It's stiff, man. Give me a break!" Ren said. "Done."

The boot groaned open.

Latif squeezed my hand.

"Golf clubs, that's it," the policeman barked, slamming the boot shut.

I closed my eyes. We were swimming underwater. Deep, deep, deep underwater. But we were running out of air, and time. Silvery bubbles rose to the surface.

The policeman asked for Ren's cab registration and licence number. Then I heard him punch Ren's details into a machine, which he described as a tracking device. The other policeman must have moved to the rear of the cab, because a tearing sound filled my ears as he removed the cardboard that covered the number plate.

"So, sir." The policeman's voice was sarcastic and insincere. "The police won't stop you again, now your details are on the grid, but," he paused, and I imagined him returning his gun to his holster, "that's only if you go straight home after dropping this lady off. Be warned we can monitor your every move…"

I felt Latif tense up in the darkness.

Then there was a strange beeping sound, followed by a chilling explanation: "We've lasered a circle onto the door – for your own safety, of course." His voice was heavy with irony. "On your way, sir."

We heard the ignition spark and the cab's engine begin to turn over. Then Ren revved the engine and pulled away. "For my own safety – my arse. Now they've got my name and licence number in their system. *On the grid!* That's not good. It's a freakin' disaster. You heard the fascist. They can track our every move if they want."

"But why would they?" Yukiko's voice was calm. "Relax, Ren. We've been given the all-clear. They've checked thousands of cabs tonight." Yukiko banged her foot on the floor. "Okay in there?"

"Yeah right. Deluxe. There's zero air," Latif shouted back.

"Hang on a minute," Yukiko replied. "I'm getting you out."

There were scraping noises. Then the lid swung open. We sat up, blinking and gasping for air.

"Those stormtroopers were hardcore." Yukiko handed Ren a lace handkerchief. "I thought they were going to kill you, babe. Are you okay?" She kissed him on the cheek.

"Nah. Those fascists gave me a real kicking."

Latif eased himself out of our bunker, slid onto the empty bucket seat, and poking his head through the partition, said: "Thanks for taking the rap, Ren. That was ugly."

When Ren turned round, his nose was bloody and swollen. "Can't say it was a pleasure, but you would've done the same for me, Lats." He pressed the hankie to his nose. The white lace blotted scarlet. "Those guys were hyped as hell."

"Is it broken?" I asked.

"Nah, mashed-up. But you guys owe me big time."

"Big time," I repeated in a whisper, my nerves completely shredded.

"Truth, fam," Latif reached through the partition and squeezed Ren's shoulder.

Ren slotted back into the grid of cabs. "'Sakes, we're crawling. Come on, step up the speed. The last thing I need is another rumble with those stormtroopers."

Travelling so slowly made me feel uneasy.

Minutes later, Ren was shouting, "No way. Game over."

"What's up, fam?" Latif's voice was tight.

My stomach clenched up. I could hardly breathe.

"The wire says Jeannie's in a scuffle with the feds." He was leaning towards the radio so he wouldn't miss a word. "She's at Speaker's Corner stirring things up. She's politicking! We're in serious trouble, bruv."

We exchanged looks, not wanting to be the first to say how serious.

"She's a friend of Mum's so she'll be on file." Latif's composure slipped momentarily. "MI5 will have her details."

"Truth! If they cross-reference the grid for friends and family. Boom! Up will come my details. We're laser-tagged, too. We're as good as caught. Damn! Damn! Damn!" He blasted his horn in sync with each damn, morse-coding his anger into the night.

"Keep cool, Ren," Yukiko said. "Latif's your friend. If the database was any good they would've taken you in. Stop being paranoid. Think straight. You were cleared. They know you haven't got any passengers on board, apart from a Japanese 'fright-fest'. So what's the big deal?"

"Ren's right. They'll chase down anyone connected to my family." Latif punched his fist into the palm of his hand.

"Even if they make the connection, they've checked the cab." Yukiko was speaking slowly and calmly to cut through the rising panic. "We're in the clear."

A gloomy silence enveloped us.

"How far is the embassy?" I asked.

"At this speed, twenty minutes," Ren replied, drumming his fingers against the steering wheel. "Should we change the plan, bruv?" He turned around. "Whaddya think? Head for a junk space?"

Latif had taken back his tablet from Yukiko. He was hunched over it tapping away. He looked up. "I'm still thinking Crunch Town's a plan. I know ways in. Trust me!" Seeing Ren's sceptical look, he added, "I don't fancy being holed up in the embassy for years until things get sorted. It'd be like prison. I can't live like that. I'd rather be on the run."

"You sure?" Ren asked uneasily.

"Yeah. Crunch Town is the only plan. I'm a CCTV specialist so I can work a route that's more or less unfilmed. Not the quickest but it's unwatched." His eyes were glued to the tablet once more. "And it should be easier now the cabbies have knocked out cameras."

I remembered our topsy-turvy route through the Pimlico grid, and in a panic found myself wondering if we'd actually make it into Crunch Town.

"Okay, guys, I've got an idea. Budge up, Dash," he said, sitting next to me and beckoning Yukiko over. "If there are blind spots, perhaps…" His fingers flew across the keyboards so fast I couldn't make out the postcode. "Yeah. Now I'm getting somewhere." A large pair of security gates filled the screen. They looked familiar. Grim, grey buildings rose up behind them. He scrolled through the many CCTV cameras listed, clicking on a few at random. A garden. A gatehouse. A hallway. Latif's face lit up. "We've smashed it!" An eerie, empty hallway. There were photos on the wall, ascending the stairway. I narrowed my eyes. Churchill, Thatcher, Blair. "That's Downing Street, isn't it?" I whispered, hardly able to believe my eyes.

"Genius." Yukiko whooped, punching his arm. "Ren. YOU. WON'T. BELIEVE. IT. Lats has breached Downing Street security."

"Now that's what I call a counter-punch, bruv."

"I'm match tough, fam. Shadow-boxing — courtesy of surveillance *sans frontières*." He winked. "They networked the CCTV cameras in a rush. I was thinking there had to be glitches, and this, my friends, is the boss of all glitches." Latif was texting *Tracker* as he spoke. "They only went and forgot to take high-security buildings off the police network."

Yukiko and I were laughing, totally gassed.

The message read: **Latif Hajjaj's ready to surrender. Go to CCTV camera 233798677 to hear conditions for Dasha's release. Two minutes or deal is off.** He pressed send. My stomach flipped.

Latif called up the tab showing the studio.

Seconds later, my parents' faces lit up. I guessed they must have heard about the text through their earpieces. "We have just received breaking news. Their eyes glinted like glass beads. "Latif Hajjaj has contacted us. The game is up. He's turning himself in and setting Dasha free. We're going live to the scene to hear his demands." The cosmetic surgery gave their smiles a special kind of craziness.

I tensed up. And then, as if by magic, the hallway of Number 10 came into view. A security guard stood at the bottom of the stairs, oblivious to his new-found fame. A second later, the PM and his team rushed into the hallway, shouting at the guard and pointing up at the CCTV camera. The prime minister's children shot in after them, waving and mugging for the cameras. The PM shouted for them to get back. A security guard picked them up, one under each arm, and whisked them out; the little girl blew a kiss to the camera over his shoulder as they disappeared from view. A minute later, the camera was shut off.

It made the strangest silent movie.

Back in the studio, my parents looked agitated. Sweat beaded Dad's forehead. My mother held up five fingers, and the producer went to camera five, which showed shots of the VJs working their magic.

Latif texted: **Eyes on you PM. Little bro's spookin' you!** Immediately *Tracker* went to an advert break.

"That's blown our cover sky high. 'Sakes, Latif if we're caught, we'll probably go down for life," Ren said.

"At least we hit back." He made trigger fingers. "It's a matter of honour."

"Yeah. But they'll GPS us real speedy," Yukiko's calm had cracked. "You've seen the films. You know, men with maggot-white faces in bunkers watching billions of screens."

"From now on things are gonna get political." He tipped up the brim of his hat with elegant fingers, his aquamarines were on full-beam. He was thriving on the high-octane buzz.

The cab was pressure-cooker tense.

We were crawling, hardly moving at all, hemmed in by cabs to the left and right.

Latif opened the window and shouted at a cabbie queueing in the bus lane. "Mate, It's Latif, Harriet Hajjaj's son. Can you help me out?" He held up the tablet. "Take this for me? It's hot, bruv. Say a brother with a ten-gallon hat left it in your cab if the feds stop you."

After the tablet was in the cabbie's possession, Ren made a circling gesture with his hand and pulled up so the guy could swing a U-turn. I watched his cab head in the opposite direction, my heart dip-dip-dashing.

"Does the wire go out to all the cabbies, Ren?" I asked.

"Yeah, why?"

"I want to get our story out there, you know, just in case we're caught." I mumbled the last words, terrified that by expressing this thought out loud, I might actually make it happen. "It's our only chance. You know, to clear Latif's name."

"To a few thousand cabbies? How's that going to change things?" Yukiko asked.

"Cabbies aren't known for keeping their mouths shut or their opinions to themselves, are they? Plus their passengers will hear it. You know, people who've flagged a ride to show support for the Hajjajs. There may even be journalists in the cabs, who are covering the cabbie's revolt. We can give them a new angle on an old story. *The truth.*"

"What, slam the truth?" Latif rolled his eyes. "Nobody cares."

"I do. The people hailing cabs do. Even the cabbies do," Yukiko said.

"For one night only," Ren said with a grin.

"We need to reframe the story. Then it's up to the public to decide which version they want to believe." I looked straight at Latif. "It's the only way to save your skin."

"That or pray for a miracle," Yukiko chipped in.

"It's risky," Ren said. "But truth needs to be out there, bruv."

"They'll be on us in no time." Latif frowned, his thick eyebrows forming an arrow. "How about we pull a three-card trick? When Dash is done with her politicking. That'll keep the feds off our backs for a bit."

Ren fixed his eyes on Latif in the rear-view mirror. "Yeah. That could work," he said cautiously. And then more upbeat. "Yeah. That could work. I like your style, bruv."

"If it flops – it flops, but it's worth a shot."

"Safe, fam. I'm on it," Ren said, leaning down towards the radio. As Ren spoke to someone in the cabbie's radio studio, Latif handed me his pay-as-you-go mobile. "You'll have to phone in. It's a bit Talk Radio – but low-fi always makes things sound more authentic." That crooked smile again. "Trust me! Remember my rep depends on you, bubblehead."

"No pressure, then," I joked.

When I took the phone I noticed my hands were shaking. I shut my eyes, took deep, measured breaths. My mind cleared. I heard Ren say: "Dasha Gold is ready to come down the line."

"In three." Ren held up three fingers and counted me in. I began speaking, hesitantly at first, until I found my groove.

"This is Dasha Gold. I want to put the record straight. Latif Hajjaj is innocent. He is neither a kidnapper nor a terrorist. He is my friend. He saved me…" I spoke in simple sentences, outlining the crazy chain of events starting with the train crash, right up until *Tracker* and the taxi revolt. The lies. The set-ups. The twists. How we'd been stitched up.

When I signed off I knew the cabbies and their fares would find a way to get our story out there, so by morning the facts would be in the few papers, TV channels and radio stations that my parents didn't own, as well as on the

Internet. My heart fluttered. I had finally changed the script.

"You dusted, Dash?" Latif asked.

I nodded. He squeezed my hand. "You killed it."

"Professional job," Yukiko said. "Ever thought of working in the media?"

Yukiko and I started giggling.

Ren was talking to radio control intently. "Okay, guys. Less gas. Next lights we pull the three-card trick."

"Musical cabs," was all Latif said in explanation, gripping the door handle ready for action. "Mirror me."

When Ren pulled up at the lights, we all jumped out and ran down the queues of stationary cabs, their engines growling throatily. Cabbies wished us well as we darted through the grid, bent over double. A few bumped knuckles with Ren. We slipped into a cab a little way down the road — the only one with its *for hire* sign on. As Ren slid into the driver's seat, the cab's owner, a black guy with dreads, slapped him on the back, and said, "Stay blessed!" Then he jogged over to Ren's cab.

Even as we slammed the doors, I heard the drone of helicopters heading our way. Sirens wailed in surround sound. Blue neon pulsed the night sky.

Ren swung a U-turn. The traffic was less heavy in this direction and we picked up speed. Latif had taken up position on the bucket seat and was directing Ren. The unfilmed route, I guessed. There were fewer get-rich-quick gits patrolling the roads as we drove out of the city.

"We're heading for the front line. Turbulence ahead.

Be ready to assume the crash position," Ren shouted.

"Doors to manual, innit?" Yukiko said, pointing at the doors. She looked like an air hostess from hell. "Your lifejackets are in the smugglehole."

We were laughing again, high on the madness of the moment.

As we hurtled east, I noticed the streets were becoming more rundown. Functioning streetlights were few and far between. Rubbish was piled high on the pavements. Crunch Town must be close now. Boards nailed to a tree said in many languages, *We want to live not exist.*

Up ahead, police were flagging cabs down. Ren picked up speed, ignoring the policeman's frantic gestures. As we shot past, I saw the policeman reach for his gun. My heart rate maxed out. We were on the radar again. Ren made an SOS call to the wire for backup. In next to no time, cabs materialised from nowhere, forming a motorcade around us, steering us through the streets in a high-speed convoy, as if we were heads of state being whisked off to an important summit meeting.

With the law, I thought gloomily.

Overhead the unmistakable rattle of a police helicopter. I heard it dip down low. Gunfire rang out. A terrifying ripping sound filled the cab as a bullet shot through the roof and sank deep into the passenger seat. Both Yukiko and I screamed. Ren cursed. The cab in front of us veered off the road and crashed into a lamppost, a jet of steam escaped from its crumpled bonnet. Another smashed into a parked car, the relentless honk of its horn blasted into the night. Ren swerved to miss the pile-up. A bullet took out our wing mirror, sending a spume of glass cartwheeling into the night.

A robotic voice was instructing the taxi drivers to stop and step out of their cabs for their own safety. A moment later, a fleet of police vans hoved into view at the far end of the street. The white vans and the black cabs edged towards each other from opposite ends of the road, like pieces on a chessboard. A few moments later, more bullets hailed down, peppering the cabs up ahead. A bullet shattered our windscreen. Ren frantically punched out the shards with his bare hands.

We swung a right. A fleet of cabs followed.

A few streets later, the street lighting disappeared. Driving through the pitch-black gave the impression we'd entered a war zone. Crunch Town proper couldn't be far now. Two outriders flanked us, tearing down the pavement. Paparazzi. They reminded me of wolves running at full stretch.

We turned hard left. Halfway down the street a police checkpoint stood between our cab and Crunch Town. I recognised the shopping mall, moored in darkness, like a half-built, abandoned luxury cruiser.

"The front line," Ren shouted. "Crash positions."

"Go hard, Ren," Latif shouted.

The cab surged forwards. "Don't worry, guys, these cabs are built," Ren yelled, as the makeshift barrier rushed towards us. He accelerated even more, crouching low over the wheel. Latif assumed the crash position, his hat tipped forward. Yukiko and I clung to each other. On impact, we shot forwards, landing on the floor in a jumble of limbs. I heard gunshots.

"Are we through?" Latif shouted. "In Crunch Town?"

"Yeah. But the feds are on us!" Ren ducked down. He tried to start the engine; the sound of a heavy smoker coughing.

Peeping out, I saw our cab had taken out the barrier, and we'd skidded to a halt in a kind of no man's land between the police barricade and the roundabout where the Crunch Town 'soldiers' camped out. Since our last trip, the gang had fortified the sentrypoint with metal shutters scavenged from the mall's retail units. A red flag with a clenched fist at its centre fluttered in the breeze. Both sides were aiming guns in our direction.

The engine spluttered uselessly. It was beat.

"We've got to head out. Stay close." Latif took control.

"I'm going out alone," I said, scrambling onto the seat. "This is my mess. The police won't shoot me, and if they do — *too bad*." I wanted to sound brave, but my voice cracked.

"Chill, Dash. No heroics. We're going out together." Latif grabbed my arm.

Yukiko took the other. "Ready, Ren?"

"We good?" Latif offered his fist, we all touched knuckles.

Throwing open the door, Latif shouted, "We're unarmed. *Don't shoot.*"

His words were swallowed up by the helicopter's deadly chop.

Gunfire rattled.

The helicopter's searchlight lit up no man's land.

"Wait up!" I tried to hold him back. "No...!"

He slipped my grip and jumped out into the firestorm of light with his hands up.

For a second, he stood alone, silhouetted against a blowtorch sky, a cowboy at a midnight gunfight. Then Ren was by his side, his quiff flattened by the helicopter's whirlwind. I stepped out with Yukiko, holding hands.

Braced myself for bullets.

Nothing.

The Crunch Town soldiers were charging forwards, using dustbin lids and road signs as shields. They were wearing hard hats and balaclavas. The tinies were sprinting down the pavements, banging saucepan lids together. For a moment we were caught up in the melee, and then Ren and Latif were hustling us out of the road. Next minute we were running down a muddy path and scrabbling through a crawl-hole into the mall. Gunfire rang out from no man's land. The helicopter buzzed above the battle.

"Head for the rookeries, Ren," Latif shouted.

Inside the mall, Latif took my arm as we sprinted towards the scaffolding. From the ease with which he navigated the wilderness, I knew he'd taken the route many times before in the dark. Whistles rang out from the scaffolding. Crunch Towners were commanding the ramparts. I twisted my ankle, but ran on. When we reached the scaffolding, we climbed the ladder at speed. My hands slipped on the rungs. Ren pulled the ladder up behind us while Latif spoke to a group of Crunch Towners, who told him to head to the top.

Seconds later, we were running along the gangway to the next set of ladders, Yukiko bringing up the rear, her widow's weeds flapping out behind her like monstrous bat wings. Four levels later, we stopped, puffing for breath.

The mall clanked and jangled as the gangs bashed metal poles against the scaffolding. The beat was hypnotic. There must have been hundreds of Crunch Towners in the derelict mall. As my eyes became more accustomed to the gloom, I saw hooded shapes silhouetted against the sky. Every now and again torches flashed in empty retail units or spaces occupied by families.

Suddenly the banging stopped. Whistles cut through the clash of battle coming from no man's land.

"Customs has been breached," Latif said to Ren, as the police entered the mall.

With a rush of blades, the helicopter swept over the mall. The plastic on the scaffolding flapped, rising skywards like angry phantoms. Paper and rubbish whirled upwards. The police moved through the storm of sweet wrappers, spotlit in the helicopter's beam. They were in full riot gear — helmets, visors, shields and guns. Faceless. Flakjacketed. Bulletproofed.

A bombardment of bricks, rubble and everday objects rained down on the advancing police lines. Shadows raced along the ramparts to defend the section the police were targeting.

The police raised their shields above their heads, edging forwards like a monstrous armadillo — missiles bouncing off its reinforced shell. Fireworks rocketed down in an explosion of colour. A petrol bomb missed the police-beast by metres. Metal poles and planks shot down like javelins. Every now and then, sorties of Crunch Town 'soldiers' raced from the foundations to lob missiles, retreating rapidly.

The helicopter's searchlights scoped the mall. Hoodies turned their backs; their shadows rising up large and sinister on the walls of the empty units. Lasers shot up towards the helicopter's cockpit. A volley of fireworks exploded around its blades. The copter wheeled away.

Down at ground level, the police continued to edge forwards. Lasers zapped their protective shell with virulent green dots. A barked command, and the front line charged forwards. The speed with which the police were running suggested they were wearing night glasses. When they reached the scaffolding a terrible roar filled the mall.

"Boiling tar," Latif said. "They do defence medieval style here."

The police retreated and regrouped, preparing for a second assault. The helicopter was hovering above the mall once more, and as the police started to advance for a second time, a robotic voice ordered them to withdraw. The command from the helicopter came again and again.

The police line stopped.

Then they began walking backwards, shields held out.

For a moment I thought they might target another section of the scaffolding, but no, they were definitely pulling out.

The ramparts rang with a victory beat.

I searched the sky for news helicopters. No sign. Weird. GoldRush Media usually arrived at a newsworthy incident around the same time as the police, if not before. From the direction of the city, I heard the throb of a helicopter approaching. Minutes later, a news helicopter hovered above the mall. I checked for the GoldRush logo, heart pounding. It was a rival news team. Even weirder.

Yukiko nudged me. Reporters were scuttling across the wasteland like rats.

The helicopter's beam scoped the ramparts. We turned our backs.

News teams were setting up beneath a rain-drenched billboard – featuring the Golds. The lights showed anchors preparing to go to air. With their immaculate hair-dos and expensive suits they looked completely out of place in this desolate scene.

A producer on the ground made a sign, and the helicopter removed its clatter.

The anchorwoman started her piece-to-camera. We could just about make it out. "Thirty minutes ago the prime minister held an emergency press conference outside Downing Street in response to the breach of his security network. He believes Tarquin and Tamara Gold have overstepped the mark by hacking into Downing Street's CCTV network. The police will be asking them to present themselves at Westminster police station for questioning. However, we are receiving as yet unsubstantiated reports that the Golds have left GoldRush Towers in a helicopter.

It is believed they are planning to flee the country on their private jet. We are reporting live from Crunch Town where it is reported Dasha and her friends are hiding out after a dramatic police chase. We hope to bring you Dasha Gold's comments on the breaking news shortly."

We exchanged looks. Eyes popped wide.

"They'll be back," I muttered.

The helicopter's lights were searching the ramparts again. Hundreds of hoodies raised their fists in triumph. We did too, taking care to keep our heads down. Reporters were fanning out, walking towards the scaffolding. The helicopter's tannoy system demanded: "Dasha, if you're out there, we want to hear your side of the story."

"Too late," Latif muttered.

The helicopter's searchlight stopped, trapping us in its beam. We turned our backs, but it didn't move on. Perhaps the TV producer had picked out Yukiko's garb, Latif's hat or Ren's quiff on their megapixel camera. We weren't exactly the most inconspicuous crew.

The press rushed forwards, questions popping like champagne corks at a premiere. I only caught a few. "What do you think of the shocking news, Dasha? What about your parents fleeing the country? What's your story?"

We raised our fists in a freedom fighter's salute. The world had to see we were friends. The paparazzi's flashguns were our witness. We had claimed the story back and it felt good — *really, really good.*

"What did I tell you, Dash?" Latif gave me that crooked

smile as he tipped up the brim of his cowboy hat. "The house doesn't always win!"

"Against the odds!" I flashed him a huge smile.

The paparazzi cameras exploded.

His Aviators reflected a million starbursts.

My heart exploded with them.

"We smashed it, Dash."

"Yeah. I can't believe it!"

"Believe it." He squeezed my hand.

"I do," I whispered. "And now we need to tell the world."

"It'll be truth for a day, Dash. Truth is a slippery thing. It don't stick."

I frowned, desperate to put the record straight. I wanted to clear Latif's name for starters. But Latif was no longer at my side; he had already slid back into the shadows.

He put his finger to his lip.

Yukiko and I lingered in the limelight. I cleared my throat, opened my mouth to speak. Stopped. Below, my parents' world was pressing in on me. But they hadn't wanted our side of the story when it mattered. The cabbies had the scoop. They'd get it out there. I turned my back on the media.

Latif stretched out his hand as I walked towards him.

"Safe," he said, putting his arm around me as we followed Ren and Yukiko along the ramparts in the direction of Crunch Town.

Acknowledgements

I am deeply grateful to:

Laetitia Rutherford, my agent, for her encouragement, patience and invaluable advice. Mulcahy Associates for their support, and Joanna Moult for her editorial comments on early drafts.

Templar Publishing for making *Stitch-Up* a reality, especially Helen Boyle and Emma Goldhawk. My editors, Anne Finnis and Emily Sharratt, whose attention to detail and insights made all the difference. Will Steele and Tom Sanderson for nailing the brilliant artwork.

Olivia Mead, Sarah Benton and the publicity team for their enthusiasm.

Dad and Mum for the space and encouragement to follow my dreams.

Eppie for her constant support.

The Martin-Niemoller-Stiftung for granting permission to use Martin Niemoller's poem.

Chima Akenzua for his parkour displays.

Oscar Stephenson for his wise words of youth.

And special thanks to Christopher for his belief, excellent advice, generosity of spirit, and for not leaving the building when the going got tough.

Sophie Hamilton was brought up in a sleepy hamlet in Warwickshire, where she spent every possible moment horse riding and going for long walks with her dog, Mopsa.

After studying history at Sussex University, Sophie came to London, and fell in love with the city's crazy cosmopolitan mix.

For years, she worked in the television industry as a film researcher and a producer. Her programmes ranged from hard-hitting documentaries to arts shows and, most enjoyably, programmes highlighting the lifestyles, quirks and foibles of the rich and famous. She then decided to swap the manic environment of television for the solitary life of a writer, and the result is her debut novel *Stitch-Up*.

Sophie loves travelling, but is always glad to come back to London. The first thing she does on her return is go for a run along the Thames to get back into the flow of things.

She is currently busy writing the sequel to *Stitch-Up*, titled *Mob-Handed*.

sophiehamiltonbooks.co.uk

Coming in 2015...

The exhilarating sequel to Stitch-Up:

MOB HANDED

DASHA is living with Maxine, but life as a civilian hasn't quite panned out as Dasha had hoped: Latif is in exile in Lebanon; *Tracker* controls Londoners, filming them day and night, and the Golds are using information stolen from data clouds to rig the forthcoming London elections.

When Latif's mum goes missing, Dasha is forced to turn double agent and return to her old life. Can everything she learned from Latif help her to outwit the manipulative, unscrupulous figures at the heart of the conspiracy... her parents?